OTHER

PUBLISHED

Apr 2004	**THE BOWLS CLUB**
Nov 2005	**THE NEW SEASON**
Nov 2007	**GOING INDOORS**

FORTHCOMING

TANTRUMS ON TOUR (HUMOUR/BOWLING)
SNUGGLETUM (HUMOUR /CHILDRENS)

THE POET'S COLLECTION

: -	**LOVE AND REFLECTION**
: -	**THE MODERN WORLD**
: -	**SADNESS AND SORROW**
: -	**WAR AND PEACE**
: -	**INSPIRED THOUGHT**

JENNER PUBLICATIONS
Inspiration from Suffolk

GOING INDOORS
Paul Hammond
First Edition

Published by
Jenner Publications
C/o Wild About Birds
Main Road
Theberton
Suffolk
IP16 4RA

Printed by
Barnwell's Print Ltd
2-6 Penfold Street
Aylsham
Norfolk
NR11 6ET

ISBN Number 978-0-9546633-8-4

Distributed by Jenner Publications
First Published November 2007

Illustrations @ Sonya E Burrows

INTRODUCTION

Reverend Percival Peabody has the unenviable task of tending to his flock in the sleepy little Suffolk village of Lower South-Borough.

Unfortunately, due to his fondness for the traditional pastime of bowling he has been roped into participating in their daily trials and tribulations.

Apart from the fact that he owns a rather disturbed moggie, has an aversion to lawnmowers and is always in the wrong place at the wrong time, he still maintains his sanity and a semblance of order.

Well, that was at least until now.

Having survived the mayhem of the summer season Percy once again gathers his temperamental, flirtatious and potentially insane parishioners as they make plans for winter.

But pursuits of passion, the love of one-upmanship, playful shenanigans and sheer ribaldry systematically reduce all previously arranged and well organized plans to total chaos.

There's no denying the fact that here indeed is a club with some extra-ordinary people, and yes indeed, even one or two who might perhaps be able to play the game.

Rooney, Russell and Roger

This is for you

ACKNOWLEDGEMENTS

I'd like once again to express my deeply appreciative thanks to all the bowlers, and non-bowlers alike, who continue to make this book possible by supporting the on-going antics of Lower South-Borough with their purchases.

I love the sport to distraction, with its competitive spirit, challenges of the green or sometimes ploughed field, the characters, personalities and great friends that the sport continues to create.

To David Ramsden and everyone at POTTERS, home of the indoor championships, a huge thank you again for giving such fantastic support.

To Sarah for taking the time and having the patience to do the initial proof reads again and again. Also for the never-ending supply of quality coffee as well as the intellectual observations, witticisms and light-hearted humour.

To all my teammate's at Halesworth Angels who now have to endure my sense of humour at a somewhat closer aspect than previously. Of course the new faces have given rise to some equally new characters so it could be an entertaining year on and off the green.

To Sole Bay Bowls Club, thank you for the original inspiration and the continuing friendships.

Getting back to bowling and having the opportunity to write this next edition of the Lower South-Borough saga has been both the icing and the cake.

Events continue to be based on real life experiences with a lot of leeway for artistic licence, interpretation and totally unrelated reality.

Once again thanks to the very patient, enduring and talented artist Sonya for creating the caricatures for this latest edition.

Thank you

Paul Hammond

CONTENTS

5.   JANUARY   A PRISION BREAK

Resolutions and turkey fishcake head for the dustbin, but dog collars are all the rage. The members start the New Year with a seafood buffet and champagne celebrations are soon to follow. But it's a re-run of bad luck as a ghost from the past returns. Rollo turns to romance and makes his mark in more ways than one as usual. Percy returns the flock to reality and soon finds everything has gone to seed. It's a crisis of confidence for the church, a dark time for the vicar and a bad case of cold claws for the cat.

6.   FEBRUARY   HOW ABOUT A TEA PARTY?

It's a month of big change, religious ramifications and peasant revolutions. The men run scared as Valentine's Day approaches, whilst it's out with the old and in with the new for the vicarage. Percy has palpitations, dilemmas and grave concerns as Rollo runs away. But it's show-time shenanigans as usual when the postponed party comes to fruition. A local business saves the day, the chef picks up a tart and things get altogether spicy whilst there's a carpet clean up for the builders. It's a bad time for Reverend Archibald, the bishop goes nuts and definitely more than bats in the belfry.

7.   MARCH   ICING ON THE CAKE

The builders finish at last and it's a time of decision for Percy. There's a marriage in the offing, moggie 'n' mouse antics and an unexpected but timely arrival by the senior clergy. Rodents run wild with the organ until the cats lend a hand and Percy conducts a 'sit in'. Heavy snowfall catches out the vicar as Jack Frost bites back with the coldest night on record. But it's business as usual and a time of grand openings. Special guests join in the chaos as local celebrities bring a whole new meaning to bowling indoors. It's back to the Victorian way of life for the club and good cheer all around.

8.   EPILOGUE

A time of changes and reflections; the season draws to a close.

MEET THE MEMBERS

THE MEN

<u>HON. PRESIDENT</u>   Ronald 'Squiffy' Regis
Former RAF Squadron Commander still living in 1942, bowls like a Barnes Wallis bouncing bomb. Now the retired club president.

<u>CHAIRMAN</u>   Bernard 'Batty' Bartrum
Dubious DIY plumber, definitely a ladies' man, always in a pickle, very inquisitive, talkative and sometimes acts a bit too rashly.

<u>VICE CHAIRMAN</u>   Douglas Doolittle MBE
Retired surgeon, a posh and wealthy suburbanite, one of those 'fair play' guys who guarantees a good game and never cheats.

<u>HON. SECRETARY</u>   Charles 'Charlie' Chesterford
Former cricketer, couldn't play, nothing has changed! He likes a tipple, is a bit of a practical joker and loves money-making scams.

<u>HON. TREASURER</u>   Reginald Trimley Esq.
Accountant, short-sighted, well meaning but easily flustered, fairly naïve in all things non-accountable, but hot on figures.

<u>HON. COMP. SEC.</u>   Jack 'Big Jim' Tuttle
One-time county legend, larger than life, eats for England, drinks like a fish, a funny comedian, everyone's favourite speech maker!

<u>HON. TOURING TEAM SEC</u>. (Position vacant)
Life beyond Suffolk has never been discovered.

<u>CAPTAIN</u>   Rt Hon. Clifford James Johnson
A traditional working class councillor, well-respected and a good bowler, but still very much 'Jack the Lad' with looks to match.

<u>VICE CAPTAIN</u>   Derek Dunstable
Quick tempered, average bowler, a fiery combination, always argumentative and never ever wrong, advisable to run for cover!

GREEN KEEPER   Patrick 'Postie' Albright
Retired postman, very keen and serious, a 'by the book' player who loves his green more than life itself; don't upset him!

Assistant GREEN KEEPER Rev. Percival 'Percy' Peabody
Very helpful, eager, accident prone, single, sincere cat owner. He can't bowl but can paint, is well meaning, loveable and innocent.

CLUB CHAMPION   Dennis 'Sticky' Ditherford
Excellent bowler, tall, slightly built, prone to talking too much, has a real tendency to fake injury. A keen 'twitcher' and a dramatist.

TOURNAMENT UMPIRE   Eric 'Chalkie' Tunstall
Retired pilot, enjoys life, plays a jolly good game, now slightly detached and never really left the war but still game for anything!

THE BARMAN   Bertie Tattleford
Double glazing sales rep., explosive, cocky, bowls well at times, an exuberant individual, well meaning at heart; a naturalist too!

COACH   Tony 'Trigger' Havershall
Council worker, serious player, all round nice guy, easily distracted and not too clever. Has some very unusual, questionable hobbies.

CLUB MEMBER   David Dimpley
Retired, humorous, easy going, brilliant bowler when awake.

CLUB MEMBER   Colin Spindleforth
Thirty-something family man with a mid-life crisis in everything.

CLUB MEMBER   Russell Cobblethwaite
Long serving, most senior member, 70 years young, still sharp.

CLUB MEMBER   Frenchie 'Wide Boy' Phillips
Silver tongued, fast talking ladies' man, always on the move.

CLUB MEMBER   James 'Scottie' McCarver
Talks a good game, but tends to lose the plot, loves his whisky.

CLUB MEMBER   Paul Jenner
Upcoming new kid on the block, very competitive, still learning.

CLUB MEMBER   Johnny Jackson
The club's hottest signing, an aspiring county and national player.

NEW ARRIVAL   Olly 'Ever Ready' Ramsbottom
Full of dodgy ideas, a definite 'wide boy' with the gift of the gab.

JUNIOR MEMBER   Timothy 'Tiny' Doolittle
The son, now 14 years old, always eager to play and to play up!

SELECTION COMMITTEE
Whoever is available and foolish enough to volunteer.

THE LADIES

CAPTAIN   Doris 'Posh' Doolittle
Impoverished socialite, vegan, questionable high morals with a liking for a tipple or two. A devout defender of womens' bowling.

CLUB CHAMPION   Sheila 'Legs' Ramsbottom
Aussie girl, cocky, sharp, definitely a match for any man around the bar and at the card table! A feisty handful on and off the green.

COMP. SEC.   Diane Ditherford
Long-suffering wife, gossips for England, unorthodox bowler with a voice that could cut glass. Has a tendency to get things mixed up!

COMMITTEE REP.   Cynthia Cobblethwaite
Forthright, warm-hearted, popular all rounder, nice lady, does a lot of charity work, but naïve with it. Still fights for her beliefs though!

PRESIDENT (ELECT)   Gloria 'Smiler' Grimshaw
Never a dull moment or a happy one, renowned for steel britches, lack of humour and stentorian personality; definately a cold fish!

CLUB MEMBER   Pauline Jenner
Wannabe mum, highly ambitious, somewhat tactless and blunt.

CLUB MEMBER   Molly Tattleford née Coddle
Long-suffering tea lady and former spinster, recently married.

CLUB MEMBER   Phllippa Spindleforth
Working class councillor aspiring to be posh, but a culinary genius!

NEW ARRIVAL   Sarah Jane Coddle
Former black sheep of the Coddle clan, self-assured, sensuous, saucy, sultry, seductive and suggestive, apparently a real man-eater.

JUNIOR MEMBER   Abbey 'Spice' Doolittle
The daughter, 12 years old, going on 22, and a wannabe model.

AND THEN THERE WAS...

ROLLO
Disturbed, long haired, maniacal, mischevious, mayhem causing, madcap, short-tempered, scheming and misbehaving vicarage cat!

MISS MATILDA BAGSHOTT (Baggie)
Gloria's posh Persian pussy, long of hair, short on temper, never preened, supposedly snobbish and a bit of a tart as well as a cat.

REVEREND ARCHIBALD (Archie)
A bulldog with a big attitude to compensate for his bow legs, cross-eyed expression, drooling mouth and inbuilt hatred of cats.

THE PARISH COMMUNITY

The Rt Hon. E. A. Thomas the 3rd	**Bishop**
The Rt Hon. M. J. Twiggle	**Archbishop**
Dr Boris Binder-Garden	**Vet**
Harry 'The Hammer' Huckstable	**Organist**
Cedric Spindleforth	**Museum curator**
Peter 'Chippie' Barryman	**Recycling manager**
Reverend Joshua Jackson	**Percy's predecessor**
Jiggy 'Snapper' Jenkins	**Paparazzi hotshot**
Jimmy 'Monkey' Murphy	**Builder**
Johnny 'Midge' McPherson	**Builder**
Godfrey Go-Lightly	**County vice-president**
Martin King	**National champion**
Tommy 'Tick Tock' Ballcock	**National president**
The Rt Hon. Lady Quinton MBE	**Ladies president (ret.)**
James 'Jamie' Gotthelott	**Store proprietor**
Sam 'Iron man' Harris	**County president**
Mrs Jones	**Local parishioner**
Sir John 'Jeremiah' Tinkleton	**Touring president**

Matilda Elizabeth Tinkleton	**Touring captain**
Tim	**Valley Tours driver**
Joshua	**Adventure World rep.**
'Boom Boom' Baker DSO MBE	**Retired air marshall**
Sgt Major Sid 'Snotty' Snodgrass	**Territorial Army**
Joe 'Dodger' Stubbs	**F. H. Promotions**
Johnny 'Greaser' Stubbs	**F.H. Holiday Tours**
Little Jimmy Blodger	**School bully**
David Van Stem	**TOTTERS manager**
Manuel "Burrito' Mondago	**TOTTERS head chef**
Dazzling Bluecoats	**TOTTERS stewards**

Even as we speak the parish of Lower South-Borough continues to flourish and grow...

****

FOREWORD

In the sleepy countryside of Suffolk, amid the ancient willows and thatched cottages of peaceful hamlets, lies the small village of Lower South-Borough.

Surrounded by picturesque duck pond, heraldic sign, carefully trimmed hedgerows and freshly swept pathways, there stands a tired wooden building with an objective lean (depending on the wind direction).

Nearby, a growing pile of bricks and timber under an old tarpaulin promises the beginnings of long awaited new construction, after many years of lying dormant.

Weathered timber seats stand proudly in front of a more robust but now aged timber framework. This is the members' 'clubhouse', a rather worn out Victorian structure whose majestic windows offer, when cleaned, a splendid panoramic inspection of the goings on outside.

The clubhouse overlooks a magnificent lawn, rectangular in shape, which on closer inspection proves to have a formidable ditch and bank much like a medieval castle but with numbers and markers attached to its structure.

The grass is short, mostly, with some threadbare patches towards its edges, but its carefully manicured form can leave the visitor in no doubt that this is indeed the village bowling green.

It is now the 1st of September, with a hint of autumn in the air as the weak rays of the sunrise over the trees. Birds still sing, the odd butterfly flutters, but the distant 'putt-putt' of a small two-stroke engine no longer disturbs the distant tranquil calm.

An ancient, battered and broken lawnmower lies in the shadow of a ramshackle, recently stained shed at the edge of the lawn, announcing to all that its days of grass cutting are finally over.

Now autumn draws on, the memories of the glorious summer have past and it's time for the outdoor greens to close for another year; for a line to be drawn under all events past.

The Reverend Percival Peabody gathers his flock for another adventure into the unknown depths of a new bowling season with all that fate may again have in store.

RUNAWAY CRANES, DEFLATED PUDDINGS,

AVENGING ARACHNOIDS, BOWLING HOLIDAYS,

RAUNCHY RELATIVES, BUILDING RENOVATIONS,

JAMMED TOILETS, ORNITHOLOGICAL ADVENTURES,

FLIRTATIOUS FESTIVE FROLICS, JELLIED EELS,

FANCY DRESS PARTIES, SUPERMARKET CHAOS,

ESCAPEE PRISONERS, DECLARATIONS OF LOVE,

Even THE FULLY MONTY makes an appearance.

Oh Yes... And of course...   CATS, CATS, CATS...

It's ANOTHER bowling season at Lower South-Borough, the boys and girls are GOING INDOORS and it's certain that the club will continue to live up to its motto...

'WHATEVER CAN GO WRONG PROBABLY WILL.'

All characters, places, and definitions within this book are fictional, although some readers may feel a familiarity and empathy with some characterisation.

CHAPTER ONE

SEPTEMBER

THE BUILDERS ARRIVE

Percy sighed.

Now it was nothing unusual for Percy to sigh.

He was after all the duly elected spiritual guide and religious representative for a rather unique group of people.

This peculiar, often frustrating, challenging, but strikingly familiar, union of 'family' were not only his congregation but also his fellow members of the local bowling club.

His sigh was more one of sublime contentment with perhaps a slight hint of relief that he had somehow survived his first season at Lower South-Borough in his dual role as assistant green keeper and Reverend of the parish.

Percy had, like many people in his vocation, taken an early morning walk to seek divine inspiration amongst the tranquillity and serenity of the new dawn rising.

The harvest festival was due and he felt a keen sense of urgency to compose a sermon fitting for such a special occasion.

His biggest problem, he pondered, was trying to create and present an oration of great magnitude, appropriate for such a splendid event but encompassing all that had passed in the previous months.

There lay his fundamental predicament.

Simply far too much had been occurring in the day-to-day events leading to this moment that he now felt he needed to write a book to record his experiences.

Now there's a thought, pondered Percy, as the idea once again struck him that he really must place all his memoirs on paper as one day he felt there would be inspiration enough to perhaps compose a literary masterpiece.

He was fairly sure that there were more than enough characters in his congregation to inspire a whole bookshelf of novels.

At that point, Percy suddenly hesitated, breaking his immediate chain of thought to contemplate the likely outcome of this rather bold undertaking.

After all, it was frowned upon for anyone in his position of servitude to show too much individual initiative.

There lay the foundation of an even larger problem, certainly with the emphasis on 'large' thought Percy with a slight chuckle to himself.

Percy reflected that any venture into the field of creative literature would attract a great deal of publicity given the outcome of previous events and the now well established popularity of his congregation with the paparazzi.

He envisaged a strongly worded letter from the bishop regarding his position and especially his vow of pious abstinence from sinful wealth.

There was almost certain to be an invitation to make a generous donation for the new church bell tower whose underpinning would be firmly embedded in the bulk of any profit that the book should make.

Percy shuddered and a chill of trepidation traversed his lower spine; it was bad enough to receive a letter from 'higher authority', worse even than a tax bill or a VAT demand, but not as bad as a surprise visitation from the diocese.

Certainly one did not want to incur the wrath of Bishop Eugene Augustus Thomas the Third.

He was an extremely devout, keenly inspirational and 'old school' devotee, known for his unbroken vow of celibacy, personal chastisement and almost fanatical fervour for poverty and self-denial.

It was never a good idea to invite one of his enduring long winded sermons on the required devotion of the Lord's 'servants' and, heaven forbid, anyone should accidentally mention the word agnostic.

Eugene Augustus Thomas the Third was likely to turn the colour of beetroot before gathering a large 'bellow like' breath and launching into an address that would escalate rapidly in terms of volume, density of speech and impressively long words.

Percy was almost positive that there were distant relatives from the bishop's family history who had held places of honour in the Spanish inquisition.

He had heard a rumour that the bishop was actually christened Eugene Augustus Tabitha Thomas by a mother whose satirical sense of humour and poor handwriting had led to a most unfortunate misunderstanding at the font.

It was a closely guarded secret, and not one any wise person should dwell upon, or consider raising in close proximity to his keen ears which were famous for their sensitivity and ability to pick up key words such as 'donation', 'religion' and 'servitude' as well as the feared 'Tabitha'.

Rumour abounded of the fate of the Reverend Joshua Jackson from Little Snoring, who had unwisely commented on the fact that the bishop's initials were E.A.T. which was perhaps unfortunate given his fairly substantial body mass and girth.

In the 'off the cuff' response that followed, Eugene unwittingly revealed his hidden secret and not long after the Reverend Jackson undertook a very lengthy sabbatical to Australia.

Percy smiled reflectively to himself and wondered if perhaps his life was best left alone, uncomplicated and safe from too many unwelcome or self-incurred distractions.

Then again, he pondered, what were his chances of staying out of the limelight given the way his fellow members of the bowling club had unintentionally grabbed headline after glorious headline?

Actually there were a couple of occasions they had been unwittingly photographed dressed in only their glory and not much else. Percy had to admit though it had been a very shrewd career move for one or two of his flock to utilise the impromptu publicity, to further their public image.

Sticking to it more like the proverbial fly to the jam they had immersed themselves in their newly acquired celebrity status appearing on chat shows, radio interviews and political debates.

Percy did think it a bit much that Charlie, currently conspicuous by his absence, had appeared on the renowned ITV television show 'Richard and Prudence', thinly disguised as a retired member of the Lower South-Borough bowling fraternity suffering from recent memory loss.

It certainly hadn't prevented him recalling with much clarity the events of the summer camp excursion or the theatricals of the club finals day.

Newly-weds Bertie and Molly had spent their honeymoon as hosts of the renowned Channel 5 reality television show 'What a Big Bother' which was probably why the show was taken off the air after two days.

Squiffy and Chalkie had been commandeered by the Territorial Army recruiting office following their notorious misadventures with the hijacked armoured vehicle from the adventure park's military compound.

Following the publicity, the T.A.'s recruitment campaign became an instant success until, in his infinite wisdom, the army publicity officer, Sgt Major Sid 'Snotty' Snodgrass, decided to film a live television commercial.

The staged re-enactment of the bowling enthusiasts' wild ride was designed to prevent any re-occurrence of the rhinoceros-like trampling and trouncing of the theme park's prized assets.

Much like an old time movie the tank had been firmly fixed and set against a clear skyline above the forest with a cinema screen behind it showing the moving film footage of the bowlers' previously epic adventure. It has to be said, on reflection, that with the engine disabled, what had seemed perfectly safe at the time, later transpired to be very a foolish misconception.

No one had taken into account the precarious perchment of the armoured amphibian on the hill top, unwittingly left in neutral, and requiring only the not insubstantial weight of the dynamic duo to start it sliding down the rather slippery overnight well frozen mud.

Two hundred saplings and three-quarters of a mile later, the two veterans sat slumped on the broken tank track, sipping 'Dutch courage' from a hip flask, surveying the ravages of another Armageddon and agreeing that retirement was definitely the order of the day.

Percy breathed deeply, a reticent and reflective sort of sigh, with a wry smile flickering across his face.

Life in this parish was never dull and perhaps he should be thankful for the merriment it brought his way to an otherwise lonely, sometimes, meagre existence as an ecclesiastical bachelor.

Then again, considered Percy, even he had not escaped the limelight altogether, in his role as spiritual guide, religious consultant and keeper of the innocent.

He was still rather over-awed, shocked but secretly flattered by the offer he had received from a Bollywood director keen to make a comedy musical out of the South-Borough satire.

At the time the vicar thought it sounded quite fun until the title of 'CARRY ON PERCY' was bandied about and the connotations of that caused him more than a few palpitations.

Nevertheless, he promised to give it his utmost consideration: after all, one never knows what the future holds or what lies just around the corner, does one?

He deliberated on his thoughts very seriously for a brief while and reached, what was to him, an obvious and inevitable conclusion.

Local reporter Jiggy 'Snapper' Jenkins really did have a lot to answer for and perhaps this year's sermon should also carry a message; a respectful acknowledgement of everyone's right to individual freedom without fear of being 'caught on camera'.

The vicar sighed deeply and in a more reflective mood returned to the more immediate point in question and the reason for his stroll as he finally neared his intended destination.

He espied the fine oak which dwarfed the corner of South-Borough Lane, the mature hedgerow that formed the boundary both to the property and the lane that led to the bowling club.

The bowling green was clearly visible and at this time of the day nothing stirred other than an occasional blackbird or foraging squirrel.

Percy set out the deckchair that he had been carrying in his right hand, making sure not to open it before his long-suffering fingers were well clear of the temperamental wooden hinges, and sat down at last with a feeling of contentment.

He reached into the small bag he had also brought with him and studied the interior with a mixture of contemplation and careful consideration.

Inside he could distinctly see his notepad and pen already awaiting his divine inspiration, but that would have to wait just a while longer thought Percy to himself with a warm feeling of anticipation.

More importantly, alongside the writing material, sat a stainless steel flask full of piping hot coffee, accompanied by a small receptacle containing sugar, a cling-film covered jug of fresh cream and a misshapen piece of tin foil in which lay a thick slice of Mrs Spindleforth's very best fruitcake.

There was also a small paper bag in which he had earlier deposited four delicious digestive biscuits, fresh baked, and sure to be over rich in butter, honey and other delightful delicacies: it was too nice a day to worry about his waistline.

He lifted out the hot flask and proceeded to arrange his miniature picnic on the clean handkerchief which he had previously laid out on the grass beside him.

Being Percy meant being 'just so'; it was important to have the sugar and milk on the right side of the flask top, the fruit cake safely to one side away from any risk of spillage and the digestives at hand for ease of dunking.

He gazed at the rather splendid array, which was sure to inspire his literary speech preparation, poured his first cup of coffee, reached for the small paper bag and got ready for some serious dunking.

The vicar could almost taste the sumptuous delights of the delicious digestives as he unfurled the folded top and stared with anticipation at the contents within.

His emotions were somewhat mixed as the tin of 'PUDDIES Best Meaty Chunks' stared back at him.

Men are not always best suited to multi-tasking and answering the telephone to the bishop's inquiry about the harvest festival had apparently led his fingers astray.

Rollo was equally in for a shock and Percy wasn't too sure how his furry feline friend would respond to a dish of digestives in place of his favourite meaty chunks.

He looked around quickly to make sure Rollo wasn't already lurking under the hedgerow or behind a leaf pile preparing for a spur of the moment demonstration of deckchair shredding.

Knowing Rollo as only he could, as an impulsive, self-centred maniacal ball of uncontrollable fur with a tail at one end and a head at the other who was definitely 'several sausage rolls short of a picnic,' trouble was almost sure to follow.

Add to that a set of the fastest, sharpest razors on legs, a keen sense of the absurd, an IQ that would have astounded Einstein and an obsessive passion for his meaty chunks in gravy, it was a foregone conclusion that Rollo would react in a manner that would involve a painful reminder of failure to supply his favourite food.

For the time being the coast seemed clear. He breathed a sigh of relief: perhaps Rollo hadn't even returned home yet and there was time enough for him to enjoy his brief interlude and return to the 'scene of the crime' before the mistake was discovered.

He breathed deeply, took a chance and settled back into the comfort of his deckchair with coffee in one hand and fruitcake at his immediate disposal close to the other.

Percy gazed around at the scenery that unfurled before him as he sipped his beverage, pausing only to remove the teaspoon that suddenly appeared up his left nostril.

The lawnmower-shaped gap in the hedgerow was almost invisible already thanks to the nimble green fingers of Patrick Albright and some nifty replanting of well-manured new saplings.

It was a day to end all days at the twilight of the summer season, with the last of the sun's strength beginning to fade, the dew starting to gather in the corners of the green and the first of the leaves beginning to fall.

Percy noted with a slight grimace that other things were also starting to plummet and it was not the best of times to sit under the horse chestnut tree.

Absent-mindedly he picked up the offending item, noting its rather large and spiky exterior and the newly formed split, apparently from contact with his forehead, through which the recently born conker now glistened.

He moved his deckchair into the warm sun and away from erstwhile dangers from above, as he contemplated the championship potential of his not long acquired prize conker.

Certainly it had all the making or merits of becoming at least a '50' or maybe even more, he reflected, depending on how much pickling vinegar he used.

He remembered well his childhood years when he had tried to bake one or two in his mum's oven, just to harden then up of course. After all, Little Jimmy Blodger, school bully, had conkers that could put a crack in hardened cement and every trick in the book had to be used if you were to stand a chance at beating him.

Percy laughed to himself, chuckling loudly as he remembered the first time he took a swipe at Jimmy's prize champion.

The slight hint of fear in Jimmy's eyes as the light caught the toughened skin of Percy's 'challenger' made it look, just for a minute as if the conker were constructed out of cold hard steel.

Jimmy had, of course, tried to remove the target at the last moment but it was too late and in the blink of an eye his '200' was split cleanly in two halves.

One piece accelerated over the hedge as if attempting to reach orbit whilst the other cannoned into the tarmac and shattered into a thousand tiny pieces.

Little Jimmy Blodger was not one to be toyed with and his mind would have, at other times, been set on thoughts of revenge, conker napping and satchel-bashing.

He didn't really have time to consider any of that as the winning cannonball continued to accelerate through an arc, hardly hesitating as it impacted the outgoing champion, proceeding to impale itself on his two front teeth.

Well, Jimmy's mouth was always a bit overcrowded, reflected Percy, and once the conker, now embedded on his front incisors, was surgically removed along with any other broken teeth, he had been sure that Jimmy would look a lot better.

Percy of course didn't stay around to find out, in the terms of the old school banter he 'legged it.'

He had thought his schoolyard antics wouldn't backfire in too spectacular a fashion even though he'd have to keep a low profile for a week or two until Jimmy calmed down and the conker season was well and truly over.

What he hadn't bargained on was the missing conkers...

After giving his hedgerow haul a good overnight soak in vinegar Percy had made good use of his mum's kitchen appliances during one of her rare absences from the cooker.

Noting quite appreciatively that she was baking a fruit loaf amongst other things, he had quickly slipped seven or eight of the most promising conkers onto the top shelf just to 'harden them off' as his granddad used to show him.

He smiled to himself ruefully, remembering the length of time that passed before he could comfortably sit down again after his dad tanned his hide with a size 10 slipper.

It wasn't for the use of the oven of course.

Percy hadn't really paid much attention to the facts as he recovered the miniature meteorites from the cooker's steel grid.

Actually they were so well baked he had to borrow the metal tongs from their normal place of rest beside the fireplace to recover them.

He couldn't help but notice they were glowing a pale red in colour and wondered if, perhaps, he had left them just a little bit too long?

Anyway, Percy had dropped the hardened missiles quickly into his blazer pocket and returned the tongs, without incident, to their rightful place without being seen by his dad.

If he hadn't been in such a rush he might have noted that eight conkers went into the oven, but only six came out.

He might have pondered on their non-appearance and even contemplated the probability of spontaneous combustion from a touch too long in the oven.

He certainly hadn't considered the possibility of two of them falling off the top shelf and nestling quite comfortably into the top of mum's cake mixture.

It wasn't until granddad was safely tucked up in his hospital bed after having his stomach pumped that the inquisition began.

Perhaps it was lucky that the other miscreant had become wedged in his false teeth, otherwise it could have been a lot, lot worse, mused Percy.

He had in fact very nearly got away with it, the finger of blame pointing quite strongly at Mr Albright's (senior) fruit emporium where some very strenuous allegations were made about his nuts, much to the consternation of the local spinsters.

It was of course, too good to last and Percy's luck ran out much at the same moment that the remaining conkers exited his school blazer pocket through the hole they had burnt in the lining.

By the time his dad had finished with him, following first an apologetic meeting with the fruit merchant, his bottom resembled the glowing conkers.

The vicar wriggled in his deckchair momentarily as he remembered the experience and pondered on how a memory from 31 years ago could seem so fresh in his mind.

It had of course been quite an experience; certainly one with a lot more twists and turns than a roller-coaster ride and with all its surprises not one he would have wanted to miss out on.

A wry smile played across his lips as he remembered some of the funnier events of the summer past.

Who would have thought that the rather brash, objective, abrupt and somewhat annoying Bertie Tattleford would win the hearts and minds of the locals as well as becoming the crowned singles champion.

Percy's rueful smile spread into a grin as he remembered the actions of Molly Tattleford, former spinster of the parish, and her overt display of seduction which subsequently led to an over-exposure of her assets in every sense of the word.

Then of course there was the legendary 'grand finale' from the outgoing president, the Rt Hon. Ronald 'Squiffy' Regis who would certainly go down in history for his dedication and commitment, not to mention his boxer shorts.

Percy chuckled to himself.

On the subject of underwear there was no doubt that Big Jim had been spared more than a few blushes for his fanciful choice of underwear, although rumour soon spread quicker than soft butter.

Talking of rumours, Percy had experienced more than a few concerning his own antics mainly due to the ongoing misadventures and grandiose misbehaviour of his equally problematic pet Rollo.

Percy glanced across the green from where he currently sat deep in reflection in his deckchair and noted that the cat in question had arrived surreptitiously and was also now deep in contemplation, actually it was virtually comatose.

From his actions and demeanour it didn't appear that he had yet discovered the error in his food bowl.

Rollo was in fact curled up in the corner of the flowerbed, his large bushy tail curled around his slumbering body as the last of the summer's warmth washed over his fur.

The twitching of his whiskers and tail indicated that he was probably having a very interesting dream.

Percy sighed again, settling into the comfortable recesses of his chair as he indulged in the extravagance of enjoying his own space and the pleasure of the late summer warmth.

The outdoor season had come to an end in a blaze of spectacular theatrics, colourful metaphors, unexpected publicity and a deserving accolade for the club.

The accumulation of fund raising, substantial donations, a triumphant tournament and a few hefty contributions from unnamed sources had been backed by a successful lottery grant bid which had reaped unexpected rewards.

That reward currently lay around the car park, pathways and gardens of the bowling club in the form of construction materials.

Actually it was more like the equivalent of the European butter mountain for builders, reflected Percy.

There were piles of new bricks stacked in large rectangular squads much like a mass of miniature Roman phalanxes whilst quarry stones rose in columns as if they were stone-age lighthouses.

The interspersed mountains of breezeblock and shingle gave the impression of a random post-impressionist mosaic.

All in all, thought Percy, the once orderly, immaculate and perfectly presented bowling club gardens now resembled an outside exhibition by a leading artist at the Tate Modern.

Lunar landscapes comprised of brightly coloured sand and cement sacks fought for pride of place underneath tightly stretched tarpaulins.

Freshly cut and treated timber supports were laid lattice-like amid the assault course lending a pleasurable smell of oak and pine to the warm air.

Ladders perched precariously along the clubhouse structure gave the impression that the hut was in the last defiant throes of fighting off an invasion.

A number of impressive items of important looking machinery sprawled around the car park of which the centrepiece was a rather majestic and imposing JCB digger.

Percy supposed that even the club's ancient 'Beast of Lower South-Borough' Victorian mower would develop an inferiority complex amid this awesome array of hardware.

The child in him was running riot and he was overwhelmed by a desire to climb into the cab of the JCB, just to have a look; of course he wouldn't touch the controls, would he?

He made a mental note to have a word with the site foreman.

There was of course all manner of merchandising and paraphernalia associated with building sites although Percy could not fathom the purpose of the polka dot boxer shorts still hanging from the clubhouse flagpole.

They did, however serve as a timely reminder of the humorous manner in which the season had unfolded and which the club had ultimately come to receive its financial benefaction.

Whilst he was sure that Squiffy could have made a lucrative foray into the financial enterprises of the underwear underworld and perhaps could have even cornered the market in autographed polka dot pants he had not even considered the possibilities of exclusive designer bunting.

Sheila being the outgoing and shrewd woman that she was, always keen to turn an unexpected reward, was ecstatic to have profited so well from the photogenic promotion of her best assets.

In a lucrative deal with 'Pretty in Pink' she not only topped up her bank balance considerably but had enough free stockings to last a lifetime.

Like many of the members she was not backward in coming forward with a sizeable donation to the club's liquid assets and it was perhaps the unexpected bonuses from their various madcap adventures that made everything possible now.

Not only could they look forward to a brand new outside clubhouse, but also the re-laying of a new lawn for next year's rinks. There would also be enough left over in the kitty to pay for a number of important local events.

Perhaps even enough money for the more costly celebrations such as the children's Halloween party and community Christmas 'knees up'.

Maybe even an overseas holiday.

Reverend Percival Peabody sighed wholeheartedly, and returned with a wishful expression to the matter in hand, that of drinking his rapidly cooling coffee and enjoying his delicious fruitcake.

He reflected again on his choice of seating as he looked in despair at the larger than life unopened conker now floating in his half-empty coffee, much like a World War II mine.

He nursed his rather tender nose which had encountered the offending object and looked across to where Rollo exuberantly played 'cat and mouse' with a piece of shiny silver paper.

Percy smiled at Rollo's antics and wondered where he could have found such a large piece of metallic paper-ware on the otherwise spic and span green.

The cat was definitely having a lot of fun chasing it around the grass as the light cool breeze lifted it teasingly into the air, and it wasn't too long before Rollo had shredded it into tinsel.

Percy laughed.

It must have been the remnants of a workman's packed lunch he mused; after all the only thing one would wrap in such a piece of foil would be a ham sandwich or a piece of fruit cake.

FRUITCAKE!

Percy glanced down towards the impromptu picnic where the flask still stood alongside his utensils and the small bag of home made digestives.

The china plate formerly adorned by Mrs Spindleforth's very best fruit cake now looked rather forlorn and bare.

A trail of crumbs conspicuously led away to the nearby shrubbery and Percy cast a look in the cat's direction that spoke volumes, none of it good.

He was a mild mannered man even at the worst of times but there were certain things a person just did not do, and one of his much respected proverbs was 'never mess with another man's fruit cake!'

It clearly was a time for action and anyone remembering the fate of Joe 'Dodger' Stubbs from Flash Harry promotions would have wisely left the immediate vicinity very quickly indeed.

Percy reached down to pick up some of the fallen conkers and advanced on the playfully unaware cat with a purposeful look in his eyes.

It would have been better if perhaps he had put down the coffee cup first, as his scream of surprise alerted the mangy moggie to the ensuing danger.

Rollo fled, as a vengeful and somewhat damp vicar pursued him in a rather bedraggled fashion.

A few minutes later, Rollo was to be found ensconced at the top end of the rather substantial and high bird feeding station in the club's wildlife garden. He had managed to squeeze his not inconsiderable bulk inside the birdhouse, much to the annoyance of the up to that moment resident and rather content blackbird.

How he had quite achieved it was questionable, but there was no doubt that he had.

His imposing and bulky frame was squeezed in so tightly that his long hair swelled out of every opening like a sponge ball. His head was extended through the front porch and a pair of wild-eyed dilated pupils twitched in a nervous fashion from left to right and back again.

Percy stood at the bottom of the table staring in amazement up the length of the ten-foot post to where the birdhouse shimmied and shook to the rhythm of Rollo's rapid breathing.

The sight of Rollo substantially wedged in such a way that a carpenter would probably be required, as well as a vet with a tranquillizer, was really all too much for the mirthful Percy.

The cat did indeed resemble a puffer fish that had just met a very large shark and had protectively inflated itself accordingly.

Percy just couldn't restrain himself.

'Ha Ha Ha' he chortled.

'Ha Ha Ha Ha Ha!!!'

****

It was the morning after.

It had taken several hours of the previous day to secure the services of a carpenter with a good pair of steel gloves as well as the on-call vet, Dr Boris Binder-Garden.

A much subdued, hungrier and deflated Rollo, somewhat relaxed, chilled out even, from the effects of the tranquilliser administered earlier, now resided on his favourite velvet cloak, formerly the property of Reverend Percival Peabody.

A large tin of pilchards in tomato sauce and a saucer of double cream had done much to restore the bedraggled moggie's demeanour; following a good night's rest on Percy's sumptuous thick quilt he was in fine fettle. Though it had to be said that Rollo's over-burdened digestion did little for the vicar's sleep patterns as twice during the night he was required to open the bedroom windows rather swiftly.

With the outdoor season well and truly over, Sunday 22nd September was set to be a very prestigious and important day.

Most of the club members of course would be there this year in particular, as the traditional closing of the green marked the last day of the old clubhouse, ever!

There were, of course, all the mementos and furnishings to remove and pack away, the kitchen to clear and the salvaging of anything worth keeping.

Percy could imagine that decisions on what should be kept and what should be sacrificed would become quite a contentious issue.

He had no doubt that Big Jim and Co. would be overseeing the packing away of all the alcohol from the club bar.

Of course there were bound to be a few bottles that were nearly empty and it was not hard to imagine that the boys would consider them not worth packing away.

It was almost certain to be a unanimous decision by the 'beverage removal committee' that it would be both wise and space saving to finish them up!

Percy could already envisage Big Jim, Derek, Charlie and Dennis at the end of the day, rolling about the armchairs amid a growing number of whisky, rum, gin and brandy bottles that had been liberated of their dregs.

It was pretty much assured that a pack of cards would somehow miraculously appear at some point and highly likely that Sheila, in passing, be drawn into the affray.

He dared not imagine the final outcome and made a mental note to ensure that Jiggy Jenkins was nowhere near the clubhouse at that point.

Percy was deep in thought as he checked the vicarage. He needed to make sure that all was as it should be; in particular that Rollo was safe and sound with ample food as well as fresh cream, not to mention securely under lock and key.

Perhaps if he had been a little quicker he would have espied the now fully refreshed moggie hi-tailing it out of the patio door having paused momentarily to polish off the half empty tin of pilchards left over from the previous night.

It was fairly obvious that the Reverend was still mulling over the letter that had arrived first thing that morning.

The envelope was clearly marked with the return address of Eugene Augustus Thomas the Third and as such Percy required a whole pot of strong coffee before he plucked up the courage to open it.

'Dear Reverend Peabody...' it began, which was always a good sign that there was indeed a likelihood of welcoming news within.

Bad news usually began with the line 'It has come to the attention of...'

At that point it was wise to pack your bags, take a vow of chastisement, hide the brandy bottle and prepare for the arrival of nothing less than the Spanish inquisition.

Percy was, nevertheless, vexed by the unexpected content of the letter and unsure of how to respond although at heart he already knew his decision.

Apparently the bishop was, for once, well pleased with the Reverend's attentive and enthusiastic pursuit of preaching divinity to the masses of Lower South-Borough.

The rapidly increasing numbers in his flock had also had a corresponding effect of significantly swelling the coffers and there was little doubt the rising bank balance had caught the bishop's eye.

Perhaps he had considered the 'Percy Effect' and the potential outcome if it were to be repeated throughout the other 42 parish communities in his realm.

Certainly the tills of the diocese would be definitely ringing in unison with the church bells at an overtime rate.

The letter included a substantial rise in Percy's payroll, almost 12p an hour, which to a vicar was rather a lot, at least enough for an extra three loaves of bread and fives fishes at the end of the week, metaphorically speaking.

However, and there was always a 'however' with anything involving the vicar of Lower South-Borough, the offer required Percy to move to the rather grandiose offices of the bishop's sprawling country estate in Upper Snoddington, much removed from the warmth and camaraderie of his own small parish.

There, no doubt, he would fall under the jurisdiction and watchful stentorian eyes of Eugene Augustus Thomas the Third's calculative and most fervent advisors.

Just the thought made Percy tremble and a tiny worry bead of perspiration broke out on his now furrowed brow.

How on earth was he supposed to say 'no' to the strongly worded offer without being stripped of his parish and deported to the salt mines of Siberia?

After all, look what had happened to his predecessor.

Well at least the Reverend Joshua Jackson would have got a suntan; all Percy would get was a severe case of hypothermia.

More importantly though, how was Rollo going to cope with the sprawling pastures of the bishop's smallholding which was closely, almost possessively and fanatically overseen by Archie?

Archie was of course better known as 'Reverend Archibald', a temperamental, drooling, cross-eyed, bow legged bulldog with the attitude of a vampire slayer, the patience of a psychopath and the personality of a zombie.

Heaven forbid, thought Percy, even the coffee house was called The Inquisitors Rest, and that was the nearest thing the locals got to any libation given the strict regime of the autocratic Parish Council.

Just the mention of a Public House or Chinese Takeaway opening would be enough to send the bishop and his followers into a panic-stricken, hysterical, fanatical frenzy much like possessed witchdoctors.

'Morning Percy, watch out for that hole!'

Percy came back to the reality of the present with a startled jolt as he paused in mid stride, aware of his raised right foot now precariously perched over the freshly dug builders' hole.

It looked rather deep and muddy around the foundations and the excavation trench was not the place for anyone to investigate too closely, especially a member of the clergy.

He stepped back cautiously onto the footpath and looked up towards the source of the vocal warning.

A number of his fellow members had emerged from the indoor arena and were apparently discussing the ongoing works for the new clubhouse.

Bernard Bartrum, Douglas Doolittle, Jack Tuttle, Derek Dunstable and Patrick Albright all stood in a judge's huddle on the slope near the entrance, whilst a frustrated looking Dennis 'Sticky' Ditherford peered out from the inside.

He could be seen clearly through the glass panel and it was obvious he was trying to open the door to come outside; equally apparent was the fact that the others were pretending not to notice.

There was little chance however of Sticky opening the heavy external, spring loaded door whilst the not inconsequential mass of Big Jim's 18 stone leant against it.

The reason for Jim's innocent amble became clear as the previously unnoticed head of Charlie popped up into view in the other window.

Apparently the long lost parish comedian and loveable rogue had resurfaced, but the others were not going to release him from the impromptu prison quite yet.

'BACKS TO THE WALLS BOYS!' came the shout from the old clubhouse.

'Has anyone seen Charlie?'

More tittering emerged from the clubhouse and Percy looked around to find the cause.

Sheila 'Legs' Ramsbottom and the now much liberated Phillippa Spindleforth were creased up with laughter trying hard not to spill their tea, which Sheila had unfortunate memories of, whilst the newly elected ladies' president Gloria Grimshaw looked on with a haughty expression of disapproval.

Gloria, also known as 'steel britches' when out of earshot, was about as near as you could get to a female version of Mr Freeze.

One was almost sure to get frostbite when shaking her hand at any award ceremony, and she always had a knack of putting her foot in it without even realising it.

'Oh look it's Pinky and Perky,' shrieked Sheila.

'More like Laurel and Hardy in a fish tank,' screamed Phillippa, with reference to the extreme contrast in the men's girth sizes.

'Oh Charlie are you coming out to play?' giggled Sheila loudly, provocatively exposing a considerable length of her long leg through the clubhouse doorway.

Charlie clearly wanted to come out to play, and the increasingly darker shade of red of his complexion was an indication of just how much.

Sheila raised the stakes and the hemline of her skirt...

Her extremely long, tanned and shapely pins were always the centre of much attention around the club, especially when she bowled. A fair length of those from ankle to thigh was now 'on show' around the door frame.

The desired affect was achieved with the usual impact.

Douglas turned red, as one of his braces twanged loudly, the flying buckle catching him on the end of his nose making his eyes water profusely.

Derek quickly gave his glass eye an extra polish.

Bernard whistled loudly, his tongue protruding like that of a hungry wolf spying fresh cooked lamb, just as Patrick, being of modest inclination, leant across quickly with a firm hand to close his mouth tightly shut.

Bernard of course had little time to retract his tongue and much later would require a good mouthwash full of salt to numb the pain.

Big Jim as per usual reached for his hip flask and stepped away from the door to get a better look at the floorshow.

The withdrawal of 18 stone of doorstop combined with the forward motion of Dennis and Charlie pushing with all their strength on the other side led of course to the inevitable.

The door opened with great gusto, Dennis, being a lightweight, collapsed in a heap whilst Charlie propelled at great speed into the open.

Charlie's face was one of desperation, hysteria, and desire all rolled into one. Suddenly released from his prison he catapulted across the grass having just enough time to identify and recognise Sheila's saucy provocative display; he reached out a hand in vain hope.

On any other occasion he might have succeeded in making contact and would have accepted the rebuke of a stinging slap across the face just for the privilege.

On this particular day, however, luck, nature and builders played their part in spoiling Charlie's fun as he arrived at the place where Percy had stood, or teetered, minutes beforehand.

Percy, now safely balanced on the edge of the footings had not yet taken in his brethren's playful tomfoolery and was trying hard not to laugh or indeed look at Sheila's brazen antics.

Clearly the ladies were enjoying the turn of the tables to the full.

Charlie felt the ground disappear beneath his feet, literally, and he was somewhat confused to find himself, seconds later, up to his ankles in wet mud whilst fending off the attention of a large wriggling lobworm.

The previously enthusiastic and pursuant blackbird was equally not impressed by his dramatic, unexpected entrance; squawking loudly he pecked Charlie's head, picked up the worm and flew off in an angry flutter of feathers.

'Er... anyone seen Charlie?' asked Sheila, as she leaned around the doorjamb with a very wicked grin as the others smiled broadly.

The ladies burst into hysterics, struggling for breath as they laughed louder and louder. Tears were soon running down their cheeks as they took full advantage of the moment and thoroughly enjoyed its mirth.

The men at the clubhouse door were not far behind...

Percy sighed.

'Here we go again,' he thought to himself, with a feeling of déjà vu.

At least, he thought, Rollo was not on hand to make matters worse than they already were.

Later perhaps he might reflect on that thought with an air of inevitability and realise how foolish the observation actually was.

****

About an hour later, events had settled down somewhat.

The men had managed to extricate Charlie from the pit; in fact he scrabbled to safety very quickly with a wild look in his eyes when Derek suggested they use the JCB to scoop him out.

Charlie now sat in the warm surrounds of a deep cosy armchair, drinking a cup of tea, and nursing a small elastoplast on his forehead.

Bernard, Big Jim, Patrick and Derek had headed off to the outside clubhouse where they were already making preparations for moving the last of the bar stock.

Over by the kitchen, Sheila and Phillippa had been joined by a number of the other ladies including Diane the competition secretary and Doris their captain.

Gloria Grimshaw had remained behind in the condemned kitchen to supervise the packing of the new, and much prized, bone china dinner service which had replaced the one previously demolished by Bernard's antics in the summer.

It was rather a tasteful set, finished in cream with an inlay of bowler's figures around the edge and an individual set piece in every centre.

Gloria would of course ensure that they were packed with the female silhouettes on top and the male underneath, just to keep the men in their 'proper place'.

Percy, having restored a semblance of order and decorum had retired to the corner of the pavilion and was even now reclining in his deckchair where he began the previous morning.

In the warmth of the mid-morning, after tea and biscuits, he had started to get quite sleepy; it wasn't long before the peace and quiet had its desired effect.

Percy dozed off...

Nothing so much as a falling leaf disturbed the tranquil and peaceful serenity of the glorious autumnal morning.

Perhaps he was already dreaming of events far ahead. The preparation for the new clubhouse, or maybe the children's Halloween party or even Christmas, as he had been invited to give a talk on the local radio show.

Whatever his thoughts he was far away.

Rollo however was a lot closer.

He was in fact curled up in his favourite spot in the flower bed, happily snoozing on top of Patrick's prize petunias, and was not bothered at all whether the green keeper could see him or not.

Once again he had made good his escape and the cunning ploy of utilising the air vent hidden behind the velvet cloak would no doubt create a mystery that would vex Percy considerably.

In his dreams Rollo was in pursuit of a mouse, the fattest, juiciest, tastiest, and most delicious one he had ever seen or could imagine. It almost looked like a hock of prime roast beef with legs attached. The attractive aroma arising from it already had him mewing in his sleep, drooling and salivating.

Over in the corner of the bushes on the far side of the greenery, the pampas grass twitched as a pair of deep blue eyes stared intently at the slumbering figures.

Anyone passing closely might have noticed that there appeared to be a large bundle of straggly beige, cream and white fur behind the piercing eyes.

Gloria Grimshaw's prize Persian pussy 'Miss Matilda Bagshott' stared intently at Rollo from behind her leafy screen with a raised eyebrow and a mischievous smile.

She was a somewhat snobbish, short tempered, often spoilt and ungraciously preened supposedly 'posh' pussy, but had a tendency to be a bit of a tart too.

Despite being the companion of such a prim and proper owner Miss Matilda Bagshott preferred the rough 'n' tumble lifestyle of an alley tomcat; not to put too fine a point on it, she liked a 'bit of rough'.

With an air of playful intent she waltzed out of the pampas, strutting and prancing like a ballerina, her hips swaying, fur fluffed and tail raised high in a question mark curl.

She approached Rollo from the rear, so there was no indication whatsoever even to his radar-like senses of the impending pampered puss on parade.

Baggie, as the alley cats preferred to call her, arrived at the tail end of Rollo's torso, sat back on her haunches and studied the slumbering fur ball for a few minutes.

Her pupils dilated extensively, as her heart pounded that bit faster, and faster still, whilst her hackles twitched and quivered; she watched, stared and contemplated.

She purred rather loudly in a mewing seductive fashion.

Rollo stirred slightly, his tail fluttering before falling back.

Baggie purred again, louder still, and licked the back of his left ear in a suggestive manner.

Rollo was too busy chasing the roast beef; he had finally cornered it in the cloakroom and was just fastening his napkin around his neck.

He remained slumbering.

Baggie sighed in a cat-like way, considered the possibilities and likely outcomes, then, being a typically forthright Persian pussy who expected and demanded attention, took the most direct approach.

She stretched her front paw, examined it studiously for a minute and then extended her middle claw which glinted in the weak sunlight much like a fish hook.

Rollo had just administered the salt and pepper and was raising his knife and fork when he was very abruptly awakened by the arrival of a very sharp needle-like skewer in his left rump.

The vicar's cat had very unpleasant memories of sharp things that stung, mainly due to his unfortunate encounter with a large bee last summer, so it was pretty much a forgone conclusion that his body would react well before his brain engaged.

The juicy mouse instantaneously disappeared in a vivid flash of colour as Rollo's eyelids shot open in shock, his fur coat expanding in all directions as he levitated fully four feet into the air with his legs stretched stiffly downwards, claws extended and trademark loo-brush tail bolt upright.

Much like a greyhound out of the starting gate, Rollo hit the ground running; in fact he took off in a madcap, insane and uncontrolled manner that left dust flying, leaves parting, flowers decapitated and grass cuttings unceremoniously thrown into the air.

Baggie looked on with a playful smile on her lips, pleased at the response, and thought to herself that this particular 'bit of ruff' looked rather sexy when aroused.

She removed the clod of turf that now decorated her head, spat out the petunias and charged after Rollo in hot pursuit.

Percy remained oblivious to the animated antics and continued to snooze.

Back at the clubhouse, the boys were busy packing up and discussing all the latest news as well as the tastiest tit-bits of the summer season now past.

Big Jim had just emerged from behind the rapidly diminishing stock cupboard with a twinkle in his eye and a near-empty brandy bottle that still promised the possibility of one or two 'snifters.'

Bernard, quick as always on the uptake, reached for a couple of small shot glasses and stepped swiftly to the bar.

Charlie, Dennis, Bernard, Patrick and the newly arrived Tony Havershall, known favourably to his friends as 'Trigger' because he was so slow off the mark, were busy helping to reduce the stock of nuts and crisps by digesting them.

'Quite a summer, old chap,' said Charlie, in between munching on his cheese and onion crisps.

'Not a bad one at all really,' replied Dennis, reflecting on his near miss on finals day whilst devouring a pack of salt and vinegar.

'Still can't understand why I didn't make any money,' muttered Trigger, referring to his failed betting coup as he picked up his prawn cocktail flavoured offerings from the clubhouse floor.

It's never wise to turn the crisp bag upside down to read the answer to 'today's joke', especially when you've already opened the other end!

'What's the time then Trigger?' asked Patrick, in a mischievous manner which was much unlike him given his normal character, but then he had enjoyed a significant quantity of coffee with a whisky top-up.

Trigger turned his wrist over to check.

'It's 11.55 and Noddy will soon be on top of Big Ears,' he said, with a gleeful smile, as his dry roasted peanuts joined the prawn cocktail crisps on the floor.

Charlie looked across with a concerned and anxious expression on his face as he questioned the suggestive answer, only to note the larger than life Toytown watch that Trigger happily flashed in his direction.

Patrick was obviously in a rare silly mood and was already hiding behind the kitchen worktop gurgling in a childish manner at his prank whilst Gloria Grimshaw looked on with distaste from behind her damp tea towel.

The derogatory snorting from behind the bar also indicated that Bernard and Big Jim had joined in the mirth and were currently in fits of alcoholic paroxysm.

'It's a present from my nephew,' continued Trigger, in his excitement, oblivious to the cocktail party buffet he was distributing on the club floor.

Charlie stared at the watch face now only four inches from his line of sight and noted that the figures of Noddy and Big Ears were indeed adhered to the hour and minute hands whilst being superimposed over a backdrop of the Toytown clock tower.

He couldn't quite make out what Andy Pandy and Teddy were doing; however Looby Lou was definitely looking somewhat sick surmounted on the second hand.

Dennis made a rapid exit, chuckling to himself en-route whilst Sheila and Phillippa desperately tried to stifle their own laughter, failing miserably.

They too made a dash for the fresh air leaving the hapless Charlie alone with Tony Havershall, who definitely did on this occasion appear to have left some of his marbles in the bag.

'I've got matching socks and underwear too,' stated Trigger in a matter of fact fashion, 'would you like to see?'

Charlie downed the nearest available tot of brandy then in a hoarse choking apologetic voice said, 'No that's alright, I've just remembered I'm late for confession with the vicar!' and raced for the door.

Trigger looked with a bemused expression on his face, and called after Charlie's fleeing figure, 'How about my vest?'

Big Jim, Bernard and Patrick peered over their respective glasses and stared at the wildly swinging door with open-eyed surprise at Charlie's speedy exit.

It would be even funnier if Charlie did actually bump into the vicar and had to spend the next two hours listening to one of Percy's sermons; he was after all long overdue for a serious confessional after his summer antics.

Patrick, with a slightly mischievous twinkle on his face, looked over to where the innocent looking Trigger now stood.

'You haven't really got Noddy and Big Ears on your boxer shorts have you?' said Patrick, realising that perhaps the worm had turned, and that the leg puller had his well and truly yanked.

'Of course not...' said Trigger in a firm positive voice.

Bernard and Big Jim sighed with relief and reached for their shots of brandy.

'I only wear Magic Roundabout characters on my underwear!' he continued, 'Florence and Dougal are my favourites!'

The tipsy two slid back behind the counter clutching their glasses and snorting loudly.

'HA! HA! HA!'

'OH DEAR... HA! HA! SAINTS PRESERVE US!'

Patrick beside himself with mirth had to sit down rather quickly on the nearest chair, which was slightly unfortunate given that Gloria had just deposited the newly washed knives, forks and spoons on it just a few seconds earlier.

'OH MY GOD!!!' screamed Patrick, standing up a lot quicker than he had previously sat down, and reaching for the fork whose prongs were painfully embedded in his well padded posterior.

For once even Gloria managed a smile and reached thoughtfully for the first aid kit and a pair of nearby pliers.

Patrick, noting that she gave the impression of a welder about to carry out repairs on some armour plating, thought better of it, made his excuses and left abruptly in search of the on-call nurse.

It was about one hour later that the men and women gathered back at the clubhouse for one final sweep of the building for any final boxes, bottles, badges, or bits and pieces.

They were all in a somewhat calmer mood and enjoying a final cup of tea before the boiler was turned off for the very last time.

It was a very auspicious moment which was to change the whole aspect of the club and it was a good opportunity for them to reflect upon matters both arising and past.

'What a season eh?' commented Percy casting his mind back to the summer.

'Yes, and what about old Dodger from Flash Harry promotions?' said Patrick, still nursing his painful, but now well-administered bottom.

There was a definite coldness in Percy's eyes as he replied, 'Well that's the last we'll hear of him, he's behind bars where he belongs!'

'Thank God he didn't have any brothers, one is more than enough for any community,' quipped Charlie, 'that's the last we've heard of Joe 'Dodger' Stubbs!'

Big Jim piped in, 'Has anyone heard from Molly and Bertie?'

The two members of the club had been opposite extremes when they first met but after one or two very big surprises they had ended a whirlwind romance with marriage and were yet to return from their honeymoon.

Dennis joined the debate, 'We had a postcard to say they were returning home this week, they've had a wonderful time and Molly says she has a big surprise for us all!'

Bernard made a typical Bernard-style comment: 'God she's not expecting a baby already is she?'

Percy looked across, 'Well whatever the news, it can only be good and we should embrace it with open arms.'

'Hear hear!' spouted Squiffy, having just arrived and entering the conversation for the very first time, 'jolly good show, what!'

The Rt Hon. Ronald Regis had been the club's most successful and popular president ever and having now retired from his position at the end of the summer held a lifetime honorary membership.

He was a typical former RAF man, and sometimes bowled a bit like Barnes Wallis, but in his day, or when on-form, he was a force to be reckoned with, as county champion Martin King had found out much to his loss earlier on in the tournament finals.

The sound of an engine running in too high a gear and being overstrained, disrupted their conversation as a tatty ancient transit van struggled into the car park bearing the motif 'Murphy & McPherson ... Builders of Trusted Quality'.

Percy noted that the first T in 'trusted' had been humorously painted out and the wording now bore a more honest and appropriate resemblance to the van's state.

It was apparent that the firm didn't put much faith in their transportation, whilst it was certain that you could not fault the quality of their construction equipment that adorned the car park.

Their reputation for craftsmanship grew with every installation, but they were certainly known as eccentric characters within the trade.

Behind the van a number of interestingly dressed workers began to arrive, a rather motley bunch of brightly coloured hard hats, string vests, denim shirts unwisely unbuttoned, decorated dungarees and cowboy boots.

Percy was unsure whether their clothing was builders 'required uniform' or they were expecting to audition for a part in the Village People later at the local theatre.

One thing he was sure about however was the unlikelihood of them ever passing an audition for the 'Full Monty'.

Squiffy glanced at his watch: 1.00 p.m. stared back.

'Looks like a typical day out with the Murphy & McPherson boys,' he observed, 'start late, finish late with 32 tea breaks thrown in.'

Percy smiled as a voice carried over from the car park 'Right lads, let's have a quick cuppa then we'll get started on the demolition.'

****

Rollo had been running for a while and even he was beginning to tire, his rump still smarted from the earlier acupuncture treatment and he had yet to weigh up the damage to his tender anatomy.

He still wasn't sure exactly what had happened, but he assumed that in curling up on the petunias he had unwittingly squashed a few bees and perhaps one of them had popped back to voice its discontent.

After a few wild forays back and forth through the hedgerow he had finally found a place that was sure to be safe from any disturbance; being enclosed it held no threat from any passing bee, wasp, dragonfly or prehistoric monster.

Rollo was now safely ensconced on the warm, padded, driver's seat of Murphy & McPherson's JCB digger.

The midday sun had warmed the cab to a pleasurable temperature and with most of the windows closed he felt fairly safe and secure, added to which he had the advantage of a prime view of the rather busy bird table.

All in all, after careful consideration, it had been worth the slight discomfort of the sting just to find this haven from which to watch his favourite entertainment, birds feeding!

Rollo began to drift off to sleep at last; his final thoughts before snoozing were 'What could possibly go wrong here?'

****

It took about 15 minutes for the builders to finish their first tea break of the day, another 10 before they were suitably attired and ready to start work.

Jimmy 'Monkey' Murphy, so named from his hay-days as a scaffolder with no fear of heights, and Johnny 'Midge' McPherson simply because he stood an impressive seven feet tall in his bare feet with broad shoulders were poring over the blueprints. Jimmy could just about see over the five feet high table, whilst Johnny had to stoop low just to fit in the Portakabin so together they really did make quite a picture. However it took a very brave or somewhat foolish man to pass a remark on their appearance.

They did, after all, employ at least two dozen beefy 'wannabe' lumberjacks, well paid brickies, pampered plumbers, and laconic labourers on their books.

'Well that's settled then,' commented Jimmy.

'Agreed,' said Johnny, 'the clubhouse goes at 2.00 p.m. you had better give the members a 30 minute warning to clear the building.'

Any other person might have considered walking around the clubhouse and immediate vicinity to warn people one at a time, but Jimmy was never one to do things by halves.

With lightness in his step he bounced out of the Portakabin, climbed nimbly onto the tracks of the JCB, swung himself up the arm of the digger and stood on top of the large raised bucket.

He raised the over-sized gas propelled foghorn up into the air and checked his watch; it was 1.59 and 55 seconds.

Jimmy counted down the final seconds,

Five... Four... Three... Two... One...

and pressed the button.

P—H—W—A—A—R—R—R —P!!!

Unfortunately the elevated bucket was only a few feet from Rollo's left ear, and the extended arm was even closer.

Beneath the digger Miss Matilda Bagshott had been preparing for an all-out assault on the main cab.

Having spent the last couple of hours stalking Rollo cautiously through the rough grass of the shrubbery she had arrived at the end of the car park just in time to espy her prime target entering the steel clad hotspot via the cabin window.

Baggie was, not to put too fine a point on it, wildly excited by the chase, and her pheromones were charging around her body like Formula One racing cars. She was besotted by the raggy, rough 'n' tumble appearance of Rollo; his wild looks, crazy antics and mayhemic misadventures had been the source of her ever closer attention over the summer months.

She had watched from a distance, absorbing every move that he made, and within her an amorous passion had grown more and more on a daily basis until finally that day she decided to give things a little 'push' in the right direction.

'Well, more of a little prick really,' she sniggered to herself.

She had got to within virtual earshot of her intended target and was about to pounce when fate and builders took a hand in her precise military campaign as the foghorn blared out.

Nothing could have given Rollo more of a shock than the equivalent of a nuclear detonation close to one of the most sensitive parts of his anatomy.

Well that was certainly how his traumatised nerve endings analysed it in his mind.

Rollo, it has to be said, had never woken or moved quicker in his entire life; he did a sensational impression of a Harrier jump jet, rising fully six feet off the warm seat, rotating 180 degrees and exiting the window of the JCB without pausing to first open the window.

Jimmy's first warning that all was not as it should be was the shattering sound of re-enforced plastic sheeting followed by the expulsion of a snarling, spitting projectile of a flying fur ball from the cab.

Rollo's thick coat protected him from any injury as he escaped through the window, but the following sound gave the impression of a very loud sonic boom which made all the nearby club members jump in alarm.

Eight cups of tea, two mugs of coffee and an orange squash left their relative containers, propelled in an upwards direction as their owners responded to the loud bang with a knee jerk reaction; well more of an arm jerk really.

A photograph at that point would have quite easily made the Sunday Times supplement 'Caption Competition.'

Six drinks actually re-orbited successfully into their waiting receptacles, whilst two, a coffee and a tea, managed to swap places, hardly missing a drop.

One managed to deposit itself in a continuous stain from navel to ankle on Big Jim's best trousers, whilst another contrived to turn Patrick's lawn shoes into a miniature Jacuzzi.

The orange juice, and it's ice cubes were the cause of even more acute embarrassment as they descended at great speed down the back of Charlie's jeans; he had been at that point bending over to tie his shoe lace.

The resulting involuntary scream was bad enough for any relative bystander, but the subsequent physical response did little to improve Charlie's demeanour; he had already had a bad day after all and it was getting progressively worse.

Standing up all too quickly he managed to dislodge the overhead hanging basket which conveniently flipped over on its retaining chain depositing a fair quantity of manure, fertiliser, dead geraniums and pansies on his head.

'E-E R-R-G-H!' groaned Charlie as he clutched his sore head, crossed his legs to prevent a lower descent of the ice cubes, and staggered off in the direction of the nearby changing rooms to make amends.

Derek, standing closest to the disaster, was by then in a fair amount of difficulty due to an over indulgence of laughing.

He snorted deeply in a chuff-chuff fashion until his attention was drawn to the fact his glass eye was bobbing up and down in-between the top fastenings of Sheila's shapely, well endowed, tightly buttoned and heaving cleavage.

Bernard, never one to miss an opportunity and being ever vigilant, as well as being the only person not holding a cup at the time, moved quickly to take advantage of the situation.

In his hurry to reclaim the wandering glass bauble, without giving Sheila any time to consider his actions, or the merit thereof, he plunged foolishly in pursuit of his trophy.

He might have been wiser to pause and ponder on the old adage 'act in haste repent at leisure.'

Bernard made contact with the intended target and was doing well until his enthusiastic shout of 'Got ya!' alerted Sheila who became alarmed at the sudden presence of Bernard's hands in the immediate vicinity of her vital statistics.

In his haste Bernard not only managed to dislodge the eye, but also squeezed it too tightly, sending it careering around Sheila's curves like a marble on a bagatelle board.

His eyes bulging already at his over close proximity to her perfectively formed assets, beads of sweat breaking out on his forehead, he feverishly sought to recover the situation, but only managed to get his thumb caught painfully under the support wiring of Sheila's bra.

In blind panic he wrenched the offending digit free, pulling the strongly elasticated and wired centrepiece outwards to release it.

T-W-A-N-G!

If Bernard had studied his science lessons more diligently he would have known that any action is usually met with an equal and opposite reaction, but today he was to prove the exception to the rule.

Firstly, the support material catapulted back into Sheila's delicate extremities with a painful snap causing her to gasp sharply with a sudden intake of breath as her nostrils flared and eyes hardened in a distinct warning sign that even a Tyrannosaurus Rex would have noticed and fled from.

Being an Australian through and through she was a real 'Jack the Lad' character, one of the boys when it came to cards, beer, ribaldry and rough necking, but even she had her limits, and a real temper to match when riled.

Bernard had refocused his attention on the glass eye, which had been caught by the elastic and was rising speedily in an arc away from the now tender and reddening cleavage; he was oblivious to his predicament and blissfully unaware.

S-M-A-A-A-C-C-C-K-K!!!

The second reaction came from Sheila, or more accurately, her right hand as she educated Bernard in a short sharp etiquette lesson, 'Aussie' style.

For a second or two you could have almost heard a pin drop; well at least until Bernard staggered back, fell over a case of polystyrene coffee cups destined for the new vending machine and promptly demolished the nearby coffee table.

'Oh well,' said Derek in a matter-of-fact voice that broke the stillness, 'that's one thing less to move.'

Bernard rubbed his sore cheek with a rueful smile: 'I suppose I deserved that!' he acknowledged and held open his hand to display the offending glass bauble he had captured.

'An eye for an eye?' he ventured humorously.

Sheila looked across with a hint of a playful smile on her lips; 'Well, next time try asking first,' she said slyly, 'you never know until you ask,' and stepped away with a wiggle of her hips.

It was a good job Bernard couldn't see the expression on her face as she tried to maintain her composure, but the others could so they couldn't help but laugh... and laugh they did, raucously.

It was as well in some respects that they were momentarily distracted from the events outside by the ongoing antics inside. The compulsive laughter sweeping through the clubhouse members and workers obscured the possibility that things could still get much much worse.

****

Over on the JCB Jimmy had stepped back in a mixture of shock, surprise and amazement as Rollo's unexpected exit caught him off-guard.

Rollo's first reaction was to escape and his second was to latch onto the nearest object, anything at all, that would help to propel him away at greater speed.

Spontaneously his claws found traction on some kind of metal girder and he reacted instinctively, racing up it as if he was being closely pursued by the hounds of hell.

Higher and higher he rose, glancing back over his shoulder again and again in blind panic as his paws firmly took him further away from that awful noise.

It became apparent to Rollo that there was no sign of an elephant or hippopotamus, not even an outraged orang-utan sitting blithely beside the cab in which he had, until a few moments before, comfortably resided.

He could see what appeared to be a small monkey leaping about in an animated fashion on the track of the digger, and there was a very large furry caterpillar crawling from under the engine mounting of the JCB.

Rollo became suddenly aware that everything he was looking at was getting progressively smaller and smaller; the sudden sight of an inquisitive kestrel hovering nearby watching him intently, made him hesitate.

So intent had he been to flee he had simply not realised that his passage of escape was not outward but upward, and he had in fact ascended the lengthy towering jib of the builders' crane; he had just arrived at the rounded tip on which he was now precariously balanced.

A cat's perception of distance is sometimes questionable. At seventy-five feet off the ground all sense of reality tends to fly out the window in exchange for self-preservation at any cost.

It is a well known fact that cats can not, will not, do not, climb forwards down a tree or a rope, their claws are simply not designed that way, so Rollo in typical fashion reversed off the tip and began backing down the structure.

It was just a touch unfortunate that he did not check his point of entry first. Having arrived safely at the top of the jib he then opted to leave via the steel cable on which the large lifting hook hung 60 feet below.

He didn't however discover that important, indeed vital fact until his back claws encountered the slippery, well greased, thick steel hawser and began to slip just as his front ones gave up the ghost on their retention of the jib tip.

Rollo begun to slide...

'M—-E—-E—-E—-O—-O—-W—-W—-W!!!'

He began to caterwaul in an increasing, expanding, and rapidly ascending crescendo as his claws hung on for dear life until sparks flews from their razor-like tips. Rollo anxiously eyed the tendril of smoke arising from near his tail and concentrated on keeping his delicate anatomy away from any risk of friction burns.

Down below Miss Matilda Bagshott stepped out from underneath the JCB engine mount, staring upwards in total disbelief.

Her tail twitched violently from side to side as she eyed the acrobatic animal antics; Rollo appeared to be performing what could only be described as a bizarre mating ritual.

She could not believe that he was going to all this trouble just to make an impact, and she licked her lips in wild anticipation of what might happen when her ruff 'n' tumble playmate arrived.

Clearly she had impressed him very much indeed!

Perhaps Baggie should have concerned herself more with where, and not how, the impact was likely to occur.

She didn't really have much longer than that to consider the various impressions that Rollo was having, or going to have, before Jimmy interfered with her train of thought.

His mouth open in utter disbelief Jimmy Murphy watched the wild antics above him, stepping back from the JCB as the image of Rollo's rapidly accelerating rump came more and more into view.

Already finely balanced on the bucket of the digger he momentarily forgot his whereabouts and proceeded to step back into thin air.

There was of course very little to worry about; he was after all very lithe, flexible and adaptable. It was probably due to his family's grass roots and especially qualities inherited from his Hungarian uncle who was a high wire trapeze artist with a travelling circus.

What was, of course, of more concern was his landing on Miss Matilda Bagshott's extremities; Baggie had, after all, a very fine tail and she took much exception to anyone altering the arrangement of any of her wayward strands of fur.

True she had rather a lot, probably enough to thatch a cottage or make several Persian rugs, but that wasn't the point, she was very attached to her fine coat and was determined that it stay that way.

Therefore when the small but compact figure of Jimmy Murphy arrived 'en masse' in a pair of size 11 builder's boots astride her bushy extremity she reacted extremely violently, much to poor Jimmy's regret.

Percy, who had wandered off back to his secluded sunspot, had been awakened from his pleasurable slumber in the very comfortable deckchair by the sound of the builder's horn. After a good stretch, feeling enthused by the peaceful rest, he had meandered back down to the clubhouse to watch the demolition.

He was much surprised, en-route, to be passed by Charlie heading in the opposite direction, shivering, legs crossed and wearing an array of garden flowers on his head, complete with bedding soil.

He did think however that the geranium looked particularly fetching, but refrained from any witticism given the colour of Charlie's complexion as well as his rather wrathful expression.

Percy arrived at his desired rendezvous and turned the corner.

Bernard for some reason appeared to be breaking up the soft furnishings with his bottom and the vicar could not, for the life of him, understand what he was doing with Derek's glass eye.

Sheila appeared rather flushed and Percy had to quickly avert his innocent eyes from her heaving, well-defined bosom; it was not right for a vicar of the parish to gaze at such delights, even covertly.

Derek seemed to be chuckling to himself, whilst Big Jim looked like he had encountered a very embarrassing mishap and Percy rather thought he really should be past that age when he required a nappy.

Several other members, male and female, as well as a motley collection of builders were all mingling around, but everyone seemed intently focused on the events proceeding in the clubhouse car park.

Percy glanced across, seeing nothing suspicious or untoward other then a smoking fur ball sliding down the crane jib and Jimmy Murphy hopping around the gravel as if trying to undertake a rain dance.

Given the experiences of the previous summer it really didn't take more than a second or two for the penny to drop and Percy did a rapid double take of the unfolding scenario.

The bungee-jumping ball of fluff was clearly Rollo in reverse drive, although what on earth he was doing was quite beyond Percy at that stage. By the look of the sparks and smoke it was evident that the steel hawser and Rollo's bottom were having a hard time deciding who was having the worst of it.

'And, heaven forbid, just what was the builder trying to do?' muttered Percy, as Jimmy Murphy's boots flew into the air unaided and he took off across the car park in his bare feet.

****

Jimmy wasn't expecting anything but gravel when he landed back on the car park surface; just for a moment he thought he had landed on a hosepipe, until the much agitated high-pitched hissing refocused his mind in the direction of maybe a large snake.

That's as far as his thought processes reached before he glanced down, just in time to witness the pride of Persia undertaking a four footed frenzied violation of his best working boots.

Twenty razor-like talons working at breakneck speed make for a fairly respectable shredding machine, and Jimmy's laces lasted all of half-a-second.

It took just a few more seconds before the tough leather of his boots began to part and when the left toecap fell off to expose his little pinkies Jimmy did the sensible thing, kicked off his loose boots and ran away very quickly.

Baggie made sure to give him a send off to remember: as Jimmy flew by she assaulted the lower 13 inches of his heavy duty dungarees, swiftly turning them into slender strips of denim tinsel.

Suitably pacified, she turned her attentions to remonstrating with her damaged appendage, briefly distracted from the main

- 47 -

event of the day by the builder's untimely arrival; talking of which, there was another event on the way.

Rollo, for want of a better expression, had reached critical mass; his acceleration was such that his poor rump had warmed up enough to resemble the space shuttle on re-entry.

He looked down in blind panic, registering the fact the ground was a lot closer than anticipated and that the JCB roof was closer still; tightly shutting his eyes, he voiced his terror and let go...

'M—E—E—E—O—O- - - -W!'

THUMP!!

At that point all should have come to a timely, inconsequential conclusion with nothing more remaining than a touch of wounded pride for all parties concerned.

Percy later reflected that, remembering previous occasions involving Rollo and the Lower South-Borough Bowling Club, this was really more of a whimsical pipe dream than an actual reality.

However, fate always seemed to have an extra ace to play.

Jimmy Murphy's guilty conscience and a rather ruffled Persian pussy were suddenly joined by a disgruntled saddle sore vicarage cat who immediately set about battering the bumblebees in abject frustration.

It had, after all taken a mere second for Rollo's disorganised descent to turn, as the members saw it, a highly amusing event into a practical disaster.

A number of things caught Percy's attention in minute detail, almost as if in slow motion, in a picturesque 'freeze frame' of multiple related events.

Big Jim, Derek, Bernard, Sheila, Phillippa, Gloria, Dennis, Patrick and Trigger were still 'in situ', paused in the middle of what they had been previously doing to watch the cats' carnival parade.

Even Charlie, still wet and on his way to the changing rooms, had paused to watch the unfolding melodramatics with an air of disbelief.

The bootless, sock-less, builder was still running hard in a deviating manner around the construction site debris with Baggie in hot pursuit.

Meanwhile Rollo had landed in a rather undiplomatic manner on top of the JCB diggers roof.

He would have finished there had it not been for the fact that his not inconsiderable body mass arriving at significant velocity was a touch too much for the stress load factor of the polypropylene roof.

The catalogue of events, if slowed down on the evidence tape of the CID investigation would have actually captured Rollo's landing as more of a...

THUMP... R-R-R-I-P... TH-U-M-PPP!!

It was, of course, the third part of that sound effect that caught the eyes and ears of everyone watching the cat-aclysm of events.

Rollo had unwittingly landed on the starter button.

VR-O-O-O-MMM!!!

The powerful V8 diesel engine instantaneously roared into life as the electronic start performed perfectly for the thousandth time; a tribute to the fact that Murphy & McPherson always kept their machine well serviced.

What was not so much a tribute was the fact that they always left their vehicles in gear.

Percy did what he always did best at times like this, he simply groaned loudly and hid behind his hands.

The outcome was inevitable; Rollo, having rebounded back onto the driver's seat, could only stare out of the cab windows in a disorganised, dizzy and docile manner as the JCB digger trundled unceremoniously forward in low gear.

It wasn't until the metal monstrosity pushed over a brick pile, flattened the adjacent stack of orange cones and trampled the car park flower bed that the members woke up to the very significant fact that it was indeed trundling their way!

Bernard was the first to react.

'RUN FOR YOUR LIVES!!!' he screamed.

Big Jim was slightly sharper than the rest.

'Women, children and alcohol first!' he exclaimed as he raced for the bar with a like-minded Sheila in close pursuit.

'Why don't we just shut the door?' stated Tony in his usual 'off the cuff' but blindly stupid, naively innocent observation of life.

Patrick and Dennis paused momentarily to consider Trigger's flawed plan and thought better of it.

Tony, as always was one step ahead of his idea and quite a few behind in common sense, reality and scientific fact. He had already shut the door and posed the next question.

'Do you think I ought to lock it too?'

The rest of the members were clearly not waiting to even contemplate a response as they each made a grab for any last remaining items of value and bolted through the back door.

Any innocent bystander would have thought themselves slightly unlucky to have apparently missed the 'sale of the century' as a crowd of people stampeded out of the rear exit balancing an array of chinaware, cutlery, chairs, framed pictures and crisp boxes.

At least one of the people presently standing in the vicinity of the mass exodus was decidedly not innocent and very much a proven opportunist.

Jiggy 'Snapper' Jenkins had a knack of being in the wrong place at the wrong time.

As the local newspaper reporter he had caused mayhem in the media over the last year by covering a number of embarrassing slip ups and exposures on the club front.

Nevertheless the coverage had proved extremely fruitful for the club's finances so they had continued to adhere to the saying 'better the devil you know.'

It was that policy that had led to the arrival of the reporter for a meeting with the newly appointed county vice-president Godfrey Go-Lightly to prepare a news feature on the new clubhouse preparations.

'Good Morning, pleasure to meet you, I'm...' was as far as the newly arrived Jiggy Jenkins reached in his introduction to the waiting official before the rear door crashed open and a deluge of people emerged like stampeding buffalo.

'What on earth...?' spluttered Godfrey as Percy followed up the rear of the miniature congregation with 'Trigger' in tow.

Jiggy was already well rehearsed and responded to the impending story with great alacrity, whipped out his 35mm auto focus.

SNAP!

The first picture impacted on the digital memory in less than quarter of a second. A crescendo of breaking glass and shattering timber announced the impromptu arrival of Big Jim diving head first through the nearest window with a large box held firmly in his outstretched hands.

'I'VE GOT THE BRANDY!!!' he exclaimed delightedly, oblivious to the danger and potential damage to his rather considerable girth.

'And I've got the Pimms and the Earl Grey,' piped in Gloria Grimshaw as she emerged in a flustered and excited manner from the newly made escape hole.

SNAP!

SNAP! SNAP! SNAP!

The photographer was clearly in his element and really could not believe his continuing good fortune.

'LOOK HERE....!' exclaimed the now very flustered and rapidly reddening county vice president as he searched for an explanation.

Unfortunately, the explanation arrived in the form of 15 tons of first grade steel and 2,000 perfectly moving parts as the gas guzzling terminator with a petrified pussycat knocked on the front door of the clubhouse.

Perhaps 'knock' was not quite the right expression to use in describing its arrival...

It didn't grind to a halt at the wooden veranda; it merely ground through the timber like the proverbial hot knife in butter.

Trigger had suggested, somewhat foolishly, that shutting the door on the immediate danger would perhaps delay the inevitable, if not avoid it altogether.

Either way the door had about as much impact in the 'detour and road block' department as a lit matchstick in the path of an inbound tornado.

The JCB digger didn't waste time trying to mount the steps it simply ploughed through them, creating a year's supply of kindling for the church restoration fund in just a fraction of a second.

The bemused and normally manic Rollo sat bolt upright on his haunches, frozen in time, claws embedded firmly in the soft furnishing of the cab's chair as the situation escalated and rapidly unfolded beyond his control.

His bloodshot, terrified and dilated pupils gave the impression of a four-legged, escapee, psychopathic, axe murderer dressed in a fur coat.

Around the clubhouse the various members, workers, visitors, on-lookers and paparazzi stared on in bemused shock, mouths gaping in a 'drop jawed' manner.

Their overall appearance resembled an oversize and slightly grotesque 'crazy golf' feature where the player had to choose the right aperture in which to play his ball.

CLICK!

Jiggy Jenkins carried on regardless as the astonishing and unbelievable events unfolded in a melodramatic chain reaction.

The juggernaut ploughed through the middle of the condemned clubhouse, grinding, shattering and splintering the interior of the formerly impressive Victorian structure with a cacophony of appropriate sound effects.

Four seconds after creating a sizeable entrance the steel 'rolling stock' proceeded to invent an equally impressive new fire exit, before trundling down the grass slope, and impacting on the adjacent hedgerow.

The 400-year-old majestic oak was simply too much for the JCB and it stopped dead in its tracks, the engine stalling as its forward momentum ceased, catapulting the shell shocked Rollo into the safety of the tree's still leafy canopy.

To the uninitiated, the building still looked relatively unscathed, secure in its foundation and structure. Only the ragged shape of the recently created access point gave away the Titan's recent arrival.

There was however a definite sagging to the roof's apex and the deep-seated groaning of stressed timbers inside simulated the sound of an ancient submarine well exceeding its maximum diving depth.

Big Jim was the first to respond, eyeing the building with a wary and disparaging look.

'Perhaps it would be better if we all moved away just in case...' he observed in cautious tones to the nearby members.

With his business partner oblivious to the incident and still running from the rampaging 'Baggie', Johnny McPherson, being the head builder on site at that moment, acted quickly to calm the nervous situation.

'It's quite alright,' he commented in a calm and professional manner...

The wooden structure creaked and groaned as the members took an involuntary step backwards.

'Those Victorian builders knew how to construct these traditional timber frames, and there's little danger at present,' continued Johnny.

Creak! Groan!

'Honestly,' he insisted, with a glance over his shoulder, 'it's just settling and there's nothing to worry about, we'll soon shore it up...won't we boys?'

The 'boys' were stepping back swiftly with very worried looks playing across their faces.

Crack! Groan! Creak!!

'Come back here, there's no need to panic...' he stated in a much firmer voice, used to having his authority adhered to.

The workforce paused in mid-step.

C-R-A-C-K!!!!

Midge looked back over his shoulder as if to reassure himself as he again added his professional support to the timber ones.

'I tell you there's absolutely nothing ...,' he began in a slightly strained tone that carried none of the conviction he intended.

Had he continued to speak he would have said '...to worry about', but he wasn't allowed the opportunity to complete his sentence.

GROAN!   CREAK!!   G-R-O-A-N!!!

The back stepping of the combined mass of onlookers appeared imminently likely to progress into a full-blooded retreat if one more thing occurred to panic the very nervous members.

C-C-R-R-A-A-A-C-K!!!

It has to be said that at that point Jiggy Jenkins captured one of the finest photo finishes ever seen from the front doors of the indoor bowls centre, where he had previously retreated in his characteristically cautious manner.

Johnny McPherson led from the back charging through the crowd, as he took advantage of his long legs, and bolted for the safety of the inner sanctum yelling the somewhat unnecessary and obvious advice...

'FOLLOW ME!!!'

He perhaps allowed his legs to lead and his brain to follow as he arrived at the other clubhouse in too much haste and with little time to comprehend that the sturdy door was still shut.

Jiggy Jenkins on the other hand, had plenty of time however to reflect on this fact as he noted the large lump now appearing on the builders forehead. He felt disinclined to lend a hand, after-all, 'Midge' was still quite safe lying down on the porch in his newly acquired outstretched position.

The press photographer kept his finger on the shutter button as the others began to arrive in a sudden rush.

CLICK... CLICK... CLICK...

Big Jim showed a turn of speed and degree of alacrity that belittled his girth and age, crossing the one hundred metre dash in under 13 seconds.

Derek was so close in following that one could almost assume, wrongly, that he was doing an impression of Jim's shadow.

The county vice-president, Godfrey Go-Lightly, was neither the fittest man, nor fastest finger first when it came to rapid decision making, nevertheless he was quick on the uptake.

He likewise fled after them, huffing and puffing, with a very red complexion and a desperate look at his rapidly bleeping wristwatch heart monitor.

Trigger, Percy, Gloria, Patrick and Phillippa also arrived at the same point in time en masse.

Jiggy later gave much consideration to the fact that perhaps his choice of a panoramic vantage point was not a wisely considered one.

The final picture in his photographic shoot was eventually to become much sought after, comprising as it did, a multitude of surprised, shocked, panicking faces in close up. One hundred and sixty four stone of body bulk tripped over the prostrate form of the fallen builder, landing on the camera.

Bernard, last to arrive, was more fortunate and able to avoid the pile up. He had with a selfless display of camaraderie, paused momentarily to grab Sheila's outstretched hand and was dragging her to safety.

Sheila trailed behind him in subservient cave woman fashion, fully extended with heels digging into the grass in her wake; she had one shoe hanging off, her blouse askew and skirt at half-mast.

She looked slightly bemused but with a hint of wild excitement in her eyes and in hindsight a rueful Bernard was to compare the situation to the mythical opening of Pandora's box.

Trigger, always the one to make a superlative and observant comment further from the truth than the possibility of the Titanic remaining afloat, continued the upkeep of his observed intelligence.

'Well that was fun,' he groaned, from underneath the very bottom of the mountain of man, and womankind.

Tiny grunted in unison and opened one eye, the other now swollen and not looking altogether very well after the collision with the clubhouse door.

'SEE!' he remonstrated in a 'told you so' manner as he glanced back at the clubhouse with an expression of hurt pride, 'that building is quite safe!'

With that pre-emptive comment, as if prompted by an autocue, the building collapsed, as did the builder, giving way to the extravagance of collective weight that surmounted his reposed form.

The former clubhouse simply gave a deep, lengthy sigh of tiredness, emitted a cloud of dust and woodworm, and then almost reverently folded up like a deck of cards, falling back on itself leaving nothing more than an enlarged timber molehill.

Atop of the heap sat a rather wide-eyed blackbird unable to comprehend the sudden arrival of several tons of best quality nesting material.

Had there been at that time a passing art purveyor familiar with the works of the aforementioned Tate Modern they might have made a fanciful comparison between the timber pile and the smaller stack of lawnmower parts nearby. Those 'parts' were all that now remained of the 'Beast of South Borough' after Percy and Rollo's previous antics of the summer season past.

Indeed the ironic symbolism between the demolished lawnmower and the intact machinery adjacent to the equally obliterated outdoor clubhouse might well have earned the visual carnage the Turner Prize for most original concept.

'Well at least we won't be short of chip bark for the garden,' mused Percy as he eyed the well-fragmented wood heap, and then as an added afterthought, 'perhaps we ought to go into the production of matchsticks too?'

Feeling uncharacteristically satirical and not inclined to sigh, a dry retort seemed more fitting to the occasion.

'I know', he added dryly, with a wry smile, 'Let's buy a few rockets and burn the whole bloody thing down on bonfire night!'

Every club member's head turned in Percy's direction, it was after all unheard of for the vicar to swear and they were quick to scan the immediate vicinity for anything heavy that may have bumped his head.

Patrick reached for his glasses, Squiffy reached for a nearby first aid kit and Big Jim even volunteered one of his precious bottles of brandy which he had miraculously rescued on exiting.

'My what a big bang, did you go to all that trouble just to welcome me or are you always this inviting to new guests?'

A voice, definitely feminine, unexpectedly spoke out from behind the wriggling and divesting mound of bodies as they sought to extract themselves from the confusion.

The unannounced arrival spoke in rich dulcet tones with a depth of almost sensual well-spoken English, the words flowing like fine cognac rich and honeyed.

Percy looked over his shoulder towards the source of the vocal intrusion but the sunlight was directly in his eyes and he was unable to distinguish more than a shadowy outline in the car park.

The falling wood dust created a fine haze that gave the illusion of an amber aura around her and Percy was almost convinced that an angel had arrived to discuss his flock's misadventures.

Percy moved away from the direct sunlight, shielded his eyes with one hand and stepped towards the apparition in order to get a better look.

A number of other members, mostly male, did likewise, noticeably most of the eligible ones, although Bernard was unable to; it appeared he was being physically restrained by a rather aroused Sheila Ramsbottom.

Meanwhile Percy had moved close enough to distinguish the new arrival. She was quite tall, slim, well proportioned in a very curvaceous way which he struggled hard not to notice;

her lengthy auburn hair appeared flame red, on fire in the haze.

She had legs, Percy was absolutely sure of that.

She definitely had legs!

He just couldn't help but note their length or the fact they seemingly reached all the way up to her neck...

The stranger continued speaking unannounced.

'Well that's quite an erection,' she purred, surveying the theatrical montage of metal and wood that stood in place of the former clubhouse...

'You certainly know how to bring the house down,' she said with a warm infectious smile radiating playfully across her face.

With that she extended her hand towards the dumbstruck vicar.

'I'm Miss Sarah Jane Coddle,' she announced to the arriving entourage as she took Percy's proffered hand.

'Y-Yes I'm sure you are,' stammered Percy, lost for words momentarily, as the soft warmth of her hand intermingled with the seductive and distinctive perfume that wafted across from her.

She paused, looking Percy over in a manner of speaking whilst holding on to his hand a touch longer than perhaps she should have.

'You may call me Sarah,' she commented pointedly at the vicar with a wink of her eye before continuing...

'So is this all your own handiwork or do you do performances for all your new guests?' she inquired inquisitively.

Percy blushed as their hands parted, but before he was able to reply he was gently pushed aside by a dozen other male bodies and a mass of hands were proffered in her direction.

'I'm Big Jim...'

'Derek's the name...'

'Patrick, Patrick Albright...'

'My friends call me Trigger...'

A number of introductions were thrust upon the newcomer rapidly in quick succession like a welcoming barrage of friendly fire.

Percy was looking over her shoulder to the other couple that were standing by the car enjoying a rather long and passionate kiss in the warm sunshine.

He couldn't help but notice that they looked very familiar.

The couple parted momentarily and stepped across the park, laughing and joking, hand in hand, still in summer clothing, looking very tanned and incredibly happy.

Percy beamed in recognition, it was the newly-weds.

Molly and Bertie looked like a teenage couple much in love as they flounced towards the awaiting vicar with a warm smile.

'Molly! Bertie! What a fabulous surprise, it's SO good to see you both and you look SO happy,' spouted Percy in an effervescent verbal explosion of delight.

'Hello Percy,' said the two in unison, laughing at their own spontaneity.

'Well, no more Coddle's but one more Tattleford,' smiled Percy in a light-hearted joke at the change to his flock, now vows had been exchanged.

'Not quite,' smiled Molly, patting her stomach, 'two more Tattlefords now.'

Bertie Tattleford, proud father to be, smiled broadly and gathered his new wife in his arms for a lengthy romantic kiss.

'Well well well...' muttered Percy, a warm smile on his face, 'who would have thought, well I never...' his voice trailing off as he turned away to leave the couple in peace.

Molly parted company momentarily to call out after Percy.

'And there's still a Coddle in the flock!'

Percy paused and looked around with a hint of confusion playing across his features, 'Still?' he inquired.

'Yes, my sister, Sarah Jane...' replied Molly.

'She's a bit of a looker too so you better watch out,' teased Bertie, 'and she's free and single,' he added with a flirtatious afterthought.

Sister?

Sarah Jane?

Percy looked rather confused; there was a familiarity to the recent unveiling of information, which he had been previously unaware of; he had always thought that Molly was a single child.

'Somebody talking about me?' spoke a sultry voice as the recently arrived newcomer stepped into view.

'I hope you haven't been asking about my age Percy?' she teased with a saucy fluttering of her eyelashes.

'Why... er... no...' stammered the rather confused Reverend, temporarily at a lost for a more conducive eloquence of speech.

'Oh,' said Molly, with a twinkle in her eye, 'I see you two have already been introduced?'

'OH MY LORD!' groaned Percy, as the penny dropped, and he gazed back at Sarah, recognising that familiar family resemblance and remembering the goings-on of the previous summer with the shy, quiet, retiring spinster that Molly had formerly been.

Well that had been until she had met Bertie of course, he reflected.

The vicar sighed, as the sisters laughed loudly and Sarah winked provocatively in his direction,

'Oh dear...' he muttered, as the other nearby onlookers joined in the revelry with peals of warm laughter; it wasn't often that Percy was lost for words.

In the background, Rollo charged by in full flight, followed by a terrified Jimmy Murphy looking back over his shoulder, who in turn was still being pursued by the un-sated and irrational Baggie.

Gloria 'Smiler' Grimshaw looked on with a disapproving look as Miss Matilda Bagshott sallied by in an unkempt and very unladylike fashion.

'What have you done to my poor pussy?' she shouted after the wild-eyed Jimmy.

Percy groaned again and reached for the 'good book'; it was going to be a long and difficult winter.

CHAPTER TWO

OCTOBER

GOING INDOORS

Percy looked at his diary and the usual pre-season knot in his stomach appeared as if by magic.

It had been a couple of weeks since the carnage in the car park and to anyone now arriving there was little evidence of previous misdemeanours.

The wreckage of the old clubhouse had been taken away by a fleet of lorries to a nearby wood yard for reclamation and would later provide enough garden mulch to supply the local village for a number of years.

Peter 'Chippie' Barryman had been the local 'recycler' for a longer period of time than he cared to remember and to be fair to him everything in his wood yard was certainly in a state of recyclement.

That included the office toilet, chip barking machinery, main entrance gate and his working clothes as well as the rather battered, authentically rusted work's van.

Peter had a knack for being able to convert recycling into a considerable profit and there was little he could not turn his hand to or transform into quick cash.

It was true to say that in the time it took him to reprocess the ex-clubhouse into mulch he would have also salvaged a tidy profit on a substantial crop of mushrooms that miraculously happened to grow on the decomposing mound.

A lot of things appeared to happen 'naturally' in Peter's wood yard without his apparent knowledge or guiding hand, thus avoiding the necessity of VAT or taxable income on his surplus assets.

More importantly for the parish, the sale of 5,000 bags of organic compost at £3.99 apiece would provide a timely and welcome contribution to the rising coffer's of the church and club funds.

The builders had already removed all the evidence of the 'collapse' and were busy laying the concrete foundations for the new development.

The misbehaving JCB had emerged unscathed from its short adventure with nothing more than a paint scrape and a cat-shaped hole in the pre-fabricated roof, which the driver had left in-situ as an amusing reminder.

Jimmy Murphy was not so amused though, he was still very jumpy around cats and often the butt of many jokes from his fellow workers on site. There was many a cat impression rising from the ditches as he passed by and even a stuffed cat toy left in his lunch box.

Percy had safely moved on mentally from that recent 'blip' and over the course of events of the last two weeks had seen neither hide nor hair of Miss Sarah Jane Coddle, although he had an uneasy sensation of being watched from a distance.

He wasn't quite sure what was better: knowing where she was or not knowing, or even why the thought of her potential whereabouts troubled his thoughts so much.

Nevertheless that was not the reason for the arrival of the feeling of panic in the pit of his stomach.

Today was the first of the month, and more to the point, the month of October.

It was, of course, the seasonal kick-start that as always began with the traditional Ladies vs. Men challenge match. The competition was more a 'supremacy of the sexes' where rivalry was closely fought for the privilege of not winning the 'wooden spoon'.

There was also the pre-arranged committee meeting to discuss and prepare the seasonal festivities.

Being the spiritual leader of the community as well as a church representative for the local children's hospice Percy was always looked upon for guidance, direction and pretty much everything else from planning to conception.

Halloween and Bonfire Night already loomed on the horizon, whilst Christmas festivities urgently needed arranging and of course there was the subject of the club's other annual outing.

Each of the two sporting seasons had its own high point, or, according to memory, varying degrees of low points, depending on how big a disaster it turned out to be.

Percy remembered all too recently the extraordinary goings on and revelations of the summertime extravaganza at the sporting pursuit's camp, which somehow, beyond comprehension, had turned out to be hugely successful.

He winced as an obvious thought occurred to him.

Given the outcome of the previous trip, and its publicity, not to mention its popularity with the paparazzi, it was inevitable that even more members would sign on the dotted line for this year's indoor season's adventure.

Charlie, as always, being one of the key instigators, had the 'inside track' to events liable to occur and, given his handiwork in the previous organisation it was relatively likely that any clue or tip that could be extracted from him would prove very invaluable to the recipient.

Having cornered Charlie in the clubhouse a couple of weeks ago and enticed him with a few glasses of brandy Percy had managed to gain a snippet of information; he was already nervous about its possible ramifications.

Charlie had simply advised him to have his passport ready and watch out for the wanton wiles of wayward women.

Almost immediately, a vision of sleazy downtown Amsterdam sprang to mind.

Determined not to panic, Percy pushed that thought to the back of his mind for the time being to concentrate on the more immediate matter in hand; the bowlers quest for the Holy Grail, the silver chalice on which were inscribed the immortal words:

The Rt Hon. Ronald Regis Challenge Cup
Ladies vs. Gentlemen
Presented to the club by Sir Ronald Regis Senior
Co-founder of Lower South-Borough BC
(est. 1952)

Percy well remembered reading about the early matches which had sparked such intense but friendly rivalry year after year, until 1982.

At that point the ladies, having lost in consecutive years for an extended period of three decades, to a rambunctious and ebullient male team were on the point of another severe thrashing by the dominant opposition.

Unwisely, at that point, a much younger and brazen Dennis Ditherford, along with his recently arrived bowling partner Charles Chesterford had, in a cock-a-hoop fashion, turned up at the tea break with a large wooden spoon.

It was about four feet in length and sported the club name on its handle, whilst inscribed in the spoon's giant scoop was the following legend:

Valiant they fought as lions from a fable
Trounced again like babes in the cradle
Fit to receive just the scraps from the table
To dine on with this the losers team ladle

Dennis had not been able to resist the temptation to brandish the article high above his head and to give his best oratorical recital of the verse in the style of William Shakespeare.

The men of course thought the whole thing hilariously funny and fell about the green in an exaggerated display of paroxysm.

Charlie, being typically an exuberant and high-spirited person could not resist the temptation to take it one step further.

'If the ladies manage to beat us I'll do a streak around the rink with the scorecard and the trophy!' he brazenly stated at the top of his voice.

One or two of the men did at that point cast a wary eye in Charlie's direction and passed on some appropriate wise words of caution.

'Er... steady on old chap, let's not get too carried away...'

But the die was very much cast, as they say; Charlie's wild and inflammatory announcement had not gone unnoticed or without an appropriate response.

The prevarication from the gentlemen was nothing less then the waving of a red flag at a very frustrated and angry bull. Indeed a more attentive 'matador' might have noted the change in his victim's stature and made a discretionary withdrawal of the flamboyant taunt.

But it was too late by then and the ladies' captain took the bull by the horns, figuratively speaking.

'Well in that case Charlie Chesterford if you manage to score a single point on the final end the entire ladies' team will parade around the green with your wooden spoon in just their underwear!!' she stated loudly and clearly in a clipped tone.

The laughter in the men's camp stopped suddenly in mid chuckle upon her announcement as if at the drop of a flag.

At that point, all the ladies turned to their outspoken captain wild-eyed in amazement wondering if perhaps it wasn't too late to offer a plea of temporary insanity.

The elderly members of the knitting circle watching from the tearoom clucked madly in disapproval like rabid hens and the purple rinsed chairwoman fainted clean away.

The newly appointed junior vice captain, Doris 'Posh' Doolittle, at that time one of the youngest VC's in the county, at 22, sensing the need to show solidarity, stepped in to stop the panic.

'Now calm yourself ladies it's only a game and we all know that men can't do two things at once, so how do you expect them to bowl if they're too busy thinking about you all in your underwear?'

The woman laughed nervously and one or two started to pick up the taunt.

'Yes come on we can do it!' spoke one.

'Let's show the men what we are made of!' quipped another.

'All hands to the braces let's run out the plank and shove them all into an early bath!' shouted a person from the back.

The laugher picked up apace and suddenly the men found themselves on the wrong end of their own joke.

The chairwoman, having recovered from her fainting fit, sensed an opportunity and decided rashly to up the ante.

'And what's more we'll put £500 on the table for the winning team, if you DARE to match us,' she challenged the men.

Charlie spluttered, '£500?'

It was, after all a very significant sum of money in those days.

He looked around helplessly at the men's team sensing that they had somehow been backed into a corner leaving little place to turn.

The now not so brash male team members nodded their heads in grim acceptance and Charlie accepted the inevitable.

'Right then, it's a bet!'

The rest of the events became engraved in the memories of every member who witnessed that decisive and final end; it was one of the most intensely fought games of bowls the clubs had ever seen.

The gentlemen, supremely confident at first, found themselves fighting a rearguard action as the ladies stormed onto the green in ebullient fashion, using all their guile, indeed every sneaky trick in the handbook, and outside it, in their determination to throw the men off balance.

With flashes of finely turned ankles in petticoats, strategically wafted perfumes, untimely pinching of proffered bottoms as the men attempted to bowl, much coughing, clattering and dropping of woods they succeeded in further distracting the already rattled men.

Suffice to say, the women's aggressive retaliation in the match led to an embarrassingly large scoop of 24 shots off the men on that crucial end; they won nearly every point, leaving the score tied with only Charlie and Dennis left to bowl to save the day.

Despite a heroic, some may say desperate, last stand 'firing shot' from the stalwart Dennis he only succeeded in breaking the scoreboard, three teacups and a toilet window, much to the consternation of the tea lady who was in the process of 'adjusting her smalls.'

Charlie stepped onto the green to a mixture of hollers, cheers, catcalls and wolf whistles from the ladies, whilst the men looked on in a subdued pensive manner, their eyes fixed and dilated as they stared uncomprehendingly at the score board.

He gazed around trying to locate his final bowl, which appeared miraculously to have gone missing and he glowered behind him with an unimpressed look.

The women watching nearby began gazing skywards innocently looking as if to all intents and purposes butter would not melt in their mouths.

Charlie spied Cynthia Cobblethwaite looking shifty and did a double take; something appeared to be wrong, but he couldn't quite put his finger on exactly what.

He looked again discreetly from the corner of his eye, noting the smart dress, prim and proper as always, and the bulging bosom which appeared to have three curves.

Charlie coughed loudly, but politely in Miss Cobblethwaite's direction.

She blushed deeply, mumbled a whispered apology and proffered the large inanimate object which materialised miraculously from her cleavage.

Muttering under his breath, Charlie picked up the final wood stepped onto the mat, sidestepped the chairwoman's attempt to tweak his posterior and prepared to play.

He balanced the finely honed object in his left hand, smiling weakly at his partner Dennis as he weighed up his options and then finally played his shot.

The whole room went as quiet as a church mouse watching the cheese fall off the trap; the intake of breath was distinctly perceptible as the wood gathered pace, drawing nearer and nearer to the white cot.

As one the entire assembled on-lookers perched further and further towards the edge of their chairs, tea cups rattling, biscuits crumbling to the floor, as the wood began to slow, then start to wobble.

It trundled to a halt close to its intended target, and seemingly appeared a lot closer than the womens' nearest wood.

As the men half rose, arms raised in expectation of a victorious round of applause, they froze in mid step; the wood clearly wobbled again and began to tip slowly, surely, to one side.

With an audible gasp from the stunned men, the wood rolled over and away from the cot, appearing now to be the same distance away as the ladies' last valiant attempt.

The shout went up.

'MEASURE!!!'

The Reverend Joshua Jackson who was at that time Percy's predecessor was also the allotted 'marker' for the day. Being the representative of the church, he was the only person who could be trusted to judge the game fairly, especially in such a delicate situation.

Joshua Jackson was visibly trembling as he picked up the umpire's kit and walked on to the green; he could feel the influential eyes of every member upon him as he stepped silently towards the two bowls.

He was stuck with a dilemma.

On the one hand, should the ladies win, he would be excluded and placed in quarantine by the men's team for the rest of his life; on the other if the men proved to be victorious he would never again receive fresh homemade teacakes, scones and bread.

It was said that you could have heard a pin drop as the Reverend Jackson knelt to conduct the measure and he did appear to be praying for divine intervention, maybe in the hope that one bowl would fall over and thus negate the need for his intervention.

Many a players face sported beads of perspiration and for the first time in the club's history the Reverend truly did have the complete, committed, undivided attention of his flock.

Seconds ticked away...

'C'mon Reverend,' croaked Charlie, with a dry husky voice.

'Shush!' hissed another.

'Give the man a chance to measure properly before we all buy him a brandy,' hinted Dennis, with an air of potential bribery.

Finally, after much contemplation, Joshua Jackson stood up and it had to be said, that in a timely almost spookily significant fashion, a shaft of light fell on him at exactly the moment he chose to speak.

He looked towards the men and they gleefully raised their heads with a knowing smile.

'The winning wood is held by...'

He paused, took a deep breath and then continued...

'The Ladies.'

One half of the crowd went wild in a delirious uproar, the ladies screaming excitedly, whooping and hollering, cardigans thrown in the air, whilst the men grumbled, mumbled and cursed, casting dark sinister looks in Joshua's direction.

It was a curious and coincidental thing that the Reverend Joshua Jackson was soon after transferred to a quiet, isolated parish far removed from anything involving sports. In fact, the Reverend's career involved a lot of travelling from that point on...

The men's entire campaign of subterfuge, guile, bluster and overwhelming bravado had not been enough to prevent the ladies from winning the match by a single shot.

The triumphant team's 'lap of honour' followed by their jubilant presentation of the aforementioned wooden spoon to the humbled men was one never to be forgotten, or forgiven. Many a dark night was spent in deep contemplation of a long awaited opportunity to chasten the ladies with opportunistic revenge.

The 'icing on the cake' was yet to follow, as far as the women were concerned. It was when the demoralised, traumatised and cajoled men turned to traipse home with their tails between their legs, that the ebullient ladies' captain rubbed salt into the wound.

'Er, excuse me gentlemen, aren't we forgetting something?' she enquired inquisitively in a firm voice, nodding in the direction of Charles Chesterford.

The men paused in mid-step with expressions of confusion and uncertainty.

Vice-captain Doris Doolittle was already one step ahead of the men and very much in tune with her captain; quick to follow her lead she confirmed the query with an off the cuff remark.

'Yes Charlie haven't you got something you'd like to share with us?'

Charlie looked across in a consternation opening his mouth to retort but stopped in mid-flow as the realisation hit home.

'Oh no...' he groaned.

'Oh yes!' confirmed the Captain.

'Oh no, no, no... seriously, you wouldn't?' stuttered Charlie, remembering his now somewhat foolish promise to perform a ritual loser's streak.

'Most definitely we would!' insisted Doris with a gleeful smile on her face.

Charlie took a step backwards.

'Come on ladies! Charlie looks a bit shy, let's give him a helping hand!' shouted the nearby ladies' captain in a feverish shriek of anticipation.

Charlie faltered then took another step backwards.

The women, in a display not unlike the rampaging girls of St Trinians, surged forward with purposeful looks clamouring and screaming for Charlie to 'Get them off.'

Charlie had no intention of removing any item of clothing, not by his own hand or with any assistance, especially female.

To put it into more precise a term he scarpered, with the ladies in rampant pursuit of their intended victim.

Nothing was said about the event from that moment forward and Charlie remained tight lipped until the present day, but it was rumoured that a pair of his Y-fronts had for some time adorned the wall in the inner sanctum of the ladies' changing rooms.

****

It was perhaps slightly unfortunate for Percy that this year's event was the marking of the 25th anniversary of that famous female victory and much like the historical campaigns of Waterloo, Trafalgar and Jutland the sleeping dog had not rested.

For years, the men had plotted, schemed and lain in wait until a suitable occasion arose in which to exact the maximum publicity and embarrassment on the opposite sex.

Therefore, the vicar found himself at the clubhouse on the morning of the fateful day in question without any pre-conception of what the day had in store for him.

Other proceedings were instead very much on Percy's mind at that particular point in time.

He had already made meticulous notes in his diary of the events needing to be discussed at length with the club committee and had decided, after much consideration, to invite them all to a soirée at the vicarage.

Percy thought that perhaps this would be a more suitable setting, within a relaxed environment, over tea and fresh cooked sponge cake in which to chat about the organisation of the urgently required impending fixtures.

With a steady flow of mildly alcoholic beverages as well as a plentiful supply of sugary delicacies to smooth the way he felt that the members would for once be too contented to fall out over any minor issues as in previous years.

Percy was still not quite sure how three of his flock had managed to spend an evening detained at 'her majesties pleasure' in the local cells because of an argument over the colour of toilet rolls for the festive party three years ago.

However, he felt that with God looking over his right shoulder he could influence the members with enough degree of righteousness to quell any potential uprising.

The Reverend paused for a second to contemplate the setting for the impending match, having previously been too engrossed in the forthcoming fixtures to take stock of his current surroundings.

He had forgotten all about the 'state of play' anniversary-wise, and had only agreed to come in early in order to ensure that all the final preparations such as the buffet table, tea room and prize draw table were laid out in full readiness.

Upon arriving, his hand instinctively reached for the main lighting switch for the indoor arena. After divesting himself of his coat he ventured into the kitchen as per usual for a cup of Earl Grey and a rather indulgent custard cream.

Finally, with priorities taken care of and thoughts organised Percy stepped into the main centre.

The fluorescent lights flickered twice then spontaneously burst into life, illuminating the room, assisted ably by the new and unexpected addition of four 1000-watt floodlights that now lit up the rear wall like a Walt Disney funfair ride.

Had he not been momentarily blinded by the sudden exposure to the intense radiation which threatened to give him second degree burns, he would not have failed to notice the impressive display adhering to the rear wall.

Nine seconds later, his eyesight fully restored, he certainly could not help but notice it.

It was probably visible from the Russian Mia space station in orbit around the Earth!

The banner stretched across the room fully one hundred feet whilst dropping a further impressive twenty feet from the ceiling towards the ground on a number of stoutly tied guy ropes.

More importantly, the message it contained gave Percy no doubt as to the seriousness of, or the likely outcome to, the proceeding events and at that point, he might have been wise to reconsider his involvement.

25th ANNIVERSARY LADIES VS GENTLEMEN
The Rt Hon. Ronald Regis Challenge Cup
PROUDLY PRESENT
THE REVENGE OF THE Y-FRONTS

Adorned along the bottom of the banner was a long line of various assorted men's underwear, boxer shorts, pants, Y-fronts and thermal long-johns, each decorated with a nametag related to an existing member of the men's team.

If Percy had any qualms about the day previously, they were certainly re-affirmed immediately; he characteristically groaned, clutched his forehead and headed off to the kitchen for a fresh brew.

The nearby cake stand sporting a large Victoria sandwich baked by the veritable Phillippa Spindleforth, proved too much of a temptation though and a large helping soon assisted in allaying Percy's fears.

It was after all 25 years since the event and maybe this was just playful tomfoolery on the men's part; a modern approach to what should be a light-hearted game of opportunity, missed chances and true sportsmanship.

Perhaps it was the Reverend's purity and innocence to the ways of life that led him to this misconception, but he really should have known better by now, given the trials and tribulations of the summer season past.

Poor Percy...

****

It was a few hours later that Reverend Percival Peabody returned to the scene of the crime, suitably refreshed, reassured having spent time in the vestry consulting the good book, and fairly sure that his presence would suffice to appease any potential uprising in the popular ranks.

There was only a couple of hours left before the big match and it wouldn't be long before the new county vice-president was set to give his opening speech to the amassed members.

The former elected representative had taken a sudden leave of absence citing medical grounds following his visit to the club last month. His arrival, had coincided with the clubhouse demolition and the unexpected antics of the members had given him great cause for concern.

The cataclysmic event precipitated a hasty retreat as he abandoned his reception committee amid a cloud of dust and competition forms. His driver was left standing in a perplexed, confused fashion screaming loudly after the departing vice-president.

The fact that the speeding vehicle had passed over the driver's toes on the way out obviously had played a part in producing some of the 'expletives and deletives' that he managed to articulate immediately after the unpleasant incident.

Godfrey Go-Lightly, who seemingly was losing his marbles, later rang from a sanatorium deep in the valleys of the Peak District to offer his sincere apologies, and to tell Percy that he had 'found' religion, met John Lennon and was having dinner with Elvis.

It was a funny old world indeed, reflected Percy, considering the turn of events that had occurred during the previous year, and somehow, at the end of it all the club had always emerged relatively unscathed, considerably wealthier and somewhat enhanced.

This recent occurrence was no exception; given the sudden vacancy at county headquarters, the now 'larger than life' figure of Jack 'Big Jim' Tuttle, had been accelerated through the ranks and endorsed as the new county vice-president.

For Jack it was a dream come true; he had many years ago, at a surprisingly young age, gained the presidency of his home county, where, for a number of years he built up a legendary reputation for his prowess both on the green and at dinner parties.

There was no one better suited to spinning a yarn; his eloquence and dry sense of humour combined with a rather earthy approach had firmly established him as a 'must have' personality at any presentation.

His stay of office had been cut short by a family crisis and personal loss to which he remained tight lipped about until this present day, but following a leave of absence he had moved halfway across the country to the tiny village of Lower South-Borough.

There he had fallen in love with the country life, but still secretly yearned for another taste of county representation; in the meantime he had fully absorbed himself in the position of club competition secretary.

Jack had apparently impressed the visiting delegates with his umpiring performance during last season's club championships and, unbeknown to him, his name had been added to the shortlist of potential future representatives of the county.

Big Jim was of course thrilled about the new promotion which was warmly welcomed by all and sundry as a step in the right direction for a well respected, much loved figure of the Lower South-Borough bowling community.

He was equally excited because it was a great reason to open a bottle of his cherished 1810 Napoleon brandy which at 74% proof, was almost guaranteed to make the occasion one to remember for all the wrong reasons.

He often joked, much to the amusement of his fellow bowlers, that he had been presented with the bottle by the great man himself and had even stolen a kiss off Josephine.

Big Jim already had an outstanding reputation for fine story telling with a natural talent for conjecture and composition or, as it was more lovingly known, a rip-roaring snorter of a tale.

In fact the forthcoming opening speech from him, which was his first in his official capacity, was bound to be one that would make the record books for its length, content and humorous appeal.

Percy smiled to himself, reached down to the door handle of the inner clubhouse and let it swing open.

Inside the scene looked remarkably like the setting for a rag trade bring-and-buy sale; people were milling about in all directions with plates, cutlery, sauce bottles and condiment sets.

'Afternoon Percy.'

'Hello vicar.'

'Ready for the revolution Rev?'

'Who do you fancy to win then Percy?'

Shouts of 'Hello', 'Hi' and 'Afternoon vicar' arose from all around the clubhouse as the seething mass of members paused to extend their warmest hospitality to their favourite religious representative.

Percy blushed profusely; in fact, he positively glowed in the light of so many heartfelt and welcoming complimentary words from his congregation.

He optimistically beamed to himself: 'Why how could anything possibly go wrong with such a warmth of camaraderie and team spirit?' he mused.

Poor Percy, how soon he forgets...

****

The top tables were already laid out for the pre-match dinner and were beautifully prepared with fine lace tablecloths adorned with the club's finest silverware.

There was a delicious smell of home cooked scones and sponge cakes already arising from the covered table near the tea urns where they awaited the attention of the members at the half-time interval.

Percy's nostrils twitched with excitement as an equally tantalising smell emanated from the nearby kitchen and he involuntarily stepped in that direction.

Inside, Molly and Bertie were in full flow, ably assisted by a team of volunteers, who were helping to prepare a veritable mountain of fresh vegetables for later.

Spontaneously Percy spouted a warm welcome to the newly weds.

'Good afternoon to the happy couple!'

'Hello vicar,' beamed Molly, as she juggled with a bowl of Brussels sprouts and a tray full of roasting potatoes.

'Hi Percy,' greeted Bertie as he walked by with an exceptionally large fresh cream sherry trifle in one hand, the other free to playfully nip Molly's bottom as he passed by her.

Molly laughed raucously and jokingly threw a sprout in Bertie's direction as she deposited the trays of vegetables on a nearby table.

Bertie was too quick for her and, picking up a nearby empty frying pan, contrived to score a six with the streamlined vegetable, batting it into the far corner of the distant rink.

Percy didn't require any further confirmation to know that the latest marriage in his congregation was a runaway success so he took time to marvel at the variety of foodstuffs being prepared for the clubs delectation later that day.

'What is that delicious aroma?' he enquired, inquisitive to have his preconceived assumptions confirmed.

'Why Reverend, are you telling me you can't recognise the mouth-watering fragrance of home cooked roast lamb?' suggested a voice from around the corner, 'or is it my perfume that's driving you crazy?' continued the distinctive vocal in a flirtatious fashion.

Percy went slightly weak at the knees; he recognized that well spoken voice long before the shapely form behind the comment waltzed seductively around the corner by the cooker.

Sarah Jane Coddle oozed across to the kitchen counter with a suggestive sway of the hips that did no good whatsoever for Percy's blood pressure.

Her flame red hair was swirled tantalisingly in a tight bun above her head, whilst a tightly fitting apron, which left little of her curvaceous shape to the imagination, clung to her from neck to knee.

The vicar noted that she was smothered in a liberal sprinkling of flour, seasoning and icing sugar demonstrating her prowess with the sieve if not with the placement.

'Well Percy what do you think?' she teased mercilessly as she did a quick pirouette, her dusty hands extended above her head like a ballerina.

Reverend Percival Peabody was a person equipped to handle most things relating to theological or spiritual matters, but most certainly was not prepared for the natural being of womankind, especially one as coquettish, curvaceous, alluring and evocative as Sarah Jane Coddle.

Percy opened his mouth to utter a contrived off the cuff reply, desperate to maintain a light-hearted dignity becoming of his position, but was cut short in the prime of his response as the twirling figure of Molly's sister revealed two hand-shaped floury imprints on her posterior.

Percy was flummoxed.

'I...er...that is...well...you see...,' he failed miserably in maintaining any semblance of continuity in the conversation and began blushing profusely.

Discretion was very much the order of the day so Percy made a swift, timely change of both subject and observation point.

He turned his attention back to the nearby newlyweds.

'How are things going with the forthcoming newest member of the family, Molly?' he inquired with difficulty, finding it hard to concentrate.

Sarah Jane laughed coyly as she observed Percy's original line of sight and, looking over her shoulder, noted the handprints behind her.

'Ha Ha Ha, that Bernard is a real rogue,' she quipped with an impish grin, 'just wait till I catch up with him!'

For some reason Percy felt a slight impulse to feel a tiny bit jealous.

His sanity was saved by the swift imposition of Molly who stepped forward to grab his arm, leading him away swiftly from her sister's clutches as she tactfully changed the conversation.

'Everything's fine vicar, three months now and not so much of a hiccup or a sign of sickness...'

As Percy and Molly headed towards the dining room door Sarah Jane smiled thoughtfully and turned around to tend to the roast lamb, humming sweetly to herself with a happy tune.

This was going to be a VERY interesting winter, she mused silently.

****

The next hour or so passed swiftly for the vicar as he moved from one member to another, helping with a hand of assistance, a wisely chosen word of praise or a discreet prayer and a plaster.

The tables were laid, the dinner well and truly ready, (if the smell from the kitchen was to be believed), with the raffle prizes assembled on the top table and the gleaming silverware of the soon to be competed for club trophy adorning centre stage.

A glance through the glazed inner doors at the arena confirmed Percy's earlier suspicions that the impending competition was being hyped up by both sides into, at the very least, the most important game of the century.

The ladies had responded to the men's taunt and an equally impressive banner now hung suspended at the opposite end of the room this time decorated with a variety of undergarments of the female persuasion with their corresponding name tags.

Larger than life pictures of the club's top male and female players through the ages now adorned the opposite sides of the room glaring at each other across the divide.

Above the men's changing rooms a huge swathe of red, white and blue balloons rose with imprinted photographs of Dennis 'Sticky' Ditherford and Charles 'Charlie' Chesterford, beneath which the legend stated 'Champions of Champions'.

The women were yet to retaliate further although there was a female work party in full swing nearby in the ladies' changing rooms and they appeared to be inflating a large dirigible.

Percy thought it wise not to stay long enough for the slowly forming words to reveal themselves as he felt they would not be too polite or kindly towards the men's team.

Perhaps now would be a good time to conduct a sermon on the principles of giving and receiving; the neighbourly practice of sharing and forgiveness; because he had a feeling that the afternoon was going to become very noisy, demonstrative and agitated.

However, before he had time to think there was a loud clanging of a bell being rung from the dining room and a bellowing call to order from a voice that could only belong to one person, that of Jack Tuttle.

'Ladies and Gentlemen dinner is served. Please take your places, charge your glasses and be upstanding for the Queen's toast.'

In orderly fashion, members appeared from all around the clubhouse, smartly turned out in their best club dress, blazers adorned with badges of office, competition awards and county emblems.

Those men selected to play in the forthcoming game were sporting crisp and clean 'whites' from shirt to shoe, whilst the ladies looked equally resplendent in their cream coloured blouses and long flowing skirts cut just above the ankle.

Percy noted that Shelia Ramsbottom's skirt looked like it had been cut just above the knee!

Over by the top table, the portly and distinctive shape of the club's newly appointed county vice-president waited in anticipation, a huge grin playing across his face as he stood proudly in all his branded paraphernalia.

The members gaily paraded past him in a humorous and affectionate show of respect, the men tugging their fetlocks and bowing whilst the ladies curtsied and fluttered their eyelashes furiously.

Jack Tuttle was certainly enjoying the moment and soaked up the compliments like a giant sponge in a wine vat.

It was unusual for the club to hold a meal before an afternoon of competitive bowling. However, given the sporting occasion, a newly promoted vice-president and the official commencement of the indoor season, the committee had voted unanimously to have a grandiose ceremonial roast dinner banquet to celebrate the simultaneously occurring events.

With a midday start to lunch, the members would have ample time to enjoy the luncheon, relax with a cup of tea and be ready for the 'off' at 2.30 p.m.

There had been a suggestion from the women's team that this would work in their favour as most of the male members were bound to fall asleep after such a hearty meal due to their age and frailty.

This had met with a rousing cheer and a firm rebuttal from the male camp, who proceeded to postulate that the ladies would hardly be able to bowl whilst holding on to their Zimmer frames.

The friendly banter, idle chit-chat, and posturing for position were broken in mid-flow by the call to order from Big Jim, who was never one to hold back when he needed to make his presence known.

'Order please ladies and gentlemen!'

Silence fell.

Jack Tuttle stood resolutely, proudly in front of his gathered members and raised his glass.

'Ladies and Gentlemen, I give you the Queen.'

The respectful reply of a hundred voices whispered back...

'THE QUEEN!'

At that point, as Percy looked over the gathered throng of his 'flock' he reflected that this was probably his proudest moment in the mixed misfortunes of what still remained a very distinguished club.

For one brief moment, they pulled together as one, in unity, in time honoured tradition, ready to take on the world, before they took on each other.

The next two hours flew by in a medley of merriment, mild banter and mixed metaphors over the top of a veritable tidal wave of perfectly prepared cuisine.

Best prawn cocktails, pursued by the most delicate roast lamb with all the trimmings, washed down by rich intoxicating sherry trifle, left only the long relaxation over coffee and mint chocolates as the members indulged themselves to the full whilst mentally stimulating themselves for the game ahead.

When all had sufficiently sated their appetites, and even the likes of Bernard and Charlie had refused the offer of third helpings of desert, finally the formal celebrations drew to a close. The tables were swiftly cleared, leaving the ensemble with only their refreshed coffees as they pondered, cogitated, digested and considered.

There remained just one time-honoured tradition to follow and, as everyone knew, there was no man better qualified in spinning a yarn, telling a tale, prevaricating or generally twisting the truth for the sake of comedy than Big Jim.

The shout went up across the tables...

'Speech! Speech! Speech!'

Never was a moment more perfectly suited to a man of Jack Tuttle's charisma and with a smile he raised a thanking hand and rose to the occasion.

'Thank you; you are most kind, thank you...'

'Unaccustomed as I am to giving lengthy speeches steeped in rhetoric,' he began, as he fished out a wad of pages from his inner pocket, 'and being a man of few words,' as the sheets unfurled like a falling toilet roll...

The audience groaned, in a pleasurable way, they knew, after all, what was coming and despite its corny repertoire the speech would still be funny and they would nevertheless laugh like children.

Big Jim peered over his reading spectacles with a wry smile and continued.

'During the war...'

Percy groaned and reached for the wine.

He was half way down his second glass by the time Jack reached his next anecdote, 'Have you heard the one about..?'

A smiling Sarah Jane Coddle leant over his shoulder with a newly opened bottle to give the vicar a 'top-up' of both the wine and her perfume.

Her mischievous expression caught more eyes than just Percy's and there were one or two ribs nudged as well as knowing looks cast in the vicar's direction.

Bertie was one of those that 'caught the look' and he chuckled inwardly. Poor old Percy, he really hadn't got a clue what was happening...

****

An hour later Percy had ceased to groan although he did have his box of headache tablets near to hand and a tot of brandy stood on standby near to his bottle of spring water, just in case.

He was comfortably settled in his favourite deckchair alongside the end rink ready and waiting in anticipation of the sporting frivolities to come, as were the other gathered spectators who must have numbered over 200.

Percy gazed around noting a multitude of local people present as well as a fair number of county officials, visitors from other clubs and more than a few members' of the regional press, including the long suffering, but well rewarded Jiggy Jenkins.

Apparently, the word was out!

The story of the 25th anniversary was a very tasty titbit for the paparazzi given the club's track record, and with the known facts they were obviously well prepared for an 'anything goes' game.

Percy cast an eagle eye around looking for Charlie, suspicion already dawning that he would have had a hand in any story or gossip leaked to the press. It appeared Charlie was making himself scarce for the time being however, and seemed unlikely to appear until the beginning of the match.

The tense atmosphere was electrifying and everyone was buzzing with the intense expectation of the events due to unfold shortly.

There had been of late, Percy thought, some very 'hush hush' meetings in secluded corners along with shuffling of paperwork and discreet phone calls in both encampments.

He could not help but feel there were a few surprises in the offing.

A sudden tap on the shoulder was another unexpected one and Percy turned around anxiously to see who required his counsel.

Big Jim stood immediately behind him sporting a big grin and more than a little impish devilment showing in his eyes.

'Here you are vicar, this is for you,' he chuckled, handing Percy a red armband and a rectangular wooden case.

Percy looked back with a blank stare and a mystified expression.

'Well you can hardly expect me NOT to play for the men's team on such an important occasion can you?' He paused and then continued, 'besides we've got to make sure those ladies don't notch up a repeat performance!' and winked knowingly.

Percy felt a sudden chill and with a worried look he asked in a concerned voice, 'What's going on Jack and what's this case for?'

But Jack Tuttle's lips were tightly sealed and he said no more.

Percy called after him in a more plaintive tone repeating the question and Big Jim looked back over his shoulder with a broad smile and a parting comment...

'WELL SOMEONE HAS TO BE THE UMPIRE!'

Perhaps it was an unfortunate omen or maybe just bad timing, but the church bell outside tolling the hour from the clock tower sounded more like the peal of the grim reaper's timepiece.

If Long John Silver had walked by at that point and handed Percy the 'black spot' it would have shaken him less.

How could he, of all people, not be familiar with the legend of the ladies only victory over the men in this competition and the subsequent fall from grace of his predecessor the Reverend Joshua Jackson?

Percy really didn't have time to consider the matter further before other events overtook his train of thought and he was opportunely distracted by the hissing of the internal P.A. system.

There was a definite stirring from within the darkened confines of the men's changing room, and the opening strains of a familiar discordant tune rampaged through the rafters.

Percy groaned in recognition, 'Oh no,' he thought, 'they couldn't possibly be!'

Apparently, they could.

A group of men emerged from the dark wearing jogging bottoms, sweatshirts, sunglasses and baseball caps emblazoned with the logo 'South-Borough Boys, Giants of the Green' as the all too familiar soundtrack of the 'Rocky' movie blared loudly out of the club's speaker system.

They marched forward into the bright light heading purposely towards the green, towels over one arm, sponges and water bottles in the other.

Behind them strode the cream of the crop of Lower South-Borough's male bowling community.

Percy could only groan, his head held in his hands as the female onlookers stared aghast with mouths open and teacups dangling on extended little fingers.

Jack 'Big Jim' Tuttle led the entourage, arms held high in salute like a punch-drunk boxer, smiling broadly as he led his troops into battle.

Percy suddenly envisaged a huge tag team wrestling match with the ladies and gentlemen lining the green on all sides, taking turns to participate in, and becoming part, of the inevitable mass brawl.

The team were dressed in their whites, which were now adorned by flowing silk cloaks of red and silver inlaid with gold, bearing their nicknames.

Clearly, the men had spent considerable time and indeed copious, amounts of personal finances on preparing for the day; the surprise was absolute.

A rousing cheer ran through the building as the rest of the male onlookers, following the lead of the circus-like parade, 'camped' it up with much enthusiasm and great gusto.

Behind Big Jim strolled the rest of the dirty dozen, Charlie, Dennis and Bertie making up the first quartet much to the crowd's delight.

Clifford Johnson, Bernard 'Batty' Bartrum, Douglas Doolittle, and master of the green Patrick Albright closely followed them.

However, the biggest roar of all came as the final, and most fantastic, of the teams of four emerged into the limelight.

Delighting the crowd with panache and presence the youthful talented combo of the Under-25s British champion Johnny Jackson and his pair's partner Paul Jenner swept into the arena ahead of the final group.

It came as no surprise to see Paul's uncle Martin King, the National Champion from Norfolk, with him.

Just behind, last, but not least, sporting the biggest smile of all, the Rt Hon. Ronald 'Squiffy' Regis, former president and tournament winner led up the rear.

To say Squiffy was the most popular of figures was an understatement, perhaps 'the people's choice' would have been a better perspective.

Needless to say, the crowd went wild.

A suitably primed section of the male audience waved dramatically, whistling, cheering, and throwing pairs of polka dot boxer shorts into the air in an exhibition reminiscent of last summer's final presentation by the former president.

There was no doubt that the men had turned out not only the best in the club but also in the county, to piece together the strongest team Percy had ever seen and he had suspicions that several temporary membership forms had been hastily registered in recent weeks.

He reflected that if Trigger were here with his betting book the odds would have been heavily slashed in the men's favour in the last few minutes.

The atmosphere was electric, perhaps just a touch too exciting for some of the more senior retired members. One made a mad dash for the toilet as fast as his Zimmer frame would carry him, whilst another twisted his braces in the middle of the Mexican wave and found himself talking in a higher pitched voice for quite some while afterwards.

Most of the ladies sat around glumly with a look of despair, however Percy couldn't help but notice that Molly was talking excitedly on the telephone handset in the kitchen and the curtains in the ladies' changing room were twitching erratically.

All of a sudden, the Reverend Percival Peabody felt a desire to be somewhere else very distant from the bowling green, and the tranquillity of his quiet study loomed large in his mind.

That pause for thought was all it took for it to be too late for him to make an escape; it was about to become the men's turn to be lost for words.

Clearly, the women planned to field a team with the helping hand of God on their side, because the strident tones of 'When the saints go marching in' flooded through the compound.

The ladies didn't go for the 'camp' and nostalgic testosterone packed impact that the men had picked but they certainly DID make an entrance.

They marched gaily out of their quarters and down onto the green creating an explosion of colour with striped top hats, pink pompoms and candy floss rah-rah skirts.

A number of men looked clearly flustered, whilst Bernard and Charlie were very obviously uncomfortable, reddening around the cheeks.

It was at that point the strutting females unveiled a bombshell. With a final twirl they whipped off their flouncy skirts to reveal 12 pairs of well-filled hot pants. The eye-opening revelation was an ambush of epic proportions, greater than the O.K. corral.

'OH MY LORD!' stuttered Percy, turning quickly toward the tea urn in need of a timely distraction.

The ladies shock tactics resulted in a number of spontaneous and impromptu expletives from the less than prepared gentlemen's team. Reverend Peabody found himself quickly reaching for the community swear box as 'JESUS CHRIST!', 'BLOODY HELL!' and other such comments reached his sensitive ears.

Bernard appeared to have collapsed with a coughing fit, whilst Charlie was definitely having trouble with his breathing and the younger players looked distinctly hot under their collars.

The desired effect had already rendered one quarter of the men's team helpless and how they would manage to play a full game with the females in such a state of undress was anyone's guess.

Heaven forbid that they should be tempted to remove anything else, thought Percy.

Big Jim and Patrick were feverishly consulting the rulebook but as of yet could find nothing referring to the manner of the uniform, only the colour, style above the waist and preferred footwear.

In the audience the Zimmer frame bound gentlemen arriving back just in time for the ladies' 'unveiling', stifled a strangulated cry then headed back to the toilet, whilst three sets of false teeth hit the floor with a clatter and Russell Cobblethwaite trapped his finger in the bar hatch.

In the turnaround of a few brief seconds the women had gained the advantage, taken the upper hand and stolen a march on the men.

Percy covered his blushes by making a valiant effort to enter into a polite conversation with the ladies' captain Doris Doolittle.

'Er, well that was a VERY interesting entrance Doris,' stammered Percy.

The vicar glanced around whilst trying to conceal his sense of awkward discomfort and in doing so his gaze rested momentarily on one or two members of the women's team.

There was a familiarity to the players' faces and, with a sense of déjà vu, he paused for a double take.

He noted the presence of Diane Ditherford, Cynthia Cobblethwaite and Phillippa Spindleforth but also the notable absence of new players such as Sheila Ramsbottom, Molly Tattleford and Pauline Jenner who had retired to the substitute's bench.

Whilst Diana, Cynthia, Phillippa and Doris were all still in their youthful years when it came to bowling, one or two of the other members seemed rather old, antiquated even, with grey hair, walking sticks, arthritic limbs and wobbly teeth being more the order of the day.

For some reason the line-up looked strangely memorable to Percy but no matter how hard he thought he just could not place his finger on the solution to the puzzle.

Before he could develop his thought process any further the ladies' captain returned his greeting with a warm smile and a subtle hint of certainty about her clipped voice.

'Hello Percy, how are you? Coming to see the slaughter of the innocents?' she mused in a satirical manner, apparently quite full of mirth that was hard to control and barely concealed.

'Well, not quite, I've been given the unfortunate job of keeping all of you in line,' he replied, pointing at his umpire's armband, 'so you better keep your ladies under control.'

Doris opened her mouth to reply, but before she could utter any further comment the ever opportunistic Charlie Chesterford stepped forward and proceeded to put his foot in it, as he invariably did every time.

He had been studying the females with some speculative interest but, once he had got his head around the distraction of the hot pants, he had given serious consideration to the developing situation and more importantly the standard of the opposition.

Having reached the conclusion that a strong draught of wind was likely to blow most of the ladies' team over he decided that it was appropriate that he and Dennis took full advantage of the situation.

'Never mind keeping them under control Percy,' he smirked with a huge grin, 'the only way to keep the ladies' team safe is to put them in a corral for their own protection and give them guide dogs.'

He cackled spuriously at his self-proclaimed humour and leant on a nearby chair for support as Dennis joined in the taunting, unable to resist the opportunity to add further insult.

'They are going to need a map, a compass to find where the cot is AND an intravenous injection of adrenalin just to reach the end of the rink,' he chortled.

Other members of the team nearby looked up with what could almost be described as tears in their eyes as they struggled to control the rising fits of suppressed laughter inside them.

Clearly, they were enjoying the spirit of the moment as one of their favourite kings of comedy was in full flow.

'I know,' laughed Charlie gleefully, 'why don't we borrow some of those metal ramps they provide for the juniors in tenpin bowling? At least the ladies' woods will have SOME momentum on them when they roll them down the slope and a guarantee they'll be heading in the right direction!'

Dennis creased up and a few of the adjacent men's team had to turn away, unable to stop the mirth escaping from their lips.

'Stop it Charlie, don't be silly,' interrupted the chuckling Dennis, 'that's a waste of time...'

'Why's that?' gurgled Charlie, sensing a punchline still to follow from his partner.

'Because they wouldn't be able to lift their woods that high in the first place!' he stuttered in uncontrollable laughter.

'Ha! Ha! Ha!'

'Oh my God that's a 'good un' Dennis.'

'Keep it up boys!'

Other members of their team were clearly enticed into adding fuel to the fire and Percy felt a conflagration was imminently likely should he not calm the situation immediately.

Immediately however, was not soon enough as Bernard burst through the male rank's brandishing a well-known and very large wooden spoon.

'Here you are boys, if you're going to stir things up you might as well use this!' he sniggered derisively.

'After all,' he continued, 'the ladies are going to need a big cup of tea to go with that generous helping of humble pie they're going to have to eat later!'

'Ha! Ha! Ha!'

That was clearly enough for the men who quite obviously had a voracious appetite for humour; they all burst into an uncontrolled mass of hysterical laughter.

All that was, except for the upstanding figure of the Rt Hon. Ronald 'Squiffy' Regis, not that he didn't like a good ribbing, or a bit of harmless fun at the opposition's expense.

He had been taking a hard look at the line-up of the ladies' team and a certain degree of doubt slowly but surely had begun to creep into his subconscious.

'Er steady on chaps, let's not get too carried away here...' he began in a quiet voice that no one heard or was inclined to acknowledge at that stage.

Percy in the meantime had noticed that the women, far from taking offence, becoming dispirited or downtrodden were actually revelling in the fervour of the situation.

Actually quite a few of them were smiling broadly as their captain spoke up in a warm and inviting fashion, 'Well if you gentlemen are so sure, why not match the stakes you offered 25 years ago and put £500 on the table?'

The Reverend Percival Peabody was dumfounded; he stood with his mouth open in amazement and his inner self sparked an imminent warning that something BIG was about to occur.

Charlie and Dennis were beyond the point of self-reasoning, as were several of the nearby male members who were still chortling merrily; not really able to match the mild retort with a suitable reply.

Money was never an issue to worry either of the pair, especially not for Bernard, being a very wealthy self-made millionaire from his long standing, if at times somewhat dubious, building and plumbing business.

'Why not make it £5,000?' he replied casting his line into the water alongside that of the dynamic duo.

Bernard was never slow in supporting his favourite mates and always one to stand up when his fellow members were called to account, especially when there was an element of gambling, financial risk or challenge thrown their way.

One or two of the men looked up rather sharply as the larger sum of money was mentioned and the younger players looked visibly paled by the sudden upping of the stakes.

'Look chaps hold on there a second...' interposed Squiffy; he was clearly a man with something important on his mind and there was a suggestion from his countenance that a penny had started to drop.

Bernard however sensed the taste of blood, metaphorically speaking, and with complete disregard plunged on in pursuit of the prize.

The close at hand Dennis and Charlie stood shoulder to shoulder in a show of bold support and threw their own 'tuppence-worth' into the melting pot.

'Anything else you'd like to add on top whilst you're at it?' suggested Charlie with a teasing smile on his face.

Perhaps you dare not add to the risk; things taste a bit too rich as they are,' chuckled Dennis.

Percy was beginning to look slightly blanched and distinctly grey around the gills, even more so because of the unnatural way that the ladies were responding to the baiting from the men; he began to wonder who was baiting whom?

Cynthia Cobblethwaite stood up quietly from behind the group of ladies' team leaders and spoke softly in a voice that would lull anyone into a false sense of security.

'OK Charlie, if you're so confident of winning how about you accept a dare from me, after all, you've known me for many years and what harm can it do to spice things up?'

Charlie was still only ready to test the water but Bernard, as reckless as ever, plunged in.

'Whatever you suggest, I'm sure Charlie will accept, won't you Charlie?' as he slapped his fellow team mate firmly on the back of his shoulder.

Charlie and Dennis responded in unison with a nodding of their heads in affirmation, feeling obliged to voice their support now.

'OK then,' said Charlie, 'name your terms Cynthia, whatever you care to suggest, as long as it doesn't involve me taking all my clothes off,' he added, remembering the original fiasco.

Percy, standing like a referee between two prizefighters, felt distinctly untoward and queasy as he glanced over towards the ladies, seeing the almost hidden look of triumph on their faces.

Doris Doolittle looked remarkably like the cat who had just found a large pot of Cornish clotted cream.

Cynthia appeared to be mulling over her reply for a few seconds before responding softly.

'If the ladies' team beats the gentlemen's team this afternoon they must promise to wait on us afterwards at supper time with fresh strawberry cream teas...' She paused as Charlie opened his mouth to reply and then continued her terms and conditions, 'in just their underwear!' she completed in a tone of finality.

Charlie and Dennis paled significantly, but pride was at stake and, as before, they had left themselves nowhere to turn; however, Bernard as always finished the conversation.

'DONE!' he beamed triumphantly.

Doris reached over and shook his hand with an air of exuberance, stating the obvious fact of which Percy was already very much aware.

'You have been!' she smirked as several of the ladies burst into light-hearted laughter.

Charlie and Dennis glowered and looked a touch uneasily around the room not expecting the response from the women to be quite so welcoming.

Bernard also looked rather confused by Doris's final comment.

Squiffy used the men's sudden silence to make himself heard at last, and with an air of desperation held up a large sepia tinted photograph of a ladies' team he had removed from the nearby club house wall.

'I HAVE BEEN TRYING TO TELL YOU THIS IS...' he began.

'THE WINNING LADIES' TEAM THAT BEAT YOU 25 YEARS AGO!' finished Cynthia Cobbbelthwaite, with a victorious expression on her face.

'B-B-But that's impossible,' postulated Dennis looking around the ladies' faces, 'you team captains are the only four original members from that competition.'

'Besides,' said Charlie, 'I was there and I don't recognise any of these ladies,' he stated with a voice that sought confirmation of the oppositions' bold statement.

Cynthia proceeded to enlighten them, 'It's simply because a lot of the ladies moved on to other clubs or counties over the years or play in other teams that you never meet Charlie.' She paused and then added, 'and quite a few have now retired professionally, but have always retained their membership of the club they were so fond of,' she completed with a proud smile.

Bernard, suddenly aware of the stakes at hand, tried to raise the spirits of the deflated men who began to look as if lightning might indeed be about to strike twice.

'Come on gentlemen, what are you afraid of?'

'Are we men or mice?'

'They may be the original team that beat us 25 years ago, but they're a lot older now.' He paused and then finished with, 'and some of them don't even play anymore!'

He beamed at them confidently and one or two briefly raised their expectations again until Doris interposed, speaking softly, but with a firmness that chilled them to the bone.

They're a ladies' team that includes nine county players, four members of the England team and a former world champion!' she lambasted the men as they visibly wilted at her words.

Doris Doolittle moved to hammer the final nail in the trapdoor through which the men had fallen so voluntarily.

'Gentlemen may I present to you the Rt Hon. Lady Elizabeth Quinton MBE, former commonwealth gold medallist, twice World Cup finalist, FIVE times national champion and president of the English Women's Bowling Association 1998 – 2003!'

The women went berserk, hands raised in rapturous applause as a slim framed, silver haired lady of senior age turned around to face the on-looking gentlemen, her blue blazer adorned with a stunning array of impressive badges and a gold medal draped around her neck.

She smiled sweetly, 'Pleased to meet you all' she said, and then curtsied in a composed manner that spoke volumes.

The men looked crushed.

Elizabeth Quinton turned towards Charlie and Dennis with a steely look in her eyes and offered a final word especially for them, 'I look forward to meeting you two on the green,' she said, 'after all I AM playing in the team against you!'

****

Percy breathed a satisfied sigh of relief.

It had taken him fully 30 minutes to de-ruffle the masses, settle the high-spirited exchanges between each team, calm a few nerves and find a happy median between the rising and falling or soaring levels of confidence.

In preparation, it had to be said that both the ladies and the gentlemen had been well matched, each creating an exciting entrance and display of camaraderie; although the women's game plan had far exceeded everyone's expectations.

Quite simply they had stunned the men with their revelations and more importantly fooled the other team into committing to a high dividend financially as well as morally with an obligation to personal subservience should they lose.

The atmosphere was already electrifying as, with the teams preparing to play their first 'trial end', the spectators settled down nervously to an afternoon of compulsive competitive bowling.

The top table dignitaries were comfortably ensconced in the better class seating; that included an extra cushion each, a hot drink holder and a bowl of peanuts.

Over to one corner several members of the press were busy scribbling notes for the next day's edition whilst Jiggy Jenkins had gone one step further and taken the liberty of setting up a DVD video camera system. He was obviously determined to encapsulate every single shot, all the members' expressions, and, hopefully one or two very lucrative pictures often only caught haphazardly on camera.

Newly elected vice-president Jack Tuttle was thoroughly enjoying his first big sporting occasion for the county; having successfully survived the nervy luncheon speech, he was preparing to settle down for an afternoon of competitive bowling.

All that was required for him to do was to give the teams his blessing and get the competition under way.

'Ladies and Gentlemen I think you'll agree it has already been an extra-ordinary day,' began Jack, 'and we have seen a tremendous level of preparation for such a prestigious event.'

The crowd murmured their supportive voice of appreciation, reflecting Big Jim's words.

'We will shortly begin the match, with two trial ends for each team, but prior to this, as is customary, we will invite every team player to play 'nearest the jack' for a spot cash prize of £50.

Everyone again nodded in agreement.

'However as this is my first undertaking as county vice-president,' continued Jack with a beaming smile stretching across his broad countenance, 'I am personally going to double the prize to £100!'

The spectators and members alike roared their appreciation of the generous, unexpected gesture.

'So without further ado,' continued Jack picking up the nearest white cot, 'it's my proud pleasure to get the game under way.'

A rapturous round of applause swept around the green and Percy noted that he hadn't heard such an appreciative, thunderous acknowledgement since the former club president Ronald 'Squiffy' Regis had marched onto the outside green on finals day last summer.

Big Jim stepped up to the middle mat and raised his hand to deliver the cot up the green towards a place of his choice but, just as he prepared to release it, he felt someone else's hand restraining his.

He looked around in surprise to see Percy standing next to him with his hand stopping the delivery.

The Reverend was smiling deeply to himself and with a knowing nod in Jack's direction, he pointed up the green.

At the far end, from the ditch there strayed a small bundle of fur, not noticeable or even recognisable to anyone unless they specifically knew what they were looking for.

Percy knew precisely what he was seeing and was 'tipping the wink' to Jack Tuttle.

Big Jim thanked Percy with a whispered reply and turned around to face the teams waiting to play.

'Could I please have the captains from each team over to the mat for an urgent consultation on a rules irregularity?'

The six mystified captains approached Big Jim on the mat.

****

Rollo had enjoyed a very peaceful day away from the unremitting pursuit of Baggie, aka Miss Matilda Bagshott.

Having decided that the safest place was within the confines of the clubhouse inner sanctum where there were plenty of people and little chance of another prowling pussycat, he had enjoyed the day doing what all cats love to do...napping.

In due course, he had awakened with a long stretch as well as a typically big yawn, which left him feeling full of energy, enthusiasm and enterprise.

In doing so, he had cast an inquiring eye over the proceedings that appeared to be occurring at the other end of the green to where he was currently resting.

Rollo recognised the formal presentation and the general to-ing and fro-ing of the gathered ensemble as one he had seen at the end of the recently past summer season.

Being a young at heart, playful pussycat he sensed an air of mischief at hand and remembered well the fun he had at the bowler's expense when he cat-napped the white ball previously.

He trembled with an intense excitement and carefully slunk into the nearby ditch furthest away from the players to await the known trundling of his intended victim on the surface of the green.

His ears were, after all very sensitised towards the sound of moving things and if he could pick up the footfall, or paw-fall, of a moving mouse he could certainly sense the lumbering of a large robust ceramic object.

Rollo heard, or sensed the thud of an object hitting the ground; he stiffened excitedly as his ears twitched and his tail flicked nervously from side to side.

He tensed his muscles and prepared to leap out on to the green.

The noise of the approaching object seemed to his hypersensitive ears a lot louder than he would have expected and despite his intense excitement he began to feel a little unsure of himself.

His ears twitched and trembled above the edge of the green like miniature radars trying to seek out the reason for the increasing noise but unable to gain any further insight, he felt a compulsive urge to explore further, raising his eyes cautiously over the ditch banking.

Slowly, surely, he peeked surreptitiously over the embankment, seeing first the team members then, more worryingly, a line of six people standing on mats at the far end of the green.

He lifted his head slightly higher, just a fraction, as the level of the noise increased and his curiosity got the better of his wisdom.

His pupils constricted against the bright lights and then gradually, as his eyes became accustomed, he took stock of the situation.

Rollo had expected to see a single object traversing the green that was innocently unaware of its appending arrest and seizure.

He was certainly NOT prepared for the sight of seven of the aforementioned 'objects' approaching rapidly like an armada of cruise missiles in overdrive.

It took just a fraction of a second for the data to transmit to his brain, the statistics to be digested, and the analysis to be translated into kitty-mode.

Far from being the antagoniser ready to pursue and capture, as had been his original intention, now he was very much the intended target being pursued in a belligerent fashion by the seven erstwhile 'victims.'

His whiskers twitched violently from side to side, his ears trembling and his furry mass convulsing in a mixture of excitement and sheer panic.

The natural desire to chase was overwhelming, despite the odds he was torn by a cat-sense of manic insanity, unable to resist the rapidly approaching and now thunderous objects.

They might as well have been a herd of large white mice stampeding up the green.

The hackles rose on his tail and body as if he had received a 9000 volt jolt of electricity; without further consideration he followed his natural instinct.

Rollo sprang over the bank like an over-wound jack-in-the-box and charged down the green.

It was perhaps unfortunate that the time taken by the vicar's cat to consider the options and make his move, was all the time it took for the seven cots to arrive simultaneously at his point of descent.

The six captains at the other end of the rinks, spurred on by a participating umpire, having been made aware of Rollo's intentions, had launched their cavalcade towards the far end with the intention of exacting a 'bit of fun', not to mention, revenge at the cat's expense.

To perhaps coin a phrase, the expression 'the worm had turned' seemed very appropriate.

Rollo landed in a stiff-legged, fur-balled, moggie-manner right on top of the concentration of cots, and proceeded to do a very fine display of 'break-dancing on marbles'.

His animated antics caused mass convulsions of hysteria at the far end as he desperately tried to find a firm footing on the slippery surfaces and failed miserably.

His legs flailing wildly Rollo impacted the green with a bump, spinning like a whirling top, all appendages akimbo as he scattered a number of cots to the four corners.

It had to be said that only Ronnie O'Sullivan could have produced a better quick-fire display as Rollo succeeded in potting one ball in each corner and two in the side pocket simultaneously leaving him surmounted over the final offender like a broody hen.

Over on the window ledge of the first floor skylight Miss Matilda Bagshott purred to herself in a self-satisfied manner as she surveyed the dazzling performance by the vicar's cat.

Obviously, he had gone to a lot of trouble to entertain and impress her with his aerobic abilities.

She watched as the now flustered and disgruntled Rollo charged off the playing surface with a spectacular turn of speed, his dignity somewhat tattered.

As he crashed through the cat flap on the other side of the green she flounced upward towards the nearby roof in order to get a better view of the proceedings, and more importantly, the fleeing cat's intended destination.

****

Finally, after 'time out' to allow for the audience to calm down, as well as the team members to recover from their impromptu entertainment, Big Jim at last managed to regain some sense of order and sensibility.

With a well-placed target central to the rinks, the undertaking of the 'nearest the jack' competition went relatively well given that most of the ladies chose to 'draw' whilst the men resorted to the age old tactic of 'firing'.

A dozen woods majestically rolled up one side of the green with demeanour, poise and elegance of delivery whilst 12 others approached from the other so fast they left scorch marks, which made for an interesting visual comparison of tactics.

Maybe it was a case of the ladies having some prior warning or perhaps a good memory from previous years.

More likely, it was a case of the men as per usual, with libido in full flow, forgetting to allow for the speed variations between outdoor and indoor greens.

Having played all summer on the challenging variable grass lawns of the local county, which ranged from their own prestigious, manicured masterpiece to others more resembling a ploughed field, they were not in the best frame of mind to adjust to the faster pace of playing on carpet.

To be honest it was more comparable to playing on glass and the slightest roll of the wood would have ensured its arrival at the other end of the rink in record-breaking time.

Most of the men's bowls simply missed everything, ending up in the ditch or alternatively rebounded and bounced their way into the spectator's gallery much to the alarm of those watching.

Others cannonballed into the coffee tables and ricocheted around as if they were caffeinated coconuts, or, worse still ascended the far bank, landing like the fallout of a naval barrage.

One of Molly's best teapots took a direct hit and shattered into a million shards to the dismay of Cynthia Cobblethwaite who was still pouring a cup of Earl Grey from it.

Another landed dead centre in the hitherto uncut baked Alaska spreading generous quantities of fresh cream, meringue and biscuit crumb base over the senior member's of the knitting circle.

A distant tinkling followed by an ear piercing scream revealed that at least one bowl had gone through the window of the ladies' toilet much to the consternation of Gloria Grimshaw who ran past just a few seconds later clutching her skirt desperately and with her bloomers still at half-mast.

Click!

Jiggy Jenkins made sure to get a shot of that one!

Whilst the entertainment value was as always very high, the damage, other than to pride, was considerably lighter and once Big Jim dared to open his eyes he was quickly able to take stock.

Percy, good old Percy, had quickly interceded to calm the nerves of the knitting circle, whilst Molly and Bertie were on hand with fresh tea, clean tea towels and a bottle of brandy, which Big Jim eyed with unbridled envy.

Sarah Jane was in rapid pursuit of the runaway bloomers and their occupant with offers of condolence, consolation and canapés.

With all seemingly restored to a semblance of sanity, Jack took the opportunity to peer through his fingers towards the green to assess the outcome, as if there could be much doubt as to the result.

Seven of the ladies' bowls rested comfortably within 18 inches of the cot whilst another wood appeared close enough to almost touch it.

Jack strode over to the target for a closer examination to check the winning wood, reaching inside his inner jacket pocket for the five crisp £20 notes as he did so.

Remembering and learning from previous experiences, he bent over carefully to closely examine the sticker on the nearest bowl.

He found himself needing to check twice because the winner's marker was adorned with the 'playboy' emblem, which rather surprised him.

Finally, assured of the correct answer, he assumed his best presidential stance, held up the financial reward and with a strident, deep voice announced his findings.

'The winner is...' he boomed with an authoritive voice, 'Bernard Bartrum!' and then added with a barely hidden smile, 'first blood to the gentlemen!'

Needless to say, the news received a rapturous and raucous reception from the men as they vented their pent-up emotion in a expression of verbal rampancy.

A particularly ebullient Bernard chirped in with a teasing comment just to rub a touch of salt into the wound, 'Looks like we've already outmatched the ladies and I've only bowled one wood!'

The retort came courtesy of Sheila Ramsbottom, from the rear of the ladies' ranks, as she was the one who particularly seemed to have the measure of Bernard as well as a particular vested interest.

'Well that's the first time in years you've scored Bernard,' she piped up in a rebellious taunt that immediately shut him up and brought a deepening shade of hue to his cheeks.

'GAME ON LADIES AND GENTS!'

The unexpected and firm address from the nearby vicar, brought the jubilation and taunting to an abrupt halt as he took the unusual step of stamping his umpire's authority on the match.

Jack looked around with a smirk of approval whilst one or two men and ladies glanced over in slight surprise; Molly opened her mouth to say something then thought better of it as a smiling Bertie gave her a playful dig in the ribs.

There was definitely a change going on in their vicar and it certainly was NOT going unnoticed in one or two of his parishioners.

The Rt Hon. Ronald 'Squiffy' Regis made a mental note to keep a closer eye on his good friend, whilst Jack thought it might be appropriate to carry an extra hip flask of the finest brandy about his personage in future, just in case.

Percy strode forward with a sense of purpose, 'Well come on then, let's get on with the game and find out whether you're bowlers or bike mechanics, the clock's ticking...'

And with that he approached Big Jim, extracted a large coin from his pocket and spun it high in to the air before uttering his final word on the subject.

'CALL!'

****

The game progressed at a cracking pace with exuberance from both sides much to the delight of the watching spectators who responded with 'OOHS' and 'AAHS' as well as rapturous applause at the appropriate moments.

It seemed only minutes before the halfway point was already looming and Percy was looking intently over his reading glasses at the large clock face above the scoreboard.

He couldn't help but reflect that after forty five minutes of play the clock showing a time of 3.15 p.m. and the score reading 30-15 in favour of the jubilant men bore a mutual resemblance.

It was a good job that it wasn't four o'clock, he mused to himself.

There was no doubt that the strength and youth of the gentlemen's team was overwhelming the experienced but much more senior members of the ladies' team who, although being the original winners 25 years ago, were no longer up to the mark fitness wise.

They were definitely flagging; in fact he could not help but notice that more than one or two were glued firmly to their chairs, breathing heavily with an air of desperation gathering around their laboured features.

Percy looked over to the kitchen and gave them a perceivable nod before checking that everyone had delivered their last wood of the current end, the 14th of 21 to play, and gave the call.

'Tea break, ladies and gentlemen, fifteen minutes rest and relaxation for those that need it,' and he gave a pointed look in the ladies' direction.

One or two of the gentlemen groaned, wanting to push on with their advantage whilst others murmured about the scourge of the 'tea break' under their breath, but all were glad of the opportunity to have some refreshment after the lengthy spell under the hot lighting.

The players walked off the green stepping towards the kitchen counter, some with a light bounce to their pace, others with a heavy trudge.

Percy noted the state of affairs with some concern and reached for his rulebook as he summoned Jack Tuttle to join him for a briefing.

Bernard, Charlie and Dennis all noted the mini 'conference' as they gathered excitedly, like schoolchildren around the counter, and pondered the cause. They exchanged loud, flattering observations on each others' match play, as always wishing to extract as much mileage as possible from the other team's misfortune.

It was quite clear that they felt they had the opposition 'on the rack' and were set on making the most of their impending revenge.

Percy and Jack returned from their whispered discussions a few minutes later to collect their own cups of tea; Jack as always reaching for his hip flask to add a small tot of libation to the awaiting nectar.

Sarah, serving from behind the counter, looked with surprise as he sneakily poured a generous tot into both waiting cups, then smiled to herself, and began undoing her apron strings as a sudden premonition illuminated her features.

'Here you are old chap, you better take a sip of this,' whispered Jack in Percy's ear as he handed him the cup, trying hard not to give the game away.

Innocently Percy thanked the president and without thinking took a large swig of the hot drink.

He gasped with a sudden choking cough as the sweet mixture hit the back of his throat, putting the cup and saucer down hurriedly as tears welled up in his eyes.

'By God that's a good cup of tea,' he croaked, innocently unaware of the addition to the mix or the fact that it wasn't actually God that had a helping hand in the brew.

Jack laughed and clapped Percy lightly on his back to assist the cough; 'Bet you're ready to give them the good news now then Reverend?'

A warmth and inner strength flowed through the vicar like never before; he felt strangely alive and effervescent, an effect which a watchful Sarah Jane Coddle noted and filed away for future reference.

Percy nodded to Jack, before stepping forward to face the members of both teams, now sitting comfortably in the lounge with hot sweet tea and succulent fresh baked biscuits residing on the nearby tables.

'Ladies and gentlemen, if I could have your attention for a brief moment please?'

Ever respectful of their Reverend, the members quickly stopped gossiping although those facing the wrong way had to be given a playful nudge, much to the dismay of Johnny Jackson who dropped his cup in his lap.

Percy waited for the appropriate moment and then, as the hush ensued he continued.

'It has come to my attention that several of the members of the ladies' team are somewhat exhausted, in a state of poor health and I deem them unfit to play further.'

One or two of the male team grinned knowingly whilst the ladies voiced weak protestations about their feebleness.

Percy held his hand up and carried on. 'Therefore, as this match is being played in the spirit of the original 25 years ago and with the same ladies' team,' he emphasised the last part firmly.

'After consultation with the county vice-president,' indicating in Jack's direction, 'I am invoking a little used rule from the original handbook that governed the 1982 match.'

Percy gathered a short breath as a hint of alarm bells circulated amongst one or two of the confident male opposition.

'Under Paragraph 2, sub-section 5, clause 14, of the umpire's handbook, in the event of a player or player(s) being deemed unfit or unable to play due to illness the Umpire, upon confirmation with a county representative may elect to declare....'

He paused again for breath as the men's team suddenly gathered on the edge of their seats now sensing the possibility of them being proclaimed winners by default, unable to contain their excitement nudging each other furiously and ready to shake hands on their success.

Percy continued.... 'May elect to declare,' he repeated louder, 'said team unfit to continue and...', at which point the men's sense of jubilation got the better of them and their schoolboy cheers drowned out the final words of their umpire.

He tried again, a little louder, 'AND...!'

The celebration continued unabated.

Jack reached behind the kitchen counter and picked up the megaphone kept for emergencies, switched it on, raised it to his lips and pointed it in the direction of the exuberant men.

'Q-U-I-E-T PLEASE!!'

Someone might as well have thrown a switch somewhere as the effect of Big Jim's interruption was as instantaneous as it was effective.

They all looked around in his direction with varying degrees of expression crossing their features as they 'toe'd the line'.

Percy thanked Jack with an inclination of his head and repeated his previous statement in an atmosphere that remained suspenseful but altogether quieter than previously.

'May elect to declare that team unfit to continue and be eligible to make suitable and appropriate substitutions not exceeding a maximum of 50% of their existing number.'

The silence from the men was deafening.

Percy turned to the nearby ladies and asked the question.

'Are any of you ladies feeling a touch fatigued or unwell, perhaps not wanting to continue in case you risk permanent impairment to your state of health?' he inquired of them, trying hard to keep a straight face.

'I feel very dizzy and disorientated.'

'Me too I really feel sick and not too steady on my feet.'

'I think I have lumbago.'

'My rheumatism is killing me!'

'I've come out in blotches, it might be the measles.'

The replies came thick and fast from the women and Percy couldn't help but laugh to himself; the 'unwell' members totalled exactly one half of their team, most of them the more senior, although Elizabeth Quinton stood to one side sturdily on both legs with her usual steely expression.

'Er, do you have any reserves on standby by any chance Elizabeth?' inquired the Reverend.

She smiled back in a knowing sort of way.

'Well actually yes we do just happen to have one or two willing volunteers,' and with that she turned towards the changing rooms and called out, 'Ladies may we have the pleasure of your company?'

The reserves emerged from the shadows onto the green and 'strutted their stuff', the men groaning at the sight of the new re-enforcements.

Sheila 'Legs' Ramsbottom led the entourage, leaving little to the imagination as to how she acquired her nickname, followed closely by a similarly attired Pauline Jenner, Molly Tattleford, and three others.

There was little doubt that they were a lot more youthful, certain to be antagonistic and to have the resourcefulness of a freshly trained Roman legion.

Bertie couldn't help but notice that Molly looked rather sexy.

Bernard was too busy estimating the length of Sheila's legs.

Percy was rather lost for words also; he plainly recognised the silhouette of the last lady to arrive as that of Sarah Jane Coddle and he blushed rather deeply.

Sarah Jane winked as she walked by the vicar, clearly giving a little flounce, which was enough to give Percy palpitations and he felt the need for a quickly muttered 'Hail Mary'.

Elizabeth Quinton gave the women a quick 'once-over' with a firm gaze and muttered her approval, 'Very smartly turned out ladies, yes you'll do very nicely indeed.'

'Well then,' she continued, turning towards the seated ensemble, 'looks like it's 'game on',' paused for a second and just for effect added, 'unless you men would like to concede?'

Bertie, as always the life and soul of a good party, felt it his duty at that point to give the men a lift and shouted across from the kitchen area from where he was just finishing the dishwashing.

'Come on guys that's a challenge if ever I heard one, are you men or mice?'

Eleven roars of approval and one squeak emerged from the male ranks as the majority stood their ground whilst eyeing Dennis disapprovingly.

'HEAR HEAR!'

'YES, GAME ON!'

'ONCE MORE UNTO THE BREACH OLD CHAPS!'

The men responded, putting down their biscuits and setting tea cups aside before stepping purposefully back to the green with lots of 'geeing up' and other appropriate comments to each other.

Unsurprisingly the ladies followed suit and there was a mad rush for the spectators' chairs as the non-participants raced for the best seats in the house.

Percy stood back and watched the spectacle unfold; feeling a deep sense of pride within as both teams competed; battling each other with dignity, skill and deference whilst at the same time sharing a light-hearted banter of verbal disrespect.

As with all battles it ebbed and flowed but as far as the men were concerned there was far too much 'ebbing' going on as the curse of the 'tea break' took its usual tenuous but tenacious hold on the game. It was an unwritten myth of all matches that any team that go into a tea break winning 'by a mile' will emerge at the other end on a long 'losing streak' and this was no exception.

The men contrived, cogitated, deliberated, ruminated and blustered all to no effect as the ladies clawed their way back into the game one shot at a time.

Inevitably, they arrived at the final end, neck and neck, with the scores tied at 45 shots a-piece, and two rinks each holding one shot attributable to their side at the final whistle.

One rink remained in action with only one wood left to play and, as luck and history would have it, Charles Chesterford once again stood centre stage with the fate of all men in his hands.

The room grew quiet, almost surreal within its silence as the hushed gathering watched and waited.

Charlie took in a deep breath.

He walked onto the mat and steadied himself.

The wood balanced in his right hand, he swept his arm back and, without thinking delivered it onto the green's surface, following through with a nervous swing of his extended limb.

He breathed a sigh of relief as the bowl began to run in a true line up the rink and he turned as if to step away, unable to watch, then paused, as an audible sharp intake of breath swept around the room.

He looked back.

'Oh no...'

Charlie groaned.

As he watched, the delivery began to angle away from its intended trajectory, running the opposite way across the green.

In 25 years Charlie had NEVER bowled a single wood 'against bias' and thus had always avoided the time honoured tradition of 'drinks all round'; a penalty reserved for anyone who had such a misfortune.

Twenty-three members took great delight as the shout went up across the rinks.

'Charlie's buying!'

'Mine's a whisky!'

'I'll have a large brandy!'

'Ha! Ha! Ha!' they laughed one and all, the ladies and the men, as one of the longest standing records in the club's history finally gave way; there was a much anticipated inauguration of Charlie's fabled wallet when it emerged in the bar later.

Some suspected that all of its contents in the notes section would still bear the head of Queen Victoria.

Most of the members were clearly distracted by the laughter and merriment at Charlie's expense, but Percy, a gentleman to the last, was resisting the temptation; he continued to watch the bowl traversing the green.

The vicar watched as it trundled across to the rink marker, catching the side of a badly bowled wood from the previous player.

He groaned inwardly as the re-directed wood careered back across the rink on a new line.

Nodding his head from side to side in an act of despair, he couldn't help but mutter 'Oh no' under his breath as the bowl somehow reached the right place and rattled into the ones already there.

The clattering of its arrival and subsequent disturbance took everyone else by surprise; as one, they looked up the green to see a number of bowls rolled this way and that, leaving just two fairly close to the cot.

A feeling of déjà vu struck Percy much like the icy touch of a cold shower and he already knew what was coming as the shout went up.

'UMPIRE!'

Big Jim stepped up to his side with the black briefcase holding the various measuring implements and whispered in Percy's ear, 'Come on old chap, I'm the county representative, so let's do this together and to hell with the outcome.'

With that, he marched off up the green, case in one hand and Percy's elbow in the other, the rest of the Reverend following at not too far a distance behind.

It was later said that you could have literally heard a pin drop in the hushed arena, and one or two swore they could hear the dripping of the leaky outside tap that the gardener used.

They all watched intently as the umpire and the vice-president stepped carefully around the two woods before Jack cautiously bent down and opened the black briefcase.

The metal catches sounded deafening to the audience as they sprang open and there was a sharp intake of breath as he removed wooden wedges to secure both bowls in their final positions.

Percy extracted the short string measure from the case and together they assessed the distance between each bowl and the central cot; it was close!

They compared each bowl and then went back a second time as the nail-biting atmosphere grew within the arena, the heat of the lighting intensified and the measure went back for a third final time!

Percy and Jack looked up at each other, confirming the result with a hushed whisper and an agreeing nod of their heads before standing up together, then turning to face their potential supporters and executioners.

They spoke together, as one, in unison.

'The winners of the Rt Hon. Ronald Regis Challenge Cup for this year are,' they paused for maximum effect and a shot of 'Dutch courage' then continued...

'THE LADIES!'

It was about an hour later as Percy and Jack finally had the opportunity to escape to a quiet corner, sit down together and mull over the day's events with a pot of tea to hand.

The celebrations continued for some considerable while and the men, having been somewhat gracious in defeat, joined in the victory drink that Charlie, for once, owned up to and paid for.

The game was played, then replayed countless times, every shot discussed with every variation becoming wilder and wilder as the alcohol flowed, dulling the players' memories rather quickly.

Together they sighed and sank back into the comfort of the luxurious and deeply padded armchairs. In the background, they heard the ladies' president giving the opposition a timely reminder of their forfeit which resulted in a large distant groan from the men.

'Well,' sighed Jack.

'Well indeed,' sighed Percy back.

'You know it's strange,' said Jack at length, 'I thought I knew most of the umpire's handbook but for the life of me I can not remember Paragraph 2, sub-section 5, clause 14.'

Percy considered the query at length before responding, 'That's no surprise really.'

'Why's that?' queried the dumbfounded Jack.

'Because I made it up!' said Percy with a smug grin to his face.

Jack stared at the vicar in astonishment then laughed loudly, closely followed by Percy.

'Ha Ha...'

'HA! HA! HA! HA! HA!'

CHAPTER THREE

NOVEMBER

TERROR IN THE TOILET

The events of the previous month had finally settled in the dust, after such an intense and exciting cumulation of THE big club fixture of the season so far.

Players had lived and relived every shot, every moment as it had occurred and virtually every second, minute by minute, repeatedly until those times had became engrained in the club's folklore.

Even now, there were instances still whispered of in circles around the clubhouse fireplace and bar in the evenings or during games whilst players waited their turn to bowl.

Amongst the whispers, the most discussed was the vicar's use of a little known rule to restore the ebbing of a promising game, thus preventing a humiliating drubbing of the respected but rather senior ladies' team.

The rumours were rife with gossip and admiration for the Reverend's impromptu umpiring and his handling of the match.

There was a hint of suspicion that possibly the rule maybe did not even actually exist; the vicar's reputation for fairness and ability to adapt to any situation was becoming ever more legendary on a daily basis.

More and more his congregation were taking the quietly spoken, inimitable and idiosyncratic yet sometimes radical Reverend to their hearts. They now held him in such high esteem that it would take a foolish man indeed to utter a single word against him in public.

It was a loyalty and affection that Percy would be very grateful for in the months ahead with their indecisions and difficulties he had yet to encompass.

One or two of his closest friends had noted subtle changes in Percy's mannerisms and were getting slightly concerned that his commitment to his beloved parish was becoming too much and they vowed silently to keep a watchful eye on his undertakings.

There had, been many frantic searches, up to now in vain, for a copy of the 1982 umpire's handbook which had long since been out of print. These searches proved fruitless, probably because Percy had acquired every copy in the county, thanks to Jack Tuttle's assistance and he now owned 17 copies of the little gem which were stashed away in his vestry closet.

Finally, the club gossip had moved on to more mundane matters such as stock lists, match dates and the price of spirits so Percy could breathe again with people's attention switching away from his personal indiscretions.

****

The weather was definitely un-seasonal, that much was for sure, decided Percy as he gazed out of the rectory window.

November had arrived in all its fabled glory; he was enjoying a quiet cup of tea in the late afternoon, taking advantage of the unexpected warmth of the sunshine.

The gentle sun reflected weakly through the window as the wonderful glow from the open log fire crackled and spat colourful embers up the vicarage chimney; it was a combination altogether too relaxing.

He had taken the opportunity to summon the various members of the indoor bowls' committee to one of Mrs Spindleforth's famous cream teas.

The vicarage study was already full of the smell of fresh baking; whilst the nearby table was laden with a sumptuous spread of homemade biscuits, warm scones and a large fruit cake.

There were pots of delicious jams in four different flavours including strawberry and raspberry alongside which sat a large tub of rich clotted cream.

The coffee pot was brewing contently in the corner whilst nearby a large tea urn gurgled away merrily just off the boil.

The vicarage's best china stood neatly piled with paper serviettes, linen napkins and cake doilies each colour co-ordinated to their appropriate section.

Phillippa Spindleforth was famous for her cooking and her luxurious spreads often left the diner requiring a week or more to recover before they could possibly face, or relish, the thought of eating anything again.

She had been asked if she would kindly prepare one of her delicious cream teas and was never one to leave things to chance.

Just to be on the safe side she had also prepared several large platters of pastries, which were now heaving under the strain of supporting such delightful mouth-watering delicacies.

There were sausage rolls in golden puff pastry, miniature pork pies with cranberry topping, fresh crumbed scotch eggs, cocktail sausages, cheese and pineapple on sticks and a whole host of other delicious 'nibbles'.

Freshly cut, thick slices of local cured bread-crumbed ham adorned a stacked platter along with cold roast beef and prawn vols-au-vents.

There was even an impressively laid out cheese board sporting more than a dozen assorted cheeses and at least six different types of cracker on which to spread the golden slices.

Curls of freshly churned butter stood in a distinctive silver salver nearby whilst there was even a small dish of colourful olives to wet the appetite.

Clearly, Phillippa had surpassed herself this time and Percy made a mental note to pass the collection bowl around those attending the sumptuous spread.

It was a princely sight and a feast worthy of a royal visit; although the guests scheduled to arrive were not of royal bloodline, they were nevertheless just as significant in Percy's eyes.

Rollo laid in a sprawling manner in his favourite place, near the log fire, stretched out on the now somewhat worn, plucked and hair-covered thick lined cloak that he had purloined from Percy some while back.

He was purring contentedly, his fur pristine for once, and glowing with the heat from the burning logs, which was the one thing guaranteed to keep him from misbehaving with the nearby delicious comestibles.

Nevertheless, he was keeping one eye open in pretence of watching for runaway burning embers, which might endanger his delicate countenance, whilst he surveyed the piled plates with their delicious and imaginative contents.

He was clearly dreaming of those ham slices falling right off the plate and into his furry lap!

Being a fairly wise if somewhat mischievous cat, he knew that this was one day he would not need to get into Percy's bad books.

A loud purr, a loving rub of his back against a nearby leg and a daft look in his eyes was guaranteed to bring a corresponding array of titbits heading his way.

All in all, he was a very happy, contented and untroubled pussy cat, although he was somewhat bemused by his constantly recurring dreams of a mangy Persian moggie bouncing four-legged through the primulas.

Percy stretched out in his armchair, enjoying the brief relaxing interlude as he studied his scribbled notes from the night before.

The beginning of November also marked the planning of a number of events requiring not only his attention but those of the club management committee and their arrival was pending.

One thing was for sure, with the reputation of the vicarage spreads preceding them, there was never an empty seat or a meeting missed by any of the committee and he was sure that it would be easy to sell seat space on the black market, or even e-bay, at a lucrative price should a member be unable to attend.

First on the list of matters to discuss was the press coverage to arrange for the official presentation of the lottery cheque for the new bowling clubhouse.

Already promised in principle to allow the work to start, the long awaited cheque for £250,000 had arrived and the club was keen to gain as much exposure as possible for the handover of the cheque to the club president.

The timing was, as always, absolutely perfect for the parish, more by luck than judgement, and they were sure to find a profitable response from the happy club members when Percy passed the plate around the following weekend to ask for help with the church roof restoration fund.

The village seemed such a peaceful, sublime and contented parish that Percy almost dared to think 'what could possibly go wrong?' but then, past experience had taught him to err on the cautious side.

There was of course the preparation of the seasonal festivities and the Yuletide party for the congregation to be decided upon, as well as organised. In fact, with the midnight mass, which was always a festive extravaganza at the church, Christmas never failed to be a very busy time for the vicar.

Percy had a 'bee in his bonnet' this year; an idea had been literally buzzing around his head for weeks and he was eager to share it with the committee.

He was sure it would meet with their approval and would make this year's gathering for the Yuletide blessing one of the best ever.

The postman had produced another surprise as well.

Unexpectedly, a recorded delivery package had arrived, marked for Percy's personal attention, and the accompanying letter had specifically requested that he undo it in the presence of the club's representatives.

Having decided after a good shake that it wasn't apparently dangerous or moving, it didn't tick or have a peculiar smell intrinsic of something with a best before date, he had done as requested in the mysterious mail and set it aside for today's gathering.

Percy's paused his train of thought for a few seconds to sup on the sweet pleasure of a cup of Earl Grey; one of his more enjoyable vices, before engaging his thought processes once again.

With Halloween looming as well as bonfire night, it was a time of year that the local children often got up to a fair degree of harmless tomfoolery and mischievousness as well as one or too 'spur of the moment' pranks.

Percy would have to remind the members to be more vigilant this year after last year's debacle when the vicarage cleaner was locked out on the church roof in her nightwear after trying to rescue Rollo who had been apparently stuck halfway up the spire.

It later transpired that it was actually a large cuddly toy cat with a cassette player on continuous playback. The fake feline had been lowered down on a fishing line from the clock tower until it sat on one of the lower turrets.

Percy made a mental note to get Mrs Jones to sellotape all of the vicarage letterboxes shut for the week to avoid the usual deposit of eggs, flour and bangers.

It was Charlie's fault really; after last year he had found out who the culprits were and placed eggs under the pew cushions where they normally sat for the Sunday service.

The youngsters had wriggled uncomfortably through the whole of the ceremony, unwilling to give the game away or lose face and Percy had taken great delight in taking his time reading the sermon.

A knowing wink from Charlie to Timothy and Abbey Doolittle, the known ringleaders, let them know they had been outwitted on that occasion and so it had progressed.

It was now more of a competition of 'one-up-man-ship' between the local children and the club to see who could misbehave the most on Halloween night, but Percy couldn't see any harm in light-hearted foolishness if it kept them out of more suspicious practices.

Percy chuckled to himself as he remembered the shenanigans the following day when Charlie had spent nearly an hour trying to start his car without success, only to find that the children had returned the compliment and stuffed a dozen fresh eggs up his exhaust pipe.

A distant ringing of an old fashioned bell rope door bell clanging merrily brought Percy's train of thought back to the immediate present; his guests had arrived.

He heard the housekeeper answering the metallic summons and a variety of voices offering warm greetings as he made a mental calculation, number wise, of all those he had invited.

Before he had time to reach a definitive conclusion, the study door opened and a large crowd of beaming faces burst in on him.

'Hello Percy.'

'Afternoon vicar.'

'Good to see you Reverend.'

'Hi Percy how's things, and where's the plates?'

He smiled broadly to himself as he rose to greet his guests and good friends knowing that the last comment could have only come from Jack Tuttle who was never one to restrain his modesty when it came to matters of gourmet appreciation.

The members of the committee arrived en masse all full of exuberance from the pleasure of the company, not to mention the roaring log fire and the fabulous spread that was unveiled before them as they stepped through the doorway.

In fact, thought Percy, several of them were positively drooling in anticipation.

Jack Tuttle, unsurprisingly given his wide girth, was first through the door, followed closely by Clifford the captain, then Derek, Patrick, and Dennis with Charlie, who were together as usual.

Bernard, Douglas, and the club treasurer Reginald Trimley were next to arrive, with Bertie, Tony and Eric just behind them. The robust and charming retired honorary club president Squiffy was last, but certainly not least.

Percy nodded with satisfaction, a full quorum was in attendance, unsurprisingly, and he was thankful that the vicarage study was as spacious as it was comfortable.

At the back of his mind he noted that the quorum actually totalled 13 and he briefly reflected on the religious and superstitious significance of that fact before dismissing it as nonsense.

As always Percy greeted his guests with a warm genuine smile as well as a firm shake of every hand presented before pointing them in the direction of the tea and coffee.

Big Jim made a slight detour past the alcohol to add a tot of the vicar's best brandy to his coffee as per usual.

The rest of the committee made a beeline for the table, which was groaning with the weight of the fabulous spread; they were already drooling with the anticipation of tasting every one of the delicacies on offer.

It only took five minutes for each person of the 13 strong gathering to settle themselves into comfortable chairs with a hot tipple and a plateful of titbits piled high.

Jack's plate now resembled a gastronomic version of the Eiffel tower as it had so much food balanced on top.

Percy was convinced it would only require a cocktail cherry to topple the whole lot into Jack's lap and a nearby salivating Rollo obviously had the same thought.

As an 'ideas' meeting it fell short of being a real brainstorming session, mainly due to the liberal intake of libation and a heady mix of fine cuisine. The use of intelligent reasoning compared to no more than a slight stir of dust in a cavernous catacomb.

Nevertheless, it was a significant step in the right direction; the last time round most of the members had fallen asleep in front of the log fire after only 15 minutes.

At times it looked as if Big Jim might need rescuing with a couple of matchsticks to use as eyelid splints whilst Derek would probably need a pole-vaulting shaft to keep his eyes open!

With a copious quantity of sweet talking, coaxing, cajoling and leading from the front, Percy managed eventually to unveil the proposals for Halloween as well as to lay the foundation for both the Christmas party and the nativity.

Percy had sprung his idea of providing a grandiose Yuletide party for the local children in need; He fancied the idea of throwing a special, traditional, old-fashioned tea party with 'live' cabaret and a 'Punch and Judy' style entertainment.

Several members passed significant glances at each other, which clearly suggested that their vicar, as much as they loved him, was slightly out of touch with the modern world and the wily ways of children.

Patrick looked somewhat alarmed at the potential proximity of a large number of minors AND wobbly jellies to his beloved green.

A mischievous look passed between Dennis, Charlie and Bernard as they anticipated an occasion to do what they did best, misbehave abysmally and have the opportunity to get away with it.

Big Jim caught the glint in their eyes and made a mental note to keep an eye on his associates.

Tony 'Trigger' Havershall, as always a tad slow on the uptake, was still trying to imagine the vicar hosting a party, which potentially involved a gathering of the local children, a large white rabbit, wooden crocodiles and plenty of pink trifles.

He was having a lot of trouble making the seasonal connection between the Punch and Judy show and Christmas in particular; he kept envisaging his Christmas tree decorated with fairy cakes, iced buns, glove puppets and miniature mannequins.

Percy glanced at Tony's eyes and sighed deeply; he'd had doubts previously about giving him the opportunity to mix alcohol with caffeine.

He allowed the members to ramble on about further ideas for the forthcoming festivities for a while before deciding that once they began to seriously consider the possibility of the nativity scene being set in an alien spaceship with Elvis as the angel that they had really had enough to drink; it was time to move on.

Percy called the meeting to order.

'My friends, thank you for coming tonight, I hope you have all enjoyed yourselves.'

A nod of the head from all affirmed they were indeed enjoying themselves and continuing to do so.

'I think we have managed to come up with some good ideas for the forthcoming festivities.'

There were a number of generous nods interspersed with some knowing looks, whilst other facial expressions indicated the likelihood of alternative plans.

Percy continued.

'However there are two key issues I wish to discuss with you all tonight, one is the presentation of a very substantial cheque from the lottery.'

A rousing cheer resounded around the room with a generous accompaniment of 'Hear hear', 'Good show' and 'Show me the money.'

'However we have a surprise package received a short while ago that I was asked to present to you all at this meeting,' and with that Percy brought forth the recently arrived postal delivery.

The members of the committee looked on in a mystified manner; Jim was more bewildered than the rest; he was having trouble looking around the large chocolate éclair he was consuming at that time.

Tony had progressed to the possibilities or handicaps involved with trying to balance a trifle on top of a Christmas tree and at that stage clearly lost the plot.

Meanwhile, the other 11 members stared at the mysterious package uncomprehendingly.

'Well go on Percy spill the beans,' prompted Dennis.

'Yes come on Reverend, what's it all about?' queried Charlie. 'It's not something rude is it?' questioned Bernard with a touch of reservation, concerned that there were still some photographs of the men's capitulation from last month in print.

'To be quite honest I have absolutely no idea at all' said Percy, passing the package around the room with its introductory letter.

'It's been posted overseas somewhere,' commented Clifford, noticing the unusual stamp adorning the front of the envelope.

The package arrived back in the vicar's lap and he hesitated for a second then, as if in mutual agreement, carefully tore the brown paper envelope open as the committee with intense concentration, leant forward on the edge of their chairs.

A bold array of colourful brochures emerged into their visual range, albeit somewhat blurred to some members; Trigger thought they looked more like a rainbow and took another swig of caffeine.

There appeared to be a number of tickets that looked like boarding passes, a quantity of property leaflets of some description, vouchers, maps and apparently, a letter of introduction.

Percy picked up the correspondence and perched his new reading glasses on the bridge of his nose.

'It's from a company called F.H. Holiday Tours, and appears to be an introduction to their firm describing the package breaks they organise for bowling clubs.' concluded Percy.

Patrick had leant over and picked up one of the vouchers from where it had fallen on the floor; he gazed intently at the large print:

FREE INTRODUCTORY FLIGHT

He blinked and read it again, but it still said the same.

'These are free flight tickets from Northwich airport,' said Patrick staring at them incredulously, 'and there are 24 of them,' he concluded, doing a quick count of the others in the pile.

Percy stared at Patrick, then looked back at the letter he held, 'It says here that F.H. holiday tours are a new enterprise and we have been selected for an inaugural introductory offer!'

'What's the catch then?' piped up Dennis.

'Yes come on Reverend there's always a punch line or hidden costs with these, they arrive through my door all the time,' said Bernard.

'Sounds too good to be true,' moaned Charlie.

Percy scanned the letter again at a furious pace, from top to bottom, but it still stated the obvious.

'There must be small print,' stated Jack, 'there's ALWAYS small print and that's where the catch will be.' With that, he reached across and took the letter courteously from the Reverend's hand.

He read it through carefully with furrowed eyebrows, finding nothing.

'It must be on the back of the tickets?' he queried of Patrick.

The green keeper nodded in agreement; with a knowing glance and an expectant manner he turned over the ticket he was holding.

The back of the travel document was blank, except to say that these vouchers were exchangeable anytime between May and October of the following year.

It wasn't often that Big Jim was lost for words but he was very close to it now.

'It clearly says that we have received FREE flights and accommodation for 24 club members to travel to Tiddlemarsh.' he stated.

'Where the hell is Tiddlemarsh?' questioned Bernard in a doubting and rather condescending manner, then offered his apology to Percy for the blasphemy.

The vicar hadn't noticed the verbal indiscretion though; he was busy burrowing through the holiday brochures.

'Found it!' shouted Percy in an excited tone of voice with a rare outburst of elation; he was not usually known for his impromptu displays of emotion but seemed more prone to verbal exhibitions recently.

He held up the brochure by the stapled centre and turned it around to show the others the impressive colour photographs of the holiday resort.

The pictures looked fantastic, with vivid panoramic shots, close-ups of luxurious hotel rooms and a fine overhead centrepiece of a pristine bowling green.

'Wow,' commented Bertie in an uncharacteristic and understated manner.

'Quite remarkable,' stuttered Clifford.

'Incredible,' enthused Charlie, whose attention seemed more focused on the photos of bathing bikini-clad beauties sitting by the side of the swimming pool.

Jack fixed his eyes firmly on the title text and confirmed the resort's identity, 'It's a place called El Torro Tiddlemarsh!'

That's a funny name for a village in Britain, what county is it in?' queried a confused Dennis.

'Not county, country,' corrected Jack, 'it's overseas in southern Spain!'

Jack's revelation silenced the others for a second and then there was a mad scramble for the brochures amid a banging of heads and shouts of 'ME FIRST!'

For once, there was a deafening silence from the collective gathering apart from the frantic flicking of pages as they all searched for the centre page spread on 'El Torro Tiddlemarsh.'

Percy sat back and allowed them all time to reflect on the offer whilst he enjoyed a few seconds respite with his cup of tea.

'It's a bonus reward because of all they publicity we created for the game during last summer!'

'It's ALL expenses paid!'

'A bowling extravaganza...'

'There's top class sports competitions and evening entertainment with special guests.'

'Tony Christie's appearing...'

'And Victor Sylvester Jnr. with his Big Band sound...'

'A luxury celebratory banquet on our arrival as well...'

The comments came thick and fast, circulating around the room, creating a spiral of rising excitement that soon became reminiscent of a group of schoolchildren.

Percy smiled to himself; quietly picking up his cup of tea, he 'retired' from the room in a fitting manner for a Reverend, too softly to be heard.

He smiled again as he shut the door gently, leaving the 'children' to their 'presents'; it seemed that perhaps Christmas had come early this year.

****

It was a few days later, early in the morning, that Percy was wandering down to the clubhouse from the rectory.

The weather had suddenly taken a severe turn for the worse and there had been the sharpest of frosts overnight, one that Charlie might imply, would do substantial injury to a brass monkey.

For once, the vicar had eaten a full English breakfast so he was full of good spirit and walked with a distinctive bounce in his step.

Percy was still remembering the delicious combination of smoked maple-cured bacon, free-range eggs, prime organic pork sausages from the local butcher, and mouth-watering mushrooms in garlic butter that he had recently consumed.

Having washed all of that down with freshly squeezed orange juice and followed it with some thick slices of malted toast he was in a manner of speaking 'fit to burst'.

He really had worked up a hearty appetite of late and he gently patted his stomach to make sure that he wasn't putting on too much weight, given the delicious cakes and jam the local ladies kept delivering to the rectory.

Perhaps he was feeling slightly rotund around the midriff, but he discounted that small fact as one that was connected directly to his recent consumption of fine food.

Wrapping up warmly in his new velvet lined winter cloak, which thankfully Rollo had not yet found, he had stepped out into the bracing cold with the thickest hat and gloves he could find as well.

Even so, the cold permeated the substantial layers; Percy gave a little shiver as his skin reacted to the cold temperature and he noted the fog of air particles in front of his face as he breathed out.

The weather forecast had reported that the temperatures overnight had hit -14 degrees Centigrade and Percy wanted to check there were no problems with the vicarage plumbing or the work at the new clubhouse.

He held two large flasks of hot coffee, topped up with a generous tot of brandy in each, with which to warm up the workers whom he was sure would be very cold and most appreciative of his kind offering.

Percy arrived at the building works and club green.

The hoar frost covered every blade of grass, leaf and branch in a fine white coating of winter's cold touch.

The residual water in the workmen's cement barrows and buckets was frozen solid; Percy mused that it would take the men a fair while to remove the shovels protruding from them. To any passing onlooker they appeared much like giant industrial ice-lollies.

Percy paused outside the worksite for a quick overview, it was after all far too cold and he didn't want to linger too long, but he was thankful for the glowing warmth of the flasks he carried.

Judging from appearances the building work was indeed progressing at a rate of knots, brickwork was rising from the foundations as far as the apertures for the new windows and sturdy corner pieces supported the framework of the roof rafters.

He was very impressed; despite the disorderly way in which the builders interacted there was no doubt that Murphy & McPherson ran a tight ship based on experience, knowledge and mutual trust when it came to producing the goods.

Percy made a mental note to thank them later in his next Sunday sermon.

He walked up to the skeletal door frame, checking first that the crisp frost underfoot didn't disguise the hidden danger of wet cement under the plastic covering, and stepped through.

There was no need for him to be concerned; the cement had been set for several weeks now and there was, here and there, evidence of a misplaced foot leaving its imprint embedded in the surface.

Unsurprisingly there was a trail of paw prints running from the doorframe across the room towards the far window space, clear evidence, if ever any were needed, of a cat's visit.

The paw marks were quite deep, so Percy concurred that the four-legged feline visitor must have arrived shortly after the cement had been poured.

His suspicions were soon confirmed, as he ventured towards the other side of the room, following the tracks of the aforementioned guilty moggie.

The reason for the cat's manic pursuit in the setting cement was soon uncovered, which was more than could be said for the poor mouse, thought Percy.

Sticking out from the surface of the new flooring were four tiny feet and the tip of a tail emerging like a modern horror sculpture.

It reminded him somewhat of someone suspended in carbon stasis in a cryonic capsule.

All things considered, it was a particularly gruesome way to go, but knowing mouser's as he did the moggie at fault had probably polished off the tiny rodent earlier and left its body to sink swamp-like into the morass.

Thinking back, he could not remember Rollo having ever returned to the vicarage in such a 'sorry state' with his fur matted with concrete sludge, therefore, for once, the culprit must have been from the village.

In a moment of light-hearted humour Percy considered that perhaps he should report the incident to the local Cat Investigation Department at the police station.

The thought passed in an instant leaving a smile in its place and, noting the sound of bantered laughter from the worker's hut, he stepped back out of the building towards the noise with his flasks at the ready.

****

Jack Tuttle, Derek, Patrick, Bernard, Charlie and Dennis were all sitting in a huddled fashion around the warm fire in the comfort of the indoor clubhouse lounge.

They were taking the opportunity to discuss the blueprints of the new development and, given that bowling had been cancelled for the morning session due to the freezing temperature, had opted for 'Plan B'.

This often-preferred option seemed to involve a large supply of hot coffee supplemented by platefuls of rich tea biscuits, chocolate digestives and custard creams.

With the knowledge that Jack always had his hip flask topped up 'just in case', it was a foregone conclusion, that the coffee would be VERY warming and the conversation very lucid in its fluidity.

The subject of the day and very much of the moment other than the surprise package holiday, was of course the brand new clubhouse facility.

At this particular minute they were all poring over a full set of the scaled blueprints and the comments, like the coffee, were free flowing and appreciative.

The clubhouse included a plush seating area, which allowed up to 100 people to dine in comfort within the brand new function suite. Jack's eye had been caught by this as it featured a luxurious bistro and bar area where the ladies could enjoy a glass of wine whilst the gentlemen could indulge in the finest spirits.

He was almost beside himself in anticipation as it purported to stock more than seven different types of vintage brandy all of which he was very keen to savour.

They all had to agree it really was a wonderful development ahead of its time, a real showcase for the club and the county.

The talk of wine and brandy combined with the copious quantities of coffee quaffed were by then having an obvious reaction on Big Jim; his large girth soon indicated to him that he should pay attention to his most urgent needs.

He jolted back to the reality of the present with the comprehension that nature was calling and a trip to the 'little boy's room' was urgently required.

'Er excuse me guys, nature calls, I need to take a break,' offered Jack to his nearby friends by way of a gentleman's 'by your leave.'

'Um that could be a problem,' said Patrick.

'Why's that?' queried the now desperate president.

'The indoor toilets are out of action whilst the builders plumb in the new water pipes for the new clubhouse,' continued Patrick.

'Oh dear that is definitely inconvenient,' said Jack, now beginning to feel a more urgent call to nature than previously.

Charlie offered an impromptu solution, 'Well there's always the outside block.'

The others looked up sharply with a simultaneous intake of breath, and looks of apprehensive fear and consternation crossing their faces at Charlie's remark.

The outside toilet block was a temporary erection, a prefab, built pre-war, although no one was sure which particular war.

The purpose of its construction had been purely as a means to an end, a functional, serviceable, if somewhat impractical, public convenience that shielded the user from nature's elements but did little else.

Its rudimentary, almost primeval structure bore resemblance to a seaside council toilet block that hadn't been updated for at least 50 years.

Jack shuddered with a feeling of dread and apprehension.

The primitive construction was fabricated from breezeblocks which were whitewashed to protect its porous exterior, whilst the lack of heating inside meant that its interior maintained an almost sub-zero temperature even in the middle of summer.

It was kept open normally during the outdoor season should any of the elderly members be 'caught short' whilst participating in a competition or match.

The middle of November was another matter entirely; any person giving consideration to its use had to be insane, fearless or desperate and preferably a combination of all three.

Jack Tuttle was VERY desperate.

Previous enterprising explorers, usually the younger set, had emerged pale-faced from its confines immediately after a brief visitation reciting spine chilling and comparative tales of Canadian winters where water freezes instantaneously in mid air.

Anyone mad enough to still venture inward would require a superhuman effort to escape its cold clutches and indeed be very fearful of frostbite on their extremities.

One innovative youngster, whose name could not be mentioned for fear of recrimination, had apparently created an ice sculpture in 23 seconds flat.

The cubicles were very cramped and constructed of painted steel sheets; there had obviously been a malicious streak within the builder as he had crammed five cubicles into a space designed to take just three.

It was rumoured that Bernard's uncle had been the man guilty of the wayward plumbing, and to whom the finger pointed at, when someone innocently asked the question 'Wasn't the toilet meant to be a unisex facility?'

Consequently, the urinals had to be scrapped, and the cubicles became the only source of relief for the members' constrained bladders.

As the facilities required sharing between the sexes a measure of discretion was required, therefore it was always advisable to make sure the sign on the entrance was the right way round to show whether the inhabitants were male or female.

The women had little choice other than to accept the option in days past, although some men, in times of desperation, had resorted to using the large holly bush around the back of the toilet block.

The now dying shrubbery to the rear of the clubhouse also reflected that it had come in for its fair share of abuse. More than one member however had stood too close in their desire for a discreet 'quickie' much to their painful regret.

The formerly proud, majestic holly now bore much witness to its frowned on mistreatment from members still using it when 'caught short'; it was missing most of its leaves from one side and was really not so much an evergreen but an 'everbrown'.

Nowadays an agonised yelp from the rear of the clubhouse often gave the game away to anyone's impromptu exploitation as the holly's sharp spikes made contact with vital sensitive parts.

The inside walls of the ancient block remained permanently damp in winter despite the cleaner's valiant continued best efforts.

Consequently, the water-based emulsion soon leached to create interesting 'post impressionist' murals on the bare concrete floor.

An unusual array of rare, perhaps even undiscovered, fungi and lichens grew in a vertical direction up the face of every interior wall.

The flora rose in a riotous explosion of colour until it encountered the bleach 'tidal mark' from Molly's determined volunteer hit squad of cleaners.

Unfortunately, it appeared that some of the bacteria were now developing a DNA based technology making them chemically resistant; even Domestos was having a tough time.

It was a fairly safe bet that new strains of mould would be discovered by a visiting microbiologist in the not too distant future and an important antibiotic even greater than penicillin would be cultured.

Big Jim shuddered as the myriad of memories flash flooded through his mind and he reached for the hip flask, in need of a final shot of Dutch courage.

Finally, he stood up, unable to resist the urgent needs of his body any longer and, turning to his fellow members, he cracked a feeble historical joke.

'Well chaps, I'm going out,' he paused and looked them directly in the eyes, 'I might be gone some while.'

In an animated gesture of almost comic status, they each sombrely shook his hand and wished him well, whilst Derek muttered a prayer of condolence under his breath and Bernard slipped a half bottle of cognac into his side pocket, as always, just in case.

Each of the members present offered their winter coats to Jack as further insulation and finally, unable to put off the inevitable any longer, he made his excuses and 'legged it' as fast as he could given the excessive bulk he carried with him.

Big Jim suited his nickname more than ever now as he struggled along the outside footpath to the rear of the club, the five coats he wore adding further volume to his girth. Despite that, he arrived at the toilet block in almost record time.

It looked grey and cold like a mausoleum as he approached and he almost expected a ghostly ghoul-like voice to welcome him from its depths.

He remembered to turn around the outside sign to indicate that the toilet block was under occupation with men present inside, just on the off chance that another desperate member, of the other sex, was also cut short and headed in his direction.

Inside the external windows were wide open, perhaps as a vain attempt on the cleaner's behalf, to dry out the damp interior. It was unfortunate that this had allowed the sharp frost to permeate the entire dour decor, now festooning every pipe with icicles whilst coating every crevice and surface with white crystals.

As Jack stepped through the entrance a sudden strong gust of wind responded to the additional opening and gusted through the building; the door slammed shut behind him with a deafening bang!

The loud noise made him jump but he trudged forward cautiously, as quickly as he dare on the slippery floor, his feet leaving footprints in the permafrost behind him.

Had he been standing outside when the door slammed shut he might have noticed a tiny brass fitting fall to the ground in a very inconspicuous manner.

As screws went it was a fairly small and average fastening, however quite significantly, it was the last screw keeping the inside handle and shaft connected to the external retaining doorknob.

Jack opted for the middle cubicle, his logic being that it just may be fractionally warmer than the rest of the ice-cold expanse.

It was painfully obvious to him that, with all his extra protection, he was never going to be able to enter the cubicle and close the door or be able to turn around. Therefore, he took the only option available to him, loosened his trousers in readiness and reversed his bulk backwards into the booth.

He proceeded as quickly as he dared; he was already shivering and goose bumps were appearing on his thighs; it really was a tight squeeze!

He grunted as his right hip came into contact with the Victorian toilet roll holder, damaging his delicate skin, but he noted that at least there was a toilet roll in the holder and it did appear to be soft tissue instead of the bulk standard greaseproof paper.

Big Jim smiled inwardly; this 'software upgrade' as the vicar humorously called it had been the club's one commitment to modernisation and had been the Reverend Percival Peabody's first undertaking on his appointment to the parish; one thing he insisted on was that the congregation had quality creature comforts.

Jack could wait no longer, time was running out with nature desperate to take its course. He gingerly unbuckled his belt, dropped his trousers and under garments, held his breath tightly, then took the plunge, sitting down sharply.

Had he been able to enter the cubicle in the correct manner he would have had time to notice the glistening of thousands of tiny crystallised ice particles and been amply warned of the presence of frost on the toilet seat.

Sadly, he had not.

It was impossible to separate the events of the next second or two, as they all happened in virtually simultaneous sequence.

Due to the intense cold and the numbness of his extremities, Jack had the opportunity to utter a brief sigh of relief and let nature take over before his senses finally completed the connection between his brain and his bottom.

The rasping sear of his posterior making a perfect seal on the toilet seat was akin to the sensation of touching the inside of a freezer ice box with his tongue.

Whilst Jim had never considered doing anything as foolish with his tongue, he nevertheless often got his fingers stuck to his frozen food packs whilst rummaging through the freezer drawers.

The sensation itself was not altogether unpleasant, but one was immediately conscious of the intense cold and the awareness of becoming firmly fastened to the offending article as if stuck with superglue.

There are not too many ways of detaching oneself safely from the ice without losing a layer of skin, unless you happen to have a supply of warm running water handy.

Jack's chances of finding anything remotely warm in the cold confines of the cubicle were as unlikely as him being rescued by the winner of Miss World.

All this flashed through his mind in the same instant that the warning of the extreme cold impacting on his bare flesh also arrived and by the time he felt its icy touch it was too late.

Naturally, he did what any man would do.

He screamed...very very loudly!

Back in the warm surrounds of the lounge the other members were luxuriating in front of the fire and contemplating the large clock on the wall as they kept a watchful eye on the time taken by their absent friend.

Even at that distance, given the sheer quantity of brick, timber, insulation and tile that separated them from the far away toilet block they still heard the blood curdling scream.

Actually, it sounded more like an anguished Godzilla who had just had his dinner stolen, than anything remotely human.

'Oh dear,' said Patrick.

'That doesn't sound too good,' said Bernard.

'I guess the seat was a bit on the cold side,' commented Charlie with a wry smile.

'It sounded a lot more like he might be in trouble,' surmised Derek, staring hard at Charlie with his one good eye.

Dennis interposed with his own response, 'Perhaps one of us should go and investigate just in case?'

'I'll go,' said Derek, rising immediately to his feet, 'er, has anyone got a spare coat?'

****

Jack was in a spot of bother...

He felt the need for speed, but with nature taking its course slowly due to the cold he couldn't yet move even if he was indeed able to and events were unfolding in not too pleasant a way for him.

His frostbitten bottom was firmly attached to the icy toilet seat like a suction cap on a glass panel and he was fixed more securely than a cork in a wine bottle.

The sub-zero temperature was at least numbing the damaged area and he was glad at least that his other more sensitive 'dangly bits' were for the time being well away from the perimeter of the seat's circumference.

With the needs of his bodily functions fully satisfied, he was, at long last, able to consider his options and act on them. He tried to raise himself gingerly in an upwards direction, but it was no good he was stuck fast, the move only producing a loud grunt of pain following his exertion.

There was no getting away from the fact that the winter weather had welded him to the toilet and he was in a complete jam!

He was grateful for the additional insulation of the borrowed jackets, but he couldn't spend the rest of the day in these freezing temperatures and there had to be some way of escaping.

Jack pondered, racked his brain, and then suddenly the idea struck home, if he couldn't detach his posterior from the toilet, well he would just have to take the offending article with him!

He reached behind him feeling underneath the bowl as he tried to locate the retainer nuts that fastened the bolts of the seat in place.

His fingertips were beginning to ice over and he fumbled feverishly in his bid to locate them.

'AHA!' he smiled quietly to himself, 'found the little blighters.'

It felt like, for once. he had a bit of luck, the toilet block seats were cheap and cheerful so they only had plastic nuts fastening them down; they were easy to grip and Jack soon had them spinning down the bolt shaft on both sides.

Thud! Thud!

The retainers dropped to the floor and Jack cried out with a self-satisfied cry of happiness.

'YES!'

With an over-enthusiastic gesture of delight Jack lifted his bottom upwards from the pedestal, the bolts sliding out of the holes in the porcelain base with ease.

He breathed a deep sigh of relief and now full of confidence stood up quickly; regrettably he had forgotten about the problem with the toilet roll holder but his memory was soon jogged as the toilet seat jammed hard between the steel wall plate and the offending holder.

The impact definitely did his delicate attributes little favour and his rekindled injury generated another deep-throated cry of pain as his body mass wedged tightly once again.

'Are you OK Jack?'

Hearing a voice suddenly calling out inquisitively from the other side of the outer door, Big Jim cut off his plaintive cry in mid yelp.

'Is that you Derek?'

The door burst open and the vice captain stepped cautiously into the opening, his one eye looking around rather wildly, not sure what to expect.

'Oh thank God, Derek I'm over here, stuck in the middle cubicle; whatever you do, don't let...'

For the second time that day the wind gusted through the toilet block and slammed the door back hard into the woodwork.

'...go of the door.' finished Jack lamely.

'Oh,' said Derek comprehending slightly too late.

Realizing his mistake, he felt the need to rectify his blunder and for once acted immediately to correct the error of his ways.

'Don't worry old chap I'll get you out,' and with that he clasped the brass fixing firmly in his hand, giving it a sharp tug.

On normal occasions, that action would have been quite sufficient to open the way and provide an escape route for the two of them; sadly this was not a normal occasion.

The inconsequential screw that hardly mattered earlier became suddenly very significant in its absence; as Derek pulled, the whole brass handle fitting came away from the door trailing the shaft behind it.

'Oh dear!' exclaimed Derek with a look of surprise at the brass fixture he held in his hand.

'What do you mean, Oh dear?' said Jack from within the confines of his steel prison cell.

'I'm afraid the knob has come off, it's, um, come away from the door,' stated Derek with an 'off the cuff' expression, trying to play down the seriousness of the situation, and then added 'oops,' in an attempt to make light of matters.

'What do you mean the knob came off???'

Jack was obviously getting a little agitated, his query was terse and not in the slightest bit light-hearted.

'For Gods sake we've got to do something Derek, I'm freezing to death in here,' pleaded Jack, slightly overplaying the state of affairs, 'and to make matters worse I can't reach the cognac,' he lamented.

Derek listened to the plaintive cries of Jack who was obviously distressed, distraught and definitely stuck.

He was also becoming a little anxious about their predicament, not to mention getting increasingly colder.

For a few seconds he considered the madcap idea of setting fire to the toilet block; that would at least warm things up, but then he realised there wasn't anything in the building that would actually burn!

'Hold on Jack I've got an idea,' ventured Derek suddenly as he espied the open window for the first time, it wasn't the biggest of windows but...

Jack just groaned, he had previous experience of his friends' ideas and they were never brilliant.

'I'm going to climb up onto the window ledge...'

Another groan from the cubicle!

'Then I'm going to escape through the window and get help!' finished Derek with an ecstatic flourish of his brilliantly simple idea.

A deep burdened sigh was heard within the vicinity of the trapped vice-president.

'Right then here we go,' stated Derek; he was obviously intent on providing a running commentary for his trapped and visually impaired friend.

S-C-C-R-R-A-P-E!

'Just moving the bin...'

CLUNK!

'Better shut the lid,' followed by a weak attempt at laughter.

C-R-A-S-H!!!

'OOPS!'

'Hold on I'll get the other bin...'

The explanation was followed by the sound of heavy breathing from over exertion.

Jack could envisage his friend trying to heave his fairly substantial bulk up onto the bin and he was hardly surprised that it failed miserably in supporting him.

'This should be better...'

Derek's comment pre-empted further scraping of something heavy and substantial across stone, accompanied by more exertive and somewhat ragged breathing, 'this one's metal!'

Jack groaned inwardly; he couldn't believe that Derek had actually tried to climb up onto a plastic bin, given his sizeable mass.

'Hurry up!' moaned Jack, further remonstrating with the addition of 'my bottom's turning blue in here!'

'OK...Hold on...'

'I'm going up,'...G-R-O-A-N... 'Nearly there,'... C-R-E-A-K...

'Almost...' CRASH!

'Are you alright Derek?' queried a very concerned Jack.

'Er... Yes, fine... the bin isn't though,' followed by a nervous laugh and then 'It's OK though, I'm up on the ledge.'

'Well for God's sake take it easy!' admonished Jack, 'you're not a spring chicken you know!'

But Derek was already otherwise engaged and just grunted back.

Big Jim had to use his imagination, but it didn't make a pretty picture as he visualised the figure of his friend doing an impression of a cat burglar, squeezing his 44 inch waistline through the 36 inch window frame.

All he could hear was the various impromptu sound effects of Derek's grunts and groans, and a few more expressive words, as his soft framework had an argument with the window's steel one.

'I'm almost there...' muffled Derek, 'nearly...just a bit further...'

'ONE FINAL PUSH...'

There was a shuffling wriggling sort of sound and then a short scream followed by a louder 'OH NO!!!'

Big Jim was getting to the limits of his tether and his exasperation was beginning to tell.

'WHAT THE HELL IS GOING ON?'

A muffled distorted voice answered back in a state of panic.

'I'm nearly through the window but my belt is caught up on the window hook and I'm stuck!'

Jack had a sudden image of Derek suspended in mid-air hanging by his belt like an overweight Christmas tree decoration and couldn't help but smile, in fact he had to stifle the desire to laugh out loud.

All things considered matters really couldn't get much worse, he decided, but then thinking something like that was probably just asking for trouble wasn't it?

****

It was, as always, the fickle hand of fate that took a hand in a completely unexpected direction.

In the corner of the ice cold cavern stood a small storage cupboard, not much to look at, just an open closet in which to store cleaning receptacles like the old metal wash bucket and mop.

On the top shelf in comparative dryness, considering the state of the rest of the building, there were stored the 'necessaries', a large deep stacked stock of soft toilet rolls in blocks of one dozen.

On one of his many excursions, exploring the wilderness of the club facilities Rollo had come across the cold confines of the outside toilets and more importantly the extremely comfortable recess within the toilet roll stack.

A pile of shredded chewed paper gave evidence of his visitation to the impromptu 'soft bed' on many occasions.

The sound of the door slamming shut had disturbed his slumber and the 'carry-on' below had belatedly aroused his curiosity until finally he could contain his unfettered interest no longer.

He stirred slowly, stretching out as if he were an unwinding foam snake, then extended his claws whilst purring loudly like an express train.

Rollo was a very happy cat, his sharp claws plucking and shredding the nearest available stack of inviting soft tissues as he rolled over onto his back in typical feline fashion.

Finally, his eyelids drew back and following his instinctual, inquisitive nature, he lifted his head up over the top of the paper roll ramparts for a better view, his ears twitching.

From his position, he couldn't see directly into the cubicles but he could see the window and, more importantly he quickly espied Derek's bottom protruding from the opening, his little legs kicking and thrashing about.

He was entranced by the sight of Derek's struggles; he appeared to be caught up or wedged somehow; Rollo was transfixed by the lurid boxer shorts slowly emerging from the vice captain's trousers.

The offensive underwear was covered in large red and pink printed lipstick kisses which were moving about like Day-Glo coloured wriggling worms as Derek twisted and squirmed.

Rollo glanced towards the door, noting that it was firmly shut, and then looked back towards the semi-blocked window which now quite obviously provided the only available exit point.

Emerging from his comfort zone Rollo sat for a few minutes using his paws and tongue to give his hair a bit of a spruce up as he contemplated the scenario.

Finally, feeling somewhat satisfied with his appearance, he leapt down to the ground and sauntered over towards the wriggling, kicking form of Derek.

He sat down under the glass panels for a minute weighing up matters before bounding up onto the window ledge and uttering a long guttural and melancholic cry.

'M-E-E-O-O-O-W!!'

Derek, oblivious to his further predicament until that moment, froze instantaneously in mid kick, his heart racing as he suddenly became VERY aware of his vulnerable position.

Not intentionally meaning to heighten the level of terror in Derek's mind, Rollo stretched out on the window ledge and raked his claws over the cold steel frame enjoying the opportunity to flex his talons.

The insane screeching of the cat's claws on the metal was enough to send shivers of panic through Derek's body and he suddenly imagined the fish-hook like weapons not on the ledge, but on his soft and exposed posterior.

In the spin of a coin the terror-stricken bowler went berserk, kicking, screaming, yelling and wriggling wildly; it was apparent that something would have to give.

R-R-R-I-I-P-P-P!!!

Derek emerged from the window like an arrow bolt, faster than an exploding champagne cork he accelerated around the corner of the outhouse screaming...

'A-A-A-R-G-H!!'

Rollo stared up at the now empty trousers hanging limply by their belt on the window clasp and purred loudly; wasn't it funny how humans always reacted to his presence.

Back in the cubicle the immobile county vice-president stood absolutely still like a piece of petrified timber, a look of horror frozen on his face as he listened to the untimely and panic-stricken departure of Derek from the window.

He had absolutely no idea what was going on other than that a cat was obviously in terrible pain and his friend had probably died an agonising death.

Were the confines of the cubicles hiding an escaped mass murderer, or even perhaps a maniacal mad axe man hell bent on foul deeds?

Even the goosebumps on his blue bottom stopped shivering.

Rollo heard a faint noise from up amongst the toilet rolls and looked upwards inquisitively with a catlike smile spreading across his features.

A tousled, scruffy, long-haired, bleary-eyed head arose from within the warm depths of the hidey-hole.

After weeks of avid pursuit, Miss Matilda Bagshott, Gloria's supposedly posh Persian pussy, had caught up with her 'bit of rough' and had been enjoying a contented canoodle in the confines of the cupboard with her new mate.

She could see Rollo perched up on the window ledge and the fluttering vacant pair of trousers above him; apparently her boyfriend had been having a bit of fun without her.

Baggie was also aware of an unusual noise coming from the vicinity of the toilets, which, to the untrained ear sounded much like the repetitive chattering of a woodpecker on ice.

She craned her head around the corner of the cupboard and spotted where the distraction was coming from. However, try as she may, Baggie could not quite make out the source of the disturbance, only that it came from inside one of the cubicles.

Her eager, imaginative and resourceful brain cells soon convinced her stomach that a number of fat juicy mice were at that moment scurrying around in the middle cubicle unable to escape.

The need for immediate action clouded her judgement and her response.

Climbing up onto the top of the toilet roll pile, she gave a little shake of her rump in anticipation, sat back on her haunches, tensed her muscles, and launched herself into mid-air.

Rollo looked on in a mystified manner; where was that mad moggie going to now?

****

Try as he might, Big Jim couldn't help but react to the combination of icy cold and fear of the unknown; despite his best efforts an uncontrollable urge overcame him.

His teeth begun to chatter involuntarily more and more loudly.

His nerves were shot to pieces, he was freezing cold, fed up, frustrated, extremely tired and on tenterhooks.

To be fair he wasn't prepared for the sudden appearance of so much as a piece of cotton wool without being prone to over-reacting.

Therefore, it was inevitable that the impressively large, playfully inflated, pudding-like personage of Miss Matilda Bagshott arriving en-masse was bound to cause an upset.

Baggy had intended landing four-square on the drop-zone of her target; that being the toilet seat which she knew was there and was also guaranteed to ensure her delicate toes didn't impact on the cold floor. She was, after all, a bit fragile and lady-like when it came to matters of keeping her extremities warm.

Unfortunately, she had no prior knowledge of Big Jim's calamitous misfortunes, or that his attempts at escape had necessitated the removal of the aforementioned toilet seat.

At the last moment, the descending Persian cleared the top of the toilet cubicle and saw for the first time that her landing strip was more of a landing dip.

S-P-L-L-A-A-A-S-H-H!!!

With an almighty cavernous explosion, the pride of Persia impacted on the ice cold watery content of the porcelain receptacle.

It was a good job that the personable, shy, embarrassed prisoner had previously had the consideration and forethought to flush the toilet.

The result of Baggie's arrival was two-fold.

Firstly, it produced, in a split second, a wildly flailing, angry, saturated and floundering pussycat with a large hairy rug of a coat that immediately succeeded in soaking up almost the full fourteen-litre capacity of the toilet.

Secondly, the effect on the pent-up vice-president was akin to the detonation of an atomic bomb in close proximity to the cubicle.

There couldn't have been a bigger knee-jerk response from Big Jim had someone dangled a £500 bottle of the finest brandy in front of him and whispered the word 'free' in his left ear.

Like a greyhound out of the starting box he exploded from the cubicle, one hand holding his trousers up to cover his dignity, the other clutching the flapping toilet lid which was banging wildly on the still attached seat behind him.

To be fair the innocent toilet door had no chance against the 18 stone mass of Big Jim in full flow and he was very definitely 'flowing'.

Bursting like a huge firework through the convenience's front panel he rent the door from its frame work, bending the mortise lock and wrenching the hinges askew.

In blind panic, uncomprehending, unwilling or unable to stop, Jack Tuttle, pride of the presidency and man of the people, 'legged it'.

He streaked down the corridor, not even pausing when he encountered the still blocked main entrance, which suffered the same fate as its toilet cubicle predecessor.

In a petrified state, spitting splinters, Jack Tuttle emerged out into the open, desperately trying to hang on to his dignity whilst his trousers became keen to assume the 'half mast' position.

The still attached toilet seat with incumbent lid continued to pursue him in close contact.

Rollo looked in surprise at the disappearing bottom of the rather large bowler before jumping down off the window ledge and strolling over to the dishevelled dripping wet form of his newly acquired cat companion.

He stretched himself up the door frame and proceeded to sharpen his claws in a playful manner as he eyed up the Persian playmate, not really sure of where in the cat book of mating rituals it required the female of the species to leap into a toilet.

Baggy, unaware of the mayhem she had already caused, and at that point not particularly bothered, was occupied with the more pressing problem of trying to extract her greatly increased watery mass from the toilet interior.

Rollo stuck his tongue out in a rude suggestive manner, ambled up to the porcelain bowl, leant over and, in an act of retribution thinly disguised as a helping paw, extended his sharpest claw then stuck it into Baggies rump.

'M-E-E-E-O-O-W-W-W!!!'

In typical aggravated cat fashion, Baggie ascended the bowl vertically, her hairy coat exploding in all directions jettisoning the liquid excess and leaving her instantly several kilos lighter.

By the time she arrived back on terra firma her partner in crime, having previously played victim and now perpetrator, had fled the scene fully aware of the potential repercussions.

He was sure that when the manic moggie calmed down later, she would appreciate his invaluable assistance and thank him accordingly; in the meantime, it was more a case of a discreet withdrawal to avoid the immediate fallout.

****

In the vicinity of their car park the Over 55's ladies team members were just arriving and were presently gathered together bantering idle gossip, chit chat and such like in a rather jovial manner.

The 16 associates of the 'blue rinse' brigade were, as always, in fine fettle, and looking forward to a competitive day of friendly bowling intermixed with conversation, coffee and cakes.

'Oh I say, ladies would you just look at that?'

The Rt Hon. Lady Elizabeth Quinton MBE had so enjoyed her participation in the Ladies vs. Men competition that she had elected to stay on for the winter at Lower South-Borough to enjoy some further good sport with her companions of the former team.

She had commandeered the services of Diane Ditherford, Cynthia Cobblethwaite and Phillippa Spindleforth and then, in good order, organised a weekly tournament for the slightly more senior ladies, or as they were fondly referred to, 'Hell's Grannies.'

Lady Elizabeth was just stepping out of her car, about to shut the door, when she happened to peer over her spectacles towards the large, somewhat dilapidated holly bush on the far side of the old toilet block.

Her attention had been distracted by an unusual movement with a very distinctive colour co-ordination which, for a moment, had her wondering whether she was watching an escapee tropical bird of paradise or similar.

She blinked, looked again with an air of self doubt, before reaching into her glove compartment for the small pair of opera binoculars she always kept there.

It only took her a few seconds to focus the powerful magnification of the finely tuned instrument, before muttering

'Well I never...' to herself and with a quiet titter, alerting her playing partners. She passed her binoculars over to Diane, Cynthia and Phillippa who were all clamouring for a look.

The rest of the women had quickly reached for their own bifocals and monoculars, whilst one enterprising woman quickly assembled the tripod mounted bird-spotting telescope she had in the boot of her car.

With a 60x magnification it was going to leave little to the imagination, whilst it became apparent to some afterwards that they wished it had.

It wasn't more than a few seconds before the scope was finely adjusted and zoomed in on the resident 'wild bird' inhabiting the holly.

At first the 'object' appeared to be several pairs of pink dragonflies, but on zooming out quickly became a montage of variously shaded puckered lips, before finally revealing itself to be a large baggy pair of flamboyant boxer shorts.

The lurid underwear was wrapped around the rotund posterior of none other than Derek Dunstable, the men's vice-captain, who was busy looking furtively around the bush in the opposite direction.

Clearly he was somewhat distressed and out of breath, but one could only guess the reason for his manner of dress.

The ladies were all too soon tittering and sniggering like naughty schoolchildren with a mixture of 'TUT-TUTS,', 'HEE-HEES,' and 'OOHS,' as they cavorted around the telescope like prancing chickens clucking over a tasty morsel or juicy worm.

Derek fitted neither of these descriptions.

Elizabeth Quinton had been brought up in the school of hard knocks, despite her fine-tuned upper class vocals and posh exterior.

She put two pairs of fingers in her mouth and proceeded to give the loudest, most air shattering 'wolf whistle' any of the ladies had ever heard, or were likely to hear again.

Several of them blushed, turned deep beetroot red and looked away.

Over in the vicinity of the shrubbery Derek almost jumped out of his skin with fright and, glancing over his shoulder, he became acutely aware that his vulnerability was suddenly exposed.

It was brought into sharp focus with the realisation not only of his unexpected predicament but also of his state of undress and he quickly scuttled crablike around the bush.

A peal of laughter reverberated around the ladies and Elizabeth, with tears rolling down her face, opened her mouth to pass further comment, but was cut off in mid-flow, gaping open-jawed in astonishment at the nearby bowling green.

Around the corner of the clubhouse and across the cherished lawns of Lower South-Borough streaked the county vice-president.

Jack 'Big Jim' Tuttle was in full flow, blinkered in vision and evidently only intent on finding a safe haven far away from the apparition of his, as yet, unseen terrifying pursuer.

His trousers gathered with both hands around his waist, much as if he was entered in a sack race, the toilet seat banging and clattering behind him, he vanished through the car park into the gardens in search of cover.

The ladies looked on in a mixture of astonishment, amazement and mystification.

They stared back up the green but nothing else followed or gave evidence to the reason why Jack was headlong in flight or indeed in the manner of 'dress' that they had witnessed.

Cynthia, who had been using the telescope at the time of the surprise arrival, appeared in a severe state of shock, and seemed to be mumbling unsurely about whether Jack would need a doctor or a plumber.

In a matter of seconds the entertainment had arrived, passed through and vanished 'stage left' leaving the ladies feeling quite uncertain what was to follow next; cautiously they made their way to the indoor arena, one hand on their woods and the other on their blood pressure tablets.

Rollo in the meantime had made good his escape and was sitting on the roof of the bird hide in the wildlife garden feeling very pleased with himself.

He could survey the entire garden from his vantage point and with it being virtually unassailable unless by use of the dodgy drainpipe in the corner, sure of his safety, the vicarage cat settled down for a much-needed snooze. It had been, after all, at least 22 minutes since his last catnap and being a moggie he did need a lot of sleep after all.

A bedraggled Baggie watched from the bedding plants, not sure whether to be angry, inspired or aroused by her misbehaving playmate.

She finally made her mind up to call a truce for the time being as her fur coat required a lot of attention and re-alignment; she rather felt the need for a nap too so she curled up under the petunias to contemplate her options.

It wasn't too long before both cats were fast asleep.

****

Percy was in the wildlife garden.

He had rounded up a protesting Bernard, Patrick, Dennis and Charlie from the sumptuous, warm surroundings of the clubhouse lounge and was escorting them persuasively towards the newly constructed bird hide.

Dennis, being both a keen amateur ornithologist and the brains behind the bird hide, skipped enthusiastically in front of the group, chiding them for being less appreciative.

To be fair, given the extremely cold morning outside the men in question would have still preferred to have been inside even if there had been a chorus line of naked dancing girls performing in the grounds.

Dennis was extremely proud of his conservation project in the wildlife garden, which was a runaway success for the visitors, both of the feathered and four-legged variety.

Since last summer's arrival of the awe-inspiring, majestic bird feeding station donated by local company Wild About Birds, Dennis had pursued even more adventurous avenues towards turning the five acres of wasted grassland into a haven for wildlife.

With feverish attention to large scale planting of new shrubbery, trees, and seasonal flowers as well as the introduction of a very significant water feature, the former grass meadow had been quickly transformed.

To be honest Dennis had in typical fashion, overdone things on a meteoric scale, with bird boxes and feeders festooning every available tree trunk or fence post in the area.

The so-called 'water feature' which began as a pond, ended up more the size of an Olympic swimming pool that required a suspension bridge to cross to the middle island.

What had started as a one-man job with a shovel had quickly mushroomed to a full-scale excavation requiring the 'borrowing' of Jimmy Murphy's JCB digger on numerous occasions.

With Dennis then having had to acquire the caterpillar-tracked excavator to tow the JCB out of the muddy quagmire Jimmy had no option but to lend a professional hand.

He was demonstrating his professional capability later the following day when he ploughed the digger's heavy bucket right through the main water pipe.

The resultant water fountain was said to be reminiscent of the eruption of 'Old Faithful', America's most memorable geyser, as the ensuing flood filled the entire excavation in 11 minutes flat.

A red-faced Jimmy returned later with a crane to rescue both the aforementioned digger and the excavator from the newly created reservoir.

He was to feel even guiltier afterwards when he found out it was his 'alteration' to the club's plumbing that had led to the indoor toilets being out of circulation and the cause of Jack's predicament.

The arrival of the crane quickly led to an escalation of ideas in Dennis's creative thinking; before Jimmy had the opportunity to beat a hasty retreat a large timber bird hide had been lifted in and placed dead centre on the middle island.

Giving panoramic views in all directions over the lake and gardens, it was the crowning glory of the ornithologist's masterpiece. However what began as a simple bird hide soon became an ostentatious over-the-top creation that was worthy of being considered a work of art.

Its recycled timber frame had been constructed from a fallen oak tree whilst its bodywork was tastefully layered in timber boarding made of sweet cherry. From the outside it looked stunning, natural and inviting and all was well with the world until Dennis decided to spend the afternoon contemplating his next proposals whilst bird-watching from its spacious core.

At that point, he clearly lost the plot.

The interior now sported wall-to-wall carpet, including underlay, night-time storage heating, a small colour television, telephone, microwave and refrigerator. Potential bird-watchers were greeted with the sight of recliner chairs, built in telescopes, a compendium of books in a mini library, a computer and an electronic pager for bird alerts. There was of course a kettle for making hot drinks, but Dennis had finally drawn the line when Jack had suggested putting up a range of optics.

Nevertheless, the whole project was an outstanding success for the club and Dennis warmly soaked up the praise of the parishioners.

By night the gardens became a sanctuary for a variety of visitors especially hedgehogs, foxes, a few deer and even a badger passing through. During the day time rabbits took a keen interest in the new plants much to Dennis's annoyance, but the sheer number of wild birds visiting the safe haven soon distracted him.

A kingfisher now patrolled the well-stocked lake, warblers sung merrily from the trees whilst a variety of finches and tits sparred for a place on the feeding stations.

There had been a number of rare bird visitors to the garden, Dennis had already logged over one hundred species, and news of the success of the conservation site had soon spread throughout the community.

It was this success that had led Percy to receive a letter from the BBC wildlife programme 'Thing Watch' inviting the club to have their conservation garden filmed for an episode of the show.

Consequently, Percy was on his way to meet the photographers and presenters of the television programme that very morning, hence the reason for his deviation to rope in the support of some of his fellow parishioners and in particular the creator of the garden.

Dennis of course was beside himself with excitement as he learnt of the good news from Percy.

With him leading, closely followed by the vicar and the others in nearby proximity the entourage arrived in a tumble at the gates to the wildlife garden.

Ahead of them was parked a large white Transit festooned with an impressive array of antennae, radio masts and satellite receivers.

Cables sprawled from the vehicle spaghetti-like and then raced off as speeding snakes down the garden path towards the bird hide's inner structure.

An elderly bearded chap was directing operations, closely assisted by a younger, taller, curvaceous woman and Dennis felt a strong sense of déjà vu.

The silhouettes looked strangely familiar.

The penny dropped.

THING WATCH!

'Of course,' he whispered to himself under his breath, Thing Watch! which could only mean that...

He looked again at the two figures and began to tremble at the knees.

'It was!' he mumbled, It was the legendary ornithologist William Snoddy and his co-assistant Katie Fumble.

He stepped forward, arm extended to offer his hand as they turned towards him.

William and Katie smiled as they met his greeting, 'You must be Dennis,' to which he nodded in response.

The others arrived in a bundle of excitement, shaking hands, swapping introductions, and offering their praise for Dennis's achievements, to which he blushed and for once was humbled into silence.

'Well gentlemen, it's a pleasure to be here, we're all set up, so shall we venture down to your wildlife arboretum?' proffered William at length.

'Why y-yes, o-of course,' stammered Dennis, 'after you of course.'

With that Dennis, Percy, Bernard, Patrick and Charlie fell in step behind William and Katie as they headed off towards the bird hide.

****

The cameras were set up everywhere in the bird hide, covering all angles and every eventuality as the lighting cast a warm glow throughout the interior.

William and Katie were busy 'mikeing up' and going through a sound check with their support team as the others looked on.

Patrick meanwhile was engaged in making copious quantities of tea, as Charlie handed round the biscuits and Bernard tried very hard not to stare at Katie's bottom.

Dennis turned to Percy with a look of awe as the realisation hit him suddenly, 'Reverend, do you actually mean that they are going to broadcast this live from the bird hide?' he asked incredulously.

Percy glanced up at him smiling broadly. 'Well it certainly would seem that way,' he beamed at Dennis, 'you are about to be famous!'

Patrick looked up from the steaming teapot, 'Can I have your autograph now before you're too busy?' he asked.

Dennis blushed and for the second time in one day, he seemed to be lost for words.

Before anyone could proffer a further suggestion the programme controller cut in, 'Ladies and gentlemen can we have quiet please, we are going 'live' in 60 seconds.'

'Is everyone ready?'

William looked up from his microphone, 'Ready here...'

Katie stood by the hatchway to the bird hide, 'All set here...'

The programme controller checked his watch, 'Right then, Dennis would you care to take your place alongside Katie?'

Dennis stared back incredulously.

'M-m-me?'

'Of course,' he smiled back, 'it's your project after all. William will introduce the programme, Katie will open the hatchway and make an introductory link, then you will take it from there, talking us through what we can see...'

Dennis gulped as Percy patted him warmly on the back, 'Come on old chap, this is your 15 minutes of fame, chin up.'

He looked across to Bernard, Charlie and Patrick who all smiled and nodded back in mutual agreement.

'Oh well, here goes then,' and with that Dennis stood up and walked across the bird hide to stand by Katie.

'OK everyone, stand by!' announced the controller, holding his hand up with fingers extended upright towards them.

'Going live in 4 - 3 - 2 - 1 -   and...'

William smiled and looked into the camera...

'Good afternoon fellow bird-watchers, we are here this afternoon at Lower South-Borough bowling club to see their new wildlife garden.'

Dennis was visibly shaking with the nervousness of the situation, but Bill Snoddy slipped easily into the vernacular of his ornithological profession and opened up with a warm oration.

It was hard to believe that the presenter used to be a member of a stand-up comedy trio who were renowned for their peculiar, somewhat off the cuff, irregular and Monty Python-like farce.

Percy had heard that one of the highlights of his former career involved dancing on stage like a monkey, but he had refused to believe it.

It must have been just a rumour after all.

He did think that Katie Fumble looked the part dressed in her camouflage fatigues and for some reason, with her richly coloured hair she reminded the vicar of Sarah Jane Coddle.

Percy had a flashing vision of Molly's sister charging over an assault course in a similar outfit with her hair streaming out behind her, and went hot behind his collar.

He clutched the good book closer to his hip pocket, muttering a quick 'Hail Mary' but the image kept repeating itself and he felt sure everyone would notice his blushing.

'And without further ado let's go over to Katie...'

Percy's train of thought was immediately broken by the sound of William Snoddy's handover to his co-presenter.

'Thank you Bill.'

'Well as you can see from our surroundings,' said Katie as she extended her left hand and invited the camera to pan round the interior, 'we are more than adequately kitted out for bird-watching in a luxurious state of comfort.'

'Bill has already introduced you all to the project and I am here right now with the man behind this extra-ordinary vision of ornithological modernisation, Mr Dennis Ditherford.'

And with that, the camera zoomed in on Dennis's terrified face as Katie put her hand around his shoulders in a comforting manner and offered him an invitation.

'Well Dennis, this is your baby...' which raised a titter from the camera crew, 'so would you like to do the honours and open up the hatch so we can take a peek and see what's happening in your wildlife garden?'

'Y-y-e-ss, of course, er Katie,' mumbled Dennis in a nervous stammer, and without further ado, glad to be out of the limelight, he turned around to push open the viewing hatch.

The camera lens panned out to encompass the whole lake and garden in its viewing screen.

There were a few gasps of appreciation from those watching.

An abundance of waterfowl adorned the surface of the lake, whilst wild birds festooned the shrubbery and feeding stations.

A green woodpecker flew by laughing derisively over the open grass meadow whilst a kingfisher emerged with a splash from the waters edge nearby carrying a small stickleback.

Song thrushes jubilantly sang in melodious fashion from the top of the Scots pine and squirrels scampered merrily around its base searching for food.

Katie stared through the hatchway with a look of admiration on her face, 'Wow, fantastic, what an achievement!'

'Remarkable,' commented Bill, 'quite remarkable,' he agreed with a smile of appreciation.

Dennis remained bashful and unassuming, enjoying the praise.

'Er... what's that over there?' piped up Bernard, looking at one of the monitors.

Percy's ear perked up and a familiar sense of nervous apprehension settled over him.

'Where are you looking?' asked Katie.

'There, over by the back of the holly tree in the distance, what is that?'

Bill stared out of the viewing hatch with his binoculars.

'Why it looks like a heron, no, wait, it's too big and it's pink, why it looks like a pair of flamingos,' he announced incredulously.

'Can we get a close up of this George?'

The cameraman nodded and pressed the zoom button on the top of his filming equipment.

Reverend Percival Peabody was becoming quite an expert in sensing forthcoming or impending disasters and he felt the twinge of one right now.

He looked at the nearest monitor, adjusted his bifocals and groaned as he raised his hands to his face.

Percy shook his head from side to side in a gesture of despairing recognition 'Oh no...'

William Snoddy was used to many sights of an ornithological nature and could identify most in a short time frame, but he still hadn't managed, as of yet, to work out exactly what kind of unusual species they were looking at right now.

'Well it certainly looks like a flamingo but it's too thick in the leg to be one,' he said. 'Can you zoom in a little more George?'

The camera operator nodded in affirmation.

Percy groaned a lot louder this time and reached for the Bible.

'Hold on George, that's much better, now just a touch sharper...'

Bill and Katie stared, and then stared harder still.

Katie shook her head in disbelief.

'But it can't be, can it?'

She screwed her eyes a little to re-focus.

'What do you think Bill...?'

'BILL?'

She called out again a little louder as he failed to respond and turned her head to look in his direction.

He was standing in a state of shock by the larger television monitor with a petrified look of unbelieving horror on his face.

Katie, none the wiser, looked into the camera and continued with the show, 'Well ladies and gentlemen it looks like we have a mystery here, maybe an ornithological first in the UK?'

She glanced around the room, but everyone else seemed

frozen to the spot, and, being very aware that they were 'live' to the nation, she continued in true professional fashion.

'OK viewers, let's see if we can find out exactly what we have here shall we?' and with that she nodded her approval to the cameraman.

'That's not a good idea Katie...' croaked Bill from over by the monitor.

Percy wondered if he could find the mains power supply socket in time.

Either way it was much too late: Katie Fumble was focussed on the viewers' need for enlightenment.

'Why not put us in the picture George, give me full zoom!'

The operator inclined his head towards Katie in a 'tip the wink' fashion and pressed the zoom.

Percy groaned one final time and crawled over to hide behind the settee.

William Snoddy was quick to join him.

They glanced at each other with a shared look of disbelief trying to imagine the footage now being beamed 'live' to 500,000 homes countrywide.

****

Derek breathed a sigh of relief, the ladies' bowling team were, at last, safely out of sight and his sense of vulnerability had eased somewhat.

After all, it was not the done thing for the vice captain of a respectable and reputable bowling club to be caught in the public arena without his trousers on, much less behind a bush in just his boxer shorts.

Especially these boxers!

He felt very open to the elements, but not half as much as his companion who stood next to him.

Jack Tuttle, pride of the county, had been very keen on making the most of his first term of office as the recently instated county vice-president and looked forward to achieving the maximum exposure for his beloved club.

He certainly hadn't planned on exposing all of his assets to the atmosphere in such a way though.

Having made his way cautiously back towards the clubhouse following his initial flight from the toilet block Jack had seen his fellow bowler hiding behind the holly bush and was navigating towards him one tree at a time.

The nettles in the flowerbed had caused him some consternation but nothing that an antiseptic cream wouldn't put right.

Finally, Jack reached the questionable safety of the larger shrubbery and at last had the opportunity to take a much-needed breather.

With his torn trousers gathered around his legs and the toilet seat still attached to his sore and battered bottom he now crouched in hiding with Derek as they discussed their mutual plight.

'What the hell are we going to do now?' gasped Jack, his breath ragged in the cold air following his exertions.

'Well it's you that got us into this mess...' grumbled Derek.

'How did you work that one out?' wheezed Jack.

'You're the one who got stuck on the bloody toilet seat!' he moaned, nodding his head in the direction of Big Jim's blue bottom.

Jack opened his mouth in retort but was cut short by an exceptionally loud scream.

'AAA-A-A-R-R-G-H-H-H-H!!!!'

He looked at his fellow incumbent with an expression of confusion and his companion stared back equally bemused.

The scream had come from behind them, somewhere off in the distance, but the only thing back there was the protection of the wildlife garden.

Together they looked over their shoulders.

It took a few seconds before their eyes adjusted to the scenario then became focussed on the distant garden shrubbery behind which appeared to be a very bright light emanating from the location of the bird hide.

Jack, being better equipped in the visualising department screwed up his eyes intently; he could just make out a familiar shape against the rather bright light.

'You know Derek,' he muttered in a matter of fact way, 'If I didn't know any better I'd say that was a television camera.'

The vice captain looked back at him with an expression of rhetorical disbelief.

'Don't be so bloody stupid,' he said, 'come on let's get out of here,' and with that the two partners in crime crawled along the line of undergrowth towards the clubhouse and safety.

CHAPTER FOUR

DECEMBER

THE HALF MONTY

Percy sat in front of the warm log fire that was busy bathing his clerical study with its radiance.

It was a time for deep meditation, personal contemplation and the urgent necessity to make a number of plans, arrangements and preparations.

December had arrived so quickly and he found it hard to believe that with so little time before one of the most important religious as well as festive occasions of the year there was still so much to do.

He gazed up at the nearby calendar; the date of the 5th already stood out as the point reached in the month.

Percy sighed deeply, over recent months, he had become troubled by a number of events that appeared to be encroaching more and more on his personal life; their presence disturbed his gentle spirit.

He was after all a man of the people, a shoulder to lean on, a voice to lead with, and a source of inspiration for so many of his parishioners.

The events of the last year seemed to have grown wilder, crazier and more unbelievable with each passing month and he continued to stay bemused by their occurrences as well as their unexpected outcome.

Somehow, and he didn't know how or why, everything not only turned out OK in the end, things even worked out for the benefit of the club and the parish.

Who would have thought that the vision of two members of the bowling club virtually naked from the waist down, appearing on national television could have done anything but harm to the traditional values of their parish.

The early sighting of the two pairs of pink legs initially, but mistakenly, identified as a breeding pair of migrant flamingos had planted the germ of an idea in the viewers' brains.

The fact that the branches and light foliage of the holly bush had initially hidden the naked truth provided a short stay of execution for which they had all breathed a deep sigh of relief.

Percy and Bill had finally recognised the pink appendages as being able to only belong to someone or something human and when the toilet seat, bare bottom and pink kisses came into sharp focus Katie's loud scream had goaded them all into swift action.

Luckily the BBC's standard use of a two second time delay between filming and transmission of footage, in order to protect viewers against vulgar, obscene or incriminating material, had paid dividends on that day.

Percy's right foot had hooked around the nearest power cable and pulled it out of the wall with a flash of sparks, immediately causing the satellite link to crash whilst Bill had rugby tackled George the film operator.

The subsequent wild flailing of the camera towards the ceiling had prevented the very questionable close up being transmitted.

Their reputations intact, Bill and Katie were later able to pass off the incident as a short circuit in their electrical equipment that caused the initial sparks and the subsequent black out.

A secret memo from head office had praised them on their swift action, which avoided a large number of lawsuits and litigation from viewers suffering from brain damage, loss of eyesight or long term nervous depression from having witnessed such a sight.

Consequently, the king and queen of conservation had been admirably rewarded with a contractual extension of THING WATCH to an hourly show that was to be broadcast weekly throughout the year.

There was however, a spurious rumour circulating that a club member had acquired the tape recording of the incident, which included the uncut footage, and had spirited it away to some hidden location.

No names had been mentioned but eyes were cast strongly in the direction of Charlie and Bernard who were nearest to the recording machine at the time Percy had pulled the plug.

Not one to miss much of anything in the wind the Bishop, Augustus Thomas the Third, who was a devout follower of the conservation show, had voiced concern over the missing footage which he was keen to see.

As an avid bird-watcher himself he wanted absolute proof of the potential appearance of a rare breeding pair of flamingos in the parish gardens.

Of course, he protested, it had nothing to do with the potential financial benefits and his interest had not been inflated by the large number of keen 'twitchers' who had flocked to the wildlife gardens in the vain hope of catching the migrant visitors.

Neither had he been influenced by the swift, enterprising, keenness of Dennis and Charlie who were charging £5 a person at the entrance gate in the name of good causes.

There was of course a large donation being made to the church roof restoration fund, much to Percy's delight, also another equally generous contribution to the clubhouse fitting out fund.

Nevertheless, Percy had calculated that the shrewd couple were probably tucking away about 40p a visitor and with 378 bird-watchers having passed through the turnstiles, they were making a quite substantial turn of personal profit.

The Reverend decided to ensure that the collection plate dwelled heavily in the laps of those two parishioners every Sunday up until the New Year by way of 'punishment' for their sins.

Dennis and Charlie had taken the extreme measure of closing off a significant area of the wildlife garden to hide their subterfuge so that only distant viewing of the breeding site was possible.

Added to that, the sudden recent alterations of the local vegetation to heavily disguise the apparent site, kept even the keenest twitcher with the sharpest binoculars, on tenterhooks.

Not one to miss a trick, as a façade the enterprising pair had banned the use of more powerful telescopes on the pretext that the sunlight reflecting on the large lens was likely to disturb the nesting birds.

Percy had no option but to deny any involvement in their scam and urged them constantly to 'arrange' for the birds to fly away in the not too distant future.

The placing of two large plastic flamingos in the reed bed by the site was the final straw however, and he had given them just 24 hours to remove the replicas, contemplate their sins, and make recompense in the church donations plate.

He had sworn all those with knowledge of the goings on to enter into a verbal agreement to 'keep stum' or else feel the full wrath of God, in the shape of Bishop Augustus Thomas the Third if they were to breach the unprecedented conspiracy of silence.

Percy shivered.

It would have been previously unthinkable for a Reverend of the parish to enter into such a sinful agreement, but the ramifications, if someone got close enough to detect the hidden truth, were unimaginable.

It began to feel as if he was becoming the male equivalent of the Vicar of Dibley and made a mental note to remind his wayward flock of the key commandments in his next sermon.

Percy was continuing to have troubled and sleepless nights, which seemed to revolve around bizarre re-occurrences. Whatever he was doing, albeit umpiring, preaching, bowling, helping in the kitchen; whenever he turned around his ever present assistant was always Sarah Jane Coddle, wearing an angel's outfit and appearing in a foggy haze lit by rays of sunshine.

It was quite a disturbing image for the Reverend; he thought that perhaps he should seek divine guidance and take a long vigil in the sanctuary of his vestry.

Percy reached for the nearby teapot and poured himself a fresh cup of Earl Grey; it was still piping hot and the scented steam rose sweetly into the warm air.

On his desk, he could see the pending list for the Christmas celebrations still requiring his fairly urgent attention; it was his last opportunity to make any changes as the members were gathering at the weekend in just three days time to festoon the bowling club hall and dining room in readiness for the festivities.

'Oh well,' He muttered to himself, 'I guess I better make a start?'

He stared at the headed piece of paper.

PREPARATIONS FOR THE CHRISTMAS PARTY stared back at him.

First on the agenda was the purchasing budget for the decorations, which, until Percy had arrived a few years ago, had been no more than £50 as the church funds were at that time barren, and the club poor.

On his first Christmas at the club, Percy had been shocked to find that the entire seasonal decoration kit consisted of 32 rolls of toilet paper glued by hand into paper chains with sellotape.

Following Percy's first sermon at the church, prior to handing around the collection plate, he placed £100 of his own money in the pot as a good-will gesture to celebrate his inaugural presentation of the Church service.

The astonished response from his new congregation was followed by a few parishioners equally willing to 'cover his money' with generous donations resulting in a Christmas 'pot' of nearly £500. Since then Percy's rise from unknown outsider to cornerstone of the community had been meteoric.

This year, with all the preceding events of the club members' extra-curricular activities and subsequent influx of donations the coffers were full to overflowing.

The clubhouse extension and rebuild was all paid for whilst the church restoration fund now stood at a record £99,997.50p just £2.50 short of its target.

Percy smiled and reaching into his pocket fished out two £1 coins and a 50p which he promptly dropped into the collection plate.

'There!' he said with a satisfied sigh, 'job done!' he finished with a happy grin on his face and began to hum a tuneless version of 'Onward Christian Soldiers'.

With a final check of all the available funds and surplus thereof, he decided, in a display of seasonal generosity to ensure this was for all his parishioners a Yuletide to celebrate.

'Maybe even my final Christmas here,' he pondered for a second, and then wondered foolishly, why he had suddenly thought of that.

He picked up his nearby pen and with a flourish proceeded to write a number of cheques from the church charity fund; Bishop Augustus Thomas the Third was not going to be happy, but that was tough luck thought Percy in an act of minor rebellion.

It was after all money from the people for the people.

CHRISTMAS CONTRIBUTION	£2,000
HOME FOR THE ELDERLY	£1,000
ORPHANS OVERSEAS	£500
CONSERVATION APPEAL	£500
CHILDREN'S APPEAL	£500

He reflected for a moment, on what would be best served in his consideration of the final payment, and then with a self-satisfied smile he wrote the last cheque.

MIDNIGHT MASS CELEBRATION   £500

Percy paused for a quick slurp of his favourite tea, and then, suitably refreshed, picked up his pen and began to write with renewed vigour.

CHRISTMAS LIST   (heavily underlined twice)

1)   ONE VERY LARGE CHRISTMAS TREE

He paused for a second before making a slight amendment...

1)   TWO VERY LARGE CHRISTMAS TREES

His pen positively flowed over the paper, like oil on a hot metal sheet, as the Reverend of the parish set about organising the finest festivities ever.

****

It was a Saturday morning like no other and the club was in a state of utter disarray.

Percy was currently away at the church organising a rehearsal to prepare the choir for the midnight mass and to oversee the installation of the Christmas tree.

Apparently, it was arriving with a crane and he was a bit concerned that, due to its size, it might have to enter via the bell tower.

Most of the bowling club members, acquainted with Percy's Christmas extravaganzas had already volunteered to assist, whilst others inspired by the generosity of this season in particular and encouraged by others had turned out also.

Over at the clubhouse it was a case of, 'no more room at the inn.'

However, from the vicar's recollection, given the usual combination of Lower South-Borough members, the more there were, the more complicated things became.

By a process of lateral thinking and the natural progression of all things, events usually went downhill quickly after that.

Had Percy been present he probably would have left at that stage and sought sanctuary in the vicarage.

Over in the kitchen as per usual Molly led the charge with a bountiful breakfast banquet in full swing; Bertie, her sister Sarah Jane, Phillippa, Squiffy and Big Jim ably assisted her.

It was hardly surprising that the ample figure of Jack Tuttle and the equally plentiful form of Ronald Regis were willing volunteers to serve tea, coffee and orange juice on that particular morning.

They would deny vehemently that it had anything to do with the thick rashers of smoked maple-cured bacon, prime beef sausages or rich patties of black pudding sizzling on the griddle.

Of course they were not swayed by the pan full of large free-range eggs, crisp golden slabs of fried bread or fresh button mushrooms swimming in melted butter.

Certainly, the mountains of golden brown thick sliced toast with fresh home made orange marmalade and hot, fruited muffins straight from the oven did not influence them either. However, it was noticeable to the ladies that most of the time Jack and Ron were conspicuous by their silence, mainly due to having their mouths crammed full of irresistible delicacies which left them unable to talk.

The stifled cries of pain as they munched into samples of the newly baked titbits only to find them too hot to digest, followed by sudden mad dashes to the cold tap made it difficult for the ladies to suppress their amusement though.

Over in the main arena numerous figures were scurrying back and forth, rushing about like busy ants unloading large boxes from full vans whilst their noses twitched expectantly at the smell of heady aromas arising from the kitchen department.

The gang were all present!

Russell Cobblethwaite had, in Percy's absence been placed in temporary charge. He was a very astute person under his greying exterior, and was one of the few people that actually had an outside chance of keeping the flock in order as they were overcome by seasonal frenzy disorder one by one.

Heading up the lighting team, responsible for erecting and placing all the interior roof illuminations, including the floodlighting for the children's Christmas party were Eric, Tony, Sheila, Paul and. Johnny.

The two younger members were a safe bet, being agile, nimble and able to work on the big ladders, whilst Eric, with his former bomber command experience should have no fear of heights.

Sheila was always up for a challenge; with youth and strength on her side she could easily dash up and down the scaffolding.

There was some doubt as to the suitability of her attire though.

Not wanting to reveal too much of her shapely assets in her famed short skirts she had instead resorted to a one-piece neoprene bodysuit that was normally reserved for the gymnasium.

Given that the skin tight, figure-hugging outfit left little to the imagination and covered her like a glove from neck to knee, Russell could see all sorts of problems arising!

Taking charge of the Christmas tree and it's decoration, Clifford and Frenchie were joined by several ladies including Diana, Cynthia, Doris and Gloria.

Clifford was the James Bond of the bowling world with his good looks; a gentleman of quality, or as some would put it, 'good breeding stock.' Then of course, there was that suggestive twinkle in his eye every time he glanced at any members of the fairer sex with that whimsical smile of his.

Consequently, he was one of the most sought after bachelors in the club and with his position on the council there were many rumours of extracurricular activities in the chambers, none of which had been proved, but many of which caused a fluster amongst the female members.

Frenchie 'Wide boy' Phillips was more of a rogue-ish character who wouldn't have been out of place as a buccaneer captain in 'Pirates of the Caribbean.'

His rough chiselled, sunburnt features and unkempt appearance made him the 'sort of chap' that most ladies would not admit to liking, but he was a textbook 'bit of rough' for many a bored house widow; that, and the fact he had a very substantial bank balance.

His usually inviting character did however show some concern over the rather eager volunteering of Gloria Grimshaw.

Sorting out the seasonal décor was typically the safest undertaking and therefore fell to the oldest and youngest members of the group or anyone who was seen as being unsafe in other areas of ornamentation.

Therefore Derek, Doris, Russell, David, Tim and Abbey found themselves grouped together around an imposing stack of numerous cardboard boxes sporting the legend 'TRIMMINGS'.

The younger children glanced at each other with a knowing look, as they perceived a number of opportunities to misbehave.

All in all everything was pretty much organised and in fine hands, thought Russell as he cast his experienced eyes over his charge.

He noted the laughter in the kitchen; Bertie was giving Molly a cuddle and fondly patting her 'bump'. It was hard to believe that the shy naïve former spinster of the parish was now nearly four months pregnant.

They were laughing at the tiny Christmas tree that surmounted the microwave with just a single robin perched precariously on top.

Percy had made a slight error in ordering the original trees. Never being one to easily understand modern technology he had not yet even become used to decimalisation or metric conversion.

He had intended to order a pair of trees of 15 metres in height, but had ended up instead with two of just 15 centimetres much to the amusement of his parishioners.

They had been expecting the delivery of a pair of fine specimens of Norwegian Spruce, not a couple of green twigs that wouldn't have looked out of place in a bird's nest.

A quick call to the well-connected manager of their local supermarket soon put matters firmly to rights though.

James 'Jamie' Gotthelott had a longstanding reputation with his shoppers as a man who was very resourceful and could, given time, find anything that his customers desired.

True, his was only a very small emporium, but one of a chain of over 2500 outlets now owned by the modern retail giant TRESCOS, who seemed to have a stake in all corner shops in every village nowadays.

Nevertheless, the parishioners were most grateful for the opportunity to have a wide range of convenience foods easily at hand given the remoteness of their hamlet, especially when it only required the merest sprinkling of snowflakes for all the local roads to grind to a halt.

Just a hint of the 'white stuff' had the parish council in turmoil with much gnashing of teeth as they tried desperately to apportion their thimble-full ration of salt to cover the needs of the village's access routes.

Needless to say, they failed miserably, hence the rapid growth of the one time corner shop into a fully fledged TRESCOS mini-mart.

Jamie was a fair and shrewd man, very amicable, rotund of character mainly due to his daily visit to the fresh cream counter, but he was as approachable as he was astute.

Local farmers, who initially heaped scepticism on the development and scorned its value, soon back-pedalled as Jamie's first move, as newly appointed manager, was to incorporate a local produce department into the store.

The opportunity to sell their homegrown produce in a modern retail outlet led to a swift turnaround of attitudes, not to mention profit lines, and the well-stocked mini-mart was soon the enviable career move for any aspiring trainee.

Row upon row of freshly picked vegetables and seasonal fruit competed with tasty looking pickles, jams, meats and fruit juices as Jamie turned the dour pre-packed ready meal racks into a veritable honey pot of healthy alternative shopping.

Overnight the shop had become a runaway success.

There had been several attempts by his bosses to offer him a promotion to larger stores, which he had resisted strongly, agreeing eventually to a once a month visit to other outlets as a trouble-shooter to give them guidance and new direction.

It seemed that anyone living or working in the village was truly blessed, and happiness, in a roundabout way, was guaranteed to befall any member of the parish. Certainly, things didn't always run smoothly or indeed anywhere near their planned route, but the outcome always seemed to be better somehow with everything as it should be; more importantly the tradition of the old fashioned community remained intact.

Strict planning, cunning use of protection orders on buildings, trees, hedgerows and even Mrs Cobblethwaite's decorative bonsai ensured there were few additional new builds to spoil the quiet neighbourhood.

'Russell?'

'RUSSELL?'

The temporary commander-in-chief awoke with a start as it sunk into his subconscious that his name was being called; he had been daydreaming.

He looked up with a guilty smile at the Rt Hon. Clifford James Johnson, who was shaking him lightly by the shoulder smiling humorously.

'Had a night out on the tiles partying old man?' joked the captain, looking at him with a mischievous twinkle.

Russell smiled back as he stretched and groaned, his 68-year-old bones creaking a little. 'What ever you do, never grow old my boy.'

Clifford extended his hand to give the vice chairman a helpful pull up in the right direction, as the newly arrived Squiffy offered a hot cup of coffee to him.

Come on old chap, this will tickle your fancy, it's one of my 'special' coffees,' he said with a wink of his eye as Russell took the cup with a welcoming smile and held it firmly in his cold hands.

'It's hard to believe I used to be a surgeon,' he said, his hands shaking a little as they warmed up rather too quickly from the piping hot coffee.

'Where on earth did all the years go Squiffy?'

His friend clapped him on the back in a gesture of gentle understanding. 'God knows Douglas, one minute we're getting ready for a new season and the next minute it's nearly Christmas,' he said as he glanced around the busy room, now a hive of activity.

'Well Russell you had better drink up and come with me,' Squiffy paused for effect then continued, 'I have a large hot bacon butty in the kitchen that needs operating on, are you up for a bit of oral amputation?'

Douglas Doolittle was a man who loved his bacon and the sensuous enticing smell was already wafting across to where he sat.

'Well don't let it be said I'd ever refuse an offer like that.' He smiled broadly and stood up in a sprightly fashion, linking arms with Clifford and Squiffy.

'Shall we go then?'

The others nodded in agreement and spoke in unison: 'What the hell, why not?' and with that they strolled across the floor as if they were off to find the yellow brick road.

****

Over in the kitchen it was pretty much business as usual, with many of the members finding any excuse for a top-up of fresh brewed coffee or a second helping of a full breakfast.

Charlie, Dennis and Bernard, who had somehow managed to escape the initial selection process, were ensconced in the seating area making hay as the sun shone, in a manner of speaking.

Charlie, ever the one to over-assess his ability to consume food and always having a mouth bigger than his stomach, was on a second serving of his favourite beans on toast, a double helping at that; the others were watching him cautiously, wary of the stomach's ability to deal with such an intake of fibre.

Dennis was in the process of nudging the nearby fire extinguisher closer to the table with his left leg, whilst Bernard was relieved to see that the 'no smoking' sign was lit.

Bertie was watching worriedly from the safe haven of the kitchen and thought it might be advisable to check evacuation procedures for the lounge area, certainly, it would be a wise decision not to serve Charlie with any more beans.

He paused for consideration but before he had time to act Sarah Jane sauntered past with a tray in her left hand atop of which balanced a mug of hot coffee and a plate of freshly baked oatmeal biscuits.

'Where are you off to with that?' he enquired in an innocent manner but knowing that anything Sarah Jane did whilst 'sauntering' was bound to be bad news.

'Er, it must be cold over there in the church, so I thought I'd just pop across and take Percy a hot toddy to perk him up,' she replied with a definite twinkle in her eye.

Bertie chuckled, 'Oh dear!', and turned away quickly pretending not to have noticed.

Douglas, Squiffy and Clifford having just arrived at the kitchen in search of 'bacon heaven', noted the three absconding less than wise men, Charlie, Bernard and Dennis and immediately imposed detention.

'Right you three, enough skiving, Dennis help out on the lights, Charlie you're with the Christmas tree erection team , Bernard go and give Derek a hand on the decorating!'

It was never wise to question a decision from the former president, and when the captain AND the vice chairman threw their weight behind the order you simply did as you were told.

The skivers scarpered...

****

It was about five minutes later as the kitchen began to quieten; the members were finally going about their various duties as Clifford, Douglas and Ronald discussed the forthcoming festivities.

There was a very definite, distinctive scream in the distance and the rumbling sound of something falling to the ground a long way off.

They paused in mid conversation.

'What on earth was that?' queried Douglas.

'Hello' said Clifford, 'felt like an earthquake, what's that all about then?'

Squiffy looked mystified, 'It sounded like it was over in the direction of the church...' but got no further.

The clubhouse door swung open a touch too noisily as Sarah Jane burst through the entrance with a wild-eyed expression, her hair slightly dishevelled and her mouth twitching in a mad smile.

She looked a bit shaken and her usual characteristic demeanour was not its usual brazen self as was indicated by the larger than life coffee stain down her midriff.

'Well it wasn't my fault,' she reasoned to the onlookers in the kitchen.

Bertie sniggered and turned away; he was not going to have anything to do with the game in play, fate had already taken a hand and it was wise not to interfere as his wife Molly had already proven a few months ago.

'But it wasn't!' insisted Sarah Jane as she approached the mystified members.

'To be honest girl I haven't got a clue what on earth you are talking about,' interrupted a perplexed Clifford.

Molly's sister arrived at the bar then paused for breath, her tousled hair and untamed expression giving the impression she'd had a head-to-head run in with a wild tiger or worse.

'Well it's like this....'

'Yes?' interposed the simultaneous statement from Douglas, Squiffy, Molly and Clifford as they spoke as one.

'Go on, Go on...'

'Well I thought I'd take a hot coffee over to the vicar...' she began, in a 'butter wouldn't melt in my mouth' manner.

'Oh?'

'And when I got there he was in the church bell tower lowering this big Christmas tree down...'

'And?' encouraged the others.

'Well he couldn't see me,' she complained in a plaintive manner, 'so...'

'Yes yes, go on, spit it out...'

'So I reached up and nipped his bum,' she concluded finally.

'YOU DID WHAT?'

'You didn't?'

'Really?'

'Well yes, and he sort of screamed rather loudly,' commented Sarah Jane in a matter of fact manner.

'Oh dear,' groaned Clifford.

'We sort of noticed that,' said Douglas.

Molly's sister wasn't finished with her confession however so she continued.

'He sort of lost his balance then, so the Christmas tree came crashing down the tower,' she explained before concluding...

'If only he'd let go of the rope?' she said, in a whimsical fashion.

Squiffy looked on with an incredulous expression and began to make an observation: 'So do you mean..?'

'Yes,' said Sarah Jane with a rather blank vague stare, 'he held on to the other end and shot off up the bell tower!'

And then added as an afterthought, 'I could see right up his cassock!'

Bertie burst into hysterical laughter from the back of the kitchen, unable to contain himself any longer, as did Molly closely followed by the others.

'Ha! Ha! Ha!'

'Oh Lord and saints preserve us!!'

'Hee! Hee! Hee!'

'What shall I do with these?' She asked innocently, as she held up the vicar's boxer shorts.

****

The fire brigade had just left.

Following the prudent and apologetic call from the county vice-president Jack Tuttle, who had been roped into the debacle as one of Percy's closest friends, the rescue party had arrived as diplomatically as possible, with their large rotary turntable ladder.

The understanding Fire Chief had without too much fuss, managed to rescue the flustered, embarrassed and self-conscious vicar, lowering him carefully to the ground whilst a fireman's belt constricted his cassock and concealed his dignity.

By the look on Percy's face, it was clear to those standing nearby that there was a storm of biblical proportions brewing and Squiffy, recognising the signs, gave the others in the party a subtle wink as if to suggest that they surreptitiously make themselves scarce.

Sarah Jane was in hiding behind the heavy curtain screen adjacent to the large oak door; being careful was not her usual way or style but on this occasion, she thought it more a case of 'discretion required'.

Peeking out from her place of concealment in a very cautious manner she caught a brief glimpse of Percy's facial expression; suddenly having a vision of Moses on the mount, casting down the commandments whilst laying about his person with fire and brimstone.

Just for once Sarah Jane Coddle did the right thing and prudently made a strategic withdrawal back to the safety of the kitchen.

With Percy taking on the appearance of a voracious wolf, Douglas, Bertie and Clifford did a fine impression of the three little pigs and left in quick order through the rear exit.
Meanwhile Molly and Squiffy, being made of sterner stuff, stayed behind to assist the exasperated vicar.

Apart from being two of his most special friends, it was obvious that teamwork was very necessary, requiring one to bribe Percy with tea and biscuits, the other to steer the conversation off any subject related to Sarah Jane.

Taking one arm each they steered the shaken vicar in the direction of the rectory, which, being the building furthest placed from the kitchen area, was theoretically the safest.

'Come on Reverend let's go and have a nice quiet rest in front of the study's log fire, I've got a lovely Victoria sandwich that needs cutting,' commented Molly, trying her hardest to lighten the situation.

Percy remained silent.

'Yes, and I've borrowed Jack's medicinal compound,' said Squiffy tapping his top left pocket, 'so I'll make you a very special coffee to wash it down with.'

Still silence from the vicar.

Squiffy and Molly glanced nervously at each other as they reached the vicarage steps; things did not look too good for Sarah Jane at that particular moment.

Perhaps she would be wise to consider joining a convent in search of pious chastisement and self-denial for the foreseeable future, because it was quite possible that a call from Percy to Bishop Eugene Augustus Thomas was in the offing.

Molly shivered as they climbed the steps.

Just the thought of the Bible-thumping bishop lecturing self-righteous sanctimonious morality whilst the Spanish inquisition cracked flails and chanted sombre muted rhetoric, was enough to put the fear of God into Lucifer himself.

Back in the church, the now upright, firmly planted and safely erected Christmas tree stood in all of its glorious might, fully 50 feet in height.

The branches halfway up appeared to be moving slightly in the breeze that sallied around the church steeple, and for a moment, the tree almost gave the impression of being alive. Some of the greenery rustled for a second, stopped and then started again; all was definitely not quite as it should be...

Once again, the needles trembled violently and then parted company as a small conical shaped head peered out into the gloom.

The grey squirrel stared at the church interior with a mixture of apprehension and confusion; he'd slept in for a couple of days due to the cold weather during which he had been disturbed by strange dreams of ground shaking earthquakes and tilting trees.

Nevertheless he had continued to slumber, as had the rest of his brood; having gone to bed in a pine forest he was therefore rather bewildered to have woken up in a stone building.

He suspiciously eyed up the latticed beams high up in the church roof with their suspended lighting, and the long variegated tubular construction of the organ on the far side before drawing a conclusion.

This was obviously an outdoor pursuits holiday park for squirrels and these were some of the rides and attractions.

He stared again at the barrage of organ pipes.

Now that looked like a lot of fun!

****

Tea, coffee and hot chocolate were in full flow, whilst biscuits, scones and cheese straws vanished almost as quickly as they were baked.

Lower South-Borough's pre-seasonal grand Christmas decorating bash was well under way.

The hall and lounge area were a seething mass of confused bedlam and semi-organised chaos as the members did what they always did best: their own thing completely oblivious to any pre-drawn plans.

At first glance, the scenario appeared to be a Health and Safety officer's worst nightmare on an epic scale with the potential to reach a catastrophe of calamitous proportions.

Russell, having fallen asleep for the third time that morning, due to an invigorating game of whist the previous night AND a glass of sherry, had been tucked up safely on one of the sumptuous armchairs by the fire in the lounge.

Patrick Albright had perhaps picked a most inappropriate time to finish his chores on the green outside. Arriving at the kitchen in search of a heart-warming Irish coffee, he had been immediately volunteered as the only available committee member left unassigned, to take charge in Russell's absence.

His first deep reservations soon pacified by half a cup of Kilkenny's finest, he surveyed the scene and decided reflectively that perhaps things weren't too bad after all...

Over by the green, the children Tim and Abbey were quite happily passing gigantic baubles, reams of thick glittering tinsel and various shaped seasonal decorations to the nearby adults without any apparent need for supervision.

Bernard, David and Derek were comfortably seated on a solid looking scaffolding tower, suitably placed on very secure platforms standing 12 feet apart in height. Meanwhile Doris supervised the sorting of appropriate decorations into buckets that the three men could pull up on a pulley system when they were ready for the next shipment.

The children were not altogether innocent, but their brief interludes of tomfoolery were soon, nipped in the bud, as Doris fished out their personal additions to the ceiling décor.

After all, she reasoned, it was hardly fitting for their splendid exhibit of Christmas craftsmanship to be attired in toilet rolls, Mars bars and Cynthia Cobblethwaite's corset.

She had not however noticed the addition of several stripy socks, an inflatable saxophone and the recently 'kidnapped' vicar's boxer shorts on the far side of the hall.

The scaffolding tower was firmly secured by wooden chocks that looked like they had been borrowed from Eric 'Chalkie' Tunstall's collection of vintage aerial memorabilia and were probably last used to hold World War II Spitfires in place on the runway.

A similar assembly seemed to be working equally as effectively over by the club's enormous Christmas tree where Charlie, Frenchie and Clifford had taken the moral high ground, leaving Doris and Cynthia to organise the decorations.

Diana and Gloria were doing their bit, discussing the men's various attributes in hushed whispers, giggling like school children and making spurious comments such as, 'Watch out Cliffee, we can see right up your trouser leg.'

Obviously the seasonal good cheer was having a timely effect on the normally dour and straight-laced Gloria Grimshaw.

Nearby, her precious, precocious and preened Persian pussy slumbered contentedly in a raggedy, fluffed-up, heap of fur, tinsel and paper chain kits. Perhaps Miss Matilda Bagshott's apparent close attention to her owner and desire to be near at hand had softened that stern haughty exterior.

Patrick reflected that maybe it WAS a time of miracles.

He sighed and laughed half-heartedly to himself; he was beginning to sound just like Percy.

Checking his coffee he noted its half-full, tepid condition and thought it was quite timely to get a fresh refill; after all, it was a very demanding role watching all the members working like this.

'Everything okay then Postie?'

Patrick looked up.

Bertie was smiling radiantly from the kitchen counter, from where emerged clouds of flour, icing sugar and fruity aromas. He like all the other members, tended to use the green keepers' nickname as an informal form of address.

'Er yes, fine thanks, perfectly fine in fact Bertie,' replied Patrick, staring inquisitively over the shoulders of the one time double glazing sales rep, 'I'll have a fresh coffee please.'

'What on earth is going on in there?' he queried, nodding his head in the general direction of the rear kitchen or at least where it used to be.

It was fast disappearing in a pea souper of man-made fog, or, in this case, very much woman made.

Bertie laughed loudly as he glanced back at his sister-in-law Sarah Jane, who was frantically baking up a storm. She was smothered head to foot in splashes of egg white, blotches of flour and smears of buttercream.

Clearly, food fabrication was being taken to the extreme.

As the frothy steam rose from the coffee maker's spout and the machinery gurgled away merrily in production of Patrick's fresh ground beverage Bertie leaned over the counter and whispered in his ear.

The expression on the green keeper's face changed from a questioning look, via a gradual process to understanding and then finally to gleeful hysteria.

'Ha! Ha! Ha!'

'Oh that's rich,' he spluttered, 'now that's a real example of the huntress being caught in her own trap.'

'Hee! Hee! Hee!'

'Hoisted by one's own petard.'

'Ssshhh,' whispered Bertie with a broad smile on his face, 'She'll hear you.'

Patrick looked over at Sarah Jane and continued to splutter humorously. 'There's absolutely no chance of that Bertie!'

At the back of the kitchen the lady in question continued to slave away at a mad pace, oblivious to her surroundings, totally focussed on the baking and her apparent desire to coat everything in white dust.

****

It was inevitable that all good things would come to an end in spectacular fashion, especially in the parish of Lower South-Borough. As always, it wasn't one particular thing, but more a spontaneous combination of a number of events arriving at a simultaneous conclusion.

The third team of volunteers consisting of Eric, Tony, Paul, Johnny, Dennis and Sheila were always the ones most likely to lose control of the situation.

Perhaps it was down to the youthful exuberance of the two youngest who, when unable to secure a scaffold tower, constructed their own. Therefore, they built one out of tables and chairs tied down to Patrick's eight-wheeled trailer, with a 10-metre length of ladder strapped to it at a 45-degree angle.

Maybe, because of Eric's navigational and fighter experience from the last war, he was not the best choice of person to place in charge of steering and propulsion.

Possibly, it was also foolish to let Dennis manage the trailer's manual braking mechanism especially when taking into consideration he sometimes had difficulty breaking into a chocolate foil wrapper.

Most certainly the spur of the moment decision to let Tony Havershall take care of wiring plugs for the lighting was the catalyst and one they would most likely regret.

The thinking process had been that it was considered safer for everyone if Trigger was on the floor where he could do the least damage, and after all how hard could it be wiring three cables into three connections?

Whatever the final outcome, it had to be said that everyone's attention was definitely not focussed on the job at hand, more a case of being absorbed by the shapely and leggy assets of Sheila Ramsbottom.

Attired in her one-piece neoprene body suit normally reserved for her strenuous workouts in the local gymnasium, she had decided that it would be the most appropriate item of clothing to wear whilst working underneath the intense heat of the arena flood lighting.

'Awesome,' muttered Paul, with which Johnny had to agree.

'Very stretchable fabric isn't it?' commented Dennis in a strained voice.

'Best undercarriage I've ever seen,' spouted Bertie.

'I really like the third chair up, it's my favourite colour,' added Trigger in an innocent manner.

The rest of the team looked around at Tony with expressions of disbelief; clearly, his picnic hamper was experiencing an ever-decreasing short fall of sandwiches.

Trigger, keen to impress, had however, already returned to the job in question, oblivious to the reaction of the others.

He stared at the wires he held; there were green, blue and brown ones and three terminals in the plug. It all seemed simple enough, but he just couldn't remember which colour cable went where.

His difficulty was possibly due to the fact Tony Havershall had never wired a plug in his entire life; he just naturally assumed that every time he pressed a light switch magical fairies sprinkled pixie dust in the glass bulb.

Being faced with such a simple, straightforward task, none of the others had even considered the remote possibility that the undertaking was beyond Tony and just assumed that it was patently obvious.

He stared hard at the wires, and finally reached what was to him the perfect decision, after all, they all connected to the same socket in the wall didn't they, so what difference could it possibly make?

With that, he picked up a screwdriver and proceeded to wire all three cables into one terminal.

****

Molly having returned from attending to the vicar arrived just as Bertie stopped to take a much deserved break from the kitchen, and, as Sarah Jane was hard set on cooking for the entire club single-handed, they had sat down in the lounge by the fire with a glass of wine each.

Bertie looked over at his newly wed bride with a warm smile, 'I love you Molly Tattleford,' he said is a simple heartfelt statement of fact.

She beamed back at him, 'I love you too' and leant forward to kiss him.

****

Percy had finally gathered his thoughts.

He had responded well to the delicate and understanding attention of Molly and Jack earlier and, following three portions of Victoria sponge washed down with copious quantities of Earl Grey, now felt re-acclimatised to reality.

He had thanked his friends dearly and sent them back to help out at the Christmas decoration gathering with a promise that he would follow shortly.

Following his terrifyingly rapid ascent of the church tower, despite screaming wildly at the time, Percy had actually found the unexpected rush of blood to his head quite exhilarating.

In fact his newly discovered interest in the thrills and spills of roller coaster rides also provided him with the inspiration for a whole new concept for the forthcoming nativity.

Perhaps it would be possible to have the angel Gabriel descending down the inside of the bell tower at midnight to coincide with the mass?

His head still spun with a cocktail of emotions: the shock of the events past, previously un-experienced anger at the cause, embarrassment at being summarily de-frocked, confusion over his emotional state and perhaps even a slightly perverse pleasure at shocking Sarah Jane Coddle for a change.

To be totally honest he was in a state of mental turmoil and he felt perhaps that a call to the bishop was in order, although the thought of that equally terrified him.

He stared up at the clock and realised it was already nearly 1.00 p.m. and it had been almost three hours since the rescue; duty called and he absolutely must attend to the needs of his flock.

With that he put his other confused thoughts firmly on the back burner for the moment, adjusted his cassock and, with one final slurp of his favourite tea, stepped out of the rectory to face the congregation.

****

Percy arrived at the door to the inner sanctum of the indoor arena leading to the green and the lounge; he paused briefly to compose himself, took a deep breath and stepped inside.

He noted immediately the presence of newly weds Bertie and Molly, sitting with a glass of wine by the roaring fire, gazing at each other in a very loving manner and apparently about to exchange kisses.

Percy blushed for a moment and averted his eyes, but just for the briefest of seconds pictured himself and the voluptuous Sarah Jane Coddle exchanging kisses instead.

He blushed very deeply and felt a warm flush of embarrassing innocence rising within him.

C-R-R-A-S-S-S-H!!!

The sudden explosion of sound came from the kitchen area; Percy looked across sharply to locate the source and cause of the disturbance.

At first glance he thought he was seeing an apparition, a ghostly white figure within a cloud of fine particles, but on closer inspection he realised it was in fact the shapely form of Molly's sister wearing an expression of shock across her normally buoyant features.

The source of the earth shattering sound appeared to be the demolition of 12 dinner plates in simultaneous disintegration.

He opened his mouth to express a mixture of concern, question and statement but got no further than that before fate intervened.

From the indoor green to the left he subconsciously heard the call.

'Ok Trigger, plug in the lights!'

THUD! THUD! THUD! THUD! THUD...

B-A-N-G!!!

M-E-E-O-O-O-W!!!

Percy stood rooted to the spot, mouth ajar, the events unfurling before his eyes; it was like the slow motion action replay of an Indiana Jones movie.

The staccato repetitive explosion of numerous safety fuse lights reverberated around the room like a machine gun, and it was hardly surprising to see one or two of the senior members diving for cover.

Perhaps, as he would discover later, it hadn't helped the situation that Molly had given all the lights a bit of a spruce up by putting them on a 'low heat no spin' cycle in the washing machine the night before?

One or two fuses were a bit too slow in responding, given their age, and row after row of previously sparkling fairy lights 'overcooked' in a fraction of a second, sending showers of sparks cascading to the floor.

RAT-A-TAT-A-TAT-A-TAT-A-TAT...

Eric over-reacted as per usual shouting, 'The Russians are coming!' as he dived under the nearest table waving a white handkerchief.

The louder explosion followed in the merest of moments as the main fuse box blew with a very loud bang, springing the metal door open and sending the cover crashing across the room.

A number of ceramic fuse holders ricocheted like Jumping Jack's flying from their recessed sockets in quick succession as if set off by a special effects expert.

Tendrils of blue smoke filtered across the green as the emergency lighting kicked into action casting a ghostly and very unhealthy looking pallor across the dumbstruck members.

Traces of powdered glittering resin flickered in the subdued eerie gloom as it cascaded slowly to the floor.

That was bad enough, in fact more than enough for anyone to absorb in such a brief moment. No one had time to consider the likelihood or consequences of any further resultant phenomenon occurring.

However, a chain of events had begun and it wasn't over yet...

Rollo had, for once, been minding his own business and at that point been curled up in the large wicker basket holding the roots of the giant Christmas tree. The piles of soft fake snow made just the perfect bedding for him to conduct the most urgent and necessary business, that of having a snooze.

As he dreamt, one eye occasionally flickered open to keep check on the proceedings in the clubhouse, whilst his tail trembled and twitched, rising into the branches above.

It rose just in time to make a convenient earth connection to the nearest fuse light as the Christmas tree's electrical decorations shattered in spectacular fashion.

Passing a high voltage charge though a recumbent cat is never a good idea at the best of times, especially one with a reputation for having the ability to leapfrog from full-on sleep mode to stark staring crazy berserker within a nanosecond.

In a fraction Rollo went through a transformation from perfectly groomed pussy to madcap manic moggie; to any onlooker at that moment he looked like all of his hair had been gelled in a Billy Idol punk rock style and then freeze dried in liquid oxygen.

There was a vague bluish halo of electrical discharge surrounding Rollo's body like a mini aura and a definite smell of singed hair in the ether as the sizzling moggie received a shock awakening.

It was perhaps a trifle fortunate for him that the fuse box blew almost instantaneously preventing any further damage to his paraphernalia other than to his now charred coat.

Rollo always had a reputation for over-reacting to unusual or unexpected events, usually a spur of the moment response to something that stimulated his curiosity, or necessitated further investigation.

Most of the time the events were of the pleasurable, amusing or entertaining type or, at worst, contained some element of 'scaredy-cat' mentality from which he always emerged safe from harm, chuckling to himself at the experience.

What he didn't respond best to was any event that he could not anticipate, especially one that was likely to cause him even the slightest discomfort or pain.

Most certainly he wasn't about to appreciate the impromptu and uninvited use of his tail to provide an earth socket for several hundred twinkling fairy lights which had decided to pop their combined clogs .

For want of a better expression Rollo threw a tantrum.

It was a particularly large one!

As tantrums went it was a humdinger, a full-on frenetic overload of frenzied spontaneity with no sense of direction, purpose or reasoning.

Rollo left the formerly secure haven of the chargrilled Christmas tree, his smoking tail extended to the rear as he travelled 16 feet before his paws even touched the ground.

He had no idea where he was heading, only the irrational reasoning that he was heading there very quickly and that any direction would take him away from the nagging pain in his tail.

A quick glance over his shoulder confirmed that it was still smoking and quite bald at the far end.

Cat reasoning usually extended to basic logic, that of 'an eye for an eye' and he was desperately keen on exacting retribution, but had no real plan on how to instigate it, therefore he just hit out as he sailed past objects at breakneck speed.

In quick succession, he sliced through Frenchie's braces causing a near disastrous unveiling had it not been for the additional belt, shredded the bottom of Cynthia's baggy woollen tights and tore swathes out of Gloria's cardigan.

He pirouetted like a tornado through the pile of paper chains, dislodging the sleeping Matilda Bagshott who woke up in a bleary eyed and confused state as she landed on the hard floor with a bump!

Faster than a ricocheting pinball, he pounced, bounced and bashed into everything that looked remotely susceptible to instant damage leaving further carnage in his wake.

Whatever wasn't breakable was tumbled over, turned aside or knocked flying as the rampant Rollo reeked havoc.

He passed the scaffolding tower carrying Derek, David and Bernard, lashing out at the metal poles but failing to make any significant impression; however in doing so he managed to hook his front claws into the thick manilla rope holding the wooden chocks in place.

He took off like a thunderbolt towards the stack of tables and chairs on the far side of the arena, with the chocks clattering and banging on the floor behind him adding further irritation.

The scaffolding tower, without its restraining wedges, rocked a little and then, with the substantial weight of the three amigos, Derek, David and Bernard atop its construction, began to wobble, only held in place by its small hand brake.

Abbey and Timothy were never ones to miss an opportunity for misbehaviour and no one was going to notice further mischievousness in the subdued haze.

They surreptitiously reached over and released the handbrake on the foot of the tower, then hid very quickly.

With the centrifugal force of the men's mass acting like a pendulum, the large erection slowly gathered momentum and began to trundle down the slight inclination at five miles per hour much to the alarm of its occupants.

Their cries of panic added to the surreal sense of the scene as Percy continued to watch events unfold with his mouth agape as he witnessed what appeared to be a scene from Dante's Inferno.

The emergency lighting had a way of making everything look garish and alien in the wisps of rising smoke, with a cat moving through it like a mysterious speeding phantom; a miniature apparition.

Rollo in the meantime continued to throw a wobbly, his dilated pupils searching frantically left and right for means of escape before spying a roof light ajar.

He made a bolt for it by way of the nearest convenient route.

That turned out to be the roughly assembled barrow based structure of furniture put together earlier by the junior members Paul and Johnny.

Rollo raced up the ladder, bypassing the workers hanging onto the struts for dear life, before using his talons to claw his way, hissing and spitting, up the back of Sheila's neoprene body suit.

A succession of screamed 'OUCHES!' and 'ARRGHS!' followed from the very unimpressed Sheila Ramsbottom before Rollo reached the lighting rig and raced unceremoniously for the exit.

Percy stared on in a speechless trance stepping zombie-like towards the kitchen counter suddenly in need of a very strong coffee, possibly a quadruple espresso, never for one second taking his eyes off the unfolding comedy of errors.

The runaway scaffold tower was beginning to gather pace and the occupants wisely decided to abandon ship.

David leapfrogged into a passing settee, to much protest from the groaning springs, whilst Derek simply grabbed hold of the Christmas tree as it sailed passed him.

The reasoning itself was very secure, the scaffolding was moving and the tree was not; therefore it had to be safer.

The reality was that the evergreen goliath was not designed to withstand the arrival of Derek's very substantial form.

Percy absent-mindedly noted that the vice captain hit every branch in his freefall descent and that he really should use a stout rope the next time he took up abseiling.

Bernard, last to leave nevertheless thought he had struck upon a touch of good fortune as the tower rolled past a long line of unplaced decorative lights hanging down from the ceiling and he seized the opportune moment to leap.

He landed perfectly, dead centre on the cable, remembering his basic army training to wrap his feet in interlocking fashion around the lower length allowing his hands to surrender the bulk of the weight to his lower body.

He breathed excitedly and glanced around in the hope that someone had noted his act of audacity and maybe even caught it on camera.

His bravado was short lived as his eardrums were assailed by a loud snapping sound from above his head.

If he didn't know better it almost sounded like...'

'O-O-O-H N-O-O-O-O-O-O-O!!!'

The lights were in fact fastened securely to the other side of the hall at ceiling height and had been cable clipped into place; sadly for Bernard they were not designed to support this unexpected arrival and proved to be his downfall as they snapped in progressive order.

Like Tarzan of old, he swooped across the green missing only the apeman's throaty call in his unscripted impression of the television hero.

He might have left the scaffold as a high flying apeman, but he certainly arrived in a lot lesser capacity, more like George of the Jungle.

In a curving arc he swept down towards the ground...

'A-R-R-R-G-G-H-H!!!'

His feet at one point trailed only two feet above the green; many an actor would have then taken the opportunity simply to let go and descend gracefully to the mat accompanied by a rapturous round of applause.

Bernard was too terrified to even consider the opportunity however and he hung on in his frozen state, as the cable passed its pivotal point; he began to ascend in an arc up towards the other side.

He eyes began to widen as he focused on his probable point of impact and half registered a mixture of 'YES PLEASE' and 'OH MY GOD' as he powered towards his unlikely landing place.

'LOOK OUT!!!'

****

Percy had side stepped in crablike fashion towards the kitchen counter, unable to tear his eyes away from the crazy circus act.

His hair on the back of his head prickled with a mixture of panic, alarm and disbelief; he was sure that any second now he would awake to find himself in his rectory bed.

He was mindful of the need to send a rescue party to the aid of any pensioners, who had been, embarrassingly caught short in the toilets when the lights went out.

CRUMP!

Percy's mesmerised walk came to a halt abruptly as he arrived at the counter stomach and knees first.

Absent-mindedly he reached for an empty coffee mug, averting his eyes from the impending escalation of disastrous events, before putting down the sugar bowl and trying again.

A flour-caked Sarah Jane looked up from a smoking tray of deflated Yorkshire puddings with a foaming fire extinguisher in one hand and a soggy Victoria sponge in the other.

It was fair to say there was chaos in the kitchen too!

She was knee-deep in flame retardant froth and, from the crazed look in her eyes, Percy could tell she was perhaps not in full control of all her faculties at that precise moment.

She stood up to face the vicar, setting the tray of burnt offerings down on the cooker hob and catching Percy on the nose with a generous dollop of foam.

'Er, don't you think it would be a good idea to let go of the trigger now?' volunteered Percy with a wry smile as he dodged the next burst of frothing fluid.

'Oops!' said Sarah with a hollow laugh that lacked any real conviction of sanity.

She let go of the activator and placed the fire extinguisher on the floor.

'LOOK OUT!'

Bernard's cry for help interrupted their interaction at that point as both glanced sharply across the hall to the source of the shout.

Perhaps, at the last moment, Bernard had considered it not a good idea to land on Sheila and had let go in the final seconds hoping to arrive safely on the catwalk that ran around the lighting rig.

After all, he'd already had the misfortune to misappropriate regions of Sheila's body before and he ruefully remembered the smack that followed so was keen to avoid a dubiously orchestrated repetition.

Whatever his thoughts, his eyes continued to focus on the form of Sheila Ramsbottom and he was in the process of considering how deliciously sexy she looked in her body suit when his body made contact with the ground.

Well, it didn't actually quite make contact with the ground straight away; it first collided with the pyramidal stack of tables and chairs.

CRASH!!

GROAN!

It was clear that Bernard wasn't wholly enjoying his day and the impact of the furniture on his torso did nothing to improve the situation.

Percy reflected on the bright side; 'Well at least Bernard would have a guaranteed place in the choir this Christmas!'

Bernard let go of the lighting cable and grabbed hold of the nearby ladder supports as he transferred his battered body from the flex before extracting his bruised extremities from the various edges of the furniture.

THUD... SN-N-A-P-P!

The first part of his escape plan had surprisingly gone very well indeed and as the ladder had already supported the lithe figures of Paul and Johnny as well as the svelte and leggy form of Sheila he had no reason to suppose it would do otherwise for him.

The ladder was old and had a tendency to house a variety of bugs, mainly woodworm, so it was only natural that the wooden rungs would not take favourably to a sturdy 14 stone of flesh and bone arriving at 40 miles per hour.

The first rung gave way with a distinctive snapping of stressed timber.

Bernard shook his head from side to side in disbelief as Johnny and Paul looked on from the gantry.

THUD... SNAP... THUD... SNAP... THUD... SNAP...

It was nearly too comical to watch, almost like an old black and white silent movie, as Bernard slid down the outer rails with his hands as the rungs gave way beneath his feet one after another.

There were 32 rungs on the ladder!!

He arrived at the bottom seven seconds later thankful at least that the youngsters previously had the common sense to place a soft mattress in the barrow just in case.

With the two lengths of ladder uprights still in his hands he almost felt like an inverted stilt walker, and he gave thanks for the fact that they were at least fastened at the top so he wouldn't have to worry about a long length of timber arriving, unannounced, on his head.

Shelia had other ideas though.

She had been at the top end of the ladder when Bernard had arrived without warning and was not over enthusiastic about the idea of spending the afternoon precariously balanced on top of a 10 metre pole. Wrapping her shapely assets firmly around the length of wood, she proceeded to slide down it like an enthusiastic firefighter.

She did very well indeed for the first nine metres until she encountered the still recovering Bernard floundering on the mattress.

'OOMPH!'

The unexpected appearance knocked the breath from his body leaving him winded, as Sheila landed, legs akimbo, square in his lap.

She looked at Bernard breathlessly with a twinkle in her eye and a touch of insanity in her expression before finally speaking.

'Well that was good for me, how about you?'

With that, she leant over and planted a smacker on his lips before laughing raucously, leaping to her feet and walking away with a swaying swagger.

Percy looked back into the kitchen with an expression of total disbelief.

'Has the ENTIRE world gone stark raving mad?' he inquired of the foam splattered Sarah Jane.

She considered his statement briefly whilst filling up the mug which Percy still held outstretched, the steam rising between them.

'Well,' she said, placing the hot cafetière safely down in its receptacle on the counter, 'sauce for the goose, as they say...'

Without warning, she leant across the counter and gave the vicar a long passionate kiss full on the lips, her hand reaching behind his head to make sure he couldn't escape.

She stood back after a few seconds leaving Percy wide-eyed, breathless and at a total loss for words, although the incredulous expression on his face spoke volumes.

'Mmmm, not bad,' she said with a playful smile on her face as she looked him directly in his eyes, 'not bad at all vicar.'

Percy fled, the noise of his flight and the clattering of the exit door finally separating the newly wed Molly and Bertie, who had been enjoying a lengthy passionate embrace nearby.

They looked up with a smile in the gloom, not yet taking in the state of the indoor arena.

'Did we miss anything?' enquired Bertie.

****

Percy stood in the pulpit, looking down the church aisle towards the bell tower and the superbly decorated Christmas tree that stood in all its glory near to the door.

To any visitor entering the sanctuary of the church it would appear as if they had entered the Garden of Eden albeit during the winter season.

The inner sanctum was dressed with seasonal wild flower arrangements trimmed in ivy and holly, their colours tastefully lit by a multitude of candlelight reflecting on the floral displays.

In glorious splendour, the pastel arrangements subtly added to the magnificence of the stunning tree, now decked with white, yellow and red trimming, which dwarfed the centre aisle.

Nevertheless Percy was unmoved by the majestic scene.

He was in deep thought and oblivious to the evocative atmosphere that filled the stone walls with a sense of grace and reverence.

Had Percy been more focussed on his surroundings he might have noticed the pair of adult grey squirrels sitting on the ceiling rafters.

He might also have spotted the four tiny grey heads popping in and out of the very top of the tree foliage where the youngest members of the family were also looking down at the vicar.

Nonetheless, the Reverend Percival Peabody remained totally and blissfully unaware of his newly acquired miniature congregation as they viewed him from afar with a mixture of inquisitiveness and curiosity.

He was pondering reflectively on the most recent events to overtake his close-knit community.

It had already been a couple of weeks since the fiasco with the interior decoration and he was amazed that no one had been hurt; in fact apart from a few cuts and minor abrasions as well as one or two bruised egos all had ended up unscathed.

As always, and Percy had a sneaking suspicion as to the source, nothing remained secret for long and the goings-on were soon leaked to the news hungry press.

The footage from the club's closed circuit television system had become a collector's item, nearly everyone had seen it at least twice, and copies of it were selling on e-bay at £100 each.

At last count there were orders for 563 DVDs of the recording and it was fast becoming a cult classic.

The black and white, grainy film lasted just 38 minutes but provided some of the funniest moments, and memories, that the club had ever witnessed.

In terms of sheer entertainment value it certainly was the nearest the village would ever get to creating an amateur production of Raiders of the Lost Ark', in a much condensed form of course.

Percy sighed deeply and leafed through the Bible to Psalms, not really taking any notice of the pages he was flicking past.

He was in another world of his own completely and he continued to ponder how miraculously the congregation of Lower South-Borough continued to lead such a charmed life.

In biblical terms, the club certainly had the Midas touch as it seemed no matter what they did, or became involved in, however ridiculous, questionable or risqué, the resultant outcome was always fortuitous.

With every incident, occurrence, or undertaking the notoriety of their members' exertions became ever more legendary to the point where one of the national papers now ran a daily news story, questionably entitled Percy's column.

The tabloid had lapped up the latest instalment and had even suggested the possibility of a Christmas promotional offer. A copy of their latest blockbuster best selling movie was to be given away with every online purchase of 'THE PASTOR'S PARTY' as it was now affectionately referred to.

Still, the income from the uncensored pirate tape had been more than enough to hire a professional display organiser to put everything right, after Molly's cleaners had finished of course.

The result was the finest seasonal showcase Percy had ever seen.

It came complete with a real sleigh and six animated reindeer prancing in realistic snowfall.

The nativity scene had been reinstated with a magnificent archangel overseeing the birth of Jesus in a life-size mock up of a manger, whilst the new Christmas tree rose from the floor until it touched the club roof.

Lights festooned every square inch of the ceiling, twinkling, sparkling and chasing in a riotous display of moving colour that quite took the breath away with their ever changing patterns.

Percy was quite sure he would have never seen anything quite so magnificent had he travelled to the North Pole and visited Santa's Grotto for real.

All too soon, the past events were left behind only to be discussed, laughed about and reflected on at late hours sitting beside the burning embers of a fading fire with a warm brandy.

For a while now the Reverend had been organising the notes of his experiences at Lower South-Borough, compiling them into a semblance of order; he felt that sometime soon there would be a need and use for them.

He continued to explore his thoughts as he stared emptily into space, focusing on some distant part of the stone wall opposite, with no comprehension of anything happening around him, indeed a 76 piece jazz band could have marched right by and he would never have noticed.

For the 20th time in 10 minutes, Percy's thoughts travelled back to the footage of recent events.

He had watched the first screening at the village hall, along with nearly every member of the community; it had been a sell out and had raised a considerable contribution for the church restoration fund.

In fact, he smiled to himself, there would soon be enough to build a new church, and probably a new community centre for the village too.

The original rough video recording had been edited, refined, elaborated with added text, subtitles, and full colour enhancement by an entertainments entrepreneur and the resulting film had been quite memorable.

There was little wonder it was selling well on e-bay.

The film had of course encompassed a much wider perspective, almost as if the director had poetic licence. The shot of Trigger plugging in the lights panned quickly to an external shot showing the blackout expanding outwards like a virus across the village and the county.

They had no idea until the following morning of the extent of Tony Havershall's electrical handiwork when the regional news ran a story speculating as to the cause of the mysterious shutdown, which caused a power loss to 50,000 homes.

Of course, there had also been the hilarious shot of Molly washing the decorations and the sight of hundreds of fairy lights spinning around inside the washing machine had many a person rolling in the aisles with tears streaming down their faces.

There was a touch of divine providence too, as the video tapes showed that the only place remaining lit during the expansive blackout was the church.

Percy had laughed, smiled, shed tears and offered applause like everyone else as the film had rolled across the lens almost to the end.

Then, in the dying seconds, the lens had zoomed into the kitchen area for a close-up of Sarah Jane grabbing hold of Percy before snogging him passionately over the counter much to his shock and surprise, which was very evident from the expression on his face.

Since then he had become a stranger in the club, a fact that had began to concern some of his closest friends. Molly, Bertie, Jack and Russell were amongst those calling often at his home to check on his health, not to mention his sanity, and the contents of his fridge.

The Reverend Percival Peabody was a deeply troubled man.

Overnight he had woken abruptly with the sudden haunting realisation that, sooner or later, the Rt Hon. Eugene Augustus Thomas the Third was going to see the footage and then the gates of hell would seem a safer, more preferable place to visit than the bishop's door.

Percy sighed even more deeply than before, and closed the good book as he finally refocused on his immediate surroundings.

The church indeed looked quite stunning and all was set for the midnight mass; after all, this was December 24th, the night before Christmas.

He wandered slowly, thoughtfully down the aisle away from the pulpit and into the chilled afternoon air, remembering at the last minute to close the door firmly shut behind him.

Without thinking, he followed his feet where they had taken him a million times previously, and he found himself passing by the glazed windows of the clubhouse lounge.

Inside he could see a number of members enjoying a very friendly game of bowls much to the amusement of several onlookers enjoying the seasonal entertainment.

Apparently they were indulging in a game of triples with Tony, Bertie and Molly on one team and Sheila, Bernard and Russell on the other.

Bernard was dressed up in a full Santa Claus outfit, whilst Sheila was very much his complimentarily attired assistant, which made for some very interesting bowling.

Percy pondered.

Bernard and Sheila... Hmm...

He hadn't seen that relationship coming; the older, wealthier but down to earth working man getting together with the younger, sexy tomboy-ish Aussie. There certainly WAS a touch of magic in the air this Christmas.

He gazed in again.

It appeared that Bertie and Molly were dressed as elves, whilst Russell was more suitably attired as Old Father Time.

At that point, Tony Havershall turned around, leaving the vicar in a somewhat confused state; why on earth was he dressed up as Snow White?

Movement in the lounge area suddenly distracted Percy's attention; there were large numbers of members present, mostly in fancy seasonal costumes and it looked like everyone had made an extra special effort to dress up this year.

He smiled proudly and a small tear welled up in his eye.

For all their misdemeanours, the ups 'n' downs, he loved all his parishioners with a deeply felt affection and a loyalty, which he knew was spontaneous, mutual and sincere.

He looked towards the kitchen and his heart gave a small, uncontrollable leap; Sarah Jane Coddle was serving tea and coffee at the kitchen counter as per usual.

Percy felt strange, almost as if a large number of butterflies were racing uncontrollably around the inside of his stomach and he had to admit to himself that he felt a little weak at the knees too.

For a brief second he was tempted to go in and join the gathering, but hesitated, 'No,' he thought, let them all enjoy the seasonal goodwill without feeling the need to put on airs and graces.

It was after all the season to be jolly, he mused quietly, as he turned away, his feet now making a crisp sound on the pebbles where the moisture was already beginning to freeze.

He glanced up towards the heavens; the sky was clear and a darkening blue, with the first stars already twinkling mischievously.

Percy sighed deeply with a feeling of hope, a touch of happiness and a sprinkling of previously unfelt emotion as he trudged lightly towards the vicarage.

He sensed tonight would be something special, a midnight Mass unknown in previous years, one to be the beacon, a guiding light for years to come, and yet, he could not put his finger on why.

He paused, just for a second.

And where the hell was that damn cat?

Rollo had not been seen since his near electrocution two weeks ago.

Back at the church two cats curled up together in the crib next to the porcelain replica of baby Jesus.

****

It was 10.30 p.m. on Christmas Eve; most of the fire had burned low in the grate, a steady stream of fading embers rising into the chimney.

The majority of the members had headed, or staggered home earlier to prepare for the days of festive celebration ahead and to get ready for the mass.

Those that remained were huddled together in deep conversation around the last of the burning logs, a bottle of vintage brandy on the table in front and several glasses standing three-quarters empty.

Around them sat the closest of Percy's friends, Charlie, Dennis. Bertie, Russell, Patrick, Clifford, Molly, Derek and Sheila.

They were deep in discussion about their favourite vicar.

'There are a lot of changes coming to the parish,' said Sheila.

'And poor old Percy is none the wiser,' smiled Bertie.

'Still?' questioned Patrick.

'Still,' confirmed Clifford.

'We must make preparations for the days ahead for the sake of our dear friend; he will need all our help and support soon,' said Russell.

'I'm one step ahead of that one,' laughed Charlie, 'whatever happens our dear Percy will not be left wanting...'

Russell looked up sharply, 'What do you mean? What have you done?' he asked half with a question, half with a demand.

'Oh don't worry,' laughed Charlie, 'this will be our vicar's finest moment, and he will never be left wanting ever again.'

Sheila laughed loudly, 'Charlie Chesterford I know what you are like, you never do anything easily or by half measures, what have you done?'

'Trust me,' said Charlie with a wink of the eye, 'just trust me.'

Patrick laughed aloud, 'and what happens if...'

Derek raised his one good eye to the heavens, 'If?'

'Yes,' repeated Patrick, 'what happens if.'

They gazed around at each other with knowing smiles as Derek spoke quietly. 'We stand together.'

As one, they raised their glasses towards the middle of the table with a chinking of glass.

'To Percy' said Russell.

'TO PERCY!' roared the others in unison, knocking back the final mouthfuls of their brandies before hurling their glasses into the burning fire.

****

It was the most perfect of nights; a crisp hoar frost covered the ground in a tapestry of tiny white crystals and tendrils of ground fog rose from the open fields nearby.

The sky was a brilliant darkened shade of turquoise blue covered in miniature stars that twinkled and glimmered in a glittering display of far away illumination.

The North Star gleamed brightest of all, dominating the skies like a large uncut diamond gleaming with a clarity of brilliance and hue.

Percy stood on the steps of the church, and gazed out in transient awe at the breathless wonder of God's creation; for a second encapsulating the full picture deep in his mind, as a memory to be treasured.

The haunting shriek of an owl calling into the night air added a sense of poignant eeriness sending a chill of excitement up Percy's spine.

To anyone who cared to look it was the picture postcard perfection of the night before Christmas, as it was always meant to be in fable and legend.

The vicar sighed quietly, at long last, at peace with himself inside after what had seemed months of having his soul tormented by deeply troubling dreams and fears.

He felt, at last, his search for inspirational guidance had finally led to a lucidity that gave reason to the rhyme and brought reconciliation at last to his disturbed spirit. It seemed like a huge weight had been lifted from his shoulders and he vowed quietly to himself to make sure that THIS midnight Mass would be the finest that the parish had ever seen.

He gazed once more over the nearby landscape and marvelled at the beauty of Lower South-Borough, the village now coated by Jack Frost's icy touch like icing sugar on a sponge cake.

No matter how many times he saw that scene, it continued to enthral him as this time of the year still felt so very special to Percy, the season of goodwill to all humanity.

The chimes of the large clock resonated across the stilled, frozen air, announcing the arrival of another half hour. Percy glanced at his watch, 11.20 p.m. the seconds were ticking by and Christmas was just about upon them.

He shivered slightly, wrapping his thick full-length velvet cloak around him as he waited to greet the imminent arrival of the parishioners.

The slightly discordant strains of the church organ caught his ear, and he smiled to himself, clearly the organist's fingers were still a little stiff from the cold.

Harry 'The Hammer' Huckstable, a one time heavy-handed CID detective of some notoriety had been a born again Christian in the service of the parish for the last twenty years.

In the past, he had resembled 'Dirty Harry' but now in the prime of his mid-senior years his genial and gently spoken nature had affectionately earned him the nickname of Harmless Harry.

He was apparently working out the kinks in his ambidextrous extremities and, Percy noted with a wry smile, was doing so to the melody of the Munsters theme.

Percy gazed briefly back through the church door towards the grandiose and stunning pine tree rising into the rafters, its mass of tinsel and lights sparkling with the luminescence of myriad pinpoint coloured illuminations.

Beyond it, and lining each side of the pews, large candles burned brightly, smoking slightly in the very light draught, casting flickering shadows over the array of flowers that bedecked every bench and stone pillar.

He could see the members of the church choir filing into the pews adjacent to the altar that stood at the head of the aisle behind his pulpit.

The choir of Lower South-Borough were a mixed bunch, mainly teenagers studying at the nearby Great Meltings, a rather grandiose Music College of Virtuoso Excellence established by the local and late composer Benjamin Britten.

They all marched in, heads lowered, wearing full length white cloaks fastened at the waist by a simple red sash, whilst their cowls were pulled up over their lowered heads in pious deference as they solemnly chanted a Latin rendition of 'Return to Innocence.'

From a distance, Percy noticed that the boys appeared to be eating very well as one or two appeared to have shot up at an alarming rate and several were looking somewhat rotund.

The soft crunch of footsteps approaching from across the driveway alerted him to the fact he had been absent-mindedly distant in mind and spirit; the first parishioners were already arriving.

A number of headlights were cutting across the car park, illuminating swathes through the light winter haze, as in the distance a veritable convoy of vehicles snaked nose to tail through the winding back roads heading towards the sanctuary of the church.

Percy felt an overwhelming sense of humility and a hint of moisture welled to his eyes at the sight. It was very reminiscent of his all time favourite film 'Field of Dreams.'

He always felt such an affinity for the humble story of the farmer who was beleaguered by a dream that haunted him with its heartfelt message.

Truly, the word of God had reached out into his community through his own unassuming piety and his parishioners having listened and learned were coming together as one for Christmas.

'Good evening vicar.'

'Hello Percy.'

'Cold evening eh Reverend.'

'Good to see you old chap.'

The warm and affectionate greetings came thick and fast as more and more of his community arrived all at once, paying their heartfelt respects as they passed by him into the awaiting church.

'You're looking well Percy, are you ready?'

Ronald 'Squiffy' Regis beamed up at the vicar as he walked up towards him, his hand extended in respectful friendship as the exchanged glance spoke of years of enduring camaraderie and mutual understanding.

'Hello Ronald,' said Percy, in soft tones, remembering the last time the two had met in circumstances that had then been reversed.

'Are you ready then Percy?' he asked again.

The vicar of Lower South-Borough contemplated just for a second and then, noting the car park now devoid of any one else turned to follow the former president into the church.

He sighed one final time.

'Yes,' he said, 'finally I'm ready,' and with that he closed the door behind him.

****

The church was packed, literally rammed to the rafters, every aisle full to capacity with standing room only at the back, whilst to the sides of the pews Percy noted a number of recognisable members of the press including Jiggy Jenkins from the local rag.

There was a tremendous air of expectancy throughout, the very atmosphere buzzed with exuberant excitement; the vicar had never seen such a prestigious turnout for his Christmas Mass and his heart swelled with pride.

It seemed almost perfect to him, the pinnacle of his career, at home with his favourite people sharing the joys of the season on what always seemed to be the most pleasurable and heartfelt time of the year.

Percy was for once, absolutely sure that here, in the centre of his small universe at last everything was as it should be, the stage set, the players cast and the spectators present for the cumulation of the years events.

With the New Year just one week away this was the moment with his 'children' of all ages that the festivities truly began, and what better place for them to begin but right here at midnight on Christmas eve.

He checked his watch, 11.40 p.m., time to set things in motion; with a sense of purpose, he strode down the centre aisle, his cassock and cloak flowing behind him as he took centre stage and all eyes followed him respectfully.

What could possibly go wrong on a night such as this? thought Percy.

As he passed the front pew his eyes caught those of Charles Chesterford who seemed to be stifling an uncontrollable urge to burst into hysterical laughter, whilst his neighbour Doris Doolittle elbowed him harshly in the ribs with a sideways 'Ssshhh,' to quieten him.

Percy recognised that look in Charlie's eyes; he had seen it before, too many times, and usually before he partook in his latest prank or some outlandish scheme.

For a second Reverend Percival Peabody hesitated, overcome with a sudden mad desire to turn around and run away before events overtook him, but then his conscience stirred, fortifying him and he stepped positively towards the pulpit.

What the hell, he thought, no matter what surprise Charlie had in store, he was ready for anything.

He reached the top of the pulpit, opened the good book to the pre-marked page as the choir stood up and Harry flexed his fingers to strike up the first hymn.

'Please be upstanding, let's sing together hymn 231, While Shepherd's watched their flocks by night...'

He raised his outstretched hands with his palms uppermost signalling his congregation to rise.

****

The ecclesiastical service flowed without a hitch through to midnight amid rising fervour and intense speculation as the Reverend Percival Peabody lifted his flock in a spiritual high never felt before.

He was in fine fettle and the television cameramen discreetly filming the event, which he hadn't yet noticed, were beaming delightedly to themselves as the show went out across the nation.

Their producer rubbed his hands together gleefully, sensing a top award for 'best live show' en-route to his display cabinet.

Every year the crew turned up unannounced at a Christmas service to film their live broadcast for the BBC show 'Songs of Praise' and following the ongoing meteoric rise of Lower South-Borough's public profile they had arrived discreetly following an invitation from the club's committee.

The producer had a fine sense for perfect timing and a knack for being in the right place at the right time; they had been ably assisted by a member's anonymous tip-off to expect something very special indeed!

So far they had not been disappointed.

Apparently, everybody in the church was 'in' on the surprise, with the exception of Percival Peabody.

After years of exemplary service to the community, the parish had evidently seen fit to reward their vicar in a way they felt befitted the occasion.

They had all been aware, for some time, of gradual changes in the man who was not only their religious representative but also their personal confidante.

The feeling was not only mutual but empathic towards their spiritual figurehead as they felt he was long overdue for a time of 'receiving' rather than 'giving'; therefore they were ALL giving him their most immediate, undivided attention.

The evening that began so reverently, continued unabated as Percy gave the hushed and respectful audience his most evocative rendition ever of the story of Mary, Joseph and the birth of baby Jesus.

The traditional Christmas carols passed through the midnight hour with the addition of a more modern touch, Bing Crosby's 'White Christmas', before finishing much to the surprise and pleasure of the parishioners with a rousing chorus of 'Merry Christmas Everybody.'

The service came eventually, to the culmination of the evening's presentation and the passing of the plate, which Percy, with a gesture of his hand, indicated to the church custodians to commence.

Over in the front pew Charlie rubbed his hands in glee with the anticipation of what was to follow, barely able to contain himself.

Certainly there was an elevated degree of expectancy amongst the congregation which even Percy could sense but not explain, other than their mood was very much influenced by the moment.

The plates were solemnly handed to Dennis and Cynthia who had been sitting on opposite ends of the front pews in readiness, the vicar looked on with feelings of hope for seasonal generosity.

Each reached into their pockets and pulled out a crisp £50 note which they placed with great care into their respective dishes as they spoke softly under their breath, 'This is for you Percy!'

The plates began to pass along the front rows with each person in turn matching the first donation and whispering the same softly spoken message.

Percy stood in his pulpit and watched the procession of the plates with a look that passed from pleasant surprise to admiration then total astonishment; he was not so far away that he didn't recognise the silhouette of a £50 note.

By the time the plates reached the fifth row the piles of notes were standing 12 inches high in both receptacles and there were still a number of pews for them to navigate before they even reached the people standing at the back.

For not the first time in his life the vicars' jaw dropped in total disbelief as the mountain of money continued to grow.

Why there must be hundreds, no, thousands of pounds in those dishes already, he pondered to himself frantically as the wooden receptacles continued to move amongst the massed ranks.

Eventually, with a chorus line of beaming faces looking on, the piled high plates reached the television crew at the back of the audience.

TELEVISION CREW?

Percy stared, open-mouthed, at the sight of the cameras and crew that appeared to be 'rolling' at the back of the church; he simply had not noticed them before and he was suddenly, abruptly, taken aback.

WHAT ON EARTH WAS GOING ON?

The programme controller reached into his jacket pocket and emerged with what appeared to be a large piece of paper which he then proceeded to place on the collection plate.

Percy felt like control of the evening was slowly, but surely, slipping away from him into the unknown.

He reached for the microphone on the pulpit, which wasn't there anymore.

It was in fact in the hands of Charlie Chesterford who now stood beneath the pulpit with the vicar's broadcasting apparatus in his hands.

'Ladies and Gentlemen if I could have your attention please.'

Charlie's voice cut across the void of the church as the anticipative and expectant audience paid attention to the improvised introduction.

All the vicar could do was look on in shocked disbelief as the evening turned around in spectacular style with him as the spectator.

Charlie Chesterford was in his element and, with everyone on his side for once, he continued to enjoy the spectacle of the moment; it was about to cumulate with a flourish.

'For years our vicar, Reverend Percival Peabody, whom we all affectionately know as Percy, has served us loyally with devotion, care, and understanding. He has given us love and compassion, support and consideration, hope and belief, willing to give his last penny to help ANY of us achieve our dreams.'

A roar of appreciation swept around the room from which none abstained.

Charlie held up his hand and continued...

'Well tonight is our opportunity to give back to our vicar a small thank you, an appreciation of our gratitude to the man we all love, respect and care about...'

He paused for effect then raised his voice a few octaves...

'THE REVEREND PERCIVAL PEABODY!!!'

The church shook from end to end with the sounds of spontaneous applause and shouts of 'Hear! Hear!' from the onlookers.

Percy felt the blood rising to his cheeks as words failed him and he blushed deeply, not used to the praise or tribute.

Charlie turned to face the vicar up high in his pulpit.

'Reverend, tonight we would like you to accept this donation from all of us, for the day you should choose to retire, please accept it with all our love and appreciation...'

Before Percy had a chance to respond Charlie continued...'And, you will find on top a cheque from the BBC for £20,000 as a fund raising donation to the community!'

'But how?' called out Percy hoarsely, 'Why?' he spluttered.

'What are the BBC donating £20,000 for?'

Percy was totally overwhelmed by the rapidly evolving turn of events.

'Why', said Charlie, 'for filming this live televised seasonal event of course.'

He continued, 'and without further ado...' as he turned to the organist, 'Take it away Harry!'

Harry 'The Hammer' Huckstable needed no further encouragement, as he struck down hard, fingers splayed, on the previously prepared key arrangement he had practiced for so long when the vicar had been out of earshot.

As he struck the first chords, the eight members of the choir's front line stepped forward in angelic harmony.

'IS THIS THE REAL LIFE? IS THIS JUST FANTASY?'

The strains of Queen's classic rock track 'Bohemian Rhapsody' rose for the first time towards the church rafters like a religious opera as the orchestral accompaniment soared above the singers' soprano synchronization.

Above them a large video screen unfurled from the hidden heights allowing the lyrics to be displayed to the waiting crowds as they watched with bated breath.

A smoke machine under the pulpit subtly projected a carpet of mist out towards the centre aisle adding a ghostly aspect to the whole scenario as large panoramic pictures of gaily-clad transvestites rotated over and around the walls courtesy of hidden film projection.

It was a good indication of what was to come...

Percy stood on the pulpit in total shock, absolutely gobsmacked, staring in disbelief as pinnacles of living fire, created by laser, spiralled up the pews behind the choir.

By now, the audience were in full swing, all participating at full volume, joining in the celebration at the top of their voices with gusto and passion albeit not all in necessarily the correct tempo or pitch.

The rock opera swelled comprehensively, rolling through the entirety of the church, expanding exponentially as it continued unabated.

The television crew were quite obviously enjoying every second!

As one of the best selling modern day rock classics the melody was of course well known; so by the time the much anticipated climax of the song was nearly upon them, everyone in the house was primed, ready, and expectant.

All that was, of course, except Percy.

Nothing could have surprised him more had the Titanic resurrected from the crypt.

From behind the chorus line eight more figures emerged through the mist as it swirled around their feet; the elder members of the choir were joining in the fray!

Similarly clad in full-length white cloaks, with hoods raised, they stepped through the angelic support act and formed two lines of four, one behind the other, at the front of the steps before the altar, facing the audience.

The front four swept back their hoods revealing not choir singers, but instead upstanding members of the Lower South-Borough bowling club.

Molly, Shelia, Sarah and Phillippa were all wearing headset radio microphones, as were in fact the other cowled members behind them but Percy was too mesmerised to notice.

In falsetto tones, the ladies threw down the challenge,

'SCAWLONMUSHE, SCAWLONMUSHE, WILL YOU DO THE FANDANGO?'

The back four, as if auditioning for Abba, stepped into the matching gaps between the ladies before revealing themselves to be Clifford, Bertie, Bernard and Big Jim as they added their reply in deep stentorian roars,

'THUNDERBOLT AND LIGHTNING VERY VERY FRIGHTENING...'

The organ host thundered and howled alongside in a musical cacophony accompanying the tantalising, teasing vocals now rising to a crescendo in melodious splendour. As one, the singers crossed their arms over their chests and looked up to the rafters whilst white light shone from below turning them into eight spot lit angels.

Percy remained frozen to the spot but kept on eye on the nearby altar, half expecting the archangel Gabriel to put in an appearance.

At the back of the church the jubilant film producer laughed excitedly, clapping his hands with joy, as he gave a nod to the nearby pyrotechnics man; meanwhile Jiggy Jenkins, normally a man never lost for words, stood speechless as the point of his pencil broke under the strain of resting on his immobile stationery pad.

For Percy everything became a stupendous, spontaneous and surreal blur of impressions superimposed on one another as all at once the various elements peaked together.

Harry was having the time of his life and hamming it up in the extreme; as the rock aria reached its crescendo he pumped the pedals hard, pulled out all the stops and kicking his stool out behind him launched himself into the keyboard with a flurry of fingers over the ivories.

Thunderflashes rippled along the edge of the pews to the rear of the singers as large synthetic clouds of smoke burst skyward and laser beams rippled through them like rampaging buffalo.

Above, on the beams a number of small grey animated objects clung on for dear life, claws embedded in the timber, eyes wide open in shock, hackles raised as if in a wind tunnel as they experienced the most exhilarating experience of their sheltered lives.

The squirrels had found Walt Disney in Lower South-Borough!

Down below, the momentum of the song was reaching its crescendo.

Exploding in a chemistry of air guitar and storming lyricism, the theme suddenly, flawlessly, changed in a perfectly executed sequential mix as the eight choir angels became chorus line sinners in a flick of an eye.

Clasping their hands across their chests like praying mantis they simultaneously ripped open their Velcro fastened cloaks and tossed then to one side revealing their hidden content.

'OH MY GOD!!!'

Percy could not believe his eyes, but the audience could and they went wild.

The eight members were dressed in body hugging black corsets, with matching stockings, suspenders, high heels and whips.

La Cage Aux Folles had found religion in The Rocky Horror Revue and was bringing it 'live' to Percy's church!

Together as one they raised their hands to the heavens with panache and gusto; wild eyed and hyper they prepared to give the vicar the biggest Christmas stocking filler ever.

The words flashed up on the screen as Harry launched full-blooded into the accompaniment, and the eight Transylvanian cross-dressing cabaret stars led the dance. As one the combined members and parish of Lower South-Borough indulged the cameras with a seasonal tribute they would never forget.

'LET'S DO THE TIME WARP AGAIN...'

Percy stood briefly in a state of shock, numbed momentarily into submission, but then, with a wry smile and a secular sense of slight insanity he thought, 'What the hell, if you can't beat them, join them...'

If it was to be his last Christmas at Lower South-Borough, he might as well go out with a bang!

He descended the stairs to a roar of mass approval, took centre stage as he retrieved the microphone and with his clerical robes wafting in the smoke like Batman's cloak, led the anarchy.

'IT'S JUST A JUMP TO THE LEFT...'

Had anyone walked through the door at that particular moment they could be forgiven for thinking they had stumbled on a secret tryst, a communion of sinners, seditionists and devil worshippers.

The congregation of Lower South-Borough were having the time of their lives and without a doubt this was the best midnight mass any had ever, or would ever attend.

For the first time in year's Reverend Percival Peabody was enjoying every moment without fear of religious rebuttal or dire consequence. Even American gospel rock concerts had nothing on this, he reflected as he placed his hands on his hips and encouraged everyone to bring their knees in tight.

The door at the rear of the church creaked slowly open, unnoticed by all except the vicar who was in direct line of sight;

he expected it to be a forgetful parishioner who had overslept and thought 'better late than never.'

He wouldn't have cared if the Pope himself had walked through the door right at that second, but it wasn't the Pope.

Bishop Eugene Augustus Thomas the Third stepped through the opening closely followed by a small procession of chastised monks from his most celibate order.

The 'Communion of Divine Pentecostal Perfection' was the bishop's personal prodigy and, by comparison, made the Cistercian monks look like raving hedonists on mind-altering drugs.

The bishop had been concerned that Reverend Percival Peabody had not replied to his offer of a promotion, and he was not one to let the Church's most respected and lucrative asset slip from his clutches.

A number of newspaper stories had caught his eye recently, and he had become increasingly disturbed by the reported goings on at the small parish. Even more so when the whispered suggestions floated in on the ether that there was apparently a new female arrival who was disturbing the natural order of balance, not to mention the Reverend's normal sense of being.

Bishop Eugene Augustus Thomas the Third was a devout, pious man and fervently fanatical about the lifestyle of his religious order. He encouraged all forms of self-chastisement and ran his diocese in the manner of a 13th century Spanish monastery where stone cells, timber board beds and ice cold showers were the order of the day.

He preached voraciously on the sins of evil; chocolate was Satan's blood money, bubble baths were un-godly and music an instrument of pleasure reserved only for Lucifer's disciples.

Worse still, was the female form, which he fervently scorned as that of the devil in disguise, put on this planet to entice, corrupt, seduce and lead into temptation any cleric not worthy or capable of resistance.

On hearing that such an ungodly creature was tempting his prized asset the Bishop had gathered his most zealous members to undertake an urgent pilgrimage.

Dressing them in their best brown hessian sackcloth he marched them barefoot along the 39 mile route to the sound of whip-assisted soul purging and mournful chanting.

The bishop was on a mission of mercy and it was going to require a LOT of mutual flagellation.

The party set off in the dead of night, to incur the coldest, frostiest, most unappealing conditions as best befitted their quest, armed only with three French sticks and a tub of raw tuna.

Appropriately, in the same time it took to create God's earth, they arrived seven days later, or, more to the point, seven nights later, and, as they swayed towards the church Eugene Augustus Thomas the Third began to have deep misgivings.

The church appeared to be alive with flashing lights and living flame; smoke rose from the eaves whilst the banshee wail of the siren screamed and howled from its core.

He had no doubt that Satan himself had risen from the pit in the confines of Lower South-Borough church and the Jezebel Spirit had been released from its incarceration.

Clutching the large rough-hewn wooden cross that hung around his neck, he led the wild-eyed, frothing and agitated monks towards the massive oak door.

Fervently muttering the first few lines of an appropriate exorcism to cast out the evil possession, he stepped forward and pushed the door slowly open.

Hell was apparently having a rave and he had arrived uninvited.

It took a few moments even for the bishop's sturdy soul to take in and accept the visual carnage inside; it was enough to tip the hardiest of zealots over the edge, more than plenty to push the religious fanatic past the point of no return.

He inflated his vast lungs like a giant bellow, gathered his voice and, throwing etiquette or sane reasoning to the wind, let rip...

'IN GODS NAME WHAT THE **** IS GOING ON!!!'

Most of the congregation were facing the wrong way but Percy wasn't and he paled visibly as he lip-read!

****

The last of the partying revellers had finally left the church amid a medley of thank you's, well done's, and congratulations to the vicar as he waited on the church step to shake their hands, wish them well and bid them all a very happy Christmas.

The television crews had long since departed, no doubt eagerly looking forward to a future BAFTA award in the New Year.

Now Percy stood almost alone in the chilled air of the cold frosty night, as he gazed up at the stars in the dark skies and considered the scene quietly; it was 2.30 a.m. Christmas Day had finally arrived and for a brief moment it felt that the whole world was silent, and at peace.

'Good night Percy, or should I say Good Morning?'

The vicar looked around as his dear friend Jack Tuttle walked out into the air, closing the church door quietly behind him. 'It was one hell of a night my friend.'

Percy smiled, HELL, he thought, was quite an appropriate choice of words.

He reached out and warmly shook his companion's proffered hand, smiling reflectively, 'Yes Jack, it most certainly was.'

'Any regrets Percy?'

He paused for a second as if to recapture the evening, the service, music, cabaret and untimely arrival of the bishop.

The words of Eugene Augustus Thomas the Third still rebounded around his head: Spawn of Satan, Exclusion, Sinful, Ex-Communication, and Devil Worshipper still remained his favourites from the not inconsiderable ranting of the rabid bishop before he and his followers had stormed out into the night.

'No my friend, no regrets, it was time for a change anyway...' said Percy with a whimsical smile.

Jack patted him affectionately on the back, 'Chin up Percy, you still have your congregation, your club and your New Year's wish to come, it's not over yet!'

Percy chuckled, 'Not until the fat lady sings!'

Jack laughed loudly, 'Good night vicar, Happy Christmas,' and with that he stepped off into the night, humming softly to himself as his feet crunched on the crisp frosty footpath.

Percy felt something cold and wet land on his cheek; he reached up to touch his face, only to discover a small chilled softness sliding down his cheek.

It was a snowflake!

He looked up into the skies with a childish grin as the air around him began to turn white with a gentle rush of falling snow, drifting in soft flurries over the expectant waiting ground.

At that second, he had never felt more perfect, more content; well almost...

'Hello Percy.'

A soft, gentle and sensuous voice rose demurely into the night's air as a shadow walked through the falling snow towards him wrapped in a dark velvet cloak; his cloak from the vestry!

The figure reached the top of the steps and swept back her hood revealing a swathe of fire burnt hair atop of a radiant smile and a churlish expression.

It was Sarah Jane Coddle.

She walked slowly up to Percy, as the snow coated her hair and rested on her cheeks, until she faced him and their noses almost touched.

'You didn't collect your Christmas present vicar.'

'Present?' said Percy.

'Yes' said Sarah Jane with a warm smile and with that she reached up with one hand to pull him closer still until their lips met whilst above she held the mistletoe with the other.

As the snow fell, winter chilled and Christmas arrived, Percy and Sarah kissed passionately on the steps of the church.

He did resist, but only for a second, and by then it was too late.

It must have been just a few seconds later, but it seemed like hours before their lips parted; She leant back a fraction, and whispered softly in his ear, 'I love you Percy.'

He smiled warmly, feeling his heart leap within him, 'I love you too Sarah.'

He clasped her hand in his and together they walked slowly off into the night as behind them the angels rejoiced.

CHAPTER FIVE

JANUARY

THE PRISION BREAK

Percy relaxed in the comfort and warmth of his study, enjoying a quiet moment of reflection and contemplation.

It certainly had been a tumultuous, eventful and never to be forgotten Christmas that would be the talking point in every club all over the UK as they watched the live footage with a touch of envy and a sense of admiration.

The midnight mass service had drawn in so many calls that the BBC had to close down their switchboard, whilst the viewing figures peaked at just over 27 million making the show more popular than Westenders and Coronation Lane combined.

There had been lavish praise for the seasonal spectacular, with a call from the Vatican, congratulating them on bringing religion into the modern age. It wasn't often that one faith congratulated the other, thought Percy.

There had of course been darkly veiled cries of sacrilege and devil worship, mainly from Upper Snoddington, not surprisingly the town where the bishop resided.

The very thought sent a shiver down Percy's spine; the unexpected arrival of the senior clergy member had certainly thrown a proverbial spanner in the works regarding the vicar's career.

A recorded delivery letter had arrived a few days after Christmas informing Percy that he was to be officially excommunicated and that his predecessor, Reverend Joshua Jackson, was being recalled from deepest Australia to take over from him.

Given the speed that the letter arrived it was certainly apparent that the bishop had not relied on the tried and tested method of walking to return home and had probably consented to using public transport.

The thought of Eugene Augustus Thomas and his devout fanatics crammed into a taxi, speeding off at high speed to The

Inquisitors Rest for hot broth brought a wry smile to Percy's lips.

There was no doubt that Reverend Archibald, the bishop's mentally challenged bulldog would have been getting a VERY small bone for Christmas as part of the general chastisement of all of Upper Snoddington.

The rest of the evening however had been a blur, and all he could remember with clarity were the hot lips of Sarah Jane Coddle as the snow fell.

Percy blushed, a crimson colour, as he recalled waking by the roaring log fire the following morning, wrapped in his thick cloak, with two empty brandy glasses by the hearth.

He had groggily wondered how he came to be wearing the cloak that Sarah Jane had 'borrowed' the night before, and he was somewhat confused by his rather raunchy dream and the fact that there appeared to be several items of ladies' apparel lying around the study.

There was a colourful bra hanging from the lampshade too!

He could remember the Time Warp of course, but he had no recollection of getting dressed up transgender-like to join the other revellers.

He had no time to consider the answers as Sarah Jane swayed through the open door way wearing Percy's dog collar and very little else!

The vicar turned a much deeper shade of red and suddenly remembered everything with great clarity.

'Good Morning Percy,' she purred in a very contented manner, 'can I offer you anything to nibble?' as she lowered the breakfast tray she was carrying onto the nearby table.

There was a plateful of freshly buttered, lightly toasted crumpets and a steaming cafetière of fresh ground coffee surrendering its delicious aroma.

Percy opened his mouth to reply, but thought better of it as Sarah Jane sat down on the rug by his side and picked up the hot pot.

'Coffee?'

The Reverend was feeling very distracted by the warm closeness of her soft skin and he struggled to maintain his concentration.

'Er, yes please, er, um, Sarah.'

She poured a generous portion of caffeine laced stimulant into Percy's waiting receptacle before reaching for the sugar bowl.

Her eyes glinted and sparkled suggestively as she looked him straight in the face, trying hard not to smile.

'One lump or two?'

The vicar laughed wickedly and pulled her close to his side under the cloak, before planting a passionate kiss square on her lips.

Sarah Jane screamed with delight, mischievously tickling him around the ribs and together they rolled playfully around the floor laughing and teasing.

Percy was new to all this, but he was a fast learner.

It was a while later when Sarah shook her tousled head free of the cloak from where she had snuggled close to his chest and surveyed the carnage.

'Well, I guess the crumpets are cold.'

He smiled at her and holding her close whispered in her ear, 'I don't mind if you serve me cold crumpets for the rest of my life.'

She sighed contentedly and rested her head back down close to his warm body.

****

It was the night of New Year's Eve with the hours, minutes and seconds of the old year fast ticking by...

At long last the vicarage turkey had been finished; what had begun most handsomely as a fine Christmas dinner before being offered sliced on a platter with chutney, then progressing to cold with salad, before filling sandwiches and finally casserole, the turkey had starred in every dish.

He had however drawn the line at making sweetmeat pies with turkey mince.

Finally, the last of the carcass was abandoned to the seagulls and the proposal made that New Year was to be welcomed in with a mouth-watering meal of exquisite proportions which Percy had invited Molly, Bertie, Jack, Charlie and a few of the others to sample.

In fact, by the time the ladies had finished, the 'handful' of guests had grown to create a minor celebrity function with most of the club in attendance.

As quickly as Christmas had arrived, it had passed and December 31st was already upon them, Percy was more convinced than ever that he should soon write a book, as he added the notes of recent events into his diary.

There had been a number of callers to the rectory in recent days, mostly the members of the parish wishing to pass on their seasonal good cheer, offer their support to Percy and to recount the progression of their own yuletide activities.

He still wasn't quite sure how Tony Havershall came to be stuck on top of the Christmas tree with a trifle in his hand or even the logic behind it.

Apparently Jack Tuttle had received a weekend activity break from his partner which involved a day out as a Formula One racing driver, an abseiling trip and the opportunity to do some rock climbing.

Percy smiled broadly to himself, just the thought of Jack's bulk trying to squeeze into a tiny cockpit, or hanging on for dear life to an overstressed nylon bed sheet or, better still, actually managing to circumnavigate an indoor rock face without pulling the whole mountain down.

Patrick had arrived enthusing about his receipt of four tickets to go to next year's Chelsea flower show and was already full of conversation about poppies, primroses, corn cockles and teasels.

He had obviously been spending a lot of time in the wildlife garden and felt the irresistible urge to go green.

Percy could envisage some very interesting floral displays arising from the grass banks of the outdoor bowling green next summer.

Bertie, who had become something of an old romantic, had surprised his newly wed bride Molly with a weekend break to Paris, all expenses paid, in five star accommodation at the famous hotel Le Passione`.

It seemed only yesterday that the two of them had met and yet in a whirlwind romance they had become the foundation and cornerstone of the most perfect relationship.

They were inseparable and Percy could only imagine the adventures that lay ahead for the two of them in what would be a very interesting journey through life, especially now a new addition to the family was less than six months away.

An image of Sarah Jane Coddle, Molly's sister, and the moment she first arrived back in September flashed through the vicar's subconscious, bringing a wry smile to his features.

Was it really such a short time ago that she arrived?

Why it seemed like only yesterday that Sarah and he had embraced on the church steps.

Well a week anyway...mused Percy and he pondered the thought of what to get her for a New Year present.

Having finally been united so close to Christmas they had both decided to exchange small gifts with each other on New Years Eve by way of making up for the lack of time to give each other presents on Christmas day.

Percy blushed: the gift he had already received from Sarah Jane was something special he would never forget, nor the fact it hadn't taken that long to open, although he wasn't sure who had done the unwrapping!

He began to feel rather hot under the collar and decided he should take a quick stroll around the garden in the chilled evening air to compose himself.

Besides, He thought, he already knew exactly what he was going to give her as his gift, and with that he walked over to the back door.

****

Molly was in the kitchen engaging in 'woman talk' and preparing the meal, a seafood supper, which everyone was looking forward to with great delight; the mouth-watering smells from the kitchen area already had one or two of them salivating at the thought.

The salvers were already awash with a wonderful array of crayfish tails, delicate brown shrimps, succulent king prawns, marinated whelks, fresh cooked mussels, jellied eels, and not a shred of turkey in sight anywhere.

Percy and a few of the other men were sitting in the study with a plate full of steaming hot lobsters, a gift from the local store owner James 'Jamie' Gotthelott, and which now awaited their immediate attention with the accompanying crackers.

'Well Percy looks like you've done us proud again,' said Jack as he slid a large claw between the jaws of a lobster cracker and squeezed hard.

Bertie ducked quickly to avoid being decapitated by the flying lobster as it flew over his head then proceeded to impale itself claw first in the plaster work.

Jack stared at the empty jaws with a look of astonishment, 'tough little blighters aren't they?'

The vicar laughed and threw another crustacean in his direction.

'I wanted to thank you all for everything you did on Christmas Eve,' said Percy.

'Nonsense,' said Charlie, 'no thanks needed, it was the least we could do after all you have done for us over the years.'

'But there were thousands of pounds in the dish,' protested Percy.

'Yes,' piped up Bertie, 'and you are going to need every penny now to secure your future my friend, after all, you will be feeding two mouths from now on you know!'

Percy smiled broadly, 'How long have you...'

'Known?' finished Bertie, 'I've known since the first day Sarah Jane turned up and I saw the look on her face, you never had a chance vicar,' and then after a brief pause he concluded, 'after all, look what happened with me and Molly!'

Percy beamed warmly, 'Well, I just wanted to say...'

'Nothing to be said Reverend,' interrupted Charlie, 'besides it was a lot of fun anyway, and it's not over yet.'

'What do you mean?' said Percy, ducking to the left sharply as another lobster claw rocketed by, scoring 'double top' on the grandfather clock.

'Well, you don't really think we're going to idly stand by and let you get your marching orders do you?'

Percy opened his mouth with a further question, but Jack leant over and stuffed a full, denuded, lobster claw in his mouth; by the time he had a chance to fully consume the tasty morsel Sarah Jane had joined them; suddenly his mind came over very vague and foggy!

Charlie glanced up at the clock: 11.44, just 16 minutes away from the magic moment and a brand new beginning.

'Better get ready every one, not long to go,' shouted Charlie excitedly.

Jack leant over and switched on the large colour television that dwarfed the corner of the study; Sarah Jane may not have moved in yet but she had brought her essentials, which included perfume, make-up, sexy underwear and a 42 inch flat screen plasma TV!

Molly arrived carrying a large bowl full of party poppers, streamers, silly hats and blow-outs then began to pass them out around the guests; more were still arriving. The large study began to assume cramped proportions.

Close behind came Dennis, Sheila, Doris, Eric and Clifford each armed with a large bottle of champagne in each hand.

One step further to the rear, Trigger followed up with an outsized metal tray on which balanced two dozen freshly washed champagne glasses.

Percy cast an eye very nervously in his direction: knowing Tony Havershall's reputation as he did it was never a good idea to mix anything fragile or breakable with a situation that inspired damage of epic proportions.

Several of the members closest to Trigger had obviously detected the alarm in the vicar's face.

Without forethought, they parted left and right, like the red sea in biblical times, opening up a clear passage to the awaiting table ensuring that he arrived at his destination without a hitch.

'I really don't know what you were all worried about,' smiled Tony as he turned around, having safely deposited the tray of glasses on the table, before promptly tripping over his own feet and nose diving head first into the awaiting blue cheese dip.

SPLURGH!

'Oh dear,' said Percy, nodding his head from side to side, as the others around the room tittered lightly, 'never say never, right shall we get you cleaned up?' as he reached for the nearest tea towel.

Tony emerged from the bowl of sauce much like the slimed creature from the black lagoon only not quite the same colour, and for an instant it felt like they were all participating in a cheap B-movie.

There was no damage done really. Trigger's façade of blue cheese was soon removed revealing his usual happy smiling face and no signs of any injury.

'Well I know what my resolution is for the New Year,' he beamed at the expectant audience, who knew better than to ask, although Charlie could not resist the temptation of the lure.

'And what might that be?' he enquired half-hopeful of a sensible response.

'Not to fall into a cheese dip for the next 12 months,' he exclaimed triumphantly, and with that he picked up the offending dish and headed towards the kitchen.

'I've just got time to fill it up again,' he exclaimed as he glanced quickly at the clock.

11.52

'Only eight minutes to go!' he shouted exuberantly.

'No, honestly, it's ok...' protested Molly, but Trigger was already gone.

'That's a very good point!' said Jack, 'have you all got your New Year resolutions ready?'

He had already made his, and there was a space on his mantelpiece awaiting the arrival of the trophy that read 'Vice President of the Year.'

There was a brief questioning pause as a number of minds present quickly racked their brains for the most obvious choice of unbreakable promises they could make to themselves.

Charlie vowed that he wouldn't play any pranks on his fellow members during the next year, a good idea in principle but one unlikely to withstand temptation.

Bernard eyed up Sheila 'Legs' Ramsbottom and promised himself that he would pluck up the courage to ask her out on a date sometime during the forthcoming year.

Sheila caught his eye and appeared to read his mind as she made her pledge to 'play hard to get' for at least six months; She glanced again at Bernard: 'No,' she thought, 'make that three.'

Bertie and Molly held hands, blushed and lowered their heads, they were so in love they had nothing else to wish for.

Sarah Jane glanced at the vicar and promised herself that she would behave herself more in public, and then, as an afterthought, decided that she wouldn't kiss him for at least three days as a show of determination that she could resist temptation.

C-R-A-S-H!

An unexpected sound emanated from the vicinity of the kitchen.

'Oh no...' groaned Percy.

'Sounds like the first resolution's been broken already,' laughed Patrick.

Tony Havershall stepped back into the study, holding a towel in one hand as garlic mayonnaise dripped down from various parts of his head.

'Anyone for dip?' he inquired cheerfully.

Big Jim chuckled loudly and fell back into the armchair waiting behind him.

'Oh dear,' tittered the vicar, and likewise sat down quickly.

'Hee! Hee! Hee!' Molly and Bertie collapsed on each other with tears of laughter.

To say the least, the room was in a fair state of mirthful bliss. 'Well it's not blue cheese!' stated Tony with an air of high spirits, 'so my resolution's intact.'

Charlie pointed out the obvious, 'Its still four minutes till midnight you plonker, the year hasn't even started yet!'

'OH,' said Tony.

Big Jim was the first to respond to Charlie's announcement:

'FOUR MINUTES!!'

He might as well have pressed the fire alarm!

'Quick everyone it's 11.56 not long to go, quick, quick, get the champagne open...fill the glasses up!'

A number of willing hands delved into the stack of bottles and were soon busy frantically untwisting wire cages; it was only a matter of seconds before gas propelled corks began to fly in every direction.

For once Percy was lucky; the list of destruction only ran to a light bulb, two ornaments and a tub of Harry Huckstable's organ polish.

Hastily, most of the glasses were filled in rapid succession with a frothing sparkling fountain of golden effervescence.

Percy, for the umpteenth time in the last week, wondered where on earth his cat Rollo had got to.

He only had the opportunity to consider this for a brief second before the answer revealed itself; Rollo charged out from beneath the tablecloth where he had been enjoying a few sneakily acquired succulent king prawns, closely pursued by several rampaging, ricocheting champagne corks.

As he reached the exit door, he lashed out with a paw hooking one of the large juicy tender whole lobsters from a nearby bowl where they were still waiting to be peeled, then disappeared around the corner as the corks thudded into the door behind him.

Percy beamed broadly. That cat was definitely up to something, he thought to himself. But he wouldn't be without him for the world.

Jack Tuttle interrupted his train of thought with an excited shout...

'60 SECONDS TO GO EVERYONE!!!'

Everyone stood up to get a better view of the television as they raised their glasses expectantly and a few streamers began to unfurl as they flew presumptuously across the room.

Percy turned up the volume with the remote control and stepped towards Sarah Jane who was standing at the back of the room; he paused briefly to pick up an unopened bottle of champagne and two charged glasses awaiting consumption.

The commentator boomed out from the set as the cameras went 'live'...

'And with the time now approaching midnight, let's go over to Big Ben where a tremendous crowd are gathered expectantly and we wait for the final seconds to count down to the hour before we see once again what will no doubt be a stunning firework display of epic proportions.'

There was a brief pause.

'Twenty seconds to go, and may we all here in London, in this magnificent setting, take this opportunity to wish all our viewers a happy and prosperous new year as the old one fades away.'

'TEN SECONDS TO GO!' shouted Charlie, jumping suddenly as several party poppers erupted in his other hand as a result of being clutched rather too tightly.

Percy reached Sarah Jane and grabbed her hand as he passed her by, dragging her towards the open door; 'Shsshh,' he said, 'come with me.'

'HERE WE GO!' stated the presenter firmly, powerfully and with a positive excitement to his voice as the hands of Big Ben edged together.

'FIVE... FOUR... THREE... TWO... ONE!!'

B-O-N-G!

'HAPPY NEW YEAR EVERYONE IT'S JANUARY 1ST 200...'

The rest of his boisterous excited statement was lost as the crowd went wild on screen and off...

B-O-N-G!

Glasses chinked noisily, with a torrent of toasts spoken or made in the space of a second. Poppers, streamers and party cannons exploded in all directions showering everyone with all manner of tinsel, coloured paper and confetti.

'HAPPY NEW YEAR OLD CHAP!'

'ALL THE BEST MY FRIENDS!'

'GOOD LUCK EVERYONE!'

'HERE'S TO THE NEW ONE YOU OLD BUGGER!'

The shouts of delight came thick and fast bouncing around the room amid the happy, joyous noise of celebration. Lower South-Borough was 'going to town' in a festive manner and the party had only just begun!

On screen a barrage of multi-bursting mortars and rockets propelled into the night skies in a fusion of colourful splendour and noisy confusion.

Percy and Sarah glanced back over their shoulders at the backdrop of festivity, soaking up the excitement of the New Year celebration briefly, before they raced off around the corner dragging each other by the hand into the adjacent room.

The smaller study was backlit by the embers of a small log fire burning in the grate; a number of large candles spluttering perfumed fragrances into the air as the sounds of the firework display and revelry from next door filtered through the brickwork.

Percy placed the bottle of champagne on the floor in front of the fire and handed Sarah Jane one of the glasses, which had miraculously remained intact and brimful during their short flight.

She was wild eyed, excited and breathing heavily from the unexpected mad dash; she was not used to Percy being so impulsive and was rather thrilled by this new side to the vicar.

'Happy New Year my angel,' said Percy quietly, as he touched his glass toward hers.

CLINK!

'Happy New Year to you too my darling vicar,' she replied in a somewhat husky voice, feeling electrified by the intensity of the atmosphere which surrounded them.

Percy paused before continuing in a voice full of emotional sincerity.

'You have changed my life beyond my wildest dreams Sarah; I have a small gift I want to offer you as a token of the love and affection I feel for you,' continued Percy, breathing a touch more nervously.

'Oh Percy,' sighed Sarah, 'that's so romantic,' as a small tear welled up in the corner of one eye.

He reached into his pocket, retrieving a small package, which he placed in the palm of his hand, extending it towards her and as he did so, he lowered himself carefully down onto one knee.

Sarah Jane could not believe her eyes.

As tears ran down the length of her face she reached to open the tiny box, which rested silently in the middle of Percy's upturned hand; the small lid sprang open at her touch to reveal a golden circle, two interwoven braids of silver and gold metal affectionately entwined.

To the front they joined then peaked in a small clasp in which sat, embedded within their grip, a sculptured diamond of hue and brilliance.

Percy stared upwards into her wide-open eyes.

'Sarah Jane Coddle, will you marry me?'

For a moment she was lost for words, taking the ring carefully from its surround and placing it on the third finger of her left hand; she was amazed to discover that it slid down easily, fitting her like hand in glove.

'But how?' she spluttered softly, trying to ask the question.

'Molly,' he replied in a simple understated answer.

'I don't know what to say;' she spoke in a quiet whisper, totally speechless.

'Say yes,' said Percy.

She gazed deeply, longingly into his eyes and placed her fingers gently on his face, softly stroking his cheek.

'YES,' she sighed.

The first resolution of the New Year was broken three seconds later.

Behind them, near the fire, the abandoned champagne bottle, overheated, proceeded to uncork itself with a loud POP! leaving a trail of fresh fizzing bubbly foaming around its neck.

Percy and Sarah remained oblivious.

****

It was a little later that they re-entered the large study; the party was in full swing with festive spirit flowing freely, and a fair amount of alcoholic spirit too Percy noted.

Everyone was tucking into the midnight feast with a passion, although Big Jim was more passionate than most, after all he did love his food.

He held a half lobster in both hands as if he were eating a hot buttered corn on the cob and the sound of his pleasurable devouring of its moist, succulent flesh could be judged by the sound effects escaping from his drooling mouth.

'Mmm!! Scrumptious... Slurp... Yummy!!!'

Nobody had noticed Percy and Sarah's quiet withdrawal from the celebrations but Molly was the first to notice their return as she saw their beaming faces; she glanced down to their clutched hands and espied the sparkle on her sister's finger.

'Oh my God,' she muttered under her breath, her voice husky with excitement, as she dug Bertie furiously in the ribs.

He turned around with a questioning glance at his beloved wife and, noticing her point of focus, gave a quick look in Percy and Sarah's direction.

'About bloody time,' he said in typical unrestrained fashion smiling broadly.

Charlie also noted the change of atmosphere in the direction of the door and stood up on a chair to get a better look; he could see Percy and Sarah clutching hands, but he couldn't see...

'Sweet Jesus!' he exclaimed, then quickly apologised under his breath for the blasphemy, just in case anyone 'upstairs' was listening.

The Rt Hon. Ronald 'Squiffy' Regis, having been one of Percy's closest friends for so long, was desperately keen to see the vicar happy.

He was sitting in the armchair nearest the door enjoying a rather large brandy when Percy and Sarah emerged from the hallway.

Being beneath the sway of the crowd, he was suitably situated eye level wise, to see the clasped hands and, more importantly the glistening bluish white transparent stone that was refracting light in all directions like a miniature lighthouse.

'I don't believe it,' he muttered to himself.

'I don't believe it,' he re-affirmed a little louder; one or two people nearby noting his candour and wondering what all the fuss was about.

For one of the senior members of the flock he showed an amazing turn of speed for his age and leapt to his feet with great alacrity thrusting his hands in the air high above his head inadvertently showering the nearest people with the bulk of his finest brandy.

'Y-E-E-S-S-S!!!'

He jumped up and down enthusiastically, spreading the remnants of his drink further afield.

'YES! YES! YES!' he exclaimed in an over-excited declaration of impassioned support.

The dramatic outbreak of celebration caught everyone's attention, as one, they all ceased to chatter and instead glanced over towards the door that appeared to be the centre of attention and the reason for the sudden disturbance.

Percy held up his free hand.

'Ladies and Gentlemen I have an announcement to make.' He paused, reflected, then continued...

'WE have an announcement to make,' he corrected.

Everyone, if they had not been before, was certainly paying attention now, it was very rare for Percy to say anything that wasn't worth listening too and this was obviously VERY important.

Percy gathered his nerves, raised his voiced a tone or two and made the proclamation.

'A few minutes ago I asked Sarah Jane Coddle if she would do me the honour of becoming my wife...'

'And I said yes!' concluded Sarah Jane in a fashion reminiscent of Molly and Bertie's interaction.

There was a brief stunned silence.

Then the crowd went crazy with a chaos of congratulation.

It was reported that the level of the noisy celebration of support actually registered on the seismic monitoring station in Bury St Edmunds 28 miles distant, and anyone passing would be wise to conclude that the revelry was a result of a drunken orgy that was best avoided.

The invited guests were indeed celebrating.

They went absolutely, stark, raving, and insanely mad with delight.

Big Jim lifted his glass high in the air and shouted across the top of the crowd.

'Three cheers for Percy and Sarah!'

'HIP HIP...'

'HOORAY!!'

'HIP HIP...'

From outside of the rectory a pair of bloodshot eyes watched intently through the cold frosted glass where heavy breathing had melted the whiteness allowing a view inside.

The eyes belonged to a scruffy, bedraggled, bearded and scrawny tramp-like figure who was clearly out of breath from a sustained period of physical exertion.

They belonged to the figure of Joe 'Dodger' Stubbs, formerly the area representative for Flash Harry promotions; well that was until the unfortunate run-in he'd had with the Reverend Percival Peabody the previous summer.

The long arm of the law had detained Mr Stubbs at Her Majesty's pleasure for a lengthy period of time; it was a detention which he had been loathe to submit to.

Joe Stubbs had escaped and he now wanted his revenge on the humble vicar and his congregation.

'Time for some divine retribution,' he muttered to himself in a deep, rough, and husky voice as he headed off to the clubhouse bearing a large heavy looking sack over his shoulder.

****

Over in the prison cells of the Bordsey Correctional Facility, affectionately known to the inmates as 'borstal for big boys', convict Number 10014 had spent the Christmas season plotting his revenge a thousand times over.

He had a number of scores to settle following his untimely incarceration in the Suffolk detention centre which, as far as he was concerned, was about ten times worse than a monastery in the stone age.

Clearly, he had not heard about the bishop's residence in Upper Snoddington.

Thinking back, his long list of minor crimes had not, to his mind, been sufficient to warrant such a situation; true it hadn't helped that the arresting officer had been the fiancé of the woman, Sheila Ramsbottom, whom he had been insulting at the time.

It wasn't his fault that she possessed long legs as well as a fiery temper, nor that she had been participating in the competition that he had disrupted. He had just naturally made some comparisons between her figure and the bowling green, one being fairly flat with a few bumps and that had been that really.

He had heard through the grapevine that she had long since split up with her police officer boyfriend, which was great news as far as he was concerned. The local constable had gained a promotion following his detention of Mr Stubbs the previous year and now worked as a sergeant with the Northwich flying squad.

What wasn't good news was that he was the same officer designated to facilitate his move from Bordsey to a secure unit designed for higher risk inmates.

Dodger just couldn't see what all the fuss was about or why they needed to move him at all?

True he had spent all day in court answering the 32 charges brought against him, but he had only sworn at the judge seven times and he really was a doddering old fool as far as he was concerned.

It wasn't Dodger's fault that he had accidentally stood on the toe of the officer behind him in court and subsequently hit him on the jaw, knocking him out, when he had spun around to see what all the commotion was for.

The judge had deemed it as an attempt to escape, which was balderdash, and Joe Stubbs told him so, in no uncertain terms.

Apparently, that put him in contempt of court and it cost him another 30 days on his sentence.

So Joe had made the most of it and called him a smelly old dinosaur!

That had added another 30 days...

It was about six hours later, when he was about to be removed from the court to the waiting police van that the bailiff had turned up on an urgent matter for the attention of the judge who promptly announced, with sadistic delight that there were another 97 charges to answer including 38 unpaid parking tickets and 13 speeding offences.

A few choice descriptive words later, as Joe decided to give the judge a piece of his mind, and he had suddenly found himself on the wrong end of a five year prison sentence with no early release for good behaviour.

On the way out he had given the court official a couple of 'V' gestures expecting him not to notice once he was out of sight; well, how was he supposed to know that the courts had CCTV?

That had added another 14 days to his tally.

All in all Joe Dodger Stubbs was a man hell-bent on settling old scores with anyone that crossed his path and to that end he had already taken steps to arrange certain retribution.

Unbeknown to most, he had a younger brother on the outside: Johnny 'Greaser' Stubbs, who had already gone to a lot of time, trouble and expense to set up the members of Lower South-Borough Bowling Club for a BIG shock, that was likely to prove very costly!

Joe smiled to himself with an evil expression and was somewhat amazed when, coincidentally, the shaving mirror cracked in two.

True he had never been the best-looking man in the world; his early misspent youth and some time in the boxing ring hadn't helped his features. He sported an off-centre broken nose, cauliflower ears and crooked teeth that probably needed some attention from the dentist given that he hadn't cleaned them for three years.

Added to that picturesque caricature, his shaven head, 'Desperate Dan' double chin, and questionable tattoos; he'd probably about fit the bill for a walk-on part in any horror movie.

To be quite candid, he was rather smelly; well he just didn't like water of any kind, and soap. Yuk! Who needed that horrible stuff?

He probably did need a shave though; his stubble was getting to the point that if he stood still for more than two minutes a robin would nest in it!

Looking in the cracked mirror he suddenly realised that he was still wearing the same clothes he was arrested in four months ago. He had never even considered the possibility of changing them, after all, that would involve using more of that horrible stuff, water!

To everyone else incarcerated in Bordsey, Joe 'Dodger' Stubbs was someone who was definitely losing his marbles, he wasn't just a 'sandwich short' he had lost the whole picnic.

It was the day after Christmas that the officer of the watch had informed him that he was to be moved the following night and, sure enough, late the next day three police officers had arrived in an armoured van to transport him to his new accommodation.

Dodger groaned aloud when he gained visual confirmation that one of his attendants was indeed the former fiancé of Sheila Ramsbottom; this was going to be an uncomfortable journey.

In due course, resisting the temptation to rise to the jibes of the escorting officer, Joe Stubbs was securely ensconced in the rear of the high security vehicle and on route to his majesty's newest 'hotel'.

All would have gone well for the driver had he not been too busy talking to his associate whilst trying to drink a plastic cup of hot coffee. With the back roads very icy and not the safest of places to be in the middle of a winter's night all had gone to pot the minute a red deer had wandered in front of them.

Swerving to avoid the startled mammal, he had been even more startled when the hot coffee cup upended itself into his lap and, in the consequential panic, he had lost control on the frost covered tarmac, proceeding to wrap the vehicle securely around a rather large pine tree.

Dodger couldn't believe his luck, he was broken free of his tether by the crash and the rear doors of the van gaped open like the jaws of a large shark, inviting him to take a sudden, unexpected, leave of absence.

He did just that; Joe Stubbs 'legged it'.

Four days of sleeping rough in the cold miserable conditions did nothing to improve his state of mind, demeanour, or temperament, especially as the only digestible food he had found in that time were a handful of potatoes, a turnip and some cabbage leaves well past their best.

He arrived finally at the gates to the club on the evening of the 31st December in a particularly foul mood, reciting repeatedly under his breath, 'You reap what you sow.'

The first thing he sought out was the local TRESCOS store; his groaning stomach was reminding him of the need for substantial sustenance, whilst the urgent requirement of a toilet was also an immediate necessity.

It didn't take long for the experienced Dodger to gain entry to the rear of the building, hauling himself over the back fence with a helping hand from the dustbin, which he left behind bent and battered, his usual brute force and ignorance gaining him quick entry to the mini-mart.

Having taken advantage of the public convenience first, which was a hit and miss affair in the dark, Joe Stubbs entered the bakery and chilled foods section like a man on a mission.

Crab sandwiches followed jam doughnuts, superseded by triple choc chip cookies and preceded by the best part of a crème brûlée.

Washing this down with a fair quantity of cheap lager and a generous helping of a good whisky he soon felt a lot better and announced his gratitude by belching so loudly that several cans fell off the nearly shelf.

It was the good part of an hour later that the impromptu burglar made his departure, leaving behind a trail of empty packets, cans and biscuit crumbs in his wake.

He half expected the local police to put up wanted posters announcing they were looking for a fat drunken man with his pockets full of digestives.

The thought made him grin wickedly and he wondered how much the reward would be.

Perhaps it would be enough for him to consider turning himself in.

He laughed loudly at the thought!

Making sure he had ample supplies in reserve he exited the store with every pocket bulging and even found time to cram an extra bag of crisps down the inside of his sock, although he had to draw the line at secreting a bunch of bananas in his Y-fronts.

As he was about to leave he suddenly noticed a large sign pointing towards the garden centre, which brought him to an abrupt halt. He pondered for a second or two as an idea formulated itself deep within the darkest recesses of his mind and, with a particularly evil expression, he took a detour.

A short while later he returned carrying a rather large sack over his left shoulder in which dwelt a large proportion of the supermarket seed stock; he had specific plans for its use and Lower South-Borough was in for a particularly nasty surprise!

He laughed again in a wildly manic manner and disappeared back into the night cackling witlessly.

****

Joe Dodger Stubbs was on route to the bowling club when he noticed the apparent revelry going on in the rectory and, out of insatiable curiosity, he crept nearer for a better look.

He could see through the frosted glass that a party was in full swing and a number of faces were very familiar. Reverend Percival Peabody came into focus and Dodger inadvertently shrunk back against the wall baring his teeth in a grimace as he recognised the vicar as the one who had given him an ice cold soaking the previous summer.

'I will settle up with you later!' he promised himself, with one final glare in Percy's direction; with that he hoisted the large sack back onto his shoulder and headed down the hill towards the clubhouse.

Breathing heavily from the exertion, and from the earlier bout of sustained over-eating, Dodger finally arrived at the large wooden gates marking the access to Lower South-Borough bowling club.

He cast a look around furtively from his concealed hidey-hole to ensure no one was watching, before forcing the gate open with a ferocious kick, but just as he stepped through the darkened entrance a familiar sound brought back tainted memories of his last visit.

'SC-C-R-E-E-E-C-HH!!!'

'Damn that wretched owl,' he cursed as he remembered his previous encounter in which he had come off second best.

He bent down to the nearby kerbstones and reached around in the gloom until he found what he needed, a good house brick; he hefted the object firmly in his broad hand and without hesitation slung it full tilt towards the screeching bird.

The startled raptor squawked in alarm and took flight much to Dodgers delight.

'Gotcha!' he smirked viciously with an evil grin on his face.

The large man-made rock, having passed through the leafless branches, continued its journey reaching the apex of its ascent and then proceeded to descend at an increasing velocity.

The only thing that stood between it and the ground from whence it came was the home of Ronald 'Squiffy' Regis, or more to the point, his much maligned glass conservatory.

C-R-R-A-A-S-S-H!

The outbuilding was double-glazed with toughened glass reputedly capable of resisting the impact of a meteor, but it hadn't taken into account the impact of Joe Stubb's temper tantrum.

Shards of glass flew in every direction as the hurtling projectile impacted a large panel and totally destroyed it, leaving plenty of ventilation and very little roof.

Dodger looked over the hedge in horror as the noise of the unexpected breakage was amplified a million times over by the still night air and open countryside.

He looked wildly from side to side in consternation, seeking the quickest possible escape route, half expecting every distant light to switch on immediately and numerous curtains to begin twitching in anger seeking the cause of the nocturnal disturbance.

Amazingly, nothing happened; for once in his pitiful life Joe Stubbs had struck lucky, with everyone at the vicarage for the New Year's Eve party there remained no one else in residence to hear his outlandish breach of the peace.

Breathing a sigh of relief he headed across the car park in the general direction of the clubhouse as best he could remember, given the darkened conditions.

He paused only twice, the first time to pick himself up after falling down the ditch that surrounded the outside green, the second to spit out the petals of the winter pansies having gone head first into the flowerbed.

Dodger was not impressed, in fact he was getting more annoyed by the second, the sack he was carrying was not the lightest of things and he was determined to reach the clubhouse with its hard-earned contents intact.

He decided, quite wisely to try a different tack and, carefully feeling his way to the edge of the garden, rediscovered the gravel path running alongside the green that led directly to the club.

Breathing a sigh of relief and now much more resolute, he strode confidently forward, putting on a bit of a spurt before walking head first into the scaffolding pole....

'A-A-R-GH!!!'

Dodger screamed out angrily, one hand reaching to nurse his damaged appendage, the other lashing out at the offending article, neither action doing much good.

He groaned, stepped sideways to avoid whatever the obstruction was, tripped over a nearby pile of bricks and promptly tumbled head first, again, down the excavation ditch for the sewerage pipes.

'U-R-G-H!'

'OH GAWD!'

Joe Stubbs was beginning to get very alarmed, he was also picking up a fine collection of bruises, abrasions, scratches and grazes.

'WHAT THE HELL IS GOING ON?' he shouted out to no one in particular, as he spat out a mouthful of cold wet sand before kicking out in angry frustration.

His knee didn't appreciate the proximity of the large iron grating leaning against the pipe and it was a fair bet which of the two objects was going to come off worse for wear.

'OUCH!!'

'DAMN AND BLAST IT!!!'

Having been incarcerated prior to the end of the summer, Dodger had no idea at all, of course, of the progressing building works that had now turned his easy access way into an assault course.

It was a full 20 minutes later, that he arrived finally at the clubhouse door.

His encounter with the JCB digger on route would probably now neccessitate the unavoidable attention of a dentist, he thought to himself as he felt the gap with his tongue and placed the damaged ivory safely in his top left pocket.

One of the few things that Dodger still believed in was the tooth fairy, and he wasn't about to lose the opportunity of a free silver sixpence.

It didn't take long for someone with his brawn to find a suitable window and force it open; he took his time because he didn't want his point of entry to be discovered too soon, after all, it would take a little while for his plan to take effect.

In fact, it was the whole concept of 'spending time' that had germinated the seed of his idea.

He sniggered to himself, proud of his little joke, 'Come on Dodger let's go and have our own little party,' he mumbled humorously before heaving the sack through the open window, closely followed by his battered bulk.

Had anyone noticed him entering the building at that point, they could have been excused for thinking that he was a demonic Santa Claus, running late, and hell bent on stealing all the presents back.

At that point, they would have probably declared themselves teetotal and booked themselves into the nearest rehabilitation centre.

It was another one of those unlikely, rare and virtually extinct opportunities that occurred at that moment in time and for Joe 'Dodger' Stubbs it was the most perfect of moments.

There was a large sign on the inner door, which, under the soft glow of the background lighting was clearly visible to him, and as it only had short words even he could understand it.

GREEN SHUT. REOPEN ON JAN. 14TH.

He clapped his hands with glee at the unexpected discovery, ecstatic that he had ample time, not only to carry out his act of retribution, but also that the plan would indeed have all the time in the world to follow its natural course.

Oh Yes! he thought excitedly, revenge was sweet.

The club was, by tradition closed for two weeks from Christmas Eve, but, on this occasion, with no county competitions until the 17th of January and the first club matches being held at other venues the earliest game was actually a ladies 'friendly' booked for the 15th of the month.

Dodger had all the time in the world.

Nothing stirred in the building, just the gentle twinkle of the Christmas tree lights disturbed the peaceful harmony with their softly harmonised and colour reflections.

Knowing he was completely safe now, he took the opportunity to switch on the main lighting inside the arena so that he could easily survey his intended target, before taking a detour via the main bar to acquire a bottle of his favourite tipple, a good flask of malt whisky.

This was going to be fun, he thought to himself as he contemplated the final outcome and imagined the look of shock on the faces of the first arrivals.

One thing at a time Mr Stubbs he muttered to himself. The 'deed' was going to take a couple of days and he was in no hurry, he wanted to savour every second; Dodger poured himself a generous tot of Scotland's finest and proceeded to lay out all his purloined victuals along the bar top.

It wasn't long before he had a sizeable pile of crisps, pork pies, mini Christmas cakes, sausage rolls, several large crème filled chocolate Santas, three boxes of mince pies, a whole cooked chicken and a large jar of Mrs McGregor's famous pickled eggs.

Dodger eyed up the last item with a look that almost represented passion, he loved pickled eggs, 'Mmm, yum,' just the thought made him realise that he was, again, ravenous.

Well, he thought, Perhaps one wouldn't harm would it? choosing not to remember the effect that the delicacies had on his digestive system.

One thing led to another, and half an hour later Joe Stubbs was curled up on a nearby comfortable settee for a much needed snooze, now much the worse for wear after 11 selections from the large jar and several substantial top-ups from the now nearly three-quarters empty whisky bottle.

It was a very warm 72 degrees Fahrenheit inside and he had all the time he needed to savour the moment.

The settee groaned its protest as he deposited himself on its well sprung cushions and Dodger reflected that everything would have been absolutely perfect had the log fire been burning in the grate.

His grumbling stomach reminded him that perhaps it was a good thing there weren't any naked flames in the immediate vicinity whilst he slumbered.

Dodger drifted off to sleep, as his final thought repeated itself over and over in his mind.

All the time in the world...

****

He took one final look around before he closed the door.

Having slept for a marathon 18 hours he had awoken with a throbbing head, a very aggrieved stomach and a number of aching parts from his various collisions earlier.

A quick 'hair of the dog' and another pickled egg soon helped to sort out matters and picking up the large sack he headed towards the indoor green pausing only to tear off a large leg from the cooked chicken just in case he got further hunger pangs.

'At last!' he muttered to himself, as he hefted the hessian bag onto the bowling surface and opened it up to examine its contents.

Pulling back the top he unveiled 30kg of Mrs McGregor's finest mountain grass seed; apparently she was a very prolific producer of many products from north of the border.

On top of the loose seed, which was reputedly so tough and durable it would grow in the Sahara dessert with only a thimble full of water a year, lay a number of sealed packets.

He pulled them out and examined their labels, smiling viciously as he thumbed though the packs; he had chosen well!

Dodger spent the next two hours doing a fine impression of an early day, pre-industrial, South American farmer, as he walked up and down the green, scattering copious quantities of the mixed seeds from his bulky hands.

He wished that somebody had been there to film the event, just for posterity of course, something to show his son when he was living a life of luxury as a retired criminal in the South of Spain.

Unbeknown to Dodger, he was getting his wish: whilst no one was at home or likely to disturb his demonstrations, the closed circuit television cameras were picking up every small detail as the recording device in the main office whirred away merrily transferring the images to its DVD recorder.

Every little action was being stored away as a permanent record!

It took a while but the exertion was worth every bit of effort; finally, Dodger stood back and admired his handy work.

The entire green lay covered in a fine layer of durable grass seed; there was a significant quantity of wildflowers and vegetables too!

Joe Stubbs was a very happy man, he rubbed his hands together in a gleeful manner; all he needed now was the right growing conditions and...

He looked around for a moment, and spotting exactly what he was looking for, headed off in that direction with a large crowbar in his hand.

A few seconds later, after some swift handiwork, the thermostat for the background heating was temporarily jammed on 98 degrees Fahrenheit and the fire alarm system permanently disabled.

He left the main rink floodlights on, after all, he wasn't so stupid that he didn't realise plants needed light as well as heat and water!

Oh yes, he remembered the final ingredient and, without further ado lifted the heavy crowbar and smashed the nearby fire alert box to smithereens.

The main circuit board lit up like the Christmas tree with flashing red warning lights but not a sound emerged from the overhead klaxons.

A brief gurgling sounded above the green, so Dodger knew it wasn't his stomach on this occasion, and then the overhead sprinklers activated in spectacular fashion.

He knew that without a detectable fire the sensors would trip them off after 15 minutes, but that didn't matter because, by then, the carpet would be so saturated that there would be enough water held in its sponge-like fibres to supply the indoor garden for a whole month if necessary.

Dodger cackled wildly and with one final glance, he closed the door and made his escape, pausing only to pick up the rest of the chicken and stuff the last pickled egg into his open orifice on the way out.

****

The escaping criminal paused again for a brief second after

exiting through the window he had earlier forced, taking time to contemplate his best route of departure.

He most certainly did NOT want to risk a return journey through the car park and building site; there was a limit, after all to how much collateral damage his body could absorb.

He turned right and headed off down the other pathway past the signpost marked 'TO THE WILDLIFE GARDEN'.

Again providence provided more ammunition with which to sate his thirst for a 'settling of scores'.

He suddenly came upon a very large, distinctive wooden structure with a number of platforms, feeder tubes and fat balls bedecking its form; he recognised it instantly from the previous summer.

'It's that bloody bird table!' he exclaimed heatedly.

'Well I'll show you who the boss is!'

Joe 'Dodger' Stubbs was never a man of many words, and often of mixed metaphors, but on this occasion actions spoke louder than observations.

He set about the wildlife station with a frenzied passion, heedless of the staples, screws, nails and splints as he tore into the wood with his bare hands.

The table was a particularly well made structure, but Joe was a man with a mission; blind hatred, ignorance, and a fair proportion of whisky, which had dulled the edges of his mind, fuelled his strength.

A few minutes later, the heavy breathing wrathful petty criminal had added 'destruction of property' to his growing list of misdemeanours.

'Right,' he thought, 'that takes care of that' as he subconsciously added doctor to dentist on his 'must visit' list; he surmised that some of the splinters, if not all, would be rather painful to remove!

Dodger turned away from the demolition derby and was about to head off into the wilderness to make good his escape, when he heard the distinct sound of someone approaching down the footpath.

'Damn!' he cursed his own stupidity. 'The annihilation of the bird station had come at a cost; obviously someone must have heard the disturbance and wandered over to investigate the cause.

The sound of feet on gravel was getting closer.

He looked around desperately for a sanctuary, searching for somewhere to take temporary refuge or to find anything that would offer protection from any potentially wrathful arrival.

Out of the corner of his eye, he spied the vague outline of a small structure; it looked ideal, remote, off the beaten track and unlikely to be investigated.

As quick as he could, trying hard not to breathe too noisily or make too much disturbance that would give away his hurried retreat, he hastened in its direction.

The building in question was none other than Dennis's bird hide!

Behind him, where the feeding station used to reside, a large deer wandered into sight, curious as to what all the fuss was about.

****

Dodger hurried inside and as carefully as he could, closed the heavy door behind him, gently lowering the latch into place and securing it so that, to any visitor, the place would seem securely locked up, therefore incapable of sheltering any vagrant.

Looking around, the structure appeared to be a large shed of some kind and, although he couldn't see much, he could vaguely distinguish a number of familiar shapes including a kitchen area and reclining chairs.

He fumbled around but could not find any source of lighting, so he wisely chose to proceed very cautiously; Dodger was mindful of those recent incidents, when he had plunged ahead regardless, with painful consequences.

Waving his arms warily around him he stepped back from the door into the centre of the room as it seemed the safest place and less likely to have any obstacles that could trip him up or cause him injury.

'MMM-E-E-E-O-O-O-O-WWW!!!'

Dodger froze in mid-step as his foot encountered something soft, squashable and obviously very annoyed by the infringement of his size 12 boots, which had already made an unwarranted intrusion on its personage.

He looked down very nervously, anticipating the worst, although his slow to respond brain did register the fact that large snakes didn't make a noise like a pussy cat and there had been no reported incidence of alligators in the immediate area for the last 5,000 years.

He turned slowly, lifted the offending foot and stepped back towards the door as a pair of large white eyes opened and stared up at him with a very angry unimpressed expression.

Miss Matilda Bagshott, aka Baggie, was a very temperamental, longhaired and posh Persian pussy, the somewhat questionable but proud property of Gloria 'Smiler' Grimshaw, the ladies' president elect.

She was also a bit of a wild cat, apt to run amok on a whim, loved playing 'rough n tumble' with the alley cats and at times had very unscrupulous morals.

Nevertheless, in recent months following her initially curious and then avid pursuit of the equally riotous ragtag Rollo, the vicarage moggie, she had suddenly found herself unable to tear her eyes away from him or his misadventures.

There had of course been a fair amount of 'chase and be chased' between the two of them, but eventually after a bit of fur flying and bloodletting they had reached a sort of mutual agreement.

One thing had led to another; that finally resulted in two outcomes, the first of which was that Baggie and Rollo had become both inseparable and insanely protective of each other.

The second was...

Miss Matilda Bagshott looked down at her tummy and the row of tiny little heads that stared back blindly with tiny blue eyes as they suckled for milk whilst she lay outstretched on the floor.

Apparently, she had been a bit of a naughty girl!

She was very proud of her 'magnificent seven' as she called them; Baggie hadn't named them yet, nor really had the time or opportunity to do so, after all they were only 10 days old.

She had been somewhat alarmed by the unexpected and sudden arrival of Joe Stubbs; she could sense his fear and to be quite honest she didn't like the way he smelt; the bad odour rankled her delicate senses.

Her hair lifted slightly; her pupils dilated with trepidation as she began to gets nervous about the safety of her young babies, but nevertheless she remained silent and unmoving; that was until the intruder placed his size 10 clodhoppers on her fine tail.

Her protesting, ear splitting caterwaul was the first alarm bell for Dodger and one he would have been wise not to ignore.

Instinctively he removed his foot from the 'alien' he had stepped on fearful it was something far worse than a pussycat.

Frantically searching amid the crisp packets, cakes and confectionery concealed about his person he found what he was looking for, a box of matches, and he fumbled desperately for one as he stepped back further.

The sound of the rustling plastic was heightened by the darkness and Baggy mewed pitifully in alarm; she could sense the large unpleasant silhouette of Joe Stubbs and was desperate to drive him away but dare not abandon her fragile kittens that were incapable of finding protective shelter.

A sudden light flared into brightness startling her and briefly Joe could see the figure of Miss Matilda Bagshott lying helpless on the floor, her injured tail twitching angrily.

He had never been keen on animals and had a particular dislike for cats, he thought they were a waste of time and money that just ate good food and made a ridiculous noise.

He muttered angrily under his breath for being alarmed by such a trifling matter and pulled his left leg back; he had decided he was going to give the offending moggie a good swift kick up the backside.

He froze in mid strike however as something moved and caught the corner of his eye; it was at first just a small shadow that began to unfurl before his eyes, gradually growing bigger and bigger, its shape flickering in the poor light of the burning match until it resembled a huge shaggy monster.

'H-I-I-I-I-I-I-S-S-S-S-S!!!'

Dodger suddenly became very, very alarmed, he could feel a hot breath on the nape of his neck just inches away accompanied by a very unpleasant odour much like rotting fish; he began to imagine a giant, man-eating, ogre with sabre like teeth, wild staring bloodshot eyes and enormous razor-like claws preparing to sate its gruesome appetite.

He started to tremble violently; not a very good idea with the match burning down rapidly to its base.

Very slowly Joe Stubbs began to turn his head around, his eyes rolling as far as they could to one side desperate to see what evil being lay behind him.

He caught just the briefest glimpse of a vast hairy creature with hackles raised in every direction, it resembled a bloated porcupine surmounted by a huge pair of crazed pupils under which was a massive gaping jaw filled with rows of glistening shark's teeth.

Whatever it was, it had a gigantic paw raised high in the air from which extended talons worse than those of Freddie Kruger.

Those teeth!

THOSE CLAWS!

Every impression flashed through Dodgers terrified mind in a split second and then the match went out.

He had never liked the dark, even as a child and he screamed loudly, again and again, as he frantically scrabbled for another match, only succeeding in scattering them all over the floor.

'AARGH'

'AAAAAARRRRRRGGHH!!!'

Joe 'Dodger' Stubbs was a complete blubbering, dithering wreck, quaking in his boots as he bent over desperately fumbling for the dropped fire starters.

That's as long as it took for the creature to strike and Dodger felt the sudden anguishing pain of a red-hot needle piercing his voluminous backside.

He was terror struck beyond his wildest nightmares; leaping upright as he screamed louder than ever before he turned rapidly, despite his bulk, and charged headfirst into the night, not even pausing to open the door, instead leaving a shattered frame and a pair of torn hinges in his wake.

'NN-N-O-O-O-O-O-O-O-!!!'

'HELP!'... 'MURDER!!'... 'RESCUE!!'... 'MUMMY!!!'

He screamed loudly in a childlike manner as he thundered down the dirt track into the darkness, his arms and legs flailing at the air.

The local police were shocked when a terrified, demented, drooling and delirious maniac burst through the station door at 4.00 a.m. gibbering about carnivorous wild monsters and begging for sanctuary, which unsurprisingly, they were only too happy to oblige him with.

Back in the bird hide, the moonlight shone through the torn doorway onto the rear of the shed where the flesh-tearing creature had lurked.

Rollo sat back on his haunches, quietly pleased with himself, his hackles lowering as he purred contently whilst inspecting his claw for any damage.

Miss Matilda Bagshott was also a rather impressed Persian pussy as she stared up from the floor in open admiration of her mate's impromptu and stunning stage performance; meanwhile the kittens continued to mew and suckle.

****

It was the morning of the 14th January; Percy was awake early and preparing to venture out into the cold morning despite the remonstrations of Sarah Jane Coddle who was still warmly tucked up under the vicar's very comfortable quilt.

He was becoming increasingly concerned about the absence of Rollo the vicarage cat whom he hadn't seen since New Year's Eve and only then when the cat was doing an impromptu runner with a lobster.

There had been a number of raids in the neighbourhood lately with tasty morsels such as fresh cooked chicken portions disappearing from unguarded dinner tables. Despite his non-appearance the cat's food bowl was always empty every morning so Percy kept filling it every evening before supper with Rollo's favourite food, 'PUDDIES Meaty Chunks' in the vain hope that he would return home soon.

Nevertheless, the missing moggie remained mysteriously absent.

He had received a couple of disturbing phone calls in the last few days; the first had been concerning the local TRESCOS mini market which, according to the police, had apparently been broken into sometime early in the New Year.

The break- in had been discovered only after staff returned to work following their Christmas holiday the following week.

Apparently, the garden centre had been ransacked too, but the only other things that had been stolen had been a substantial amount of perishable foodstuffs and a weird concoction at that.

Jam doughnuts and crab sandwiches just did not go together! One of the shocked cleaners was still receiving psychiatric help in hospital for post-traumatic stress following her regular visit to clean the public conveniences.

For the time being, they had put the break-in down to a travelling vagrant with a warped sense of humour and an unhealthy appetite.

The second call had come from the police cells in Upper Snoddington near to the Bishop's monastery, where they had not so much detained, but placed in solitary confinement, the crazed form of Joe 'Dodger' Stubbs, in a strait jacket for his own safety.

As his prison record indicated that he had previously had a bit of a run in with the locals at Lower South borough they naturally contacted Percy to see if he was aware of anything that could shed light on Dodger's deranged mental state.

Percy was shocked to hear the former promotions manager had in fact escaped prison in the first place. However could not assist them with their enquiries other then to re-affirm what they already knew.

Sarah Jane did her absolute best to entice the vicar to stay indoors but even fresh cafetière's of coffee and the most seductive fluttering of her eyelashes for once did little to deter him from his duty.

Wrapped up in his heaviest thickest cloak, armed with gloves, scarf, wellies and a flask, Percy stepped out into the morning light pretending not to notice Sarah Jane's half naked body wrapped flirtatiously around the door.

He smiled and resisted the temptation to respond in kind mischievously wishing that he had a snowball to hand.

Percy sighed, a much happier vicar for once, and strode off down the slope towards the clubhouse but abruptly paused on route when he noticed that there appeared to be something inherently amiss with the wildlife feeding station.

The bird table was no more; in fact there wasn't a part of it left that was large enough to even cover an A4 sheet of paper.

Something was clearly amiss and Percy though perhaps it would be wise to ring for assistance just in case.

Percy delved into his cloak pocket and produced the brand new mobile phone that Sarah Jane had given him as a New Years Eve present; he wasn't a man much used to modern technology but he could appreciate convenience.

He soon discovered that mobile phones weren't best suited to using with fingers encased in thick woollen gloves; it also took him nine attempts at dialling the number he wanted before he realised that he actually needed to turn the power on first to obtain a signal.

There were 45 text messages waiting from Sarah Jane, all apparently sent in the last 10 minutes; clearly, she was missing him.

There was a button marked 'read' which he pressed; he only got to the third message before he began to feel very hot under the collar and by the fifth he was positively blushing a deep scarlet.

Percy could foresee big problems and even larger phone bills if he should ever be away for more than a single day.

A few minutes later the vicar, feeling comfortably reassured, continued on down through the wildlife garden towards the clubhouse; he had managed to locate Jack Tuttle as well as Charlie, Bernard, Eric, Patrick and Bertie, so help if needed was on the way.

However, the closer he got, the more he realised that all was definitely not as it should be.

As he approached the bird hide, he noticed the first clear evidence that this was more than a casual act of vandalism and it appeared there was more than one party involved.

What remained of the shed door swung open in the breeze, hanging on to the framework by just one very stressed hinge.

There were several pieces of timber missing from its structure and when Percy took a closer look, he got the strange impression that someone had actually gone through the timber of their own volition.

But that was ridiculous wasn't it.

Who on earth would want to do such a stupid thing?

They would have to have been in a blind panic or taken complete leave of their senses to consider such a notion.

He couldn't help but feel though that the roughly hewn and splintered edges of the door left a silhouette that was somewhat familiar.

There were very distinctive lacerations up and down both sides of the door's supporting framework. Percy began to get the impression that Rollo might have had a paw in this.

He left the bird hide to continue his journey; meanwhile back inside, from underneath the warm seclusion of the armchair, nine pairs of eyes watched his departure.

Percy finally arrived at the clubhouse car park; he could see there had been some sort of a scuffle in the builder's yard, almost as if children had been playing 'war games' but there didn't appear to be much damage.

Which was more than could be said for the gardens!

The winter pansies were virtually all decapitated, polyanthus coppiced just above ground level, wallflowers torn up by their roots and a two-metre wide carriageway steamrollered through the crocus beds.

There was a trail of muddy footprints heading off in a meandering manner across the green towards the club windows; Percy thought it actually looked as if someone had stopped to eat the grass at some point.

The vicar was feeling very nervous by the time he placed the key in the clubhouse door, but the sound of running engines announcing the arrival of several vehicles in the car park re-assured him that re-enforcements had arrived.

Feeling much bolder, he stepped though the door and was relieved to see that initially everything looked fine. The master alarm was still showing an 'ALL CLEAR' signal and the fire control board was indicating a row of green lights.

He checked the doors one at a time...

The offices were all ok!

The toilets were spotless and unoccupied too! The only sound disturbing the peace was the running water from the cistern as it flushed the waste traps.

Percy moved on to the lounge and kitchen area as he heard the voices of Big Jim, Bernard and Bertie arriving at the front door.

There did appear to be some evidence of illegal midnight snacking in the lounge area, empty crisp packets and sandwich boxes lay strewn across the floor whilst someone had obviously taken a liking for mini Christmas cakes as there were only two left in the otherwise empty box of 12.

He made a mental note to have a word with the cleaners and to also check the signing-in book so as to locate the guilty parties.

Oh well, he thought, if that's the worst of the problem, then there's nothing really to worry about, as he opened the door to the bowling green.

He was rather taken aback by the fact that the main overhead halogen lights were burning intensely; they were all on; the electric bill was going to be horrendous, and just look at the effect the heat was having on the poor grass.

Why, it would take them all day to cut it...

He turned towards the bar, noting at once the presence of a three quarter empty bottle of malt whisky and the remnants of a chicken carcass.

Really, he thought, this simply wouldn't do...

GRASS!

The previously logged item resurfaced from his subconscious and moved to the top of his agenda in big red flashing lights, interrupting his train of thought.

GRASS!!!

This was the indoor bowling green!

What the HELL was grass doing in the indoor arena?

He turned to retrace his steps, noticing for the first time that the soft underlying deep pile carpet felt a bit wet and his feet sloshed as he walked.

Percy glanced down, it wasn't carpet at all, it was five inches of the lushest, greenest, grass he had ever seen! AND it was growing out of the saturated and sodden mush that used to be the carpet.

The vicar was completely lost for words. In his wildest imagination he had never seen or imagined such a sight; he had heard of Tom Jones waxing lyrical about '*The green green grass of home*', but this was ridiculous.

He glanced across the tabletops towards the bowls playing surface, or, at least where it used to be.

Certainly, it was the right colour, but that was as close at it got to representing a playing surface anymore.

The grass stood as much as 12 inches deep in places and there was a fair sprinkling of ox-eye daisies, ornamental clover, cornflowers, and wild poppies mixed in with it; many were in bloom and Percy thought briefly that it looked very fetching!

Here and there, he recognised a few patches of chives as well as what appeared to be spring onions and he was absolutely sure that if he looked hard enough he'd probably find a few new potatoes in the ditches as well.

Percy was, for once, totally, completely flabbergasted.

In fact, the last time he had been so completely taken by surprise was when the previously innocent Mollie had flounced into the clubhouse with tea and biscuits for the then stubborn Bertie.

Just the thought was enough to bring beads of perspiration to Percy's forehead.

He heard the others arriving behind him and then grind to a halt suddenly; so he looked around to see their reaction.

Bernard and Bertie were suitably stunned into silence.

Jack Tuttle, aka Big Jim, tried to look on the bright side as per usual and opened the conversation with a humorous repartee.

'Well it looks like the Lollo Rosso are ready but the Frisee hasn't done so well,' and then added as an afterthought, 'Did we plant any Rocket?'

Eric, and Patrick the green keeper had also arrived, joining the visual affray with an altogether different take on the situation.

'Bit deep for a landing strip' observed Eric: well he did still live in the reality of World War II most days.

Patrick stooped down, plucked a few blades and examined them closely, 'If I didn't know better I'd say it was Mrs McGregor's finest mountain grass seed.'

Big Jim had the last say on the matter however...

'It's a shame Jimi Hendrix isn't still with us, we could have staged a Woodstock reunion.'

Percy tried very hard to picture the image, but try as he may, just couldn't imagine a bowling green fill of hippies, smoking grass and preaching free love whilst practising with electric air guitars.

Perhaps they should invite the bishop.

He laughed loudly at the thought.

****

The following morning brought a much more practical resolution to the matters in hand.

All club games for the next month had been hastily re-arranged and moved to another local club where the Hillsworth Eskimos were based.

Patrick was taking full advantage of the situation to test drive the new sit-on power mower, which had been purchased as a replacement for the former 'Beast of South-Borough.'

The old mower had never recovered from Percy's attempt to give the adjacent lane a 'short back and sides' stylised crew cut. Whilst the blades had tried gallantly to carry out his wishes, they had little impact on the large flint stones that made up the bulk of the footpath's constitution.

Percy, of course, had been hanging on for dear life, and unable to do much to salvage the situation or the mower. It wasn't until the runaway mechanical monster had ground painfully to a halt in a large deep puddle hissing, snarling, spitting and steaming violently that he had found the will power to let go of the clutch and throttle.

It was clear that the carpet and the surround were totally ruined, but Patrick had thought it a great opportunity to test the new appliance, and, who knows? They might even be able to have a 'roll up' on the cut grass before the smell of the dank carpet got too bad.

Well, he was always one to maintain a sense of optimism!

Elsewhere more repairs were already under way with a replacement bird feeding station being constructed phoenix-like out of the ashes, or in this case splinters.

A new door had already been ordered for the bird hide from Peter 'chippie' Barryman.

Percy decided to leave the club members to sort out the vegetable patch, after all there was little he could do, and he had a very repetitive memory of a very saucy Sarah Jane awaiting his amorous attentions at the vicarage.

No doubt there would be hot coffee and crumpets already waiting.

He checked his mobile phone as it vibrated suddenly inside his left pocket; message number 127 had arrived!

It was still very cold and frosty as the vicar headed home...

Home?

With the new vicar arriving soon he would have to give some serious thought to where on earth he was going to live. After all he had responsibilities now, a bride to be who would require his undivided attention as well as expect him to be the provider of the proverbial loaves and fishes.

The Christmas collection would, after all, come in very handy and he was still amazed to think that he was at that time the only person in the parish unaware that the growing bond between Sarah Jane and himself had become public knowledge.

He pondered reflectively.

Just where was that confounded cat hiding?

The cleaners had recently been voicing concerns about the possibility of mice in the church, and a number of nibbled pews as well as animal orientated ramblings heard in the rafters had them convinced of a potential infestation.

Rollo was needed very urgently, after all his ability as a 'mouser' was second to none.

'M-M-E-E-O-W-W-W'

Percy glanced up as he passed one of the largest bird feeders; he recognised that pitiful call anywhere.

Rollo was hanging from the bottom of the substantially sized metal feeding tube, with the rest of his body dangling in free-fall almost like a bungee jumper who had changed his mind at the last moment.

Percy smiled to himself at the cat's predicament; he must have been out on the prowl and been unable to resist the temptation of taking a charge at an early morning mouse nibbling at the feeder.

Apparently, Rollo's paws had made contact with the ice cold metal and had become instantaneously frozen to the steel leaving him welded to the spot.

Rollo mewed pitifully again.

Percy laughed loudly, poor old Rollo.

A few seconds later, the Reverend Percival Peabody was heading home at a fast pace, with a giant steel feeder under one arm and a still attached shaggy bagpuss of a cat under the other.

The vicarage fireplace summoned.

CHAPTER SIX

FEBRUARY

THE TEA PARTY

Percy was in the vicarage, taking stock of life and pondering on the possibility of publicising his memoirs. He could not believe it was the beginning of another new month already and so much had already happened previously that he had hardly time to consider the future.

Sarah Jane Coddle was out with sister Molly catching up on some 'strictly feminine' shopping in the city; apparently Northwich had a fabulous new shopping centre and Sarah had Percy's debit card!

A letter had arrived from the bishop formally announcing the arrival of the new vicar, who was to take over the religious duties of the parish with immediate effect from the 1st February.

Percy glanced up at the clock and smiled to himself, that meant he had been already been excommunicated eleven hours ago!

It also gave Percy just 30 days grace, in lieu of untaken holiday, in which to pack then remove himself, and all his worldly possessions from the vicarage of Lower South-Borough; including, as the bishop had put it, the daughter of Satan!

Percy sighed rather heavily.

He had no idea yet what he would do or where indeed he would go to.

True, they were financially comfortable for the immediate future thanks to the generosity of the parish, and, with their pooled savings they could afford a small mortgage, enough to purchase a pleasant enough cottage.

Of course, they wished to remain with all their family and friends in the community but Percy thought he would find it very hard to pass daily by the church that had been the centre of his universe until so very recently.

His last duty for the parish was to oversee the previously postponed vicarage fancy dress tea party to raise money for local children who had been, for some reason or other, unable to enjoy or afford the festive season of good cheer.

The original proposal had been for a fund raising event by way of actually holding a children's tea party complete with live entertainment and a traditional show such as Punch and Judy.

A number of the committee members had been somewhat alarmed, or at the very least slightly concerned about the idea of encapsulating 80 or 90 pre-teen or just 'coming of age' teenagers in the immediate vicinity of food and fun.

Nevertheless, they had agreed to 'give it a go', so the two events were combined into one with a fund-raising members' fancy dress party and an invitation to the teenagers as well.

Dennis, Charlie, and Bernard had volunteered to take on the role of party organisers whilst Big Jim had also added his name, purely to keep an eye on the aforementioned known pranksters; Tony tagged on because its sounded like a lot of fun and he loved lime flavoured jelly.

Previously the original prestigious inaugural event had to be cancelled at short notice due to unforeseen circumstances, but had been pencilled in again for early in the New Year.

Well at least he would make sure his period of religious servitude would go out with a bang not a whimper, Percy promised himself.

It seemed rather appropriate that the proposed party date fell on Saturday February 14th, not only because it was St Valentines Day but also that the preceding day was the feared Friday 13th, a double whammy.

Percy glanced across to the roaring fireplace and, more importantly, the empty velvet cloak that lay by it, showing no evidence or indication of use for many a night.

Where on earth was that cat sleeping? thought Percy with an air of concern.

Rollo, having recently spent an entire evening 'thawing out' from his permafrost induced attachment to the bird feeder, had arisen early the next day, eaten the contents of his food bowl and disappeared with a whole salmon that had previously been defrosting on the kitchen work surface.

Percy's mind continued to drift.

It had been nearly 10 days since the unexpected and shocking discovery of the indoor bowling centre's conversion to a floral garden worthy of arboricultural praise.

The police, who had taken away the videoed evidence from the CCTV recording system as well as recovering fingerprints from the abandoned whisky bottle and the remaining uneaten mini Christmas cakes, had finally pieced the whole jigsaw together.

The announcement of the villain as none other than Joe 'Dodger' Stubbs came as quite a surprise to the Reverend, but not as much as the tale of Dodger's demise and the manner of his detention.

Apparently, he had been incarcerated in the poshly named Upper Snoddington Infirmary, which was in reality an asylum for the temporarily unbalanced or criminally insane.

Percy found it hard to believe until he saw the pictures of Joe Stubbs, now a wild-eyed jabbering wreck and he wondered what on earth could have happened to have transformed the man into such a state.

He only wished they had CCTV outside the building as well, as he was sure there would be a tale to tell; perhaps they had some mad, shaggy, mythical monster stalking the wildlife gardens?

At the committee meeting Percy raised the point in 'any other matters' but was chided jokingly by the others for talking about the bishop in such a way.

The vicar sighed reflectively and let his mind drift further.

It had taken the club's entire membership five days, dressed in waterproofs and waders, to remove the vegetation, uproot the old carpet and remove every vestige of anything capable of absorbing moisture.

During that time, despite several dehumidifiers, the water vapour had risen like an extreme Indian summer haze under the hot lights, turning the air inside into a humid, sauna-like, jungle atmosphere.

Big Jim had lost 10 lbs in weight, although Charlie joked that he had probably just dropped his wallet.

Percy smiled.

He could still picture the image of Patrick 'Postie' Albright, the clubs green keeper, traversing the indoor green mounted on his new, until then unused, lawnmower, their replacement for the Beast of Lower South-Borough.

It certainly was a beast of a machine, twice the size of its predecessor with twin rotary cutters revolving along a cylinder fully six feet long encased in a steel framework that was driven by a three litre diesel engine producing a mind boggling 200bhp.

A well-sprung tractor style seat surmounted the massive machine from which the driver steered his sturdy mount with a confident expression and a strong pair of hands.

Percy thought it more a case of the driver, with a plaintive tone, simply advising the 'beast' on a suitable direction, as he was sure that, given the chance it would simply do its own thing regardless of any instruction.

That brought back some not so fondly remembered moments from the recent past of his last excursion with the original mower and Percy smiled ruefully at the recollection.

Patrick had eagerly nursed the new mechanical monster into life and roared off up the rink flailing the illicit greenery into submission as he showered nearby onlookers with a cloud of grass cuttings.

Whilst members dived for cover in every direction, Big Jim picked up the abandoned steel collection bucket that Patrick had forgotten to attach, pursuing him with a mixture of grunts and free speech, some of which had the ladies blushing.

Subsequently a rather bashful Patrick had returned in the other direction at slightly less than 50mph, covered in daisy heads and cornflower stems, but not a sign of a single grass stem flying indiscriminately in an airborne manner.

Nevertheless the potential of the new 'Beast of Lower South-Borough' was aptly proven when after two successful bouts of circumnavigating the green Percy appropriately pointed out that Patrick had not only removed the grass but also most of the carpet flock and now only the underlay remained.

'Oh well,' laughed Patrick, 'it's all got to come up anyway,' and with that, he surged off back up the rink.

A trail of sparks in his wake on the return trip was a pointed indication that he was down to bare concrete in places.

Percy had a sudden vision of Patrick attempting to shred the old vicarage Christmas tree into chipped bark for the garden; the image of him riding up and down the elongated length of pine tree like a mechanised, madcap beaver was too much to imagine.

He thought it prudent to stop the green keeper at that point before he did some permanent damage, more to the concrete than to the new mower, judging by its performance.

They decided at that point, they would just have to remove the rest of the carpet the old-fashioned way, with hard graft and all hands on deck. After all, it would still probably take weeks to drain all the water away, with the lower levels and the cellar more like a swimming pool.

In the meantime, the builders had arrived to assess the damage.

Jimmy 'Monkey' Murphy and Johnny 'Midge' McPherson eyed up the additional work speculatively and began totting up the overtime in £ signs.

With the priority of the outdoor club facility to finish building on schedule, they dutifully completed their report and announced their findings.

The indoor club was out of action for the rest of the season!

It would be at least May, with the return of the good weather, before they could expect to properly ventilate and de-humidify the room successfully.

The earliest they could expect to get a new carpet fitted would be July; the supplier's entire stock had been recently purchased by Totters Leisure Centre for a scheduled relaying of all their bowling green surfaces following the recently completed World Championships.

However, a sympathetic phone call from the Leisure Centre Manager, David Van Stem, a highly regarded Dutch entrepreneur, had offered the club members free use of their facilities at Totters until the end of the current season.

The proposal had met with great delight and a fair deal of relief for a number of the bowlers involved in important county competitions; the revised venue was not only one of the best in Britain, but it was only a short 30-minute journey away by car.

Tony Havershall had suggested, quite thoughtfully, that perhaps it would be a good idea to contact ERIC, the Eastern Railway Intercity Company to see if a special service could be laid on to the holiday resort from Lower South-Borough.

The committee had of course welcomed his wonderful idea but had, in the nicest way possible, pointed out to Tony that Lower South- Borough didn't actually have a station and there lay the flaw in his elementary proposal.

As Tony's next suggestion seemed to involve the use of hot air balloons, the committee wisely closed the subject and moved on to the next matter, which appropriately happened to be the forthcoming benefit tea party for the teenagers.

Percy had summarised the particulars that had been previously discussed and invited the events committee to update the meeting.

The disclosure first of all that the event was to be held on Valentine's Day met with a number of shocked, almost fearful, expressions on several of the men's faces and rueful glimmers of expectation on the ladies.

There were obviously a number of people who either feared or delighted in the potential amorous inclinations of the most romantic night of the year; after all, with music, food and the heat of the moment anything was possible.

Charlie seemed to be perspiring just a little, perhaps at the possibility of being cornered by any of the number of single widows or available spinsters that ardently desired his more permanent fixture in their residence.

Bernard seemed to be of mixed emotion, as did Shelia 'Legs' Ramsbottom.

When the moment came to ask for volunteers to help set up the event there was a generous showing of willing hands raised until Reginald Trimley, the faint of heart, naïve and well meaning accountant had asked the question 'Err isn't that Friday the 13th?'

The previously raised hands had dropped more suddenly than the temperature at night time in the Antarctic until Percy had stepped in with a masterful recovery stroke.

'Because our venue has been put out of action by the unforeseen circumstances of the break-in, we have been offered an alternative venue!' he announced.

The entire committee, and invited guests, paused in mid-retraction...

'We have received a call from David Van Stem, General Manager of the championship bowling venue TOTTERS, who has informed me that he has generously offered us the use of one of his function rooms.'

A loud cheer of appreciation resounded around the lounge.

'Furthermore, we will have the services of his catering staff as well as his renowned entertainment stewards the 'Dazzling Bluecoat's.'

The cheers got louder as the members foresaw less responsibility falling in their direction, which could only mean more time for them to enjoy themselves or in most cases eat more, drink copiously and dance outrageously.

Lower South-Borough's members were well renowned for their ability to party and with the practical pranksters in their midst nothing less then organised anarchy was sure to follow, much to the delight, as always, of the local paparazzi.

As the drink flowed there were sure to be a number of uninhibited exhibitionists arising from the more senior age group.

One thing was for sure, thought Percy to himself, it wasn't a case of whether the event made the front page, just a matter of which infamous member was its centrepiece.

TOTTERS' Head Chef Manuel 'Burrito' Mondago, had earned himself the nickname of 'The Jalapeno Pepperer' following his distinctive personalised style of creating outstandingly spicy or savoury dishes of great distinction with tasty, mouth watering and flavoursome fusions.

It was widely commented that his creative skills for zesty foods stemmed from his fiery hot-blooded and sometimes stroppy personality, which in turn originated from his part Mexican, part Spanish hereditary bloodline.

Manuel was a very talented and masterful chef who cooked with a natural flair and an expansive range of culinary ability.

His real passion was for any cuisine of an oriental nature, from tortillas and paella, to vindaloo and sushi he always did it 'par excellence'. But he was also an extra-ordinarily talented master chef when in came to preparing sumptuous buffets, luxurious spreads and superlative smorgasbords.

Given that he was a father of seven children, he had a love for, and experienced familiarity with, family events.

As far as Percy was concerned it sounded like the catering had just become a very small matter to worry about given the capable and safe hands of TOTTER'S chef.

He made a mental note that it might be a warm gesture of gratitude to express their thanks by inviting Manuel Mondago on their forthcoming club Spanish holiday.

Percy was sure he would jump at the chance to visit one of his ancestral countries and it would be a good idea to have somebody along who could actually understand and speak the language.

Tony 'Trigger' Havershall was slightly worried however when he heard Percy describe Manuel as being a multicultural linguist as he wasn't quite sure what it meant.

He voiced serious concerns and pondered whether it was perhaps a type of Italian Spaghetti.

Trigger was particularly confused about ancestral homes as he had only previously heard of Persimmon locally.

Finally, sure he had the right notion he asked what he thought was a pertinent question of the vicar. 'Does multicultural mean I'll have to try lots of foreign food,' He queried, 'because I think I've only been immunised against measles and smallpox!'

That brought quite a few titters from the members present, who knew all too well about Tony's slight lacking in the world of intellectual terminology.

Percy considered the matter further but struggled hard to reply due to an outbreak of mirthful tittering.

Finally he managed to get control of his humour faculties and after telling Tony he would explain it to him later on, Percy returned to the matters in hand.

On reflection, perhaps they should ask David Van Stem as well; after all, he was going to a lot of trouble to help them out with the rest of the season's bowling fixtures.

His mind wandered further still as he considered volunteers for the evening cabaret and had a sudden visualization of Manuel undertaking the infamous Swedish chef sketch from The Muppet Show!

David Van Stem was a tall, well built, jovial and likeable guy, very much a character like Big Jim, always keen to help, crack a joke or partake in a humorous, light hearted scam.

Perhaps he'd make a good impresario? pondered Percy.

A nudge on the shoulder brought him swiftly back to reality and the ring of smiling faces reminded him that his concentration had again wandered; well it was hardly surprising given that he had so much to think about at the moment.

'Well, I guess I can leave the rest of the organisation for the event in the capable hands of our volunteer organisational committee,' he said, nodding his head in the general direction of Charlie, Big Jim, Dennis, Bernard and Tony.

Then with an afterthought added, 'And you'd better go along as well Derek,' he chortled deeply, 'just to keep an eye on them.'

The rest of the room fell about laughing and Derek, for once, smiling at the mickey-take, did the next best thing and stuck his tongue out.

****

It was now just a couple of days away from the party and only a single day more until the new replacement vicar turned up at the church.

Percy's predecessor Reverend Joshua Jackson had been originally recalled from the remote desert community of Alice Springs, in Central Australia, to take up the reins of the ungoverned community.

The Reverend had however fled in terror to the salt mines of Siberia where, obviously feeling safe and secure from the bishop's far-flung tentacles, he had not only declined but also been rather rude and abrupt in his reply.

On receiving the message, the rather incensed bishop attempted to placate his rage by placing his size nine sandals directly across the rear of Reverend Archibald from a distance of 30 paces.

It was a shame that he hadn't opened the window first!

Reverend Archibald may have been an ageing, drooling, cross-eyed, bow-legged bulldog but he still had the shortest fuse of any animal ever born.

His psychopathic response, matched with the dogged determination of a vampire slayer and the aggression of a bloodthirsty zombie meant that it was never wise to rile him.

He had endured a particularly pressing day pursuing the young, feather brained and very annoying baby chicks in the poultry run only to bump heads with the biggest, ugliest, grumpiest rooster he had ever come across.

Retiring to the nearby protection of his armour plated kennel, he had sat down to lick his wounds and was rather surprised to find no less then 72 beak sized hen pecks in his posterior.

It was therefore the final straw when a large, rather unpleasant smelling strappy object had landed very heavily on his most tender of body parts.

Frothing wildly at the mouth Archibald had snatched up the offending item and charged off up the garden at a fast loping run, pausing only to utilise the cucumber frame as a springboard.

Eighty pounds of snarling angry canine beefsteak arrived with a gnashing of teeth and raucous growling through the now empty pane that the flying sandal had previously vacated of glass.

The members of the 'Communion of Divine Pentecostal Perfection', who were then going about their duties in the nearby gardens, ignored the rising screams and yelling. They simply put the increased noise levels down to exuberance and excessive self-flagellation.

They were, nevertheless highly impressed by the bishop's obvious level of devotion.

An hour or two later, following the establishment of an unstable truce relatively maintained by the number of Boneo's in Reverend Archibald's food bowl, the now more reticent bishop pondered his options.

The Rt Hon. Thomas Esq was a very proud and stubborn man, not one to be trifled with, challenged head on, or indeed to be deviated from his chosen path once his mind was set.

'Right!' he thought, 'that's it! If no one is prepared to pick up the poisoned chalice then it falls to me to take the bull by the horns!'

It was time the miscreants of Reverend Percival Peabody's community were given a severe and stern talking to in good old-fashioned Christian vernacular.

Perhaps he should borrow a couple of lions from the local zoo just to emphasise the point?

He rang the bell cord to summon his monk-in-waiting...

Eugene Augustus 'Tabitha' Thomas Esq. was going to Lower South-Borough.

****

Percy was at a loose end so he had decided to wander over to check on the progress of the indoor arena and the building work at the new clubhouse.

He hadn't inspected the builder's site for quite a while and he was sure that it must have progressed some considerable way since last he ventured in that direction.

After all there were only a couple of weeks to go before the inaugural opening by the National President Tommy 'Tick Tock' Ballcock, and Percy, like many others, could not wait for the official commissioning.

Apart from which Tommy was also the former World Champion and was booked to perform a virtuoso bowling display against their current club elite as well as a charity 'short mat' bowls demonstration in the local TRESCOS.

The Reverend had taken the roundabout way to the clubhouse via the wildlife garden to benefit from the relaxing atmosphere of the grounds first. The clubhouse was still a hive of activity and, as he stepped through the main doors into the reception, he was amazed to see just how much the members had achieved in such a short while.

It had always been a case of 'all hands to the braces' in times of need so there had been no shortage of volunteers; even the builders had downed tools and mucked in with the members.

Though it was quite possible that the widely spread knowledge of Lower South-Borough's famous kitchen breakfasts and homemade cakes had perhaps again swayed them just a little.

Nevertheless, they had got stuck in with a passion.

A pair of diesel generator pumps on loan from the fire station soon had most of the water drained away.

Local bird-watchers were somewhat bemused by the sudden five feet rise in the water level at the lake when there hadn't been any rain for at least nine days.

There were also a few raised eyebrows as to why a large number of spring onions and chives were floating around the margins and it wasn't long before speculative dark tales of sinister séances, witches' covens and flagellation of naked bodies with root vegetables drifted through the local pubs.

All the same, there was enough merit in the rumours to have Jiggy 'Snapper' Jenkins camping out in the woods for three consecutive nights but disappointingly, the only footage he obtained was that of a courting couple canoodling on the park bench.

Most terrifying of all had been the rumour that The Goodies were secretly planning to re-introduce the ancient art of 'Eckie Thump'; that resulted in every black pudding in the immediate area being immediately confiscated by the local police, just as a precaution.

Having the builders on site proved a tremendous asset to progress as the fire doors proved just wide enough for them to reverse one of their mini diggers through.

With their assistance and, more importantly, their heavy transportation equipment, every trace of the indoor arena's organic infection had been removed and the entire room stripped bare, back to its concrete floors and plaster walls.

It took only a few moments for them to hook up a couple of grappling hooks before the entire remains of the sodden indoor carpet, including underlay, was ripped from its base and trundled out of the exit towards the waiting dumper trucks.

Not all the members made it off the mat on time.

Trigger was having a fabulous time riding the mat like a bucking bronco as he hung on for dear life whilst Dennis thought it highly reminiscent of his youth when he used to surf the waves of the wild Pacific breakers.

A dozen super-heaters blasted warm air into the void whilst an equal number of dehumidifiers drained litre after litre of water from the moisture-laden atmosphere as fast as they could empty the buckets.

Percy breathed heavily, feeling beads of perspiration breaking out on his forehead; it was more like the Sahara desert in monsoon season, if that was at all possible.

He wouldn't have been at all surprised to have seen a camel in a raincoat pass by.

The inside looked strangely peculiar and barren without all the carpeting, much like the unfinished building outside, with just bare concrete everywhere.

Most of the members with matches to play were rescheduled by now, over at Totters Leisure Centre.

Percy was already having a difficult month trying to amalgamate the events past and those yet to come. With Valentine's Day just around the corner as well he was, like most of the members, wondering about the immediate future and its many possible implications.

His breast stirred with a strange conflict of interests and he had to admit he had enjoyed the last few weeks languishing in the passionate and loving arms of his bride to be, Sarah Jane Coddle.

He also felt a yearning to be back at the helm as his congregation's religious mentor and already missed their playful, sometimes misguided, but always genuine remonstrations.

This Sunday coming was to be the first time he would not be attending; in all the years of service, he had never missed a single one through holiday, illness or any other reason.

Yesterday a late night visit from Mollie and Bertie had been most welcome and they had discussed several notions until the early hours; Percy was quite surprised at one or two of the suggestions, he had no idea quite how strongly his parishioners felt about the plight of their vicar.

Sarah Jane had joined them late into the evening and naturally, the conversation had turned towards the subject of marriage.

They had both become excitedly animated about the way Molly and Bertie had described their dream wedding, and honeymoon on an old-fashioned sailing ship in the sun drenched Caribbean.

It wasn't too long before their exuberance overcame rationality and the vague suggestion at the back of their minds became a foregone conclusion. Percy being at heart the quiet, until recently very shy, country vicar had envisaged just a small service at the church.

Recent events had suddenly made the ideal venue 'out of bounds' and of course he could hardly officiate at his own wedding could he?

Despite the Vatican's continued interest in Percy's success with his congregation, it would be unthinkable for the Catholic church to offer to marry the couple; a mixed denomination service was hardly appropriate and pre-marital relations, were likely to be frowned on.

He looked over at Sarah Jane and caught her eye.

She smiled back with that knowing glint in her eye and the decision was made, just like that.

They were getting married overseas!

It was Percy who came up with the perfect idea, they were, after all, going on holiday to Spain in the summer and what could be better than sun, sea, siesta, sand and...

The slamming of a door somewhere brought Percy back to the reality of the present and the awareness that he had once again been daydreaming.

Dear oh dear, sighed Percy to himself, he really must try to concentrate, but that was one thing that clearly eluded him at the moment. The haunting dream that kept drifting in and out of his sub conscience remained very feminine in shape, something akin to Bo Derek, but with red hair.

He turned and stepped out into the open air, after all, everything was very much in hand at the clubhouse, so perhaps there was something he could help out with at the new building.

His mind wandered again, 'And where the hell was that cat?'

Percy was beginning to get extremely worried about the absence of Rollo.

Not too many miles away Gloria Grimshaw was having exactly the same thought about Miss Matilda Bagshott her prize Persian pussy.

****

The evening of Friday 13th was drawing closer by the second.

Molly was just locking up at the club and getting ready to join her husband Bertie over at TOTTERS in preparation for the Valentine's party the following evening; it all sounded very exciting.

Wasn't it strange, she thought to herself, as she placed the key in the front door and prepared to lock up the building for the night.

The day had passed without incident, argument, disaffection or anything untoward, and in the end everything had been achieved or surpassed.

The clubhouse was on course for full restoration, with the damaged fabrication removed, and everything pristine, proper and prepared for the decorators to move into in six weeks time once everything had finally dried out.

Molly shook her head from side to side.

What on earth was all the fuss about Friday the 13th anyway, she pondered as she pocketed the key, did one final check of the door and stepped away down the path towards her car.

She was lost in thought, pondering the whys and wherefores of the so called day of bad luck as she passed the ancient shed that within in its dark, creepy, suspect interior hid the whims and pleasures of Patrick Albright, the club's green keeper.

Her thoughts were distant and she had little time to react as a strong hand grabbed her suddenly, thrust her roughly into the open shed, and shut the door violently behind her.

Molly had little time to scream as she gazed anxiously about her in the dark interior; there were spider's webs everywhere and she really didn't like it.

A small flicker of flame caught her eye.

What on earth was that?

The small glow grew suddenly into an incandescent flare and then began to hiss louder and louder, before fading back to emptiness for a brief second.

B-A-A-N-N-G-G-G!!!

The small firework was the largest banger available over the counter without requiring a licence for performing special effects.

It shook the building, made the floor shudder, rattled the tools in their holders and created a fine shower of dust that filtered down from the rafters.

In the final flash of the firework, Molly noticed hundreds of pairs of tiny eyes reflected in the bright light and opened her mouth to scream...

There were spiders in the shed...

LOTS OF SPIDERS!

BIG SPIDERS!

'AR-R-R-R-R-R-R-R-RGHHH!!!'

Outside the door Johnny 'Greaser' Stubbs smiled evilly and rubbed his hands with glee. He was very annoyed to find that his older brother had been incarcerated in the local asylum and he couldn't wait to exact his family's revenge on the members' of Lower South-Borough.

He had already put wheels in motion and there were going to be more than a few shocks lying in store when the unsuspecting bowlers boarded F. H. Holiday Tours airbus for their trip to paradise in the summer.

'Airbus?' Johnny laughed at his own terminology, a pre-war Tiger Moth biplane would seem more luxurious than the preferred means of travel he had arranged for the unsuspecting passengers.

Johnny had simply been passing by to check on the outcome of his brother's handiwork and could not resist the temptation for a touch of personal retribution when he saw Molly, all on her own, leaving the clubhouse.

He laughed to himself and walked away with a light step as the screams diminished into the distance behind him.

****

It was the evening of the party and most of the members were gathering excitedly in the function room. The whole purpose of the celebration was to raise money for local children in need, which was a worthy cause that every member wholly supported; every one of them was bringing a teenager along as their guest for the evening.

Percy was already at the venue, passing on his sincere admiration and thanks to David Van Stem, the General Manager of TOTTERS and their Head Chef Manuel 'Burrito' Mondago.

The room looked absolutely fantastic!

The walls were decorated with what seemed miles of decorative streamers and large inflatable hearts, whilst a multitude of balloons in festive pinks and reds covered a net above the floor. Similarly, coloured thickly set tinsel wound up every post and pole whilst several members of the Dazzling Bluecoats waited at the entrance to meet and greet new arrivals.

They looked sensational in their sparkling, sequinned, colour co-ordinated outfits that glittered from head to toe; they even had glitter in their hair and on their faces.

There were others serving at the soft drinks bar and standing by the buffet table waiting to assist the guests once the function got under way.

Percy looked across at the festive fayre with a barely disguised hunger.

The food appeared truly sumptuous, a mind-blowing array of tasty titbits, mouth-watering morsels and creative cuisine that would delight guests of all ages.

Tables groaned under the weight of freshly cooked, finely honed and deliciously formed starters, main courses and desserts.

Deeply bronzed chickens competed with bread-crumbed ham hocks, roast leg of pork and a saddle of best beef.

There was of course a more refined buffet for the adults present including a large bowl of punch, obviously alcoholic judging from the colour of Big Jim's nose; he was already sampling it.

Quiches, savoury spare ribs, sausage rolls, scotch eggs and vol-e-vents fought for pride of place with chocolate covered strawberries, raspberry cheesecake and lemon meringue roulade.

For the children, there was an impressive display of sugary sweet delicacies that only they could appreciate, that included a large number of lime jellies topped with candy cream.

Percy eyed the array dubiously, he wasn't sure that children and jelly mixed very well, especially as he knew the characters of some of the younger guests very well.

He could imagine the likes of Timothy and Abbey Doolittle let loose on the sumptuous buffet and smiled inwardly; the Dazzling Bluecoats would certainly have their work cut out for them tonight!

After the events of the pre-Christmas decorating party he wasn't too sure that the youthful high spirits of Johnny Jackson and Co. would be contained either.

It was a little like asking Billy Bunter to behave with Bob Cherry's latest food hamper whilst the Famous Five went walkabout.

He paused briefly to consider the more senior members and gave up at that point; it really was a lost cause trying to prevent the inevitable.

Still, he reflected, at least the evening's entertainment should be suitably appropriate.

There was a large pair of curtains stretching across the whole of one end of the function room. That must be the stage, Percy mused to himself.

He wondered what the committee had in store for the guests.

He didn't think they would actually decide to opt for a Punch and Judy show.

No, he reflected, they were a little more adventurous than that, so they had probably booked a stand up comedian and maybe even a few clowns, or possibly even a juggler to impress the younger guests with their prowess and agility.

****

The room was already filling rapidly and he noted a number of recognisable faces, or in some cases, bodies.

Sheila Ramsbottom, ever the exhibitionist, had chosen a leopard skin print to show off her shapely assets in her role as Jane, whilst a fake fur covered monkey on a chain proved to be none other than Bernard in the role of Cheetah.

He could see now that Russell Cobblethwaite was dressed as Desperate Dan, Derek as Popeye, Eric as Darth Vader and Patrick as Long John Silver, complete with a stuffed parrot.

Marilyn Monroe, Betty Boo and Tina Turner also joined the gathering throng as did the Blues Brothers, the Invisible Man and a well bandaged Mummy.

Percy rubbed his hands together with delight, he could not believe how much trouble the members had gone to; he could see the younger children such as Abbey and Timothy laughing, joking and apparently having the time of their lives.

Bertie with a now recovered Molly arrived together as the Parisian couple Esmeralda and The Hunchback of Notre Dame.

As per usual Bertie had tended to overdo things and it looked more like he had the mattress, and not the pillows, stuffed up the back of his jacket.

The former tea lady was looking much more relaxed and recovered after her recent ordeal. Her screams had luckily alerted Ronald 'Squiffy' Regis, who lived nearby, and after hearing the large explosion, had hurtled across on his golf buggy at a mind boggling five miles per hour to investigate the cause.

He had very quickly freed the hostage with a hefty looking pair of bolt cutters and escorted her safely home with the assurance that it must have been some kind of a teenage prank.

Percy wandered over to Gloria Grimshaw who appeared to have arrived as Mary Poppins.

'Good evening Gloria, nice outfit. Were you inspired by the musical?' enquired Percy.

She looked back at him with an air of scepticism, 'What outfit?'

He swallowed nervously, and flushed with embarrassment; he really should have known better than to think that Gloria would actually dress up.

Still, he thought, maybe when the spirits flowed she would lighten up just a touch and perhaps actually even enjoy herself just for once...

'What she needed was a man in her life!' Percy muttered with a mischievous smile and his brain immediately began searching the membership for likely candidates; after all, it was St Valentine's and there was no time like the present to initiate introductions.

Leaving a rather confused Gloria in his wake he stepped lightly around the gathering throng making small talk, exchanging well wishes and engaging in whimsical light banter.

Reverend Percival Peabody was thoroughly enjoying himself, he had not a care in the world, neither troubled conscience nor furrowed brow imposed on his pleasant train of thought.

Actually, there were so many thoughts whizzing merrily around Percy's mind, that he could probably have done with a railway station.

He gazed spuriously around the room taking in its entire content with one swift glance, almost like a photograph and his sharpened intellect took several immediate facts into consideration.

A number of notorious faces were missing!

Percy's inbuilt processor pigeonholed every guest into its appropriate cubbyhole and came up with the absentees.

Charlie, Dennis, Big Jim and Derek were conspicuous by their absence.

Two thirds of the entertainment committee were not in attendance and that was far too many to be a coincidence; there was something in the air of which they were obviously aware and Percy wasn't.

He had been around far too long not to sense when a game was in play and this had the distinct feeling of a complex chess match rather than mere tiddlywinks.

Percy stepped resolutely towards the nearest exit. If a game was a-foot he needed to find out what the plan was before it was instigated, although he had a distinct impression that it was probably too late.

As he neared the door, it opened to allow the large girth of the recently appointed county vice-president Jack Tuttle to emerge through its opening.

He was dressed in a big smile and an oversize set of shocking pink 'Teddy Boy' drapes.

With bright blue brothel creepers, lemon and green striped socks and matching waistcoat, complemented by a large lariat style tie he was an absolute riot of colour impossible to miss.

Taking into account his substantial frame one could be forgiven for thinking that Bigfoot had arrived following a run-in with a carwash full of paint.

'Good evening BIG Jim,' sniggered Percy as he took in Jack's unsubtle take on his rock 'n' roll childhood.

Jack continued to grin broadly, looking much like he was having trouble resisting the temptation to burst into hysterical laughter and waved Percy away as he then stepped around him and bounced into the crowd.

The Reverend looked on in a bemused manner before turning back to the waiting door, through which burst the impressively curvaceous figure of Snow White.

She sported a fine mane of black hair in which a large pink ribbon resided, whilst her flowing white dress and black bodice were instantly recognisable as her trademark image.

Of more concern however was the fact that six large teddy bears in dwarves' outfits were strapped around her form in a variety of inappropriate poses whilst a seventh appeared to be sleeping in her overly large cleavage.

Percy did a double take!

The rouged cheeks and brightly coloured lips looked a tad overdone and it defied belief that a womanly and feminine figure such as Snow White could look that rough.

Tony 'Trigger' Havershall smiled back through the garish lipstick.

The penny dropped as Percy remembered the similarly dressed member on the bowling green prior to Christmas; he really must have a word with Trigger about his wardrobe.

The Reverend opened his mouth to say something, but words failed him as Tony likewise flounced by in the wake of Teddy Boy Jack Tuttle.

He also seemed close to a paroxysm of hysterics.

This was all too irregular, thought Percy, something was definitely going on and he needed to get to the bottom of it very quickly.

He glanced at the large shape of Trigger's posterior dressed in white and thought a tactical change of word more appropriate.

Checking that the exit was this time finally clear the vicar dodged through it and took the nearest available route to the manager's office.

It was time he availed himself of the services of David Van Stem and, more importantly, his CCTV security system; there was an urgent need to track down the whereabouts of the juvenile delinquents known as Charlie and Dennis.

Rounding the corner, he spied the plush, uniformly contoured and superlative lines of the championship indoor arena where a number of bowling lanes marched off into the distance towards a giant illuminated scoreboard.

Surprisingly the middle lane was brightly lit by the under-slung floodlighting elements that dwarfed the ceiling with their numerous casings.

There were four people standing on the rink at the far end studying a large compact head of 15 woods, above which the scoreboard read 17 – 17 after the 20th end.

The game was tied on the last end with one wood still to play, as it rested on the mat at the near end, and they were either debating tactics or potential outcomes.

Percy instantly recognised the unmistakeable figure of David Van Stem the Centre Manager and, given the presence of a large white hat on his comrade, what had to be the form of Manuel Mondago the head chef.

The two of them were obviously enjoying a pleasurable relaxing game of pairs following the madcap rush of last minute preparations for Lower South-Borough's fund raising party.

Percy raised a hand in the air in a warm gesture of greeting as he stepped down onto the green's surface.

'Hi David, Hello Manuel, have you seen...'

Percy didn't really get time to say much more than that before his fairly active and already attuned brain alerted him to the identity of the other two players.

He had been subconsciously analysing the tactical data that his eyes were steadily inputting from the moment he had arrived at the rink's boundary. However the well-disguised figures, in the shape of Stan Laurel and Oliver Hardy, hid their identities remarkably well until they turned to face the unannounced arrival of the vicar.

Charles 'Charlie' Chesterford and Dennis 'Sticky' Ditherford had been located!

Rather than appearing guilty, they looked however like they were hanging on the punch line of a lengthy and very amusing joke.

'What on earth are you two doing here?' questioned Percy, directing his query at the two comedians.

'Oh, nothing really, just enjoying a roll up,' commented Charlie with a feigned air of innocence.

'Yes,' said Dennis, following up his partner's repartee. 'We thought we'd wait until the action really started before joining the party so we'd make more impact!'

'Really?' said Percy in a disbelieving and disparaging manner.

'Yes, really!' said the two nodding in unison with fixed grins looking much like the cast of Punch and Judy that Percy had been expecting to arrive on stage shortly for the evening's entertainment.

'The only impact you two clowns are going to make are when you land on the stage in about 10 minutes time to announce the cabaret!' stated the Reverend in a most uncharacteristic 'matter of fact' way that spoke volumes.

'But we're not going on stage?' queried Dennis.

'Yes you are, even if I have to plant a religious size 10 boot firmly on your backsides to get you there,' stated Percy in a tone of finality that dared defiance.

'But...' started Dennis.

'No BUTS!' said Percy unwaveringly.

'But...' repeated Charlie.

'NO BUTS!' confirmed Percy in an affirmation of his resolve.

David Van Stem and Manuel Burrito Mondago looked on as the showdown unfolded, sniggering hugely behind their raised hands; the mirth of the unexpected turn of events obviously tickled them immensely.

Charlie and Dennis looked at each other and then back at the vicar.

'But we haven't finished our game.' whined the two comedians in unison.

'Really?' questioned Percy.

'Really,' affirmed the two defendants, sensing a possible reprieve.

'Right then,' said Percy with a steely gimlet look to his eyes as he stared at them for a second or two, before turning around and marching off resolutely back up the green.

He reached the end of the rink, turned around on the small rubber mat and hefted the remaining bowl in his left hand, bouncing it up and down in his palm with a degree of considered antagonism.

'SO THE GAME'S NOT FINISHED?' queried Percy in a loud voice to the small gathering at the far end.

Dennis moved quickly to nudge Charlie sharply in the ribs, but he wasn't quick enough to prevent the reply.

'No, not finished!' affirmed the Oliver Hardy look-a-like.

Percy raised an eyebrow questioningly towards the Centre Manager.

David Van Stem was still far too busy relishing the approaching moment and half stood in a stooped manner laughing riotously from behind the form of Manuel.

The chef was likewise revelling in the impromptu entertainment and unable to contain the tears of merriment streaming down his face.

David's hand appeared in the air from behind the chef waving a white handkerchief in a symbolic gesture as the two continued to crease up much to the perplexed consternation of Laurel and Hardy.

'Right then,' muttered Percy to himself, spun the bowl lightly in his palm one final time before drawing back his hand and delivering the large inanimate object at great speed up the green.

David and Manuel wisely dived over the edge of the rink still laughing insanely, clearly experiencing a form of hysterical apoplexy, whilst Charlie and Dennis looked on aghast.

The rapidly approaching ballistic missile shook them out of their stupor at the last moment and they made a mad dash for cover as it reached the stationary target.

C-R-A-A-A-S-H-H!!!

Anyone wishing to carry out scientific research as to the possible outcome of an irresistible force meeting an immovable object would have been wise to have made a close study of the outcome.

A split second later all that remained on the green was the hastily abandoned white handkerchief, property of the recently present Centre Manager.

Two others emerged over the top of the bank, arms waving pitifully in the air above where now lay the shocked and recumbent bodies of Charlie and Dennis.

'Looks like that's a dead end then?' queried Percy as the back-spinning white cot rolled progressively faster down the sloping rear corridor towards the televised commentary box.

'Right then!' exclaimed the Reverend with a firm tone of affirmation, 'We'll call that a draw then shall we?'

He rubbed the palms of his hands together in a dismissive display and stepped off the green, parting company with a final comment passed over his left shoulder.

'And I'll see you two on stage in exactly 10 minutes!'

In the distance, David Van Stem and Manuel Mondago continued to express uncontrollable hilarity, and made no attempt to hide it.

'HEE! HEE!'

'HA HA HA HA HA!'

****

The Reverend Percival Peabody was feeling very pleased with himself, not only had he stamped his authority on the two biggest usual suspects he had also nipped any potential shenanigans deftly in the bud.

He had paused for a moment to briefly answer the call of nature and to freshen himself up before rejoining the party; after all the cabaret was imminently due and he didn't want to miss the show, whether it be, after all, Punch and Judy or possibly a festive comedy spectacular performed by the Dazzling Bluecoats.

Percy of course wanted to enter into the spirit of the event and had earlier brought along a travel case, which he had deposited, in the gentlemen's washroom as a convenient place to change.

He lifted the bag up on to the nearby shelf and smiled into the large mirror as he began to unpack his chosen apparel.

A large curved pipe followed a monocle and deerstalker hat onto the surface, closely followed by a lengthy tartan cape with matching three-piece suit; the waistcoat came complete with a large fob watch and chain!

Poetic licence was the order of the day, or the moment, considered Percy as he produced one of Sarah Jane's make-up bags, and it was only a matter of seconds before he sported the dark image of a large curling moustache, lengthy sideburns and over exaggerated eyebrows.

Eight and a half minutes later the vicar had disappeared from view and Sherlock Holmes had arrived at the party, although there was a suggestion of Inspector Clouseau thrown in too!

Percy made a final check in the mirror and with a theatrical flip of his cloak over his shoulder, gripping the shank of the pipe firmly between his teeth, the excited religious detective stepped out of the convenience.

The game was a-foot!!

****

As he approached the doorway to the hall, he noted his timepiece and reflected that at 8.59 and 45 seconds he was perfectly poised to enter the party at just the right moment.

A muffled voice confirmed his opinion as its message drifted though the closed exit doors.

'Ladies and Gentlemen and gathered guests, if I could have your attention please.'

Apparently the cabaret was about to be introduced.

Percy hastened his step towards the entrance and reached for the door handle, after all he didn't want to miss any of the event, did he?

Reaching down, he twisted the handle and stepped confidently through into the function hall; the room was full of talkative people, adults and teenagers alike, all in fancy dress of a bizarre, outrageous or flamboyant nature.

The atmosphere was electric, seemingly buzzing with an air of expectancy; rather too enthusiastically for just a variety show perhaps, thought Percy, nevertheless he selflessly congratulated his flock on such a positive and energetic display of anticipation.

Just for a second he wondered if perhaps he was still in for a shock surprise but quickly dismissed the idea as, on cue Dennis and Charlie, aka Laurel and Hardy arrived on stage.

Eric 'Chalkie' Tunstall, having temporarily removed his Darth Vader helmet, stood centre stage in front of the large curtain with a radio microphone held firmly in his hand.

'Ladies and Gentlemen can I have your attention please?' he repeated as he raised his other hand in a gesture for silence in the ranks.

Charlie and Dennis were looking rather nervously around the stage.

Over to one side Percy noticed a ruffling of the side curtain and two heads popping through briefly to watch discreetly; they belonged to the Centre Manager and Head Chef.

Percy began to feel somewhat alarmed; if they were watching from the sidelines then something was definitely amiss.

The stage curtain on the other side parted a little and a tripod mounted camera eased surreptitiously forward pointing in the direction of the presenter.

Percy instantly recognised the flashy, ring-covered hand as that of local reporter Jiggy Jenkins and began to have a sinking feeling deep inside. There was absolutely no way that the reporter would be here to cover a charitable good news story unless he had prior knowledge of something big and, more importantly, the likelihood of a front-page scoop.

Eric continued with his introductory commentary.

'Thank you all for supporting the fancy dress party tonight in aid of Children in Need, for which we have already raised £5,000 from ticket sales, donations and the raffle.'

A rousing and intense round of applause acknowledged the crowd's approval.

'Furthermore we have a number of our local teenagers joining us here tonight to help us in our celebrations. Therefore it seemed only fitting that we allow them the opportunity to choose the manner of entertainment for tonight's show.'

A slightly more restrained and nervous applause followed that revelation.

Percy had a sudden revived recollection of the previous year's coach trip and invitation to one of their youngest members Timothy Doolittle to select the music for the journey.

Dennis and Charlie were beginning to look desperately about for a safe haven on stage and it was patently obvious they not only were aware of the impending entertainment but had also played a major part in its orchestration.

'Heaven forbid,' panicked Percy, 'in God's name what the hell have those two got up to this time?'

A sudden thought filled him with deep dread.

'Oh my God they haven't booked Iron Maiden!'

Just the sheer contemplation of the satanic rock band's on-stage rituals was enough to send shivers down his back and had his left hand reaching for his mobile phone; they were going to need quite a lot of ambulances.

This was not music for the faint hearted!

At worst Percy had previously expected maybe an Elvis Presley impressionist or possibly even a presenter with a karaoke machine.

'We did contemplate having a mobile discothèque,' announced Eric.

The announcement was greeted with a large number of cheers from the younger members and a few deep-seated groans from the more senior element.

Charlie and Dennis began to nervously, cautiously sidestep towards the far end of the stage, discretion being the better part of valour in their eyes, regardless of the consequences.

Beneath the curtain a subtle film of fine man-made mist began to drift over the stage front; Percy recognised the signs, he still remembered the midnight Mass service!

'JESUS CHRIST! they HAVE booked Iron Maiden!!'

He muttered apologies under his breath for the blasphemy and thought that perhaps a comment of 'holy smoke' might have been more appropriate.

Turning on his mobile phone, Percy quickly dialled 999, just for a second pondering whether he should in fact be dialling 666.

Eric on centre stage waved his hand from side to side in a negative gesture, as Charlie and Dennis reached the furthermost edges of the podium.

'Don't panic we haven't got a disco,' then as an afterthought almost as if sensing the Reverend's nervous disposition, 'or a heavy metal band either!'

Percy paused in mid dial.

'So without further ado or further elaboration of an introduction, here to introduce themselves, hot from their worldwide comeback tour I am proud to present to you tonight's star entertainment!'

Almost on cue the curtains swept back in a bold statement of unveiling.

A suspenseful silence already hung over the arena like a storm cloud waiting to break; there was a tense, nervous and expectant anticipation tinged with fear of the unknown in the air.

As such, the audience had little time to take in exactly what had previously lain behind the grey curtain but was now fully exposed to public scrutiny.

On both sides of the darkened void two massive columns of speakers rose like rocky towers spiralling towards the heavens as the induced fog rolled across the stage floor and spilled over its edge.

Four microphone stands stood amidst the swirls spaced equidistant from each other whilst fake lightning flared intermittently over the vague background of a New York skyline at night.

Nothing would have surprised Percy more had a flock of vampire bats emerged from the darkness, or ABBA had risen, reborn, from beneath the stage.

The pregnant pause between the fearful expectation and the visual reality was just enough for the members to take stock of their life insurance policies as a 30 foot long pink neon sign flickered into life across the backdrop with the ominous message PLEASE FASTEN YOUR SAFETY BELTS.

Percy recited a short prayer of atonement under his breath and foolishly reached for the seat belt that wasn't there, as did a large number of the other senior members.

The more youthful element were however chattering excitedly amongst themselves and pushing through to the front of the crowd; they had recognised the logo and realised in awe its reality.

There was very obviously a consensus of opinion from the teenagers that this was going to be mega, fab and cool.

There was a flicker of movement on stage as the shadowy outline of four semi-clad females walked up to the microphones whilst a fifth stepped centre stage with her back to the audience, one arm raised in the air.

She was the only member visible as a small spotlight snapped on overhead illuminating her in a boldly coloured outrageous and gaudily coloured cat suit.

Percy's jaw dropped.

What the hell was the Pink Panther doing on stage?

The speaker stacks crackled into life with a mounting introductory crescendo of organ music as the Panther spun on her axis, mike in hand, and a 10,000 watt vocal introduction boomed through the building at 110 decibels, cracking Derek's glass eye in the process.

'LA-A-D-I-E-E-S AND GENTLEM-E-E-N WELCOME ALL THE WAY FROM N-E-E-W Y-O-R-R-K!!!'

Percy was totally oblivious to the introduction; the guest singer introducing the band was none other than his bride-to-be, Sarah Jane Coddle.

A hand appeared from nowhere with a large tot of brandy in a small glass; Percy took it and knocked it back in one gulp, which wasn't easy to do with his mouth still wide open.

Nevertheless, most of the burning liquid made it inside and he gagged at the intensity as the fiery fluid hit the back of his throat before descending quickly down inside him.

'PLE-E-E-A-S-E GIVE A BIG WE-L-L-COME TO...'

Percy put down the now empty glass then, on reflection, held it out to Long John Silver who was standing at his side brandishing a near full bottle of five star brandy; a refill was very quickly on its way following its predecessor.

'THE S-P-I-C-E-Y G-A-L-S!!!'

With an explosive, earth shaking, ear splitting, cavernous roar a line of pyrotechnic thunderflashes exploded in quick fire succession across the stage front and Percy's last vestige of an old fashioned tea dance was blown out of the back door.

Colourful floodlighting kicked into high gear, smoke belched thickly in front of miniature wind turbines and lasers created stunning time tunnels as the four famous Spicey Gals stepped up to the microphones and began to sing.

'WELL I'LL TELL YOU WHAT I WANT, WHAT I REALLY REALLY WANT...'

The Pink Panther wiggled her bottom, pointed in the vicar's direction and mimed the words at him in a suggestive manner before flouncing off the stage.

****

It was about 30 minutes into the show and Percy along with one or two of the organisation committee had retired diplomatically to the bar further down the building for a reflective observation of the evening's events.

It had been, after all, a tremendous success much to Percy's shock and surprise.

He was not much experienced in the world of pop trivia and he had no idea that the Spicey Gals were such a massive attraction or sported such a huge following from all age groups.

Apparently every person in the room with the exception of the former vicar of Lower South-Borough not only knew the introductory song but also owned a copy.

The pink clad panther sat on Percy's lap and stared at him with an expression of hopelessness.

'My dear Percy there is so much I will have to teach you...'

He looked back at Sarah Jane with a sheepish expression, he wasn't quite sure whether to kiss her, stroke her head or give her a saucer of milk!

Big Jim still looked a little wild-eyed and slightly the worse for wear.

'Well it's a good job I slipped a bottle of something a bit stronger into the bowl of punch on the adult's table.' he stated loudly with a slight slurring of his words.

Charlie laughed loudly. 'That's funny, so did I,' he announced.

Dennis raised his left hand guiltily. 'I'm afraid I did too,' he admitted.

Patrick roared with laughter, nearly falling off his chair and the others joined in raucously.

'No wonder everyone started dancing so quickly,' said Percy.

All in all, the party had been, and continued to be, a runaway success judging by the noise emanating from the reception hall down the corridor.

So far, there had only been one incident of near cardiac arrest arising from one of the most senior ladies getting carried away with juggling olives into her mouth.

She had been doing spectacularly well until she accidentally introduced a large pickled onion, which promptly lodged in her throat necessitating an on-the-spot demonstration of the Heimlich manoeuvre from Sheila who was a trained first-aider.

One or two had embarrassingly lost the top set of their dentures when the fireworks went off whilst Russell Cobblethwaite's full set was found the morning after, firmly attached to one of the microphone stands.

There was some consternation when the cleaners discovered a wooden leg, later the following day, sparking off a search of the venue for a stranded one-legged guest in a state of disarray.

It was with a sense of relief they realised 30 minutes later that it actually belonged to Long John Silver who had spent so long leaning on his crutch singing 'Yo Ho Ho and a bottle of rum' that he hadn't noticed when his false leg dropped off!

Certainly it had been very amusing when Sporty Spicey had swung her microphone stand through 360 degrees and removed Jiggy Jenkin's badly fitted hair piece clean away from his head.

Poor Timothy 'Tiny' Doolittle would take several years to live down his embarrassment...

The incongruous image of Gloria whirling him around the dance floor attempting the foxtrot was bad enough. But the visual image of Tiny being clutched tightly to her heaving and buxom chest whilst leaving his feet sweeping a full three feet above the surface of the wooden floor was a haunting nightmare.

Big Jim laughed heartily as the story was recounted once again by Charlie and he gave the nearby Derek a hearty mirthful, if somewhat alcohol-induced slap on the back.

Luckily for Derek his glass eye landed safely dead centre of the punchbowl with a distinctive splash; less fortunate was that he spent the next hour with a cocktail cherry in its place before Percy felt it necessary to point out the oversight to him.

There was much consternation amongst the members consuming the beverage that the eye remained missing after the punchbowl had been fully drained; a playful Dennis was lucky not to be lynched when he produced it from his top pocket 15 minutes later.

'Well,' said Percy with an exaggerated sigh, 'Come on you lot, it's time we rejoined the masses for the grand finale,' as he checked his watch and found that only five minutes of show time remained.

With a few grunts and groans, not to mention some very unhealthy staggering, the members of the Lower South-Borough Entertainments Committee gathered themselves and lurched back down the hall towards the reception.

If the noise was any indication, the party was indeed in full flow and there could be little doubt that every member was singing backing vocals at the very top of their out of tune voices.

Percy was already conjuring up a mental image of a fancy dress clad overspill from Universal Studios feasting on a buffet whilst at a rock concert and the picture was a touch disquieting.

They reached the vibrating doors that were trembling with the resonance of the Spicey Gals latest song being introduced by their lead singer.

Jack Tuttle, being the county vice-president and a gentleman led the way, stepping through the door as he half turned to Charlie Chesterford with a questioning expression.

'I didn't know the Spicey Gals did a song called FOOD FIGHT?'

The airborne green jelly caught him flush on the forehead before trickling slushily down his face and he looked up in surprise as the sweet dessert reached his taste buds.

'Mmm, lime, my favourite,' he announced with a smile.

Percy looked underneath Big Jim's raised arm and noted the cream cake carnage that ensued inside the hall as the Spicey Gals incited a confectionery riot.

The club members and guests had apparently needed very little encouragement to take the fun-filled party to extremes.

Pauline Jenner ran past them screaming wildly with a chocolate éclair stuck up her left nostril, whilst Sheila Ramsbottom sat in the middle of the dance floor with a happy confused expression and a sherry trifle sitting upside down on her head.

Percy glanced over at David Van Stem who had just joined the committee members at the doorway; he was wearing an insane, childlike, expression about his face, and was struggling to remove a sticky jam doughnut from his right ear.

Manuel, the chef, was close behind him but looking slightly the worse for wear. This, Percy concluded, was probably due to his easily identifiable form becoming the recipient of half a dozen custard cream tarts.

Percy groaned.

'I think we had better go back to the bar,' he concluded as he turned back to the others, but they were already on their way there.

****

It was the following morning; the first Sunday without Reverend Percival Peabody summoning his flock to attend communion.

Back inside the vestry, the Rt Hon. Eugene Augustus Thomas busily prepared for his very first service at Lower South-Borough.

He had been debating for some while now, the best approach to take with his planned 'rescue' of the corrupted, misled, wanton and wayward souls of the vicar's former parish.

He already envisaged himself in the manner of their saviour, leading the lost and forlorn flock back from their garden of despair to the Promised Land.

A 'softly softly' attitude had been discounted quite sometime ago and he had decided, eventually that he would drag them back, kicking and screaming, in a manner more befitting their blasphemy.

Finally it was time to give the heathens' their wake up call!

The bishop was now busy building up a substantial head of steam as he contemplated the vengeful wrath of a full-blooded end-of-the-world sermon.

As he straightened his best hessian cloth sacking about his impressive personage he was already practising the delivery of his most apocalyptic hellfire and brimstone lecture.

By the time he reached the church, the vestry door slamming shut behind with a thunderous echo like the trapdoor of Satan's pit itself, he was fired up with a fervour for reclaiming his parishioners.

As he climbed the steps leading up to the pulpit, the bishop was already writhing with pleasure at the thought of delivering a lecture full of eternal damnation.

Fully convinced that he had settled on the right sermon, with the need to salvage all the souls he could from this congregation's corrupted, contaminated, seedy squalour he reached the top of the pulpit.

Turning around in a dramatic, theatrical manner, he slammed his Bible onto the bookstand with a loud crash that shook the rafters, as he opened his lungs to bellow the first words of saviour's speech.

'SINNERS REPENT!!!'

Bishop Eugene Augustus Thomas the Third looked upwards and outwards with a an expression of zealous obsession expecting to see the congregation quaking in their boots, praying for forgiveness.

He stared out, with a look of disbelief, across the church pews that seemingly panned out into the distant recesses of the vast church.

They were empty; not a person attended or paid heed to his call for confession or cried for salvation.

In fact only one small group of occupants now resided in the entire vast emptiness of the church.

On the oak beam above him sat a family of squirrels.

Having vacated the former residence of their Christmas tree

in the previous month they had now moved into the luxury self-contained upright apartments of the church organ pipes.

Admittedly, it was a little harder for them to collect food but the scaling of the church bell ropes every night certainly improved their fitness.

On the other hand, their new accommodation was weatherproof, spacious, high-rise and featured piped music throughout the building.

The faint tolling of the bells during the witching hour also had the locals spreading fearful tales of dark magic at work.

One of the young squirrels lent over the beam and looked down at the bishop's shiny bald head; he didn't like the way the sun reflected off it.

Eugene Augustus Thomas was not impressed by the parishioners' boycott and even less so by the acorn which bounced painfully off his forehead. Nevertheless, he had come prepared to preach, and preach he would, if only to attempt the conversion of the heathen rodents.

He mounted the pulpit steps, opened his book to a pre-marked page and began his earthy oration to the watching squirrels.

Another acorn arrived soon after.

****

Back in the empty vicarage all of Percy and Sarah Jane's effects stood ready boxed in preparation for their removal.

Nearby the newly arrived Reverend Archibald stomped uncomfortably around his new quarters, he didn't like the smell of cat that emanated from the study, nor its implications.

He hated cats, and always chased them at any given opportunity, as long as they were smaller than him of course.

He was therefore, much aggrieved to find seven purring, mewing balls of fluff pummelling the brand new blanket in his much treasured and cherished wicker basket.

Already grouchy from being forcibly moved from his safe haven to this unknown residence, Archie was in a particularly foul mood; he had double vision in his crossed eyes, a bad case of 'drool' and his bow legs had developed gout.

He advanced onto the furry invasive creatures but was slightly confused as to which one he should chase first as he could see 28 of them. Archie was so engrossed on selecting his first victim he paid scant attention as to how on earth they came to be there in the first place.

****

Rollo had been sneaking back and forth to the vicarage for weeks, during Percy's absence, helping himself to a large number of the vicar's provisions, mainly of a fishy nature, until all that remained were a few cans of baked beans and one pack of mushy peas.

Finally Rollo, now a proud father of seven kittens, had returned home with the whole litter to present his lively entourage to Percy unaware of the Reverend's recent relocation.

There were three females, Wispa, Tara, Minky, three males, Thomas, Podge-Podge, Smudge, and a rather confused Much-Ado who thought he was a tortoise.

The proud parents had escorted the tiny, mischievous litter of mini-moggies over to the vicarage and then Rollo had gone on ahead to check out the lie of the land whilst Baggie tended to the needs of her wayward munchkins.

Finding the study window open Rollo had quickly taken advantage to gain a bird's eye view inside and was rather pleased to see a brand new woollen blanket as well as an expansive wicker basket.

It was almost as if the Reverend had been expecting him to turn up with a large number of uninvited guests. With a final check from the windowsill Rollo left in search of Baggie, eager to begin ferrying the children into their new home.

He was so eager to renew his bond with the kittens he failed to notice the dark dog-shaped shadow pass briefly across the kitchen doorway further down the hall.

Thirty minutes later the job of re-homing the family was nearly complete, having deposited the last kitten safely into the soft receptacle of the basket Rollo had hesitated briefly by the open window.

There was something different about the vicarage that Rollo just couldn't work out but it was very much like the distinctly pungent and ugly smell of D-O-G.

He had naturally assumed that the vicar must have just had a visitor with a preference for one of those disgusting creatures, although, for the life of him he couldn't understand why on earth anyone would want a companion that was unable to even provide its own entertainment and didn't use a litter tray?

Nevertheless, he had carried the children, one at a time, in relay with his companion Miss Matilda Bagshott, up onto the ledge of the open window and taken turns in dropping them safely onto the soft blanket below.

Rollo and Baggie, as the Persian pussycat preferred to be known, were now perched precariously on the window ledge, purring softly to their mewing clan below them.

They were quite content sitting there, preparing to jump, playing their favourite game of 'dare' with each other when the Reverend Archibald stalked angrily into the room and made a beeline for the basket.

Archie was having enough trouble keeping an eye on the 28 real and imaginary kittens that already bounced around his playpen and had absolutely no idea that other larger visitors were watching him intently.

He would have been wiser to retreat whilst he had the chance, but the possibility of others watching him hadn't even remotely entered his mind.

Rollo lost the game of dare but succeeded in landing on Archie's back just a split second before Baggie arrived.

The howl of anguish could be heard several miles away and some of the more elderly of the village residents were convinced that the bishop had resurrected the Hound of the Baskervilles.

Archie went berserk!

He charged around the room in blind panic before making a mad dash out of the door and around the other vicarage rooms in a desperate attempt to dislodge the unwanted passengers.

Despite the awful smell of dog Rollo and Baggie were actually quite enjoying the exhilarating experience and determinedly hung on tightly with their sharp claws as the thrilling rollercoaster ride continued.

They leaned back on all fours as if riding a surfboard, letting the breeze waft through their shaggy coats at speed giving the impression they were inside a wind tunnel.

It couldn't last of course, and together they leapt off Archie's back onto the study desk as he passed it by, scattering the bishop's papers everywhere and spilling a cold cup of tea over the computer keyboard.

Reverend Archibald was none the wiser; he could still feel the presence of the now absent claws and continued his headlong charge eventually finding the back door before disappearing through it.

The now somewhat damp computer sparked and fizzled with crackles of short-circuiting electricity, flickering into a number of spontaneous un-requested actions before its fuses finally blew.

The screen briefly displayed a final note before becoming permanently blank.

MESSAGE SENT

Unbeknown to the bishop, his recently updated and highly informative private diaries had just been e-mailed to Archbishop Matthew James Twiggle, one of the most senior member's of the church hierarchy.

The failing computer had also emailed enquiry forms to every recipient held in the bishop's junk mail file requesting a brochure.

Unfortunately for him that included a number of wine merchants, limousine suppliers, two Viagra stockists and a latex rubber company with questionable special offers.

There were indeed more shocks in store for Eugene Augustus Thomas the Third.

CHAPTER SEVEN

MARCH

ICING ON THE CAKE

Percy sat in the sumptuous comfort of a brand new armchair facing the outdoor bowling green, or at least where he assumed it should be.

It was extremely cold outside, in fact the coldest March on record with a heavy fall of snow that had continued for several days now resulting in a thick layer of the white stuff covering everything in a uniformity of colour and surface shape.

With the wind chill factor, temperatures had plummeted steadily and today already stood at minus 20 degrees Celsius with a forecast of even colder conditions overnight.

Percy shivered involuntarily.

He briefly recollected the 'adventure' of Big Jim and Derek in the outside toilet the previous year and considered it likely they would have encountered a polar bear had they been there this week.

In fact if anyone now needed to visit the Icelandic hellhole, given the current weather conditions they would be better off giving serious consideration towards building an igloo around a plastic bucket; it would be warmer and a lot safer.

Percy shivered again.

He wasn't actually cold, far from it, he was exceedingly warm, like toast in fact and it felt rather bizarre staring at the swirling blizzard from the inside of Murphy & McPherson's best triple glazed windows.

The Reverend was in fact sitting on one of the new chairs in the recently finished, furbished and completed clubhouse; it was ready at last.

He had not been able to resist the temptation to wrap up in his best cloak and brave the elements in order to take a sneak preview of the long awaited flagship of Lower South-Borough. His shoes stood by the front door, keeping guard like a pair of toy soldiers; after all, it wouldn't be good to trail slushy footprints through the clubhouse on its brand new carpet, even though there were voluminous sheets of plastic everywhere.

There was even one covering the chair that he presently rested in and he felt, to some degree, like an uncooked oven-ready chicken sitting on the supermarket shelf.

By his side stood a small cafetière of coffee which he had taken the liberty of preparing earlier; it was very good coffee, he decided.

A notepad and pen rested on his knee, balanced in preparation for whatever action he felt inclined to follow.

Percy was having a private moment far from the maddening crowd in which to ponder, deliberate, consider and take stock of all recent changes in his life.

These last two months had been tumultuous, turbulent and twisting like a rollercoaster on a never-ending spiral of turns changing more rapidly than the traveller could anticipate the next bend.

He still found it hard to believe that he was no longer the Reverend of Lower South-Borough, although to all intents and purposes he might well have been as the entire community still regarded him as their one and only religious confidant.

In three week's not one member of the congregation had attended the Sunday service held at the church by the bishop.

Instead, all the people of the parish had gathered with him on the bare concrete floors of the indoor bowling arena to share prayers and common words of gratitude for the lives they shared together.

The room, although bare in fixture and fitting was never barren in spirit.

There had been many rumours circulating about candles burning late into the night at the church, of bells tolling at unearthly hours, aberrant, almost insane, religious rantings through the empty building, interspersed by a number of repetitive painful cries.

Harry 'The Hammer' Huckstable the church organist had snuck into the basilica a couple of times whilst the bishop was absent; just to make sure that nothing untoward was going on.

Mysteriously, all that he could report were the presence of a large number of acorns rolling around the floor near the pulpit and quite a few dead twigs in the vestibule.

He did mention that it now looked like the bishop had taken to sleeping in the adjoining vestry instead of the vicarage.

Harry didn't investigate any further as there was something rather horrible, all fat, slobbery and bowlegged, snoring by the altar.

Percy made a note on his writing pad.

1) CHECK THE VICARAGE.

After all, if the bishop was otherwise occupied then it was a good time for Sarah Jane and himself to remove their packed possessions. A number of the men had volunteered to assist and Patrick had offered to hitch up a trailer to The Beast of South-Borough to move the heavy boxes.

He was getting very concerned that he had not seen Rollo for a number of weeks now and, as much as the manic moggie was a pain in the proverbial rear, he still loved him and Percy missed his riotous antics that always brought a wry smile to his face.

The Reverend made another note.

2) FIND THE CAT.

A number of the club's members thought they had spotted the shadowy figure of the church cat around the gardens and Patrick swore that he had actually seen Rollo dragging the vicar's cloak clean across the green.

It was later found with a number of cotton socks, the top half of Russell Cobblethwaite's thermal long johns, Trigger's Noddy cap and Gloria Grimshaw's best woollen tights in the bird hide.

There were also a large quantity of empty pilchard tins, dried cat food packs and a half mangled carrier bag full of PUDDIES Best Meaty Chunks.

Given those facts and also a chicken carcass, a number of cream cartons and a half-eaten salmon, apparently the one that went missing from the Christmas celebrations as it still had a miniature Santa decorating it; the culprit was fairly identifiable.

'Or was that culprits with an S,' pondered Percy.

Gloria had being complaining recently that she had misplaced her pussy, much to the consternation of the older male members; it would seem that Miss Matilda Bagshott was also conspicuous by her absence.

Percy sensed a conspiracy going on here and made an adjustment.

2) FIND THE CAT(S).

Talking of conspiracies, he recounted the recent ramifications of Joe 'Dodger' Stubbs' interference with the seasonal festivities and even more recently the mysterious episode of Molly's uninvited 'lock-up' in Patrick's old tool shed.

The aforementioned criminal was safely under lock and key in Upper Snoddington's Infirmary in a still tattered, shattered battered and bruised state, both of mind and body.

He picked up the pen again and proceeded to make another addition to his growing list.

3) WHO LOCKED UP MOLLY?

The flurries of fresh snowflakes against the window and the background howl of the icy cold wind outside reminded him of another important task to attend to before suppertime.

4) CHECK THE HEATING OIL LEVELS.

The indoor club relied heavily on a emergency back-up heating system that was oil fired and could be initiated when the weather conditions became too fierce or sustained for the background storage heaters to cope with.

It was after all a very large room and there was only so much the main system could do, besides, the oil-heated radiators provided instant, controllable heat unlike the storage system, which required long term planning on time activation.

Percy paused to pour himself a fresh mug of coffee, allowing his free hand to doodle absent-mindedly on the pad as other matters ventured into his thoughts and out again.

Two sugars and a dash of cream later he took his first sip of the sweet, deliciously hot, nectar and, refreshed, glanced down to take stock of his tasks for the day.

He smiled broadly to himself.

Items 5, 6, 7, 8, and 9 all said two words.

Sarah Jane!

Percy settled back into the comfortable recesses of his armchair and a warm glow passed through his body that definitely was not the coffee, even though it was very tasty indeed.

It seemed hardly a few short weeks since Molly's sister had appeared unexpectedly at the building site and proceeded to first influence, and then finally change, his life to such a high degree.

It had indeed been a most peculiar and eventful season; he reflected.

Reverend Percival Peabody was, despite everything, a very content man.

He glanced around the new clubhouse and soaked up the luxuriousness of his current surroundings.

Despite all the hindrances, headaches and hiccups the builders had, true to their word, finished the construction on time; in fact two weeks ahead of time.

Outside all trace of surplus brick, timber cut-offs and steel scaffold had been removed along with sand, gravel, cement bags and all manner of paraphernalia indicative of building sites.

Percy laughed out aloud as he glanced back out of the window.

It really didn't matter anyway did it: he pondered, looking at the snow falling more heavily than ever, you could have hidden a double-decker bus full of building implements under the white blanket and nobody would have noticed.

He had seen the gardens prior to the sudden, unexpected arrival of snow and had been very impressed indeed with the level of re-sculpturing, landscaping and additional improvement to the whole area surrounding the new clubhouse.

There was little doubt that the builders were to be congratulated on their achievements.

Perhaps he should recommend to the bowls committee that they extend the club's hospitality and good fortune by inviting

Jimmy Murphy and Johnny McPherson to the free Spanish holiday in El Toro Tiddlemarsh later that year.

Percy decided it was time to stretch his legs and used the excuse of returning the coffee pot to its rightful home to take a lengthy detour around the completed venue.

He was amazed.

There were now separate ladies' and men's changing rooms built into the clubhouse, rather than the older timber sub-divided unisex facility they had all previously shared with some degree of embarrassment.

On a number of occasions there had been some near disastrous revelations of the fleshy kind as well as indiscreet exposure of radical underwear selection and some untimely embarrassing involuntary noises; not always from the men either!

Percy still remembered a number of unexpected and perhaps more opportune first liaisons that had arisen over the earlier decades, none more so than that of Russell and Cynthia Cobblethwaite who had now been happily married for a number of years.

Of course their lives did get a little hectic when the grandchildren Abbey and Timothy came to stay during holiday periods.

Then of course there was the more unorthodox and unlikely partnership of Doris and Douglas Doolittle; she had caught his attention in a rather delicate manner when demonstrating the best way to 'chip shot' with a pitching wedge. He had to admit, sometime afterward that it had been a fine stroke if not perhaps the luckiest one'

Squiffy, who had been on hand at the time, responded with alacrity and a large bag of ice cubes hastily scavenged from the bar area. Even though Douglas, a retired surgeon, had to agree afterwards that it had been the right action to take, but it was nevertheless hard to differentiate between which outcome felt the worst.

Big Jim, arriving with the first-aid kit in tow, concurred that both sets of screams did indeed sound remarkably similar.

Once the swelling had subsided and Douglas's voice returned to its more baritone origination Doris had invited him out to lunch at the golf club by way of apology and that really was that; another perfect match.

Percy's mind wandered further, first to Molly and Bertie then, before he realised it, to himself with Sarah Jane; funny how it always seemed to come back to her, no matter what he was thinking or doing, reflected Percy.

He gave himself a little shake, cleared his thoughts and continued his grand tour.

The men's washroom area was a joy to behold, comfortable seats, well-lit mirrors complete with shaver points, a newspaper stand, heated hand towel rack and real soft toilet tissue!

'Hallelujah!' muttered Percy exuberantly.

He glanced into the ablutions' facilities area further; there were hot showers, a drinks fountain and, heaven forbid, even a bidet!

He was sure the ladies' quarters would be equally superb but he still felt shy about a number of feminine concerns so chose not to take a peek!

Percy did note, however, that every room he ventured into featured a number of tiny loudspeakers projecting background music, no doubt to help the players relax before and after the event.

He made a mental note to make sure the compact disc player was kept under close scrutiny at all times to prevent further re-occurrences of such music related dramas as the previous coach trip.

Passing through the trophy room it still surprised him to see just how many accolades and achievements the club members had accomplished over the many years. There was indeed a fine display of impressively burnished cups, adorned shields, engraved crystal goblets and team photographs commemorating their successes.

A central feature caught his eye over on the ladies' display wall and he wandered over for a closer look, smiling broadly as he approached and recognised the particular trophy that hung there.

It was a pair of fashionable, if now dated in style and somewhat antique men's Y-Fronts under which the in-captioned legend read Ronald Regis Challenge Cup 1982.

Charles 'Charlie' Chesterford's notoriety from that famous match would remain until antiquity.

Passing back through the central lounge he began to feel a deep seated feeling of pride for his congregation's wonderful, remarkable achievements in such a short time; yet it was touched with a pang of sadness that perhaps he would not remain to enjoy its reward with them.

To the left, lay the plush offices for the club management and he paused briefly, putting his head inside to observe the new function suite.

It was no surprise at all to find every conceivable modern facility including an impressive 20 foot projector screen and surround sound; it would be like being at the movies.

Now there's an idea for fund raising, thought Percy, before kicking himself for being foolish; after all, he wasn't likely to be here was he?

He stepped back out and took a minute to fully admire the stunning glass fronted lounge that provided ample viewing of the club's bowling green; it ran the full length of the clubhouse enabling every lounge resident to enjoy the visual experience.

They certainly wouldn't enjoy much today! sighed Percy as he looked through the glass to the world outside; the snow continued to fall.

He looked across the green to where a terrace area provided a generous picnic area for the summer visitors, or at least it would once the weather improved.

Percy had seen the blueprints, and knew that it also sported a bouncy castle, and mini bowls green for the children, as well as a spectacular play fort for the cats.

The builders having had a fair amount of excessive timber and a humorous manner had decided to give the bowlers the opportunity to restrain the moggies whilst games were in progress. There was probably also some element of trying to placate the pussycats following the builders run-in with Rollo and Miss Matilda Bagshott during the club's demolition phase.

The resultant construction had provided more rooms, tunnels, niches and nooks than the average castle as well as a roof-top sunning area.

Percy had little doubt that Rollo would be enjoying the benefits of that for some time to come; he also had a sneaking suspicion that 'Baggie' might be joining him.

The Reverend had nearly reached the end of his impromptu inspection and, reaching the kitchen area, reflected on the memory of Molly Tattleford, one time spinster of the parish, serving coffee whilst absentmindedly dressed in her best tea cosy.

He remembered the mayhem caused by Bernard with his playful slap on her rump and laughed to himself at the thought that it was more likely to be the 'shy' Molly to provide a teasing slap now.

As fast as Percy considered one outcome another popped into his thought pattern like one tangent following another.

Bernard...

Now there was an unexpected possibility...perhaps he had bitten off more than he could chew with the Australian tomboy Sheila Ramsbottom.

Bernard could soon be ruefully waving goodbye to his long standing bachelor-hood, but he would be sure to have a very interesting and challenging life, albeit a fiery one.

Percy chuckled.

It was time to write that book, he decided, and he made a definite decision to use the forthcoming holiday in Spain to begin his preparations.

His ramblings and journey of exploration continued.

The new kitchen area was a vast expanse of sparkling stainless steel seemingly capable of furnishing fast food for the crew of a battleship.

There were all manner of accessories; in fact, you couldn't accessorize the kitchen any more if you tried!

Pride of place took centre stage in the form of a state of the art coffee maker; not just any old machine either, but one that offered a selection of no less than 10 different types of Arabica coffee beans to grind!

Percy still remembered the time Molly, in her naivety had mixed up the instant coffee and gravy granules. Poor old Dennis had consumed half a mug in one mouthful before he realised the error of her ways. His subsequent expression of distaste and rejection of the supposedly sweet offering resulted in a voluminous expulsion over most of the nearby committee.

They could easily have auditioned for a part in a Caribbean musical after the event whilst Dennis's taste buds had taken two weeks to recover their full sensitivity.

He turned on the nearest tap cautiously, all too aware of the likely water pressure from the new plumbing, and gave his coffee pot a thorough rinse.

The cooking facilities were also extremely impressive, and Percy had no doubt that Molly, Bertie and Sarah Jane could look forward to a host of culinary concoctions freshly prepared within its confines.

He chuckled again, more loudly this time.

There was after all very little chance of anything remaining within the kitchen's recesses when the three chefs were placed in the immediate vicinity of flour, eggs, icing sugar or anything of that messy consistency; it was a guaranteed recipe for fun and frolics.

He remembered the hand shaped floury pattern on Sarah's bottom in her last kitchen adventure and the later chaos with the fire extinguisher; it was a thought that produced a wistful sigh from the pondering vicar.

Sarah Jane might never have the opportunity to make a similar mess if they had to move away.

He gazed one final time around before drawing his thick winter cloak tightly around his body, stepping out into the blizzard and pulling the door firmly shut behind him as the snowflakes swirled around his feet.

Where did all the time go to? he reflected as he stepped out into the whistling wind, shivering as its cold touch induced a sharp gasped intake of breath and made his eyes water with the shock.

His toes also felt the extreme cold; he had left his shoes in the new clubhouse and locked the door behind him.

'Oh drat!' muttered Percy, realising he had turned the Yale lock on the way out and there was no way of getting back in.

'Well, there's nothing else for me to do is there?' he muttered to no one in particular as he addressed his toes apologetically.

With a sense of purpose, Percy trudged off towards the vicarage leaving only a foot trail in the virgin white snow behind him.

****

He was shivering, tinged with a shade of blue, and exhausted by the time he finally arrived outside the old, but inviting rectory.

There was little sign of life.

Luckily Percy had retained his front door key, so, with shaking fingers he placed it in the awaiting lock, allowing the door to swing slowly open with a creaking groan as a flurry of fresh snow flew into the hall.

Inside was almost deathly quiet, lacking the usual inviting welcoming warmth and fragrance of good home cooking that normally greeted any guest.

Percy clucked angrily at the change of atmosphere.

His home had always been a welcoming haven to any visitor; they were always sure of receiving a genial offer of hospitality with a warm fire, hot drink and a wholesome meal.

There was little doubt that the vicarage had been unoccupied for a while and the cold atmosphere inside was almost like the brushstroke of death itself.

Percy 'tut-tut'ed to himself.

'Botheration,' he spoke out loud, 'and nuts to the bishop!' added as an afterthought.

With Sarah Jane visiting Molly and Bertie she would be well entertained and there was no immediate need for him to rush back.

It was time to relight the fire in the old home, Eugene Augustus Thomas could go to hell, and to blazes with the consequences! concluded Percy, with a chuckle at his little joke.

A short while later Percy had the coffeepot brewing on the stove, lights on throughout the house in an inviting manner and a log fire blazing merrily in the previously empty hearth.

Its iridescent light sparkled and flickered around the room bathing it in a warm glow; the vicar of Lower South-Borough was home and that was that as far as Percy was concerned.

If the bishop wanted him out he would have to remove him forcibly, mob-handed.

Not only that, thought Percy, he'd have to deal with Sarah Jane Coddle with a rolling pin. Just the image of that alone made him smile.

The cupboards unsurprisingly were almost bare, although he did find a can of chunky vegetable soup and a thick crusty loaf that wasn't quite stale so he wouldn't have to worry too much about shopping until the next day.

He felt a metallic thud by his left foot and glanced down as a solitary tin of PUDDIES cat food rolled out from under the kitchen sink where it had been hiding before his toes had disturbed it.

Percy leaned over and picked up the object.

'Rollo?'

The vicar sighed and felt another deeper pang of sadness.

He was missing Sarah Jane and now he was missing that damned cat too!

He sniffed emotionally and wiped away a small tear from the corner of his left eye.

Instinctively, almost without thinking, he reached for the tin opener, removed the lid off the can and proceeded to deposit its rich gravy covered meaty contents into a large bowl that sat nearby on the draining board.

A few minutes later, fully prepared, Percy walked back down the hall to his study, where the roaring fire now awaited his eager toes.

In one hand he held a deep bowl of steaming hot soup which smelt delicious and made his mouth water with anticipation; he hadn't realised just how hungry he actually was.

As he passed through the doorway he placed the bowl of cat food in its usual place near to the fireplace then, in a moment of whimsical compassion spread his best winter cloak nearby where Rollo used to sit and shared so many fights for possession of his previous one.

He sniffed again as another tear welled up in his eye and looked up from the material offering as a larger than life longhaired ball of fluff with feet padded through the door.

'Hello Rollo,' muttered the vicar, his thoughts distant.

It took a brief second for the realisation to hit home.

'ROLLO!!!' he exclaimed noisily.

The moggie in question mewed extremely loudly, bouncing towards the vicar with a huge question mark tail, enormously wide eyes and an expression of a big grin formed on his features, if cats could have a smile of course.

With only a momentary hesitation Rollo leapt full tilt into Percy's lap, narrowly avoiding the chunky vegetable soup and proceeded to do what contented cats do best, knead and paw the soft receptacle with great gusto, not to mention a few sharp claws.

'M-E-O-W-W'

A questioning catcall reached the vicar's ears, but it wasn't from the already boisterously purring pussy cat in his lap, it came from the hallway.

Percy looked up as Miss Matilda Bagshott made an entrance.

The ragtag scruffy Persian Pussy flounced into the room with a similar display of greeting offered towards the vicar and an expression of proud contentment playing across her features as Rollo gave her a 'told you so' look from Percy's lap.

'Well I never,' exclaimed the vicar, 'I had a feeling you two were up to something...'

Baggie mewed again in a more attentive expressive manner and looked back to the doorway as seven fully-fledged kittens announced their presence.

They tumbled through as a riotous explosion of tornado-like fur balls, a rough house of toppling twisting and turning Tasmanian devils.

'My oh My,' muttered Percy, 'You two have been busy haven't you.'

The kittens stopped playing abruptly, mainly because they had run into the food bowl, which had been freshly filled with meaty chunks and gravy just a short time ago.

If there is one thing kittens love more than fighting, it's eating, and they set about the innocent bowl with great gusto.

Baggie purred contentedly and without further ado made herself extremely comfortable on the thick velvet cloak that had only recently been deposited adjacent to the roaring fire.

Rollo looked up at Percy with questioning eyes.

The vicar gazed back with a knowing expression. 'Yes, go on, go and join your family,' He said after a sigh and short pause.

Rollo jumped softly off the vicar's lap, onto the floor then, with a thankful but loving glance back at Percy, proceeded to nestle down alongside Baggie and together they stretched out, paws extended together, to luxuriate in the warmth of the fire.

It wasn't long before seven very full kittens left behind a very empty dish and proceeded to clamber all over their waiting parents with a few squeaks of protest and cries for attention.

Seconds later, they were all fused together in a welter of indistinguishable coloured fur as each found its ideal niche and settled down contentedly in it; before long they were all fast asleep.

Percy looked down at the cats and stretched out himself to wiggle his cold toes in front of the roaring fire.

He had a feeling that there was something he should be doing, but he just couldn't think what on earth it was.

It wasn't much longer before he too was fast asleep, snoring lightly as the temperature plummeted outside and the snow continued to fall.

****

Percy slept long through the night, warm by the heartily blazing logs, and content with the knowledge that Rollo had returned, but his dreams were full of swirling mists in which there were Sarah Jane, Big Jim and many figures running around the green being pursued by the demon bishop in a JCB digger.

As he slept the snow began to ease, the skies turned darkest crystal blue and the stars shone brighter than ever. Degree by degree the barometers temperature gauge dropped until finally it reached minus 25 degrees centigrade and could go no further.

Jack Frost was very busy that night, but Percy slept on oblivious.

Over in the clubhouse the combined forces of the builders and members had done a fantastic job in clearing the bowling rinks and in fact the whole clubhouse. Some might have said perhaps they had been a little over enthusiastic.

The carpet was no more, tables, chairs and furniture all placed in store, and the bar stock moved into the new clubhouse for safe keeping; after all the new facility was ready to use so they might as well stock it up now for the opening.

Only the offices, which were on a higher level, were untouched and therefore remained fully functional for the committee to use, indeed, they continued to be the only part of the building still heated.

With the bowling area completely devoid of anything damageable and now stripped to bare concrete, there was little left to do, therefore only the dehumidifiers remained, drawing water from the surrounding air.

All that remained now was the task of pumping out the big cellar, which was a long job that needed tackling from the outside and good weather to replace all the pump fittings damaged by the impromptu flooding.

The water still lapped just below the casement at the top of the underground stock room stairs but had nowhere to go.

And that was the way it should have stayed, had Percy not fallen asleep, because he would have remembered that his last duty was to return to the clubhouse and switch on the oil fired heating.

Unfortunately, Percy was not compos mentis and nature in his absence took its natural course.

There was a traditional double wooden hatchway to the cellar with little insulation to protect the interior from the cold; normally the heating would suffice and besides the cellar normally didn't have several thousand litres of icy cold water in its confines.

The water had been chilling for a number of days and by nightfall had began to freeze hard with the surface soon beginning to take on the semblance of hardened steel; unfortunately this steel was expanding.

The plastic pipes circulating water through the basement didn't take too kindly to being squeezed, squashed and generally restricted to a smaller and smaller diameter.

Eventually they got tired of the constriction and expressed their discontent by first splitting open then discharging their contents into the already overfull store.

Benefiting from the additional insulation of the plastic the water inside hadn't quite reached freezing but nevertheless it was very very cold, and wouldn't need much convincing to become a solid state.

Meanwhile the water levels rose.

Five minutes later the water was pouring over the hatch combing and spreading across the bare concrete floor of the lounge area.

Within ten minutes it had found its way under the door jamb and was flowing around the protective bank surrounding the indoor rinks; or at least it was until it found the short step down onto the green.

Like most indoor bowling surfaces it was set a step or two lower with a ditch around its perimeter and then a dividing wall to restrict flying woods from escaping, not that it ever prevented the members of Lower South-Borough from launching a few into orbit.

Like a greedy child the water flowed quickly down into the ditch before rising over its lip and quickly consuming every square inch of dry concrete.

A number of spare beer mats gave chase across the top if it, propelled by the flow like a racing flotilla playing dodgems on the top of the water.

The temperature continued to plummet and the water's surface was already begin to show a shimmering of frostiness; it didn't help that the skylights had been left ajar to reduce the humidity either.

A short time later the split pipes themselves froze solid putting a sudden end to the waters impromptu bid for freedom but not before a generous depth of six inches covered the bowling green from one end to the other.

Within an hour it was iced over and by morning, even with the temperature rising by comparison to a tropical minus nine degrees centrigrade, it resembled a blue sheet of wrought iron that glistened with a white frosty sheen.

Oblivious to the fact, Reverend Percival Peabody continued to slumber.

****

It was 7.30 the following morning, when Percy finally awoke. In a slow, stretching, yawning motion he emerged in a manner that announced to the wide world that he had slumbered long and deep.

His extending legs pushed towards the dying embers of the fireplace and the dozing moggies that still curled by its edge in a massed bundle of fur.

His foot reached Rollo's resting face and un-intentionally gave him a little prod with its biggest tootsie. The cat in turn raised one eye open questioningly, eyed the large plump pink digit and noted that Percy really must get some time in with his darning needle, before going back to his second favourite occupation.

It was lucky for Percy that toe clawing fell into third place behind sleep and mouse chasing, otherwise the vicar might well have received a rude awakening.

Percy glanced at his watch in a still semi-comotose and blurry eyed manner, noting the second hand was creeping around the clock face but not really being able to distinguish which of the blurred numbers the others were actually sitting on.

He rubbed he eyes with a clenched fist and gave a shake of the head, which reminded him that he had been sleeping rather near the table lamp.

He shook his head again, slightly more cautiously this time, and glanced again at his watch: 7.31 stared back at him in an accusing manner.

Merciful heavens, thought Percy in astonishment. Had he really slept for more than 10 hours!

He stretched his arms into the air with a groan as his bones creaked and his rib cage stretched outwardly to allow more flow of life into his awakening body.

Percy half-turned to one side as if to suggest to Sarah Jane that a nice pot of coffee wouldn't go amiss, then laughed to himself for his foolishness as he remembered where he was.

No doubt there would be fresh filter coffee awaiting when she awoke from under her snug featherdown quilt if Molly and Bertie's hospitality was anything to go by.

There would probably be a rousing plateful of crisp smoked bacon, over-easy eggs, real pork sausages and fresh button mushrooms steeped in butter as well, surmised Percy.

And warm toast with chunky home-made orange marmalade to follow, he added with an afterthought.

The vicar's tummy growled appreciatively at the mouth-watering contemplation and Percy reached a decision.

He would take an early morning stroll down to the clubhouse and then, in a roundabout way, ensure his walk took him tantalisingly close to the residence of Mr and Mrs Tattleford. After all, if he made quite sure he was noticed they could hardly not invite him in to join them for breakfast could they.

Sarah Jane was bound to be very pleased as well thought Percy, and he licked his lips in anticipation; she always liked to demonstrate her affection with lots of kissing and he could already feel 'first contact'.

Feeling quite rejuvenated he rose out of the armchair with a bounce in his step and headed for the curtains, which he drew back with a bold sweep to allow the morning sunshine through the windows.

A grey ice-cold day looked in through the frosty glass from the very white garden.

Percy had forgotten all about the previous night.

'Oh bother!'

He pondered briefly, and then shrugged his shoulders in a gesture of acceptance; he would just have to wrap up warm wouldn't he.

Ten minutes later a very snug, well-insulated vicar stepped out of the door into the breathtaking freshness of the unseasonably cold spring day. He had paused briefly to stoke up the fire, adding another log or two, also taken time to top up the kittens' saucer of milk as well as to purloin a tin of the bishop's best Spam for Rollo and Baggie.

Happy that they were warm, well fed and catered for, he had proceeded to also acquire a thick wool jumper, overcoat, gloves scarf and bobble hat from one of his packed boxes before sliding into his wellies and slipping out of the door.

Percy hadn't realised quite how cold it actually was until his glasses frosted over, but at least it had stopped snowing he noted appreciatively as his feet sank ankle deep into its overnight carpet.

He picked up the pace of his walk to shake away the fingers of cold percolating around his nether regions noting with curiosity how the tiny droplets of moisture in his breath froze at each exhalation.

Breakfast summoned him strongly from the nearby village and Percy strode forward determinedly, in the direction of the clubhouse; he also had a strong feeling that there was something he had forgotten to do, but wasn't quite sure what it could be.

Ten minutes later he had a very vivid and instant recollection.

As he approached the clubhouse Percy couldn't help but note that the outside standpipe for the garden hose was crisply white with a coat of frost and that a number of icicles hung down from its rim where dripping water had slowly frozen.

It just shows how quickly things can happen if they aren't wrapped up well, protected from the cold or kept nice and warm, thought Percy to himself.

By a gentle process of word association his mind, now quite awake, began to formulate a link within his sub consciousness.

Ice...   Frozen water... Keep warm...   Heating...

HEATING?

The penny dropped as he reached the clubhouse doors.

'OH MY GOD!' he suddenly realised, that the one thing he was supposed to have done the previous evening still remained unaccomplished.

Quickly fumbling for his keys, he selected the right one on the third attempt, inserted it in the lock, turned it firmly and pushed the door open. It was not a good sign, there were definite sounds of groaned resistance from a frosty seal being broken around its framework.

The air inside was freezing cold, with no perceivable change from that outside, but the hallway leading past the offices to the indoor arena looked as it should be and Percy's heart rose a beat in the expectant half hope that all was well.

He stepped briskly towards the inner door, his right hand fumbling for the light switches as his left pushed it open, and without warning his feet flew up into the air, landing him with a bump hard onto the surface of the floor.

THUD!

Percy groaned loudly, thankful for the well-padded protection of his jacket, jumper and coat, as he looked out over the arena, the lights flickered into life with an eerie glow.

The entire room was covered in a thick sheet of ice, reflecting a blue-ish white tinge in the lights' glow, whilst hundreds of freshly frozen icicles of varying lengths hung from the steel work above.

Every piece of bare metal was coated with a thick film of frosty whiteness, whilst an impressive column of frozen water rose majestically out of the cellar hatchway into the air like a geyser captured in suspended animation.

Reverend Percival Peabody was lost for words, looking around here there and everywhere for an answer or excuse, finding none.

With a deep sigh he gingerly hauled himself to his feet, hanging on tightly to the door handle, before reaching for his mobile phone and pressing the present dial-up for Bertie Tattleford.

A few calls later Patrick, Jack, Bernard, and the rest of the committee members were alerted and en route, as well as on foot.

As the yet unsalted road was certainly not safe for vehicles that early in the morning and it was still well below freezing, it was nature's pre-ordained transportation that set them all on their way.

Percy put his phone away, pulled his gloves back on and headed back to the entrance to await their arrival.

'Oh dear Oh dear,' he thought to himself, 'What have I done?'

****

An hour later, they were all congregated back at the vicarage.

Had the bishop returned at that particular moment he would have found himself severely outnumbered by a host of heathens and beaten a hasty retreat with his best hessian sack.

The conversation over a pot of hot coffee hastily rustled up by Molly and topped up by Big Jim with his hip flask soon had the ideas flowing, although the more the liquid consumption went on the less the practicality of the ideas held sway or common sense.

It was true that many of the members had other distractions mainly of the four legged variety; as Rollo and Baggie noted from the warmth of the thick cloak adjacent to the freshly stoked log fire.

The well rested kittens were now very active and extremely playful, relishing in the indulgence of the numerous adult companions that now dwelt in the study.

Wispa was currently scaling Patrick's inside leg hanging on by her young claws to the swaying fabric with grim determination whilst the green keeper smiled and grimaced alternatively depending on whether the tiny talons found bare flesh or not through the material.

Podge-Podge was squatted legs akimo on top of Bernard's unruly hair, playfully spitting and hissing at Minky and Smudge who perched on either shoulder trying to usurp the young pretender.

Tara was in the process of traversing the curtain pelmet, albeit very precariously alternating her tenuous grip between one paw and two whilst Percy watched nervously and as a precaution moved the coffee cups from beneath the kittens' potential landing spot.

Thomas was only distinguishable by the vague shape of his body moving around underneath Big Jim's woolly jumper as he explored the strange darkness unable to find the sleeve cuff that he had previously entered by.

Much-Ado was upside down inside the fruit bowl playing with its contents, still a very confused kitten who thought he was a tortoise.

Rollo, becoming caught up in the spirit of the moment, biffed Baggie playfully on the ear who responded likewise and, with a suddenly flailing of paws both set about each other in a good-natured wrestling match. It ended abruptly a few seconds later as their actions succeeded only in tangling them both up in the soft cloak like a large sausage roll.

For a brief moment Percy imagined all was as it should be and that this was after all a simple tea time gathering of his friends and newly expanded family.

He sipped his hot coffee cautiously and let the spur of the moment party continue for a few more minutes, unwilling to disturb the cats playful antics.

Finally Percy opened his mouth to speak needing to get the conversation back on track, but before he could utter a word another euphoric shout caught everyone's attention.

'I'VE GOT IT!'

The laughter ceased immediately as each looked across at the cause of the unexpected distraction; even the kittens paused in mid-play with a questioning glance of mystification and puzzlement.

The cloak continued to rock back and forth by the fireplace as Rollo and Baggie persisted in pursuing their struggle in a more confined manner unheeding the muffled distraction.

'I'VE GOT IT!!' repeated Tony 'Trigger' Havershall in an excited voice that spoke of an imagination working overtime.

Percy was already awaiting a suggestion involving space aliens, whilst the look on the others' faces clearly suggested they were equally preparing themselves for some outlandish or bizarre proposal.

'THE VICTORIANS!' shouted Trigger as he continued to enthuse about his sudden brainwave but unable to get all his words out in an order that made particular sense, 'Remember the Victorians?'

Percy stared back somewhat alarmed, with a sudden illogical inkling that perhaps Tony was envisaging raising the dead from the local cemetery.

That was one religious practice that he had absolutely no knowledge of whatsoever and there was little doubt that it would not go down well with the bishop no matter how much it increased the local population and thereby the congregation.

The other members looked at Tony in an equally perplexed manner.

It was almost possible to hear the noise of wheels, cogs and tiny motors whirring frantically inside his head as he tried desperately to elaborate on his idea in a manner that currently eluded him.

Jack tried to help him.

'Yes, go on, The Victorians, what about them....?'

Tony continued to prevaricate in a flustered manner until Sarah Jane stepped over with a fresh coffee strongly laced with alcohol, providing him with the breathing space required to calm down and to allow his mouth to catch up with his brainwave.

He gulped back a large mouthful of the sweet nectar, swallowed it gratefully and breathed deeply before continuing.

'The Victorians used to celebrate in the winter,' he slurped another mouthful before continuing. 'They held festivals on ice whenever it turned cold and their local lake froze over.'

Tony continued unabated.

'They made it a big party, with live music from a brass band and ice skating and...'

'Roast chestnuts...,' interrupted Jack with a large smile as he warmed to the idea and introduced food into the equation.

'And hot jacket potatoes....,' added Bernard as he also picked up the thread of conversation.

'We can play curling as well,' piped up Patrick, 'and we might even be able to muster some bowling. After all it'll be just like playing on a very fast green.'

Percy smiled broadly and clapped his hands together in a visual display of congratulation.

'Well done Trigger, well done indeed.' He applauded his approval and the others quickly took up his lead in providing a rousing round of physical appreciation.

They roared their approval vigorously, energetically and enthusiastically as Molly and Sarah leaned over and kissed Tony on opposite cheeks simultaneously.

He blushed madly, his face beaming with the biggest smile he could muster as he, for once, became the welcome centre of attention.

'Hear Hear!'

'Well done old boy!'

'Jolly good show...'

Tony 'Trigger' Havershall had come good.

****

Over in the church the rather grey-faced, bleary-eyed, haggard and unshaven features of the bishop stared out over the pulpit at the once again empty pews.

His sackcloth robe was looking rather threadbare by now; with the lack of heating, nothing more than potato stew to sustain him and long sleepless nights accentuated by Reverend Archibald's constant monotone snoring, he was beginning to have regrets about his rashness.

Former delusions of grandeur, inspired by an image of his aura-encapsulated figure leading the congregational flock back from the gates of hell like Moses through the Red Sea, now faded into a more jaded scenario.

He longed for the secure comfort of his brick cell and timber bed and more importantly the embellishments that were bestowed with his position, namely the deep pile carpet, sumptuous settee and well stocked wine cabinet to which he never openly admitted but secretly indulged in the pleasures of.

There was in Bishop Eugene Augustus Thomas the Third a dark secret never revealed to the outside world, but one that he surreptitiously enveloped himself in from time to time.

He told himself that by offering and tantalising his soul with the devilish temptations of the corrupted world outside he would be better placed to understand its decadent debauchery and thereby preach against its sins.

Having thus convinced himself of the necessary sacrilege he therefore fully indulged in the immorality of alcohol, rock music and thick dark chocolate, whilst still berating the evil temptation of loose women.

There were some days that he not so much 'dipped his toes in', more a case of totally immersed himself, but still none were any the wiser as to what went on behind the door under the stairs behind the little red curtain.

The bishop shivered in the cold and considered it perhaps was time to send a message back to the monastery at Upper Snoddington summoning members of his order to attend to his bidding.

There still remained, of course, the problem of Lower South-Borough and what to do about the wayward vicar or indeed its current vacancy.

He had no time to consider further as another acorn hit him squarely on the forehead before bouncing onto the growing pile below.

Above him the squirrels squealed with delight as they again indulged in one of their favourite pastimes, whilst beneath them the irritated bishop considered the best way to disguise the purchase of an air rifle in his outgoing accounting receipts.

****

The clubhouse, despite the deep snow and cold icy weather outside, was a veritable hive of activity, the message was definitely out; just about everybody from the village was now in attendance and fully entering the spirit of the occasion.

Clearly, the committee members had spent the previous hour ringing around every single member of the community with the proposal for their Victorian party on ice and the suggestion had definitely fired the imaginations.

The inclement and difficult driving conditions did little to dissuade the locals from reaching their desired goal; the excitement of a 'spur of the moment' seasonal carnival was in effect like a red rag to a bull and they were en route in whatever mode was available.

Some just simply wrapped up warm and trudged off across the fields in a more or less straight line towards the bowling green, although the somewhat curvaceous manner of one or two foot tracks clearly indicated that they had partaken of a liberal quantity of brandy first to insulate their inner being.

Dr Boris Bindergarden the local vet arrived on skies dressed head to foot in a thick fur coat cleverly attached to boots and hood by a concoction of zips that left him looking like an Eskimo.

Harry 'The Hammer' Huckstable, Percy's church organist, took it one step further, hitching up the Christmas Santa sledge from TRESCOS store to a team of farm horses before ferrying in a number of guests.

Peter 'Chippie' Barryman, the village recycling centre manager won the award for most inventive method of transportation however. He simply chained together all the oil drums that had been previously cut in two for the village BBQ, then placed them 'line astern' and towed them like a flotilla of battleships down the back roads with his very large tractor.

The vehicle benefited from heavy snow chains therefore the weather conditions presented little problem to Peter's mode of transportation, a fact he gave great consideration to before charging across the hilly fields. The 18 passengers sharing the nine drums equally acknowledged the chain's firm grip as they hung on for dear life and screamed delightedly in response to the impromptu fun ride.

The builders Jimmy 'Monkey' Murphy and Johnny 'Midge' McPherson, who had been staying nearby at Mrs Jone's guest house whilst completing the renovations, were also called upon for their services.

Within half an hour of the mobile BBQ drums arriving they had them welded on tripods, topped up with charcoal and fully serviceable.

James 'Jamie' Gotthelott, the local storeowner was as always a quick thinking, act on impulse type of guy, so he had quickly raided the vegetable display rack and stocked up the seasonal sleigh as Harry harnessed the horses.

Their arrival with the shop's entire stock of jacket potatoes, roasting chestnuts, chicken portions, hot dogs and a full set of accompanying sauces met with rapturous applause.

Much to the delight of Big Jim and the older committee members Jamie had also packed a substantial quantity of all the necessary ingredients for eggnog; certainly enough to formulate a large vat full.

The wicked smile on Bertie's face was a firm indication that he had remembered to bring the keys to the stock cupboard for the main bar; his wink in Percy's direction only re-affirming that the beverage was indeed likely to be extremely alcoholic.

The sight of Molly setting out several large glass bowls complete with ladles was equally a reliable clue as to the forthcoming arrival of mulled wine in copious quantities.

Percy groaned with the memory of more recent events and was at that point very thankful that there was little remaining in the club still breakable, liable to damage or likely to cause serious injury.

He glanced around the room doing a mental calculation of the number of people present, the amount of alcohol in the store and the likelihood of some, if not all, of the adult community likely to become pleasantly inebriated.

After a quick recount, he came to the conclusion that all 200 guests would be paralytic in 73 minutes.

It was a good time for him to check out the sleeping capacity of the newly constructed club facility, he decided, after all, with the function room, pool table and deep pile carpet they could all probably fit in quite snugly until the following morning.

Peter Barryman was never one to wake up with a clear head either, remembered Percy, so it would be an interesting and somewhat entertaining journey back for the tractor driver and his passengers.

With a smile on his features, the former vicar of Lower South-Borough headed off to ensure that the heating was definitely switched on in the new clubhouse, 'After all,' he muttered to himself, 'it would not be a good idea to make the same mistake twice would it.'

As he reached the door though, he was momentarily distracted from his mental ramblings by the arrival of Sarah Jane, his bride to be.

She was very warmly wrapped head to toe in one of Percy's thick winter cloaks but appeared to still be chilled as her arms were wrapped firmly around her midriff.

He approached her quickly with a look of concern on his face as he spoke.

'Are you OK darling?'

She beamed back at him with one of her disarming smiles that never failed to melt his heart and make his legs go wobbly at the knees.

'Of course I am you silly thing,' she chided with a teasing, loving reply, sighing contentedly in the knowledge that Percy as always paid such attention to even the tiniest things that might affect her.

'But you looked as if you were perhaps feeling the cold,' he said, querying her further as he nodded towards her tightly crossed arms.

She looked down.

'Oh that,' she replied with a look of mischievousness and loosened her grip on the cloak slightly.

A pair of tiny heads popped up through the gap now conveniently offered and the movement around Sarah Jane's folded arms clearly suggested that they were not alone.

Wispa and Tara stared opened eyed in awe, their little ears twitching excitedly at the colourful, lively, noisy atmosphere of their new surroundings.

The wriggling and jiggling inside the cloak quickly signalled to the others within that there was something of great interest outside. Their insatiable curiosity soon had another four kittens looking around eagerly in anticipation of a great adventure ahead.

Much-Ado remained curled up within the warm confines of the cloak, he was, after all, still convinced he was a tortoise.

Sarah Jane glanced back at Percy, a little more sheepishly this time.

'Well we couldn't leave them all alone at the vicarage whilst we enjoyed the party, could we?'

He pretended to consider the fact seriously for a second and then, as she began to look slightly worried, leaned across and kissed her affectionately, full on her lips.

'Of course not my angel,' Percy agreed, laughing as she blushed, and then with a slight pause asked, 'but where are mum and dad?'

She sniggered loudly and gave a knowing nod over her shoulder.

Percy stepped past and looked behind her, resisting, for once, the temptation to give Sarah Jane a playful nip on the bottom.

Rollo and Baggie were quite happily sitting on the trailing tail of the thick cloak, purring contentedly and twitching with excitement from the sleigh ride through the snow on the back of the cloth carrier. With Sarah being a little smaller in height there had been just enough of Percy's cloak draped on the floor for the two cats to seize upon the opportunity of a free lift!

'HA! HA! HA!'

The vicar was clearly tickled by the ridiculously funny image, and he laughed loudly to himself, as he continued on his way and contemplated the future. No matter what else happened he was certainly going to have a very interesting life with never a dull moment.

****

It was about an hour later that Percy returned from his travels. Having roped in the help of one or two members they had ensured that the heating had been switched on and enough blankets, sleeping bags, comfy seats and warm abodes awaited any that cared, or needed, to stay overnight before attempting their journey home.

Stepping in from the still freezing conditions outside he made his way quickly to the indoor arena, eager to see how the high-spirited members of his congregation had managed to progress matters during his absence.

Near the doorway he noted a number of pairs of ice skates lying in readiness; it would seem they had come up with a number of ways to take full advantage of the frozen conditions and were quite literally rejuvenating the spirit of a Victorian ice festival right down to the minutest detail.

'Excellent,' said Percy to no one in particular.

'Very good indeed,' expressed Percy, addressing the walls as he took one step forward then hesitated midway; his spirit of adventure already rising within him.

He rubbed his gloved hands together with a gleeful expression, and after considered contemplation for all of two seconds reached down for a pair of the skates.

'Well why not?' he concluded.

It took just a few minutes before the vicar was suitably attired; he checked his appearance in the mirror, zipped up his warm red jacket, adjusted the bobble hat with its matching scarf, straightened his reading glasses and prepared to 'make a go of it.'

It had been quite a few years since he had last donned a pair of ice skates, but he was quite sure that he hadn't lost his touch, in fact he quite fancied that, in his best winter clothes, he closely resembled the male lead from Torvill and Dean.

Percy cautiously straightened up and made a final address to the brickwork before gingerly pushing himself out into the centre of the hallway and turning around to face the inner doors.

'Right then here we go!'

Taking care not to fall over, he took a short step, bent his legs, extended his arms and with a playful scream slid down the small icy slope that now bore a semblance to a mini ski ramp.

'W-H-H-E-E-E-E...'

Percy was clearly in a very light-hearted frame of mind.

He gathered pace quite quickly, perhaps a touch more than he had anticipated, having not really allowed for the speed in which he would accelerate given the downward inclination of the slope.

Normally it would be carpeted and he had never previously given consideration to how steep the slope actually was or indeed how long it was either.

Percy couldn't quite work out exactly how far he was from reaching the internal doors as it all seemed a little blurred, distorted and for some reason quite out of focus.

'Now why should that be?' he considered to himself before very quickly in an almost instant telepathic response realised the obvious answer.

He was still wearing his reading glasses!

The vicar had, earlier on, been reading the instructions on how to ignite the new heating system and he simply hadn't taken them off afterwards.

The doors appeared to be arriving in a very quick manner and Percy felt that it might be prudent to prevent any injury that was likely to occur should he impact, nose first, on the soon to arrive framework.

'WH-O-O-O-A-H!!!'

He extended his hands out in front of him like a train buffer and braced himself for the impact.

It never arrived...

As he rapidly approached the entrance Percy could hear a number of voices chattering excitedly; one or two of them were instantly recognisable and it appeared as if Jack Tuttle was talking to the Rt Hon. Clifford James Johnson.

In an instantaneous blur the conversation registered on Percy's consciousness but gave him no time to contemplate a response.

'Jolly good show what!'

'Rather spiffing don't you think?'

'I wonder where the vicar's got to; he's been gone for over an hour?'

'We better go and look for him, just in case...'

Both doors swung open inwardly as eager hands grasped their handles and gave them a stout pull in the opposite direction.

Percy had barely time to acknowledge the fact that the passageway was no longer barricaded by the woodwork before he sailed through it at tremendous speed following the beneficial acceleration of the icy incline.

'OH NOOO-O-O-O!!!'

The Reverend Percival Peabody, former vicar of Lower South-Borough, guardian of the good book and preacher to the parish made quite an entrance!

****

More or less the entire congregation had turned out to attend the festival on ice, or PERCY'S PARTY, as the revellers were now lovingly referring to it.

In the vicar's absence, they had been very busy indeed.

Eric 'Chalkie' Tunstall had gathered together a number of his fellow retired veteran RAF musicians to form an impromptu brass band of sorts and they were, at that particular moment in full flow.

Ronald 'Squiffy' Regis, their now retired honorary president, was heading up the musical entourage much as if he were leading a military charge across the battlefield.

Swinging his prize trombone side to side like a battle flag, he forged ahead of the vanguard romping it up with a surprisingly good rendition of 'When the saints go marching in...'

Douglas Doolittle, being a one-time surgeon, still had nimble fingers and clearly showed his dexterity by virtue of a performance on the saxophone, which featured a display full of flair and vigour.

Russell Cobblethwaite was having the time of his life; he had borrowed the junior drum set owned by Timothy 'TINY' Doolittle and was hitting everything in sight he could land a drumstick on.

On more than one occasion that also appeared to include Cynthia Cobblethwaite's bottom; she was standing nearby with Gloria Grimshaw and Diane Ditherford adding the more refined musical constraints of tambourine tapping.

In Gloria's case it was more a case of tambourine bashing; she was whooping, hollering and doing some kind of tribal rain dance; much to the amazement of several members, she was actually laughing.

Phillippa and Doris were however showing some concern and looking anxiously up at the ceiling fearful they might actually start to see the beginnings of a cloud formation.

Tony Havershall surprised everyone by turning up with a very fine banjo, which he clearly knew how to play; it was just slightly unfortunate that he appeared at times to be playing a completely different tune to most of the others.

Nevertheless any discordant off key clash of melodies was easily compromised and overwhelmed by the members' infectious enthusiasm.

Dennis 'Sticky' Ditherford had boldly, but unwisely volunteered to play the big bass drum, as he used to play a few notes in the school orchestra many years ago. He forgot to mention that the previous experience had been the glockenspiel and had not taken into account the sheer size or weight of the massive percussion piece.

One or two of the other members, seizing the opportunity for a bit of harmless fun offered to assist him into the strapping and in doing so took most of the drum's weight on their own hands to prevent Dennis realising his predicament until it was too late.

After securely fastening the monstrosity firmly to the bird-watcher's willow-like frame they nodded to each other in agreement, counted to three and let go suddenly.

With a loud cry of shock Dennis had lurched forward as the bass drum dropped to the floor hauling him high into the air leaving him stranded four feet off the ground with arms and legs flailing about.

If it wasn't for his agitated extremities he would have looked like a beached fish.

The hysterical, tearful and riotous laughter from the participating jokers took at least 15 minutes to die down before they felt reticent enough to help lower him back down to the ground.

Nearby Jiggy 'Snapper' Jenkins made sure to capture the moment for posterity, in fact he was taking a lot of pictures and just for once in his life not for financial gain; the club's antics had made him very wealthy indeed and as with everyone else, he was here to support Percy.

A much calmer Dennis, now more appreciative of the humorous antic, joined the back of the band, near the ladies where he felt safer and now sported just a triangle in his hand.

Meanwhile the bass drum was set back on the bandstand to await the much more suitable presence of Big Jim to add its big beat to the already noisy and enthusiastic cacophony.

Former Desert Rat Derek 'Big Bang' Dunstable was not one to let the Air Force musicians steal all the limelight and thunderous action though.

Previously having served as a sergeant during the war, he had been one of several members who had attained an honorary promotion through the ranks at a 'mock up' ceremony during the CAMP EISENHOWER campaign of the previous summer.

Squiffy had, at the same simulation, transformed from Squadron Commander to Air Marshall Ronald 'Boom Boom Regis in deference to his real war time superior.

At that military enactment they had both emerged more or less unscathed and equally matched, but now Derek saw Squiffy stealing a lead in their lifetime battle for supremacy.

Without hesitation, he took up the challenge, sweeping an unclaimed French horn from the makeshift bandstand and charging after the marching throng with an accompaniment of deep-throated brassy farting noises.

The ladies to the rear looked over their shoulders with a degree of alarm whilst the fragile Mrs Jones, seated nearby, nearly fainted clean away and had to reach quickly for her handkerchief full of smelling salts.

The vet, Dr Boris Binder-Garden who had been standing in the immediate vicinity serving hot dogs, rushed forward with a small spray can of cat litter deodoriser just in case, whilst Molly leaned over as she skated past and emptied a case of double strength mint Tic Tac's into the tuba's funnel.

Derek immediately took on the appearance of having swallowed a swarm of bees, turning extremely red faced, huffing and puffing before violently exhaling down the funnel mouth; consequently every member of the congregation partook of a Tic Tac and some lucky ones even got two.

Sarah Jane Coddle who was serving over at the main bar, eyed the nearby Charlie and Bernard suspiciously, having grave misgivings about the numerous off-white oval tablets now floating in the mulled wine.

Last, but not least, to be caught up in the fever pitch music extravaganza Harry Huckstable, the rather talented if somewhat outrageous church organist, imposed himself in grandiose fashion on the bandstand.

It was entirely possible that he could have physically manhandled the entire church organ out of its framework and installed it on the stage had he been of the mind to. However, he had thankfully settled for acquiring a still rather impressive old-fashioned piano from the local school, which he'd dragged all the way to the clubhouse on a sheet of thick plywood.

Big Jim had looked at him in showed awe upon his arrival with piano in tow and had tried, unsuccessfully to mentally envisage Harry's huge form astride a runaway upright piano surfing down a snow-covered hill on a six feet square timber block.

With Harry now tinkling the ivories and the variable qualities of the brass band filling the room with their lively energetic accomplishments there was indeed a very distinctive buzz of excitement.

Jiggy Jenkins couldn't help but notice there were already some very interesting musical harmonies and reached for his earplugs as he observed the church choir beginning to warm up in the distance.

The half drum BBQ's were already set out on their newly constructed tripod framework at one end of the room, heat rising into the cool air creating a misty atmosphere as the delicious smell of hot dogs, baking potatoes and roasting chestnuts drifted mouth wateringly through the gathered throng.

The external fire doors had been left wide open to keep the temperature low, after all everyone was warmly wrapped up and the last thing anyone wanted was for the ice to melt too quickly.

Jimmy and Johnny, the builders, had obviously taken their task to heart; they had already constructed an open brick pit in the garden outside and, with a hearty, red glowing, charcoal fire roaring away, had a hog roast on the go.

A number of games were in play across the icy waste that had replaced the former indoor green.

There was in fact a very competitive, if somewhat challenging game of bowls ongoing in the middle rink where the now slightly tipsy Charlie and Bernard were trying their best to adapt to the very fine touch required to keep their bowls out of the ditch.

They soon realised that having no ditch to physically stop any wayward woods made life very interesting indeed as their first played bowls continued to trundle about the ice long after the last had actually been played.

Meanwhile Molly, rising to the challenge, continued to skate in spirals and pirouettes around the arena gracefully weaving in and out of them like a mouse in a minefield.

Several of the flock were having a dance and they were indeed 'cutting a rug' in a splendid manner.

There were games in progress in every corner of the ice field; the children Abbey and Timothy were having a lively altercation over a skittles match whilst others were simply enjoying a leisurely skate, like Molly.

Bernard noted that several of the ladies were attempting to revive their school day hockey skills as a ceramic puck flew past his left ear, whilst Charlie stared in amazement as an empty Zimmer frame sallied by unattended; obviously one or two of the older members were trying their hand at curling and hadn't quite got the right idea yet.

His observation was quickly re-affirmed as Lady Elizabeth Quinton drifted by in a spray of ice, screaming excitedly as she pummelled the floor with the yard broom ahead of a curling stone.

A number of other sideshows were performing too.

A group of volunteers had thrown together a makeshift glove puppet theatre with a little help from a pair of the window curtains and several of the men would find they suddenly had numerous odd socks in the weeks ahead. Nevertheless the younger children of the village were highly delighted and screaming their enthusiastic support.

Somehow, the members of the congregation had even managed to secure the assistance of Cedric Spindleforth, Colin's father and curator of the village museum of historical artefacts.

The result of which was that they managed to acquire a steam driven Wurlitzer organ from its dark recesses which, having trundled merrily down the track on a tractor tow, now whistled away in an infectious melody of old tunes as puppet figures danced up and down by its side.

From every angle the continually evolving scenario was one of a picture perfect festive Victorian party and all had to agree it was quite a magnificent sight.

Here, there and everywhere the kittens were having fun, causing chaos and participating in every event too.

Wispa and Thomas were still trying to stand up on the ice, their little paws flailing in every direction as they failed to find any purchase on the polished surface.

Thomas, having found his feet, was avidly pursuing a bowl up the rink whilst Tara play fought with a knocked down skittle as Minky sat in one spot spinning around and around getting dizzier by the minute as she chased her own tail.

Smudge was having a wonderful time sitting on the Wurlitzer organ trying to tap all the metal vents as the flaps lifted up to release a small cloud of steam and eject a musical note.

Podge-Podge, unsurprisingly was over by the hot dog stand gnawing ferociously at the tail end of a tasty sausage that, as of yet, was still too hot to eat.

Nearby, the attending Boris Binder-Garden kept a watchful eye on the youngster. Smiling down at the playful kitten he thoughtfully trimmed another piece of cooked sausage and set it to one side so that it was already cooling.

Quite a number of hot dogs subsequently served up that afternoon appeared to have one end missing.

Much-Ado was off on an adventure, having finally decided that he wasn't after all a tortoise but actually a mountain lion had spent a considerable period of time climbing up a nearby curtain one claw at a time.

Finally, he had, by some stroke of luck, reached the summit and was currently perched precariously on a steel beam in the roof space.

He was, at that point in time in a world of his own and currently stalking a large, hairy, wild-eyed wildebeest to which he was in the process of raising his paw before spitting at in a catlike hissy fit.

The mouse stared back at the kitten over the small piece of cheese it had purloined from the festival down below, and decided it didn't like being considered a wildebeest.

In fact, it didn't really like the noisy intruder at all!

Picking up the spare chunk of blue cheese it had also sneakily acquired, the mouse left by the nearest available exit, sliding down a large long icicle that hung suspended on the underside of the beam.

The tiny rodent dropped virtually unnoticed to the floor below.

It paused for a second to gather its wits, pick up the dropped cheese and to decide which way it was going to run, and that's about all the time it took for its plans to go somewhat astray.

At that point in the proceedings several things occurred more or less simultaneously, all of them focused on the point of landing selected by the mouse.

Much-Ado, being unskilled in the art of hanging onto to the slippery surface of a icicle strove desperately to retain a grip with his tiny claws. However, he had yet to develop the steel hook-like hold of an adult cat and only succeeded in slowing his descent, rotating around and around the icy spike in a downward spiral like a helter-skelter.

As if caught in a vortex the kitten descended to the point of no return and then with a tiny yelp slipped and fell.

Baggie, who had been partaking of a leg of chicken under one of the BBQ stands, witnessing Much-Ado's precarious ascent with growing alarm, was already sitting up, tail twitching, as her kitten began to slide down the inverted frozen limb.

By the time it entered freefall Baggie had engaged aft thrusters and rocketed like a bat out of hell towards the drop zone, her eyes firmly fixed on the descending youngster.

Rollo on the other hand, had not witnessed the kitten's perilous trip but had caught sight of the mouse from the top of the bandstand and had been watching it with growing interest for the last five minutes.

He had spend most of the winter pursuing this particular pesky rodent around the rafters on many occasion but had never been lucky enough to get within striking distance.

Just the thought of that juicy morsel in a catnip kebab made his mouth drool in anticipation.

Rollo was already wound up like a tight spring and, when the mouse took what seemed to be a foolish leap into space, he seized the opportunity, launching himself into orbit from the canopy.

He hit the ground running five metres later and catapulted towards the middle, his eyes never leaving the falling target.

It was already a four-way race to the centre point, which only lacked a large X marking the spot, when the vicar of Lower South-Borough made his grand entrance.

Percy sailed through the open doors at great speed, arms flailing and shouting a warning to any and everybody in his line of travel.

'LOOK OUT!!!'

Jack and Clifford stood either side of the access each holding a door open with their hands as they stared agog, jaws open in disbelief at the vicar's unexpected entrance and manner of arrival.

Big Jim gave a quick look back up the hallway just to be on the safe side, after all there just might be a JCB digger following and he hadn't had time to secure the brandy!

He sighed with relief a moment later as he discovered his sudden fear to be unfounded and looked back in bemusement at Percy's progress.

The vicar was very obviously being watched over from above.

Nothing as of yet impeded his epic adventure on skates; he had somehow managed to avoid any collision or accident and even accomplished a double twist with half axle as he leapt over the children's skittles, much to their delight.

Percy couldn't help but notice, as he performed his impromptu spiral, that the event appeared to be going very well indeed and the hog roast looked very appetising; he wondered if there was any way he could deviate in that direction without falling over?

Rollo and Baggie had half turned their heads in mid charge as they were distracted by the vicar's scream and, recognising his voice, momentarily lost their concentration.

The same thought occurred to both cats at the same time, not only was Percy careering out of control at great speed across the ice, but he was also hurtling in their direction.

At that point time ran out.

The mouse arrived safely on the ice with the cheese still in its paws and an elated grin across its tiny face at its daring, risqué escape to freedom.

Its expression changed seconds later as Much-Ado landed squarely on top of his head squashing his features into the soft cheese.

He groaned and looked out from under the kittens rump, his eyes blurred from the soft Gorgonzola; his dulled senses noted that something very large was arriving at great speed and he gave a very loud panicking squeak!

Rollo and Baggie approaching from opposite ends of the compass had the briefest of seconds to acknowledge the mouse squeal before they realised the situation and by then it was far too late.

C-R-U-N-C-H!!!

Back-pedalling feverishly, their paws gouging large fissures in the ice, the two cats collided in an eight-legged embrace that shook several large icicles loose from the ceiling as, at the last moment, the kitten and mouse scrambled clear of the crash.

Rollo and Baggie sat back on their haunches, stunned into senselessness by the impact, their eyes rolling from the skull rattling collision as the descending ice columns crashed around them.

Both opened their mouths to utter a questioning meow but were left speechless by the arrival and departure of Percy who sailed straight through the middle of their parted legs narrowly avoiding tails and ice towers.

A stunned audience, assuming that this was part of some carefully orchestrated cabaret stunt, applauded wildly and enthusiastically as the steamrollering vicar executed a deft right hand turn in a shower of ice spray and sailed past the BBQs snatching a fresh cooked chicken leg from the surprised vet.

With a broad wild grin Percy took a large bite of the poultry piece before waving it high above his head like a trophy, implementing a 360 degree spin and turning sharply towards the door from which he had first emerged.

His huge smile turned to one of panic as he suddenly became aware that the escape route was now blocked by the arrival of two newcomers.

He recognised them immediately; on the left there was the national president of bowls and former World Champion

Tommy 'Tick Tock' Ballcock who was due to arrive for the grand opening of their new clubhouse.

They had been expecting his arrival and it looked like he had made it to Lower South-Borough earlier than anticipated.

Percy certainly was NOT expecting the eloquent, impressive and awe-inspiring figure of the Rt Hon. Matthew James Twiggle, the most senior Archbishop in England to be standing there.

The vicar had never met the noble clergyman but had heard of his legendary prowess in performing Sunday services; he must be here at the bishop's summoning.

Percy groaned as he swerved sharply to avoid a collision, and, still brandishing his chicken leg as he passed them by, detoured into the bar area where a suitably prepared Sarah Jane stood ready with several large cushions.

With a shower of ice particles, the vicar landed safely in his girlfriend's open arms who, as always, never missed an occasion to place a large smacker of a kiss right on his lips.

Behind him, the archbishop and the president looked on with smiles of amusement as the crowd continued to applaud Percy's performance.

Back on the ice another pair of lovers, two cats of great notoriety, were coming to grips with their senses once again.

They gave each other a quizzical, deep, expressive look and it was clearly obvious that something unsaid had passed between them, other than the vicar, as Rollo raised an eyebrow and indicated in the direction of the fire exit doors.

Baggie glanced over to where the mouse was now beating a hasty retreat with its cheese, before giving her partner the nod.

Rollo stood up, and turned to face the mischievous rodent, giving his body a serious shake that sent a ripple all the way up his fur from tail to nose tip, padding the ice like a rampaging bull and setting his rear half to shimmying with a highly nervous twitch.

The mouse recognising the danger signs began to back-pedal a lot faster, reversing out of the doors so as to keep an eye on the impending protagonist.

Without warning Rollo charged, showering his proud partner with a cloud of ice, as he put on a sudden spurt and stormed after the mouse with an impressive turn of speed; showing much wisdom the rodent dropped the gorgonzola and ran for its life.

****

It was many hours later that Percy sat around the still warm, but fading embers of the charcoal pit with a large steaming mug of hot chocolate.

Sarah Jane sat beside him, wrapped up warm in his thick quilted cloak whilst kittens and cats alike snuggled on its hem as it draped near the fire.

Behind them the village congregation continued to party on unabated but in a more subdued form of revelry, following the afternoons liberal intake of food, drink and frolicking.

A number of people, including the surprise guests, were in deep conversation over by the hot dog stand, whilst the strains of 'Carousel' wafted into the ether from the distant Wurlitzer.

It was the most perfect of evenings and of endings...

Percy looked across to Sarah as tears of happiness and sadness combined, trickled down his cheeks; she was crying too, but sported a large contented smile.

They laughed then reached across and held each other's hand tightly as the cats stared up at their gesture of unity.

'Well,' queried Percy?

'Well...' said Sarah in a quiet reflective voice.

They stared out across the icy wilderness at the millions of stars shining in the cold blue night skies.

It was a brave new world, but they faced it together.

EPILOGUE

The church was packed.

Every possible seat was occupied; all the pews filled to overflowing and not even space left at the back where normally standing room only remained.

The choir stood ready in their very best finery whilst Harry 'The Hammer' Huckstable sat with fingers poised over the organ keys.

By his side in a very large wicker basket lined with a thick velvet cloak sat Rollo, Baggie and the seven kittens all purring contentedly and, for once, behaving impeccably.

There was an overwhelming presence of excitement and knowledgeable suspense running through the congregation; it was the first Sunday in April and the entire village was in attendance.

Standing by the altar at the front the Archbishop the Rt Hon. Matthew James Twiggle cast a knowing eye over the choir and prepared to give them timely instruction.

In the front rows sat every member of the Lower South-Borough bowling club fraternity including Tommy 'Tick Tock' Ballcock who had stayed on for this special occasion.

It had been a fortnight of surprises following the arrival of the two celebrities and the village was still in a state of shock after the announcement that a new vicar was taking over with immediate effect.

Apparently the bishop had been sent back home on a leave of absence following a number of inadvisable revelations in his on-line diary which the Archbishop had somehow acquired.

The big freeze had passed as quickly as it had arrived, but the memory and press coverage of the hugely successful Victorian Festival on ice remained engrained on everyone's subconscious.

There was no doubt that this had been Percy's finest hour.

The ice was all gone now, but the memory remained, as did that of the grand opening day of the new clubhouse, which had been a tremendous occasion; a stunning accolade suitably endorsed by the legendary World Champion who had taken great pride in cutting the ribbon and declaring the venue opening.

He had further delighted everyone by announcing that he was to stay over for a few weeks and that he would be giving a display of 'short mat bowls' at the newly refurbished Trescos the following month.

Jamie was already rubbing his hands with delight and anticipating record sales.

Percy had not been seen since the opening and rumours abounded that perhaps he had been instructed to take a leave of absence, but Sarah Jane remained tight-lipped about the matter when asked.

Now she sat at the front of the congregation alongside her sister Molly who was glowing radiantly with her very visible pregnancy, next to her sat the very proud husband Bertie Tattleford.

Primed and waiting down by the steps the now infamous paparazzi figure of Jiggy 'Snapper' Jenkins knelt with his camera ready to take the first picture of the new appointment; once again he had a scoop!

A sudden hush swept through the building as the archbishop nodded to the choir leader and turned to face the congregation.

He paused for a second to gather his thoughts, took a deep breath and then without further ado launched into his announcement.

'My dear friends of Lower South-Borough I am delighted to see so many of you here today and nothing has given me more pleasure than seeing the community spirit that you all show today and enjoyed together when I first met you all at your recent festival.'

He paused for the words to sink in.

'You are all a glowing example to all on how community life should be, experienced together, helping, sharing, understanding and caring.'

Several of the members turned misty eyed whilst a sense of pride swept through the gathered congregation.

The archbishop gave them a further few seconds to gather their thoughts before continuing his address; it was clear that emotions were running high.

'You have for years created and enjoyed a unique community spirit under the gentle guidance of the Reverend Percival Peabody and he will be a hard man to replace.' He paused for breath, 'But I am bound by my duty to act upon the request of Bishop Thomas the third.'

The audience tensed.

'Therefore I ask you all please to be upstanding and give a warm welcome to your new vicar.'

The adjoining vestibule door behind the pulpit creaked opened and swung shut with an audible thud of heavy oak returning to its frame before the light fall of footsteps at the rear of the preacher's tower made the audience tense expectantly.

On cue the choir softly swept into a harmonised a cappella introduction, which sounded vaguely familiar to many of the waiting audience.

Harry Huckstable, with typical fervour launched into a storming, tub-thumping, powerhouse introduction, striking the chord keys hard as he kicked the pedals violently and let rip with his own unique rendition; it was Elton John's 'I'm Still Standing.'

As the melody pumped strenuously through the towering framework several squirrels rose up out of the organ pipes lifted on the powerful jets of air pressure with surprised looks on their faces.

Speechless, the congregation looked on with stunned, incredulous expressions and a feeling of déjà vu as the new vicar of Lower South-Borough reached the top of the pulpit then turned to face the congregation.

It was Percy.

The crowd went wild.